"Don't say it," Samuel warned.

"Say what?"

"Don't say you're sorry again."

"How did you know what I was going to say?"

He smiled. "A good attorney learns to read faces well. He has to know when someone is lying and when someone is being honest. When someone is ready to make a stand and when someone is ready to apologize. We've both said 'I'm sorry' too often, because we've needed to. Isn't it time to stop?"

"Yes."

"I think so, too." He took her hand again and curved her fingers over his. "This would all be so much easier if you didn't look as if your dress might fall apart at any time. It keeps taking my attention from what I need to be thinking about, because I'd be a fool not to watch to see when the tatters win."

"Such words are sure to turn any woman's head."

Samuel's fingers tightened on hers. "The way you look is sure to turn any man's. You've got a softness about you, Cailin, that belies the steel within you. Your eyes are filled with a sensuality that's hard to ignore."

"Can you?"

"I don't know." He released her hand and sighed. "I honestly don't know."

"The children—"

"Forget the children." He pulled her into his arms and claimed her mouth with a feverish kiss. . . .

Dear Romance Readers:

In July of 1999, we launched the Ballad line with four new series, and each month we present both new and continuing stories set everywhere from medieval England to the American West—the kind of passionate, romantic stories you love best, written by the most grifted authors. At the back of each book, we tell you when you can find subsequent books in the series that have captured your heart.

First up this month is **After the Storm,** the final book in Jo Ann Ferguson's heartfelt *Haven* series. When a mother in search of her children finds them with a man who has become like a father to them, will he become a husband to her, as well? Next, talented Kathryn Hockett introduces us to the third proud hero in her exciting series, *The Vikings.* Raised to be a scholar, he never expected to be an **Explorer**—until the fate of a young woman falls into his hands, and her love burns in his heart.

Men of Honor continues with Kathryn Fox's emotional tale, **The Healing.** Can a desperate woman on the run from her past fall for the mounted police officer who intends to bring her to justice? Finally, Julie Moffett concludes the *MacInness Legacy* with **To Touch the Sky,** the gripping story of a woman born to heal others who discovers the strange legacy that threatens to harm the one man she has come to love.

These are stories we know you'll love! Why not try them all this month?

Kate Duffy
Editorial Director

Haven

AFTER THE STORM

Jo Ann Ferguson

ZEBRA BOOKS
Kensington Publishing Corp.
http://www.kensingtonbooks.com

*For Tom and Sue Miele
who have helped more people
than they can even imagine.*

*Thanks to Sheila Hogg for her help so I could get
the pronunciation of Gaelic words right.
It makes such a difference.*

One

"Do I have to finish these carrots?"

Samuel Jennings looked up from the stove where he was dishing out food for himself. At the table, three red-haired children were waiting for his answer. He saw a smile twitching on the boy's face, but the two younger girls wore hopeful expressions.

Six months ago, he could not have imagined having three kids on the farm he had bought after he left Cincinnati. He had been quite content to live alone here. Yet, when he had heard about an orphan train coming to the village of Haven along the Ohio River, he had gone to look for a lad to help him with some of the farmwork.

Instead of one, he had returned to Nanny Goat Hill Road with three children. Ten-year-old Brendan Rafferty and his younger sisters, Megan and Lottie, had been willing to help, but the girls were so young there was little they could do other than weed the kitchen garden.

"I thought you liked carrots, Brendan," Samuel said, adjusting his gold-rimmed glasses, then reaching across the table to do the same for Lottie's smaller ones. He had not been certain if Delancy's General Store could order spectacles small enough for a child who would not celebrate her fourth birthday for another month.

"I thought I did, too." Brendan toyed with the orange slices on his plate.

Megan piped up, "I like them."

"No, you don't." The boy flashed his sister a frown.

"No, I don't," she said, looking down at his plate.

Samuel chuckled under his breath. Even after half a year here, the Rafferty children sometimes banded together to help each other as if they were still without a home. Other times they fought like puppies with a single bone.

"Do you like them or not, Megan?" he asked and watched as she grinned, revealing the spot where a pair of teeth had not yet grown back in.

"I do, but I don't want Brendan's."

Lottie bounced in her chair and said, "I don't want mine neither. Dahi doesn't want'm neither."

"I thought Dahi liked carrots," he replied as he put the lid back on the pot. At first, he had been unsettled by Lottie's comments about a friend no one else could see, but now he was as accustomed to having this invisible Dahi around as he was to everything else about the children.

"I wanna give'm to Bunny."

"Bunny?" Samuel sat at the head of the table. Now none of the children was looking at him. When Brendan scowled at his younger sister, Samuel hurried to say, "I suspect that's what I heard scratching in the larder earlier on my way in from the barn."

"Brendan taught it!"

He tried not to laugh. The little girl always mixed up words when she was excited. "How did he *catch* it?"

"In a box." Lottie would not be subdued by anything as commonplace as a wrongly used word. "It's cute, Samuel. Me and Dahi like it a lot. All brown and fluffy, and it has big ears and the littlest tail and—"

"And it needs some carrots for its supper," he said,

knowing the little girl could go on and on when she was so enthusiastic her green eyes sparkled like faceted emeralds. Leaning his elbows on the table, he smiled. "There are plenty of raw carrots in the root cellar. Your bunny will like them much better than cooked ones."

"So we can keep it?" Megan's eyes, a shade bluer than her sister's, now glistened with anticipation.

"If you build a hutch for the rabbit out by the chicken coop. You can use a crate and put that unused piece of chicken wire in the barn around the box to give the rabbit a place to get some fresh air. That way it won't dig out or hop over." He winked at Brendan. "Rabbits leave round, brown balls in their wake, so it needs to have its hutch moved often."

As the children excitedly discussed how they would put together the rabbit's house, Samuel began to eat. He preferred having supper in the kitchen, using the dining room only for Sunday dinner. The vegetables fresh from the garden were a nice change from the dried-out ones they had eaten during the spring and early summer. Just the thing growing children needed.

He laughed silently. Now *that* was something his mother would have said. Somehow, he had become both father and mother to his kids. That was how he thought of them now—his kids. Whenever he heard someone mention them as "Samuel's children," he was pleased. The children had adjusted well to their new lives far from the slums of New York City, much better than some of their other companions on the orphan train.

As he noted how carefully Megan cut her vegetables, he was curious as he had been so often. These children had nice table manners and spoke politely to all adults. Not what he had anticipated when he brought them to Nanny Goat Hill Road. He had heard how the street children could be as bold and rude as an attorney with an open-and-shut case.

The Rafferty children had taken to life on his small farm down the river from the village of Haven as if they had spent every day of their lives here. Funny how he found it difficult to recall the months before they came here. Now they were so much a part of his life he could not imagine them not being on the farm.

"Finish up your milk," Samuel said when the chairs being pushed back on the uneven floor interrupted his thoughts. "You're going to need every bit of your energy to build that hutch."

"I'm strong." Brendan pulled up his sleeve and flexed his left arm. The merest hint of a muscle was visible.

Samuel squeezed it gently as he did each time Brendan asserted it had grown bigger. "Very good, but another helping of carrots would really help."

"Me and Dahi—" began Lottie.

"Dahi and I," he corrected gently.

The littler girl giggled, then said, *"Dahi and I* are real strong, too." She held up her pudgy arm, which had been shockingly thin when she first arrived in Haven.

Squeezing it as he had Brendan's, Samuel complimented Lottie on how well she was growing. He glanced at Megan, but she did not move. Maybe he had been fooling himself when he believed the children had acclimated themselves completely to this new life. Brendan had for the most part, because he had come to Haven with his best friend, Sean O'Dell. Lottie had, which was no surprise, considering her age. Megan was the most sensitive of the three, the one who always tried to make sure the other two were happy. It was almost as if she wanted to replace their mother, constantly worrying if they were warm enough or if they could see when they went to meetings at the Grange Hall in Haven.

He wanted Megan to remember she was a child. It was an uneasy compromise at best, a rope he had to cross with caution so he did not tear away the tenuous connections he

had made with her. Most of the time he was successful,
but he had to take care with every word he spoke. Otherwise, he might bring on again the endless bouts of tears
she had cried during her first two weeks at Nanny Goat
Hill Farm. Then, only her brother and sister had been able
to comfort her. Samuel's attempts at solace had made the
situation worse.

As the children cleaned their plates and emptied their
glasses, Samuel called after them not to let the door
slam . . . a warning that had become as automatic as
breathing. He chuckled. The children were not the only
ones who had had to adjust and discover how to live this
new life.

Glancing out the window while he washed the dishes
and dried them before stacking them on the shelves he had
raised just enough to keep Lottie from breaking even more
glasses, he saw the trio was concentrating on their project.
He was not sure where the rabbit was, but he suspected
Brendan would have made sure it could not escape. The
lad had an eye for detail that impressed Samuel, and Brendan could argue logically about anything.

All the skills a good attorney needed.

Samuel wrung out the dishcloth and dumped the dirty
water. There were other skills an attorney needed, as he
knew so well. He smiled. He did not miss the work he had
left behind in Cincinnati when he came here. Petty differences and arguing about property rights once had intrigued
him. No longer.

He picked up the newspaper that had arrived in Haven
this morning. He ignored rest of the mail, including
the letter with a return address of Jennings & Taylor. It had
been sitting there for more than two weeks, but he was not
curious enough to open it. He was not even intrigued why
his former law partner had not changed the name of the
practice when Samuel left. That answer was simple. Theo
expected him to give up here and return to Cincinnati. The

last letter from Theo had been filled with questions of why
Samuel wanted to live such a spartan life on a river-bottom
farm, and didn't Samuel know he was wasting his education among cows and corn? Theo had not been satisfied
with his answers, so Samuel saw no reason to go through
another explanation. Eventually Theo would realize he
needed to look for another partner.

He carried the newspaper into the small front parlor. The
farmhouse had six rooms on the first floor. A kitchen, his
bedroom, a guest room, and at the front, the dining room
and a double parlor separated by a pair of pocket doors.
Those doors always remained closed, because he preferred
the cozy front parlor, with bookshelves covering two walls
and its eclectic collection of furnishings.

Smiling, Samuel sat in a chair covered with the same
blue paisley fabric as the sofa. Another chair's dark blue
brocade was now half-hidden beneath a crocheted blanket
that hid the stains left by spilled ice cream and pie. This
parlor was filled with so many happy memories. When he
had bought the farmhouse and the acreage around it, he
had shipped his favorite furniture from Cincinnati to use
along with the pieces left behind by the previous owners,
who had decided to head west. A pair of Regency marble-
topped square tables were set on either side of the sofa.
Atop one was a gold clock with a charger and a Roman
chariot that had come from France. Over the slant-topped
desk in the corner, a barometer offered an excellent tool
for predicting the weather. The children particularly enjoyed checking it each day, and Megan was already showing a real interest in how it worked.

He looked out the window but could not see the children.
He heard their voices through the front door, so he settled
back to read. Before the children entered his life, he had
enjoyed the newspaper with supper every night. Now he
was kept busy making sure they ate as they should and that

they washed up before going to bed in the two bedrooms under the rafters at the top of the stairs.

He flipped through the first pages, for the news was old by the time it arrived. Gossip and the telegraph brought news faster to Haven than the postal service could deliver the *Enquirer* down the river from Cincinnati.

Hearing a yelp from outside, Samuel put the newspaper under his arm and went out onto the porch. It took him only a moment to calm Lottie and remind Brendan to let his little sister help as much as she could.

"But don't let her use the hammer," Samuel added quietly as Lottie skipped away.

"Or the nail." Brendan now wore the very superior smile befitting an older brother. "She drops it as soon as I start to swing the hammer."

"Maybe each of you should hold both the hammer and the nail for yourselves." He thought of smashed fingers and tears. "That way, if any fingers are hit, they'll be your own."

"Girls shouldn't use hammers anyhow."

He laughed. "Where did you get that idea?"

"Sean—"

"I can't believe Sean said something like that. Even if he'd felt that way before he came to Haven, he would have learned differently as soon as he came to live with Emma and work at the store. She uses a hammer whenever she needs to."

Brendan kicked a pebble across the grass. "Sean told me Jenny Anderson says girls don't use tools."

"Is that so?" He tried not to laugh again. The Anderson girl was the daughter of the owner of the livery stable in Haven. Both Brendan and his best friend were sweet on her, and Samuel suspected Jenny played one's attention against the other in an attempt to keep them interested.

He lost all desire to laugh as the bitter thought unwove in his mind. For heaven's sake, he should not be labeling a young girl with the same hypocrisy Beverly had shown. An innocent flirtation was different from an intentional ruse.

Quietly he said, "Jenny needs to think again. Every woman who comes to the meetings at the Grange Hall works side by side with her husband or parents. Farmers' wives and daughters have to pitch in with all sorts of chores around the farm."

"Jenny doesn't live on a farm."

"True, but we do."

Brendan said softly, "I wish we lived in town. Then I'd have someone else to play with instead of just my sisters."

"We'll be going into Haven tomorrow evening for a meeting at the Grange."

The boy screwed up his face. "But we have to wear good clothes for that, and I can't play in good clothes." He turned when he heard one of the girls shout his name, and he ran back across the yard.

Samuel sat on the old chair on the porch. The upholstery smelled of damp and humidity, but it was comfortable after a day's work. Propping his dusty boots on the railing, he opened the newspaper and began to read by the day's last light. The summer days were growing shorter, so he would have to finish most of the paper inside after the children were in bed.

Lightning flashed, but, for once, Megan did not come running for comfort. The little girl was deeply afraid of thunderstorms. Tonight, she must be too focused on building the rabbit's cage to notice the approaching storm.

Ignoring the distant thunder that could be barely heard over the children's voices, Samuel opened his newspaper. He had read only halfway down the third page before he saw *it*. Her name. Her married name.

He folded the paper and let it fall onto his lap. With a curse, he snatched the page away from the others, crumpling it. This is what he got for trying to fool himself.

Beverly had decided to make herself a life in the highest realms of Cincinnati society, so he should have realized her name would appear in the gossip columns sooner or later. That this was the first time it had since he had left Cincinnati almost a year ago only proved that she and her besotted husband had returned at last from their grand tour of Europe.

"What's wrong, Samuel?" asked Brendan as he came up the steps.

Forcing a smile, he replied, "Nothing important."

"You made a mess of your newspaper."

Samuel picked up the balled page and tossed it to the boy. "Tear it up in strips. Your rabbit will enjoy making a nest out of it."

"Thanks! Do you have more wire?"

Although he was astonished that the pieces in the barn were not enough, he said, "Look around for some more. There may be another section. If not, we'll pick up some tomorrow when we go to Haven."

Brendan jumped down from the porch and ran to where his sisters were intent on their project. When he called to them, they all raced off toward the barn. Megan paused to allow her sister to catch up, then they ran hand in hand. At the barn door, Brendan hushed them as he always did, for he wanted his cow to be able to rest.

The boy spoiled that cow as if it were his own babe. He planned to take it to the county fair next month, and Samuel guessed Brendan brushed it more than he did the horses.

Samuel sighed. Why was he letting thoughts of Beverly intrude tonight when he should be thinking of the future and fun things like the county fair? Her time in his life was in the past, left behind him when he moved here. He wanted no part of fancy gatherings and jostling to see which person could be the grandest or the richest or be owed the most by those around him. Even before Beverly burst into his life—and his heart—he had become disillusioned with his life. Now he was happy.

Or he had been until he had seen her name. Her married name.

Lightning crackled, much closer than before, and thunder rattled. Not thunder, Samuel realized, but a buggy coming along the road leading to the house and barn. It rolled to a stop under the tree.

He came to his feet as he recognized the passengers. As always, Alice Underhill, the village's schoolteacher, was dressed in unrelieved black. Her skirt was not dusty with chalk as it was during the school year. Handing her out of the buggy was Reverend Faulkner. That they were together forewarned Samuel that the reason for their call was to talk about the project to establish a public library in Haven.

He was not surprised when, as soon as he had greeted them and seated them in the parlor with some lemonade Megan had made earlier, Alice said, "You know there is going to be a town meeting on Wednesday."

"Yes." He leaned back in the rocker by the front window. It was not comfortable for a man of his height. More than once, he had thought of giving it away, because it was too well-made to break up for firewood. It was here because the children enjoyed rocking in it. He wished he had not sat here, because each time he looked at his guests on the sofa, he saw the Majolica fountain set beyond the woodstove. Its blue and gold decoration would have been better suited to a fine Lexington Avenue mansion in New York, but he had not been able to leave it behind. His parents had bought it on a trip to England and had intended to give it to him as a wedding gift. He had enjoyed the gift, just not the wedding.

Why was he letting a silly society newspaper piece about Beverly unsettle him so? He should have been better prepared for seeing it. After all, he had had over a year to get used to the idea.

"Are you coming to the meeting on Wednesday?" Alice asked with an impatience that suggested she had spoken to him several times while he had been lost in his thoughts and had not received an answer.

"I'm not sure. It'll depend on how much of the corn I can get harvested before then."

"Samuel, we need you to be at the meeting."

"Why? I've said all I have to say about the library."

"You need to say it again." She leaned toward him. "Samuel, I know you're a man of few words, but that may be the very reason why your words and the good sense behind them are heeded." She glanced at Reverend Faulkner, who was sitting beside her on the sofa. "Do tell him how much we need him there."

"I don't understand," Samuel replied, pushing his other concerns aside as he focused on the reason for their call. "I thought everyone, including the mayor, had agreed the library would go ahead."

The minister sighed. "The diphtheria outbreak has unsettled people."

"That was last month, and there hasn't been a new case in more than three weeks."

"True, but folks are leery of creating any reason to gather in town until they're sure the sickness won't break out again."

Samuel shook his head. "That's absurd."

"Is it?" Reverend Faulkner folded his hands on his knees. "The outbreak came after the Centennial Day celebration."

"Which hardly anyone from River's Haven attended, and look what happened out there." He could not keep from glancing out his window where, on a sunny day, he could see a reflection off the windows on the highest floors of the massive building that had, until a few weeks ago, been the center of a utopian community. Diphtheria had ravaged the Community, leaving more orphans who were being taken care of in Haven or sent to relatives back east.

Fortunately his kids had not sickened. He had watched for signs of the horrible sickness because Sean O'Dell had been one of the first to become ill. Sean had survived, but others had not.

Alice nodded. "I have been trying to tell folks that, but no one wants to listen. They're frightened, and they don't want their children coming into Haven to visit a library."

"What about school?" Samuel asked. "No one is considering keeping their children from that, are they?"

"We have almost eight weeks before the harvest is in and school can begin," she replied.

The minister patted her hand. "And to find a new teacher now that you're about to be wed."

A warm glow of happiness coursed up Alice's face, and Samuel looked away. He forced his eyes back to where Reverend Faulkner and the schoolteacher were now talking about the plans for her wedding. He kept a smile on his rigid lips. Giving folks more reason to gossip about him would be stupid. When he had not attended any of the weddings in Haven this summer, there had been veiled and quite candid questions about why he had stayed away.

He had stayed away because he did not want to make a further fool of himself.

The front screen door crashed open, and Megan ran in, crying, "The chicks are out!"

"Damn," he said when he saw her sister and brother behind her, then glanced at the minister. "Sorry, Reverend."

Reverend Faulkner gave him a sympathetic smile and stood. "No need to apologize. Do you want help gathering them up?"

"I have three helpers." He frowned at the children, who now wore expressions that suggested they had no idea how the chicks could have escaped as a thunderstorm approached.

"Do you need some help with your helpers?"

Samuel chuckled. The minister had raised quite a brood of his own, so he understood how a child's help could create more trouble than anything else.

"No, I think my helpers will be just the ones I need tonight." Motioning for the children to precede him, he paused in the doorway. "I'll try to get into town for the meeting. I know the children would like to have some time with their friends. Brendan must have mentioned Sean O'Dell at least a dozen times today, and Megan gave me a wistful look when she spoke about her friend Kitty Cat this morning."

Bidding his guests a good evening, and knowing he was being a poor host, Samuel rushed out into the yard to scoop up several of the two dozen chicks that were skittering in every direction. He nodded to Reverend Faulkner's wave as he and the teacher drove back to town. They would be lucky to get there before the storm arrived, for thunder resonated around the house.

Samuel was about to put the chicks back in the chicken coop when he discovered how they had escaped. One section of the wire was missing. He twisted the ends together, creating a much smaller coop. Putting the chickens in, he stood to see Brendan and the girls rushing toward him. Megan was carrying four chicks in her apron, and Brendan held two more. Lottie just jumped up and down in her excitement.

He put a hand on her shoulder to keep her from bouncing on a chick. As he placed the chicks in the pen, he asked, over the rising wind, "Does anyone want to explain how this happened?"

"Bunny needs lots of room. He's glowing big." Lottie smiled with pride.

"You used *this* chicken wire?" he asked, not bothering

to correct the little girl. Catching a chick racing past him, he put it back inside the coop.

"We thought it was all right. You let the chickens wander about." Megan's lower lip began to quiver as her eyes filled with tears.

He ruffled her hair. "The chickens, yes, but the little ones might wander so far they couldn't find their way back."

"Then they wouldn't have their mothers any longer."

Keeping his oath silent, Samuel nodded. Just when he thought the children had adjusted to living here, one of them made a comment like that. He sighed. He could not blame them for missing what they once had had. After all, he did.

"Let's get all the chicks rounded up and back in the coop," he said, giving Megan a smile.

She started to return it, then squealed when thunder clapped.

"Megan, will you take Lottie inside and help her get ready for bed?" Samuel asked, taking two more chicks from Brendan.

The little girl nodded, gratitude brightening her eyes. Taking her sister by the hand, they started toward the porch.

Suddenly Lottie tugged away and ran back to say, "Dahi will help you."

"Thank you." Samuel smiled. "And thank Dahi."

Giggling, Lottie ran back to where her sister was waiting fearfully on the porch.

"She's silly," Brendan announced as he cornered a trio of chicks by the coop. He was almost buffeted from his feet by a gust of wind. "There's no one named Dahi here."

"She believes there is. Why not let her have her fun?"

"Because it's silly."

Samuel had to agree with that, but he did not answer as he chased some chicks away from the road. Pulling his shirt out of his denims, he used it as Megan had her apron to hold the fluffy balls. He brought these back and made a quick count as lightning flashed overhead. All but one were there. When another bolt struck the river directly down the bluff from the farm, he grasped Brendan's arm and hurried the boy up onto the porch.

"The rabbit!" cried the boy.

With a groan, Samuel ran back out into the yard. He picked up the small hutch. Seeing the last chick cowering beside it, he set it atop the wooden crate. He put the chick in the coop, then hurried up to the porch.

Brendan dropped to his knees and peered into the crate. "He's all right."

"And he'll be fine here."

"I should check on—"

"The animals in the barn will be nice and dry. You can check on them in the morning." Opening the door, he said, "In the house, Brendan!"

As the boy hurried inside, lightning flickered again. A motion near the road caught Samuel's eye. He peered through the thickening darkness. He saw nothing moving but the tree limbs swirling in the wind. Pulling the door closed, he twisted the lock, so the wind could not snatch it open.

The storm seemed to have energized the children even more than the runaway chicks. It took him longer than usual to calm them down, and he made certain the chapter of the fairy-tale book he was reading them was a short one. They were jabbering like irritated crows when he sent Brendan to the room across the landing and tucked in the girls.

He was bidding them good night from the doorway when he heard a furious fist banging on the front door. He frowned. Who would be knocking on the door at this hour? At this time of year, when the beginning of the workday came so early, people stayed close to their homes.

"Go to sleep," he said when Lottie popped up with a curious grin. "In the morning, I'll tell you who's calling."

"But—"

He laughed. "If the caller is for you, I'll let you know."

"And if it's for Dahi?"

"He'll be the first to know."

The girls' giggles followed him out onto the narrow landing. Glancing in to see Brendan blow out his light, Samuel hurried down the stairs.

He tried to shake off his uneasiness but knew callers at this hour usually brought bad news. The last time someone had come out here after dark was to let him know about the diphtheria outbreak in Haven.

Thunder sounded like the tolling of doom. Shaking off his grim thoughts, he tried to persuade himself that this visitor was probably the minister or Alice, coming back to retrieve something they had left behind. He glanced into the parlor, hoping to see a glove or an umbrella.

Nothing but his treasured books and paraphernalia he had brought from Cincinnati. Including that ugly fountain. He was no longer sure why he had insisted on bringing it along. Self-flagellation had never been his idea of a good time.

Samuel opened the door, just as a fierce gust of wind drove rain through it. He did not get wet because someone was standing on the other side. A woman, he realized in astonishment when lightning flashed to give a hint of her appearance. A woman he did not know. Her dark gown was so tattered it flapped in the wind. She held her skirt to her by pressing a small bag against her leg.

"Is this Samuel Jennings's house?" she asked, her voice slurred.

Had she been drinking? He grimaced. There were tales of the drifters who looked for work during the harvest. They worked until they had enough money to buy liquor for a drunken spree. "Yes. Who are you?"

"Are you Samuel Jennings?"

He frowned. "Yes, but who are you?"

The woman opened her mouth. No sound emerged, and she wobbled like a feather tossed about by the storm. Her bag fell to the porch and popped open, revealing a hint of something lacy inside it. He caught her as she collapsed. Her face pressed against his chest, her heated breath rapid and shallow through his shirt.

Was she ill? If so, he could not allow her into the house where she could infect his children.

"Miss?" he asked softly. "Miss, can you hear me?"

She groaned, and her head lolled across him so heavily that he knew she had lost consciousness.

Samuel did not hesitate. He could not leave her with the rabbit on the porch in a thunderstorm. If he put her in the parlor—and kept his children away from her—she might recover without passing on whatever was afflicting her.

Lifting her senseless form into his arms, he was astounded to discover she must be almost as tall as he. Her kerchief had concealed the top of her head in the darkness. As her arms dropped along his, her ragged shawl drew back to reveal a worn gown that once might have been black. It was now a dull gray. Over it was a white apron, that was, in spite of the rain, unblemished and starched. Had she put it on just before she knocked? That made no sense. But then, neither did her swooning in his doorway.

He kicked her bag into the house, so it would not get soaked, then carried her into the parlor and placed her on the sofa. A small sound came from her when her head touched the cushions. It could have been a moan or a sigh of relief. Her eyes remained closed, and her face was almost as pale as her apron. Pulling the blanket off the chair, he draped it over her.

Now what?

No one had ever taught him what to do when a strange woman fainted in his arms. Determined to find out if she

was liquored up or sick, he put the back of his hand against
her forehead. He yanked it back. She was as hot as the
inside of a stove. What sort of fever had she brought with
her? He needed to get Doc Bamburger out here, if the doctor had recovered from nearly dying after his own bout
with diphtheria.

Samuel turned to go into the kitchen to see what he could
find to make a posset to draw out the fever but halted when
he saw Brendan standing in the parlor doorway.

"Brendan," he ordered, "stay away. She's sick and—"

The boy ran toward the sofa.

Samuel caught him and lifted him off his feet. Setting him
down by the door again, he asked, "Didn't you hear me?"

"Yes, I heard you, but—" He struggled to escape from
Samuel's hold.

"She's sick, and I don't want you near her. I don't need
you getting sick, too."

"I know, but—"

"So go back to your room and to bed. I'll tend to her.
When she wakes up, I'll find out who she is and contact
someone to come and get her."

"But, Samuel—"

"Off to bed, Brendan."

The boy planted his feet, his gaze rocking from Samuel's
face to the woman on the sofa. "No."

"No?" Never had Brendan disobeyed him like this.
"Brendan, I think you should go to your room."

Grabbing Samuel's sleeve, he said, "No. Let me stay.
Please."

He frowned, noting how the boy's thin chest was heaving
as if he had tried to lift a tree out of the ground. "Why do
you want to stay here where this stranger could—"

"She's not a stranger."

"What?"

Brendan looked up at him, his mouth working. Through
a sob, he said, "She's my mother."

TWO

"Your mother?" Samuel wanted to believe he had heard wrong.

Brendan slipped past him and rushed to the sofa. Kneeling, the boy put his hand over the woman's and leaned his head against her arm. Tears ran down his cheeks. He wiped his sleeve under his nose as he sobbed.

Watching, Samuel could not think of a word to say. A condition Theo, his onetime partner in their Cincinnati law firm, would have found unbelievable. Samuel had always prided himself on being able, when he chose, to speak his opinions in any situation. He had been wrong, because his mind was blank now.

As Brendan untied the kerchief on the woman's head and lifted it off to dab it against her rain-soaked cheeks, red hair fell down over her shoulders. It was the same vibrant shade as the children's. Beneath summer freckles, their skin possessed the same pale coolness of hers. Only a few freckles decorated her nose and high cheekbones. Had she had as many freckles as Megan when she was a child? Or was that an inheritance from their father?

Samuel gripped the back of the closest chair, recoiling as if someone had struck him in the gut. Mother? Father? These kids had come to Haven on the *orphan* train. If they had parents, what had they been doing on the train?

"Brendan?" He was unsure which question to ask first.

"They said she was dead." He wiped his nose on his
sleeve again. "They said she was dead."

While Samuel fished his handkerchief from his pocket
and held it out, Brendan continued to stare at the woman.
The sound of soft footfalls was Samuel's only warning before Megan pushed past him to stand behind her brother.
Lottie wrapped her arm around Samuel's leg and stuck her
thumb in her mouth, a sign she was as agitated as her weeping siblings.

Brendan took Megan's hand. She stretched out her other
hand to touch the woman's cheek. When the woman
groaned, Megan whirled in panic.

"What's wrong with Mama?" she cried.

Samuel stepped forward, with Lottie clasping his leg.
"She has a fever, so she must be sick. You need to stay
away from her until we find out what's wrong. If she has
diphtheria—"

"No!" cried Brendan, jumping to his feet. "Don't say
that, Samuel! Mama is here! Mama is alive! She's not going
to die now."

Taking the boy by the shoulders, he bent to look directly
into Brendan's eyes. "She's very ill, Brendan, but she's
here and out of the rain now, and we'll do all we can to
make sure she gets better."

Brendan threw his arms around Samuel's shoulders and
pressed his face against Samuel's already drenched shirt.
Looking past the boy, Samuel held out his hand to Megan.
The little girl clutched it as if she feared being sucked away
by the storm.

Over their heads, Samuel stared at the motionless
woman on the sofa. He stepped forward and motioned for
the children to move aside. For a long moment, they just
looked up at him. Then, glancing at each other and sharing
some message he was not privy to, they edged away.

"Brendan," he said quietly, "I know it's still storming,
but the worst of the lightning seems to have passed. Will

you take the wagon into town and bring back Doc Bamburger . . . if he's well enough to come? Tell him it's important. Otherwise, I wouldn't call him out on such a night."

The boy ran out of the parlor without answering. The front door slammed against the wall as he threw it open.

On the sofa, the woman mumbled something.

Samuel did not try to figure out what she was saying. In her fever, it could have been anything or nothing of importance. What *was* important was getting her quarantined somewhere away from the children.

He lifted her into his arms again. Before he could ask, Megan stood on tiptoe and adjusted her mother's head against his chest.

"Thank you," he said softly. "Megan, get your mother's bag, which is out in the foyer, and bring it to the guest room."

The little girl regarded him through tear-filled eyes. "Will she be all right, Samuel?"

"Please do as I asked. Then go upstairs." He looked down at the littlest child, who was watching him with wide eyes. "Take Lottie up with you and say your prayers that your mother will be fine."

Megan hurried to her sister. Grasping Lottie's hand, she ran into the hall and picked up the bag. She stuffed the lacy clothing back into it and, with Lottie trying to keep up, raced to the guest room at the back of the house.

Samuel followed, trying not to jostle the woman. Not the woman, but Mrs. Rafferty. He murmured his thanks as he met Megan and Lottie by the stairs. Telling them he would come up and get them as soon as their mother woke up, he watched Megan lead her sister to their room.

Samuel looked from Lottie's confused face to the woman in his arms. Had Lottie even recognized her own mother? She had been so young when she had last seen her. He grumbled a profanity under his breath. Why had this woman deserted her children and now obviously come searching for them?

More questions he needed answers for.

He carried her into the extra bedroom. Placing her on the bed, he lit a lamp and set it on the table by the bed. He grimaced when he saw how her wet clothes were soaking into the coverlet. If he left her in those clothes, she could take a chill that might be fatal in her weakened condition. If he started to remove them and she woke, she could cause all kinds of trouble for him. A woman who left her young children to fend for themselves in New York's slums might have come after them only because she had heard they were with him and wanted to extort something from him in exchange for not hurting the children again.

It was not easy to believe that pretty face could hide such a horrible intent. She was not beautiful, but her face, which resembled Megan's would, if she was smiling, offer a warmth that would draw people to her. Was she as stubborn as Brendan? Could she be as silly as Lottie? Were Megan's easily hurt feelings a legacy from her mother?

"What are you thinking?" he asked himself. He should not be letting his gaze linger on her features when he needed to be thinking about other things. Things like getting her out of those wet garments, and things like how stupid it would be to trust her.

He picked up her bag and tilted the contents onto the floor. Nothing but a change of underclothes and another surprisingly clean apron. Not even a hairbrush. Why had she traveled with so little? That was another question he would not get an answer to until she regained her senses.

Samuel drew back her soaked hair and undid her collar, watching her face to make sure she did not come awake with a screech that would upset the children more. A collar button fell off in his hand. Tossing it on the table by the lamp, he hoped the rest would not follow suit. Her dress was ragged from long wear, but he had nothing for her to wear. On the morrow, he would send Brendan to the Baileys' farm and see if their daughter Rhea could bring some clothes when she next came to clean the house.

As he carefully drew the apron and dress from her, she did not awake. But the sight of her curves hidden so sparsely beneath a chemise and petticoat nearly as shabby as the gown awoke something in him that he had not expected. He tried to ignore everything but undoing her shoes and setting them on the floor. His gaze kept slipping again and again to the length of lissome leg revealed by rips in her single petticoat. A sensation he had thought he had submerged for good when he left Cincinnati blasted through him as he put his arm around her waist to lift her enough so he could pull the covers out from beneath her. Her breast pressed against his arm while he tugged the bedding aside. He cursed. He did not want to find her appealing. Not her or any other woman. Hadn't he learned how a woman could use her seductive ways to persuade a man to do just as she wished until she tired of the sport?

His fingers glided up her back when he leaned her onto the pillows again. A simple, commonplace motion, but again the heat spread through him, compelling and demanding.

As he drew the covers over her, he released the breath ready to burst from his lungs. She was certainly not the first woman he had met since he had come to Haven, but none of the others had caused this unwanted reaction. Although the children had not said much about their father, he knew their parents were wed.

So why was he acting like this?

He was spared from having to answer *that* question by a knock on the door. He looked over his shoulder to see Brendan with Doc Bamburger. The doctor was much thinner than the last time Samuel had seen him, but his steps were firm when he came to the bed.

"How long has she been senseless?" the doctor asked, setting his black bag on the floor.

"Since just after she got here. About five minutes before I sent Brendan for you." Samuel stepped back to let the doctor do what he could.

"Hmm . . . nearly an hour, then."

An hour? Had a full hour passed since she had dropped into his arms at the front door? A mere hour that had changed his life far too much.

He went to where Brendan stood in the doorway. He put his arm around the boy's trembling shoulders.

They said she was dead. Brendan's words resonated through his head. Who had told the children their mother was dead? And why had the children been put on the orphan train to Haven? He hoped the woman would wake and be able to explain.

Cailin Rafferty did not want to open her eyes. As long as they remained closed, she could pretend the last year had been a nightmare. She could believe she was on the small farm in southwestern Ireland where she had been born, and where her children had been born.

She drew in a deep breath. A smile teased her lips as she savored the fresh, green scent of ripe fields after a rain. It had been one of her favorite smells each summer. She had lived on the few acres all her life, first with her parents and then, after her mother died, with her father, and then with her husband as well.

The slow roll of the hills rising from the sea would be glistening beneath the sunshine, and the children would be outside, their light voices sounding like birds in the trees. She would bring them in for their evening meal and a tale of the little people. The raw dirt floor would be warm at summer's end as they curled up on their cots, pulled from beneath the bed she had shared with Abban.

Abban Rafferty . . . She could remember the day she had first seen him at the tavern around the bend from the farm her family had tilled for generations. He was a tall man with no extra flesh on him. He might be less muscular than the other men she had seen all her life, but he had a refinement about him that intrigued her. He was not a farmer or a fisherman. When she heard he had come from America to see the lands his grandfather had left before the Great Famine, she had listened, enrapt as he described his journey with such an odd accent. Then he had delighted her in other ways. Abban had asked her father for her hand. The wedding had been a grand one, as fine as the wool coat Abban had worn when they spoke their vows to love each other and only each other until death separated them.

Their love had blessed them with three children, the youngest born after Abban had to return to America. He had received a letter from his family in New York, requesting that he come back immediately. He had told her that he would send for her and the children and . . .

Cailin moaned as fingers brushed against her forehead, sending a debilitating pain through her. She gripped the bedding. With a gasp, she opened her eyes to stare at a quilt far fancier than anything she had ever had in Ireland.

She did not recognize this room that was as magnificent as the quilt. She looked for anything—even a single thing—that was familiar. The whitewashed ceiling was bright in the sunshine, and the pale yellow walls glowed with warmth. A double window was raised. Filmy curtains floated in and out with the vagaries of the breeze. A tall dresser was set between two doors. Next to a washstand containing a beautiful pitcher and bowl both painted with blue flowers, a mirrored table had a small stool set beneath it. Before she had left Ireland, she would not have known what the marble-topped table with small shelves set on either side of the mirror was. She had learned it was called a dressing table.

She winced, recalling the shame heaped on her when she had not known enough about the furnishings the rich who lived in New York surrounded themselves with. The other servants had laughed at her mistakes while she struggled to earn money for herself and her children. Yet she had learned being belittled was not the worst thing she could endure and survive. Not by far.

"Can you talk?" asked a tenor voice not far from where she was lying.

Cailin turned her heavy head to look at the man. The lower half of his tautly sculptured face was darkened with whiskers. As she raised her gaze past his nose, she could not keep from staring. His eyes, behind gold-rimmed glasses, were as green as Abban's. She had not thought she would encounter another green-eyed man here along the Ohio River, so very far from Ireland.

"Who are you?" she asked, her voice little more than a croak as she pulled the quilt up to her chin.

"Samuel Jennings." He held a cup up to her lips. "And I hear you are the Rafferty children's mother."

She did not take a drink as she clasped her hands in front of her and closed her eyes in fervent thanksgiving. Even though her head ached so hard she could have believed she had been struck by a horse trolley, she summoned up the energy she had left and whispered, "The Rafferty children? My children? They're really here?"

"Yes."

His answer was so reluctant she looked up at him again. "I was told when I arrived this afternoon in Haven that they'd been placed out with you."

"When you arrived *this afternoon?* It's long past 'this afternoon.' "

"What? How long have I been here?"

He put the cup back onto its saucer so hard it rattled, and the tray beneath it almost tipped off the table by the bed. "I think the better question would be—where in hell have you been?"

She stared at him. Her first impression of him having a kind expression must have been wrong. His eyes glittered with a hot fury that added blue sparks to the emerald.

"Are you just going to lie there and say nothing?" He crossed his arms over the front of his stained cotton shirt. "Or are you trying to devise some lie to make me think better of you? Don't waste your time. Any mother who abandons her children on the street—"

"I didn't abandon them!" she cried. She moaned and put her hand to her throbbing head. Her throat burned with her outcry. Weak tears seared the corners of her eyes, but she would not allow them to fall and let Samuel Jennings discover how his words lashed so painfully at her.

"They thought you were dead."

"Dead? They were told I was dead?" She snarled her father's favorite curse under her breath. How dare Mrs. Rafferty lie to her children when she knew very well how much it would hurt! Or had that been the reason for the lies? She had learned the hardest way a Rafferty cared nothing for another's feelings, unless it got that Rafferty something he or she wanted. "You must believe me. I didn't know they had been sent out of New York until a couple of months ago."

"Months?"

"It took me this long to earn the money to follow them. Trust me. I recall every day they weren't with me."

"The Children's Aid Society would have arranged for the children to be returned to New York, if you'd asked," he said, but the fury in his eyes tempered a bit. "They told me when I first met the children that any child could be sent back to them if the placement didn't work."

She shuddered, then groaned as the motion thudded again across her forehead. "I didn't want the children traveling back to New York alone."

"They would have sent someone to escort the children back."

"No, that's not what I mean." She struggled to sit, then halted. She wore too little to slip out from beneath the covers. Heat slapped her face when she wondered if this stranger had undressed her. She looked past him. Surely he would have let his wife tend to her. Where were his wife and the children?

"Here." He held out a white shirt. A man's shirt, she realized. "It's the best I can do for you right now."

"Can't I borrow something that belongs to your wife?"

"I'm not married, Mrs. Rafferty." His expression became even colder. "This shirt is the most appropriate garment I have for you to wear."

She stuck one arm in the fine linen sleeve but was stymied. She could not put it on without first sitting up, and she could not sit up without putting it on first.

When he offered to help, she almost said no, then faltered. He cared about her children. That much was already clear. She had to let him assist her when she was unable to do anything herself.

She nodded and found herself cradled against his strong arm beneath the sleeve of his simple dark green cotton shirt. It had been rolled up to his elbow, and the warmth of his skin brushed her nape. He slowly raised her. When her head spun, a groan escaped her lips. He paused, holding her against his chest. Something crackled beneath her ear. Papers. She ignored them as the manly scents of hard work and bay rum filled her senses. She closed her eyes, once again longing to turn back time to when she had believed those aromas would be part of each night.

She had been wrong.

"I can manage alone," she said, pushing herself away from that strong arm before she could let herself be seduced again by something unreal, something coming only from her silly, lonely heart.

He released her, and she fell back against the mattress. Renewed pain sliced across her forehead as the empty sleeve struck it. Propping her heavy hand on her brow, she waited for her eyes to focus and the room to stop spinning. She had not guessed she was so weak. How ill had she been?

As if she had asked that question aloud, Mr. Jennings said, "Maybe now you'll admit that you need help."

"Yes." Her voice was as shaky as her hands. She added nothing else while he leaned her back against the pillows he had plumped and helped her put on the shirt. She hastily pulled it closed in front of her. She would button it when she was alone.

He stood, and she found herself staring again. He was shorter than Abban, but taller than she was. She had become accustomed to being the tallest woman, her head rising over even some of the men's. Athair had despaired of her every finding a man to wed, so she guessed her father had been as pleased as she was when Abban asked her to wed.

If Athair ever learned about what had happened in the past year . . . She did not have to think about that long. She knew what her father would have done. He would have seen Abban dead, but he would have been too late.

"Are you all right?" asked Mr. Jennings.

He leaned toward her again to straighten the quilt. Beneath his cotton shirt, his shoulders were well muscled and moved with a lithe ease. His shirt was tucked into worn denims, so she guessed he was a man accustomed to hard work. When he smoothed the quilt around her, as if she were a babe, his fingers were calloused. Yet, they were not stubby and possessed the same grace as his other motions.

"Tá mé go breá," she replied when he stood as straight as a soldier again. Before he could ask, she repeated in English, "I'm fine."

"You're lying."

"Yes." Arguing about what was obvious would gain her nothing, and what little pride she had left was useless. "I feel like my head is going to explode at any moment."

Handing her a cup of water, he waited until she had taken a sip. Then he asked, "What else have you being lying to me about?"

"Nothing!" She moaned at her own raised voice and rested her head against her palm as the pain swirled through it.

The cup was plucked from her fingers as her hand trembled. Closing her eyes, she sagged into the pillows. She had never been this weak. She had to overcome whatever had sapped her, because she needed to be strong now. Stronger than she had ever been.

"Maybe you should try to sleep," Mr. Jennings said.

Cailin opened her eyes, not wanting him to leave before she had answers to the questions haunting her. "My children—my children . . . how are they?"

"They're well, and they'll stay well if you haven't brought some sickness into the house to infect them."

She stared at him, wide-eyed with horror.

His frown eased, but not completely into a smile. "They've shown no signs of becoming ill since your dramatic arrival in the middle of that thunderstorm. Why did you come out in it? The children aren't witless, so I wouldn't have expected their mother to be. You proved me wrong."

"It wasn't storming when I started out from Haven."

"The walk isn't long, no more than a few miles."

"I got lost or . . ."

"Maybe you lost consciousness along the way?"

Cailin whispered, "It's possible. How long have I been here?"

"You arrived two nights ago. It appears your fever has broken." He put the back of his hand against her forehead as if she were no older than Lottie.

The thought of her youngest sent anticipation flowing through her. "May I see the children?"

"Tomorrow."

"Tomorrow? Mr. Jennings, they are *my* children, and I want to be certain they're all right."

His mouth became a straight line. "You may rest assured, Mrs. Rafferty, I haven't been beating them daily since their arrival."

How many more things could she say to insult this man who had opened his house to her children . . . and to her? Telling her empty arms to be patient for a few more hours, she said, "Forgive me. I shouldn't have spoken so. It's only that I haven't seen them in so long."

He sat on the side of the bed, startling her because he had been the model of propriety since she had opened her eyes. She tried to keep from thinking about him undressing her down to her smallclothes. Locking his hands around one knee, he said, "I have some questions of my own if you believe you're well enough to continue this conversation."

"Yes . . . yes, of course." She clasped her own fingers together.

Mr. Jennings spoke with obvious education, more than she would have imagined a farmer to have. Then she reminded herself how little she knew of American farmers. So little in America had matched the eager expectations she had enjoyed while she sailed across the stormy Atlantic and into New York harbor.

"I take it from your words," he said, "you've known where the children were for some time."

"I went to the Children's Aid Society a couple of months ago." That was stretching the truth a bit, because she had gone more than three months before, but she could guess, even when her head was hurt so badly, what his next question would be.

He asked, just as she had assumed he would, "How is

it the children were gone for so many weeks before you missed them?"

"They weren't living with me."

"Where were they?" Again his eyes slitted, and she wondered if he was thinking the children had been taken from her in New York. They had been, but not as he must assume.

Quietly, Cailin said, "I'd left them with my husband's family while I sought work so we could have a home of our own. New York City was so expensive, we soon spent every coin we brought from Ireland." She did not dare to hesitate before she added, "I saw them only on my half-day each week, for I was working in a house many blocks from where they were staying. Then, one afternoon I came to visit them at Mrs. Rafferty's home, and their grandmother told me the children were elsewhere visiting with friends."

"And you weren't suspicious?"

"I should have been, but I was so glad the children had new friends, I never questioned her, even when the children weren't there the following week or the week after that." Staring at her folded hands, she whispered, "I was just glad they were happy."

"But . . ."

Cailin looked at him as steadily as her aching head would allow. "But my children had been turned over to the Children's Aid Society. The people there were told my children were orphans." A sob bubbled in her throat, but she did not let it escape. "And my children obviously were told I was dead."

"Why would their grandmother do such a thing?"

"I've asked myself that a hundred times over each day." Even though she did not let any tears fall, she took the handkerchief he held out to her. A linen handkerchief she had not suspected a farmer would own, but, again, she reminded herself how little she knew about American farmers. How many more times was she going to be betrayed before she realized how different this country was from the Irish countryside she had known all her life?

His voice became gentler. "The children told me that not only were they told you were dead, but that they were being sent to stay with someone you'd arranged for them to live with."

"What? That was a lie!" She did not give voice to the plagues she wished would fall on everyone in that house where social standing meant more than anything or anyone.

"Of course it is, I can see now. They were put on the orphan train by the Children's Aid Society and sent to live among strangers."

She closed her eyes and whispered, "They must have been so frightened."

"They were." He did not give her a chance to respond before he added, "It appears both you and the children were fed many lies by their grandmother." He appraised her anew. "What did you do to incur such wrath?"

"She wasn't pleased with discovering she had a daughter-in-law and grandchildren from Ireland." She looked down at the handkerchief so he would not guess she was revealing only part of the truth. She must be as careful when speaking with the children. She could not let them know the appalling thing their father had done—the very act that she had been blamed for by his mother. A child should respect his *athair,* even if his actions were wrong. How many times had she spoken of what a wonderful man *do athair*—your father—was? She had believed that at the time.

"There must be more to all this than that." His frown returned. No one could accuse this man of hiding his emotions.

Knowing she had to bring this conversation to a close before she said something that would reveal more than she wished him to know, she said, "Mr. Jennings, I thank you for all you've done in watching over my children and me, but this is a problem I have to deal with myself."

"Quite to the contrary. Your problem became mine the day I brought the children here from Haven. I won't have them hurt so badly again."

Cailin nodded cautiously. "I understand." She must take care he did not use words to trip her up and cause her to betray herself and her shame. "I don't want them hurt either."

"You might find in here some answer to the riddle of why your children's grandmother sent them away." He held out a folded sheaf of papers. "These are the papers I was given by the Children's Aid Society the day the children arrived. I haven't read them since, so I don't know if you can discover some clue to the truth."

"If the Children's Aid Society had any idea they had been lied to, the children wouldn't have been here."

He nodded. "I thought of that, but if our situations were reversed, I can assure you that I would scrutinize every possible page for any hint." He set the papers on the table when she did not take them. "I can understand if you want to wait until you feel better to read them, so I will leave these with you."

"Thank you." She stared at the papers. If there was a clue among the many words, she would not be able to uncover it. Although she recognized most of the letters, she could not decipher the combinations written in a neat hand. She gasped when she heard young voices through the window. "My children!"

A wry smile tilted his lips. "They stayed quiet longer than I'd guessed they would." Standing, he said, "Mrs. Rafferty, I'll go and quiet them so you may rest. The doctor said that would be the best thing for you."

"The doctor? A doctor was here?" Her fingers grasped the quilt. She would have drawn it to her chin, but it was tucked in too tightly at the end of the bed.

"Your modesty wasn't compromised during his examination, I assure you." He paused, then said, "Doc Bamburger wouldn't have allowed that."

A flame scorched her face, and she looked down at her hands. As she released her grip on the quilt, she said, "Forgive me, Mr. Jennings. I shouldn't have suggested otherwise."

"Of course you should have."

Cailin's head snapped up as she met the abrupt amusement in his eyes. "Pardon me?"

"You don't know me from Adam, so you don't have any reason to trust me."

"Except that you've taken care of my children." Her lips curved in a smile. "Or so you assure me." Another screech came through the window. "It sounds as if they're hale."

"And tormenting each other as only siblings can." He motioned toward the tray. "I'll leave this here in case you're thirsty."

"Thank you." She was unsure whether she could lift the cup on her own because a thick lethargy was dropping over her. "I appreciate all you've done for us, Mr. Jennings."

Only when he took her hand did she realize she had raised it in his direction. His fingers were warm and rough-skinned and broad—just perfect for a farmer. Again a pulse of something exciting rushed through her, but this time she had not been thinking of her children. She had been thinking of him.

She slid her hand out of his and curled her own fingers around it to hide how it trembled anew. Not just with the weakness left from being ill. It was another weakness, she feared, one she had hoped she had banished forever.

"You're welcome, Mrs. Rafferty. I—"

The scream coming through the window was obviously one of frustration.

Smiling, he said, "If you'll excuse me, I'll go and figure out what's got Lottie upset now."

"Lottie . . ." she whispered.

Mr. Jennings must not have heard her because he walked out of the room, shutting the recently painted door behind him. His footsteps grew distant, and then she heard him call to the children. Their eager voices revealed how happy they were to see him.

Cailin leaned back against the pillows, then slowly slid down onto the mattress, so she could stare once more at the ceiling. She had found her children. That was all that mattered. She had found her children. And now . . .

The pain erupted once more, but this time not across her head. This pain came from her heart. While she had been searching for the children, she had been able to put aside her grief at what had been waiting for her when she arrived at Mrs. Rafferty's house.

Although she did not want to remember, the scenes emerged from her memory. She had been tired and filthy after traveling from the harbor. Her attempts to look her best had been stymied because she had not been able to take a real bath since she boarded the ship for America. As soon as she entered the front hall of the house, she had known all her paltry efforts had been wasted.

The fancily turned spindles on the staircase and the thick rugs on the brilliantly polished wood floors were only the beginning of the splendor. Dark red velvet curtains were drawn back from a wide doorway opening off the hall. Gold tassels matched the thick braid along the curtains' edges. Not curtains, she had learned later, but portieres that could be released to keep drafts out of the parlor. That day, she had not considered that. She had been too awed by the grandeur around her.

When a maid led her into the parlor, Cailin saw more furniture in this one room than would be found in several houses in Ireland. She had never seen a table with a marble top or so many prisms hanging from a lamp. The sofas—for there were a trio in the room—were covered with flowered fabric, the deepest shade matching the velvet curtains. Pictures hung on the wall above a black hearth with a mantel supported by what looked like golden women wearing little more than a drape of fabric.

Behind her, she had heard Brendan and Megan whispering in astonishment. She hushed them, not only to remind them of their manners, but because Lottie slept in her arms.

They had been kept waiting a long time, standing in the middle of the luxury but not daring to sit after the maid warned them to touch nothing. At the time, Cailin had blamed the maid for failing to deliver the message quickly, but she had learned later that leaving unwanted guests unmet in the parlor was a sign of contempt.

She had known the white-haired woman was Abban's mother the moment she entered the parlor. Mrs. Rafferty possessed the same self-assured motions, but she had not been wearing Abban's easy smile.

"Who are you?" her mother-in-law had asked.

"Cailin Rafferty."

"Rafferty?"

She should have noted the stiff sound of his mother's voice, but she had been too eager to see her husband again after almost four years of separation. So she had answered, "Yes, ma'am. These are Brendan and Megan, and the youngest is Lottie—Charlotte," she had corrected when the woman's scowl tightened.

"Charlotte? That's my name."

"Yes, ma'am." She hesitated, for she had thought Mrs. Rafferty would say something else. When the older woman was silent, Cailin added, "They are your grandchildren. Is Abban here? He has never seen our baby, and—"

"You cannot be his wife."

"Excuse me?"

Mrs. Rafferty looked down a nose that was as patrician as Abban's. "You heard me. If you think you can crawl in off the boat and invade this house, you're sadly mistaken. Leave now, or I shall ring to have the police called."

"If you'll call Abban instead, he can tell you that I'm being honest."

"No. Leave, or I shall have the police arrest you."

Shocked, Cailin had set Lottie on the closest sofa. She heard a sharp intake of breath but ignored Mrs. Rafferty as she dug into her bag for the papers that confirmed that she and Abban were married. The priest had read everything aloud before the wedding, so both she and Abban had a chance to be certain this was the step they wanted to take.

Holding out the crumpled pages, she said, "This proves that I'm being honest."

Mrs. Rafferty had taken the papers, scanned them, and then reached for the bellpull. Before Cailin could speak, she said, "Be silent, you silly girl. I'm not ringing for anyone but a maid to take these children to rest while we talk."

Bidding her older children to follow the maid who answered the bell, Cailin had reluctantly placed Lottie in the servant's arms. She turned back to speak with her mother-in-law, but not before she saw the maid's nose wrinkle in disgust as she fingered the thin blanket around the little girl.

That had been the last time she had seen all three children together.

And the last time she had believed happiness awaited her in America, for Mrs. Rafferty's next words were, "Before you say anything else, I have something to say to you. My son is dead."

Three

"Good morning!"

"Good morning!"

"Good morning, Mama!"

Cailin woke as the bed bounced along with the happy voices. With a cry, she held out her arms. Her three children tumbled into them like a litter of puppies. She hugged one, then the next, pressing her face close to theirs, drinking in their luscious scents, remembering every moment she had held them close. She had treasured those memories, when she had feared she would never see them again, and she treasured them even more now when her children were in her arms again.

She stared at each of them as they sat in front of her. She would never take the sight of their charming faces for granted. Not ever again. Her memories of them faded to tepid copies of these vibrant children. Brendan, who looked even more like her father than before, and whose dark eyes could go from one emotion to another in the midst of a single word. Megan, who—as always—watched over her younger sister, making sure nothing happened to her. Lottie, who had grown from a baby to a little girl since Cailin had seen her last.

All those months had been lost and would never be regained. Megan had two more missing teeth on top, and her second teeth on the bottom were growing in to tower over the others. Brendan had a scar on his elbow that might have been a recent scrape or the remnants of a deeper wound. And her dear, dear Lottie had not grown too big to fit into her arms . . . if Lottie still liked to cuddle.

With a start, Cailin wondered if the differences were only physical. The children had suffered the greatest blow any child could—believing they had lost both father and mother within weeks of each other after their arrival in America. She had been not much older than Brendan when she had lost her own mother, and the pain still lingered. She had been among friends while she grieved. Her children had had only each other.

"Look, Mama!" cried Brendan, jumping down off the bed and tugging up the sleeve of his clean, well-pressed shirt. "See how big my muscle is now."

"It is *mór.*" When he gave her a quizzical glance, she said, "It is truly big." She had become accustomed to using English after she married Abban, and the children understood very little Gaelic. In New York, with the other maids, she had spoken Gaelic, a comforting link to home. "You've grown a foot since I last saw you."

Lottie looked over the side of the bed. "He's got only two feet, Mama."

With a laugh, Cailin drew her youngest closer. "I mean he has grown so tall. And look at you!" She had hidden her shock at seeing spectacles on Lottie's nose, but she would ask Mr. Jennings about them as soon as the child was out of earshot. "You're a big girl now."

"Almost as big as Megan!"

Cailin held out her hand to her older daughter. With a heart-wrenching sob, Megan threw herself into Cailin's arms and wept. Stroking Megan's hair, which was curly just like Cailin's, instead of straight like her brother's and sister's . . . and their father's, which had been a brown so light it was almost blond, she said nothing. Megan had never been able to hide anything she was feeling, and that had not changed.

Cailin knew she should say something to the children. She had been awake half the night trying to decide how she would explain what had happened. If she had devised some wise words, they had fled from her head the moment she opened her eyes to see her dear children.

"I have missed all of you so much," she whispered. "I've missed seeing your smiles and listening to your laughs while I told you stories before bed."

"Mama," said Megan as softly, "Mrs. Rafferty told us you were dead."

"She was mistaken, *a stór.*" How she wished she could spill all the anger in her heart, but she must not. There had been enough sorrow already. She would not create more for the children by telling them of their grandmother's treachery.

"Her name is Megan," Lottie announced, sitting cross-legged on the bed. "Samuel says we all should speak directly."

"Correctly," Brendan said with a roll of his eyes. "Mama, Lottie always talks like this when she's excited."

"*A stór* means darling, and Lottie is just learning more new words, right?" Cailin tapped Lottie on the cheek, the motion almost sapping her strength.

"Oh." The little girl considered it for a moment, then said, "Dahi and I like that word."

"Dahi? Who is Dahi?"

Before Lottie could answer, Brendan said, "Mama, we've got a rabbit! We caught it yesterday, and Samuel let us keep it. We built a house for it. As soon as you're better, I'll take you to see it."

"And I'm going to take it to the fair." Megan grinned through her tears.

"Who told you that you could take *my* rabbit to the fair?"

"You've got your silly old cow to take. Samuel said I could take the rabbit if I wanted."

"I didn't say you could!"

Although even their spat was a wondrous sound to ears that had missed every aspect of their voices, Cailin said quietly, "Arguing will gain you nothing. Can we talk about this when I'm up and about?"

"Are you still sick, Mama?" asked Megan, as always the one most concerned with someone else's welfare.

"I'm getting better every day." She smiled as she had not since she had reached Mrs. Rafferty's house in New York and thought her journey was over. "Just seeing the three of you is the very best medicine I could imagine."

"I wanna show you the rabbit," Lottie said with a superior smile at her sister and brother.

"I want to see your rabbit. We'll all go and see it together."

Cailin took Megan's hand as Lottie cuddled next to her. Holding out her other hand to Brendan, she blinked back tears when he grasped it. She had been afraid he would think he was now too old for such a show of affection. Closing her eyes, she said, "Thank you."

"For what?" Mr. Jennings's voice intruded on the perfect moment.

Straightening her borrowed shirt, which was now buttoned properly from top to bottom, Cailin said, *"Dia duit."*

"That means good morning, Samuel," Brendan added, grinning. "See, Mama, I remembered it! *Deartháir.* Brother." He pointed to himself, then to his sisters. *"Deirfiúracha.* Sisters. And mama is *máthair."* He pointed to her. "And papa is *athair."*

"Yes, your father is *do athair."* She put out her hand to calm Lottie, who was bouncing about again and babbling. "Hush, Lottie," she added. "Let your brother finish."

"My father is *mo athair.* Right?"

"Yes."

Brendan glanced at the man in the door, and she flinched before he added, *"Mo athair.* Samuel, did you know I could speak Irish? See how much I remember, Mama?"

She did not answer, other than giving him a tremulous smile, for her gaze could not escape Mr. Jennings's cool one. Brendan had called him Samuel but had looked toward this stranger when he said the words *mo athair.* Only when Lottie jumped off the bed and ran to him did his eyes warm. If his questions had not shown her how much he cared about her children, the grin he offered Lottie would have.

Again her opinion of him had to be adjusted. He might treat her with a polite chill—and why not? She had arrived at his house so ill he had had to send for a doctor. But he had a warm heart that he had opened along with his house to her children. She owed him more than she doubted she could ever repay. If he had not been willing to take all three children, they would have been separated, and she might have taken far longer to find them.

Everyone was astonished when Samuel offered to have the three children placed out with him. Three children for a bachelor!

The strange voice within her head startled her. She had forgotten those words until now. Why hadn't she remembered them last night before she asked Mr. Jennings about his wife? Her head had throbbed then. It was better now, so why couldn't she recall the woman who had said those words? She searched her memory, but she could not put a face with the voice. In astonishment, she realized she could remember nothing but desperation from the time the train stopped at the station in Haven. There had been a small town and people, but they were all faceless, and the buildings might have been any color. She did remember the sound of thunder spurring her feet to reach her children before the storm broke around her.

"Good morning, Mrs. Rafferty." Mr. Jennings set the tray where he had put the other one yesterday. When had he come to retrieve that one? "I trust you'd like some breakfast, for you haven't eaten since you got here."

Lottie clambered across the bed and picked up a piece of toast off the tall stack. Sitting back on her heels, she started to take a bite. She paused, and with a glance at Mr. Jennings, she held it out to Cailin.

"Thank you, Lottie," she said, trying not to pay attention to the luscious aroma of the toast. "Will you eat breakfast with me?"

With a giggle, the little girl plucked another piece of toast off the pile and handed it to her sister. She offered the next to her brother. When she held out a slice to Mr. Jennings, he took it with a smile and a quiet "Thank you."

Again he sat on the foot of the bed, as if it were the most natural thing for him to do. Again Cailin said nothing as the children pelted him with questions between bites of toast and the jam he helped them serve themselves. The questions were about the upcoming fair, and he answered them with a patience she admired.

She did not eat, even though her stomach was painfully empty and she could not recollect when she had last had any food. She sat in silence, the toast quivering in her hand, and watched how her children treated Mr. Jennings with respect and good humor . . . and love. They clearly were at home here, and she wondered how they would feel about leaving this house and him.

When he looked over their heads, she met his gaze evenly. He turned back to the children. Not hastily, as if he were embarrassed to have her see him glancing toward her. Rather as if he had dismissed her as a problem he did not want to deal with when he preferred to chat with the children. His smile was warm as he spoke with them, keeping them from arguing about one matter or another with a skill Cailin had to admire.

"Do you have children of your own, sir?" she asked at a pause in the rapid conversation.

Mr. Jennings was clearly reluctant to look at her, and she wanted to tell him that he could not continue to hide behind the children and act as if nothing were out of the ordinary. When his gaze swept over her again, she knew she had misjudged him. He was not chatting with the children because he wished to pretend she was not here. He was doing so because he was trying to govern the powerful emotions visible in his eyes.

She clutched the covers and the long hem of the shirt beneath them. She hoped he could not hear the frantic thud of her heart.

"No children but these," he replied. "In the past six months, they've come to consider this house their home."

"You have a way with children."

"I've learned." His smile grew warm again as he clapped Brendan on the shoulder. "I've had good teachers."

"It's good to see that they've been happy, Mr. Jennings."

Lottie dropped onto her stomach. She leaned both elbows on the bed and swung her feet behind her. With a grin, she said, "You should call him Samuel, Mama. Allbody does."

"Everybody," Samuel corrected quietly.

When she did not answer, unsure what to say, for it was almost as if two men sat on the bed—the one who was so chilly to her and the one who had clearly won her children's love—Samuel laughed. He ruffled the little girl's hair and teased, "Quarter-pint, you know that's what I usually say when I meet folks."

She giggled. "I was faster than you."

"You were." Looking over Lottie's head, he flashed another of those warm smiles, but this time at Cailin. "I guess I've said that too many times in her hearing, but she's right. Samuel is more comfortable."

For whom? She did not ask. The question sounded spiteful, even in her head. Samuel Jennings could not help the fact that his smile could have lit up a ship's deck on a moonless night.

"And her name is Cailin," announced Megan, reaching for another slice of toast.

"Whoa there." He put up his arm between her eager fingers and the plate. "No one has another piece until your mother finishes her first slice. Then you can have another when she does."

Megan sat back on her heels. "Hurry up, Mama. I'm hungry."

With four pair of eyes watching her—the children's eagerly and Samuel's with amusement—she took a tentative bite. She chewed with care, almost as if she had forgotten how to eat. The first swallow was tough, and she was glad for the cup of tepid tea Samuel offered her. When she took another bite, hunger surged over her, blanking out every other feeling. She ate the toast at a pace for which she would have chided Brendan.

"Now?" asked her son as he poised his hand to grab the next slice.

"Brendan, you have better manners than this," Cailin said, then smiled. Even scolding her children was something precious now.

"Which he hasn't lost since you last saw him." Samuel arched a single brow, a skill that had always impressed her, because she never had managed to perfect it. She guessed her tone had been too cool. "Brendan, offer your mother a piece, and then—"

A door opened beyond the bedroom. The sound of a screen door closing was followed by firm footsteps.

"That must be Rhea." Samuel glanced at Cailin. "Rhea Bailey. She lives with her folks on a farm just up the road. She comes in to help with the cooking and cleaning a couple of times a week."

"She does a fine job of ironing." She touched Brendan's sleeve. "This is nicely starched."

"Samuel does the laundry," her son replied.

"You do?" she blurted before she could halt herself.

"Every Monday." Samuel smiled. "Or every rainy Monday, I should say. If Monday is sunny, then laundry gets pushed back a day. Now, when the harvest is ready, I don't have as much time for laundry. Because all their other clothes need washing, the children are wearing their school clothes today, which is why they look so nicely pressed."

"School . . ." she murmured. Her children were going to school! She fought not to weep with joy. At least one part of her dream for America was coming true. Her children were being given a chance to learn their letters and numbers. They might even be able to write their names.

"What did you say?" Samuel asked.

"Mama has always wanted us to go to school," answered Brendan before she could.

Samuel wore a puzzled expression now. "Then why didn't you send them before they arrived here?"

Cailin was spared once more from answering when a woman who was not much taller than Brendan peeked into the room. The young woman's pale blue eyes widened, and her brows rose nearly to her blond hair.

When Samuel came to his feet, clearing his throat as if he had swallowed a large piece of toast, Cailin wondered if her face was bright red. Nothing indecent had happened, but his sitting on her bed gave that suggestion.

"I brought over a dress, Samuel," said the woman who must be Rhea Bailey. She held out a light blue gown with a simple skirt. "It ain't going to be long enough by a long shot."

He grinned wryly. "I didn't consider that."

Rhea laughed, startling Cailin. Then the blonde looked at her and said, "Men!" and Cailin laughed, too.

Cailin put her fingers to her lips as Samuel's gaze aimed at her again. Offending her host with such a reaction was beyond rude. When his lips quirked with a smile, she relaxed.

"I'll have to think of something else," he said, and thanked Rhea before the young woman left.

Rhea stuck her head past the door again and said, "Megan, you promised you'd help me knead the bread this morning, didn't you?"

"But I want to talk to Mama."

"Mama?" gasped the young woman, staring at Cailin. "I thought . . . that is, I assumed . . ."

"It's all right," Samuel said. Without a pause, he went on, "Megan, a promise is a promise. You can come back and talk with your mother after you've helped Rhea."

Cailin took her daughter's hand and squeezed it. "I'll be right here, *a stór.*"

Megan smiled.

As she turned toward the door, Samuel said, "Don't forget your apron this time, Megan."

Her nose wrinkled. "I don't want to wear it."

"You don't have to wear it. Just go and get it and have it ready in case Rhea has some other chores for you."

She nodded before she followed Rhea out of the room.

Samuel walked back toward the bed. "I know. I spoil them."

"Some spoiling is good for a child." She drew up her legs and stretched her toes. Locking her arms around her knees, she did not care about her unladylike position. She needed to stretch her muscles after the long train ride and the days of being sick. "It makes a child know he or she is loved."

Again that single eyebrow rose. "Your opinion is different from the women in Haven, who have told me it is bad for a child."

"It can be, if it's done too much."

"And how much is too much?"

"I don't know. I never have gotten to the point where I

believed I loved my children too much." She smiled at Brendan and his younger sister.

Samuel motioned toward the door. "Brendan, you've got your chores in the barn, and, Lottie, you should check that your rabbit is doing well."

"Mama," Brendan asked excitedly, "did you know I have a cow of my own?"

"I heard you say something about taking a cow to a fair, but that's all."

"I've got my own cow." His chest seemed to swell two sizes as he said with pride, "Samuel lets me take care of her all by myself, and I'm going to take her to the fair to be judged." He grinned so broadly that she laughed.

Cailin wondered how many different ways she would see signs of Samuel's affection for her children. When Brendan left, his sister following to feed the rabbit, she said, "I cannot thank you enough for your kindness to them, Samuel."

"They make it easy."

"They do." She was so glad to be able to agree with him. "And I can't thank you enough for your kindness to me as well."

He gave a nonchalant shrug. "Folks in Haven look out for each other. That's why I settled here last year."

She glanced around the room. The furniture appeared as if it had been standing here for years, because it fit the room so perfectly.

"You look surprised," he said.

"I assumed you'd been here for a long time if you were able to have children placed out with you by the Children's Aid Society."

Everyone was astonished when Samuel offered to have the three children placed out with him. Three children for a bachelor! She silenced the voice in her head. Until she knew where she had heard those words, it was worthless thinking about them.

"No one stays a stranger long in Haven, so there would have been several to speak on my behalf." He laughed, astounding her again. "People mind their own business and yours as well, but only out of caring for one another. I'm told that it isn't unusual in a small town."

"So you didn't live on a farm before?"

His face closed up again, and she knew she had asked the wrong question, although she could not guess why. His answer was terse. "No, I lived in Cincinnati."

She was curious what sort of place Cincinnati was, but did not ask. Clearly this was not a topic he wished to discuss with her, and she had something else she wanted to talk to him about.

"Lottie is wearing spectacles," she said.

He nodded. Picking up the plate, he held it out to her.

She took the last piece of toast. Once she had started eating, she found she did not want to stop until her stomach was full, a sensation she had nearly forgotten. She started to take a bite, but he lifted it out of her hand. When he slathered it with more of the strawberry jam, he handed it back to her.

"If you're going to eat cold toast," he said, his smile returning, "at least have it be good-tasting cold toast."

"Thank you." She took a bite and savored the flavor of the jam and fresh butter.

"It must be quite a shock for you to see Lottie wearing glasses," he said, as if there had been no pause in the discussion.

"A big shock."

"Within a few days of her arrival," he said, leaning one hand on the footboard, "I noticed she was squinting at everything. I thought at first it might be the bright sunshine, but it quickly became clear she was having trouble seeing."

"I was afraid that was so, for I had noticed her squinting when we were crossing the sea to America. I wanted to take her to see a doctor in New York, but I wasn't sure where there was one."

"Doc Bamburger examined her. Now if we can just convince her to stop using words she doesn't mean . . ." He smiled. "She wants to be as big as her sister and brother."

"Who is Doc Bamburger?" she asked, although she wanted to hear more about her youngest, who had been speaking like a baby when Cailin last saw her. "Will he be willing to tell me if her eyes might get worse?"

"He's the doctor in Haven, and I'm sure he'll be glad to assure you—as he did me—that there's no reason to think she may become blind."

Again she flinched. "I'm glad to hear that."

"Doc Bamburger is a good doctor. He got the village through diphtheria with only a few deaths."

"Diphtheria?" She sat straighter. "You have *that* here?"

"It was in Haven earlier this summer, but no one in this house got sick."

"Thank heavens."

"My thoughts exactly." This time when he smiled, she did as well.

"As I've already said, but I doubt I can ever say enough, I appreciate you taking such good care of Lottie and making sure she can see. I feared what I might find when I got here. Anyone can see how well you've taken care of the children. Far better than I was able to."

"Our situations are quite different."

Her shoulders stiffened, and she closed her eyes before sudden tears could flow from them. That remark sounded too much like Abban's mother when she had looked down her nose at Cailin and denounced her as a liar. *No Rafferty would marry riffraff like an ignorant Irish farm girl.* Those words had plagued her for the long weeks of her grief at the dashing of her dreams.

"Cailin?"

At the concern in Samuel's voice, she shoved aside the

tentacles of those memories. She opened her eyes to discover him so close to her, as he searched her face while he waited for her answer, she hardly dared to breathe. His breath, flavored with strawberry jam, brushed her face, and his lips were only a finger's breadth from her mouth.

They were alone in this room with, she noticed with abrupt uneasiness, the door closed. Caught up in her conversation with Samuel, she had not seen Lottie or Brendan close it. Or had they? Had Samuel closed it after they left?

Her daughter and his hired girl probably were just beyond the door, but they might as well have been on the far side of the ocean. She could think only of how this strong, quiet man, who was not afraid to show his attachment to her children, possessed an undeniable male charm. As his hand rose toward her, she was torn between cringing away and lifting her own hand to touch it.

He put his palm against her forehead, shattering her delusion that he was as mesmerized as she. She should be grateful he only wanted to see if the fever had returned, but she could not be. For a moment, she had imagined his hands holding her as gently as he did one of the children. But she had not wanted him to hold her with a parent's care. She had imagined him holding her far more intimately.

"No fever," he said. "Is something else wrong?"

"No fever at all?"

"None at all. You're as cool as a spring morn." Samuel regarded her with confusion, and she could not blame him. How could she explain that it would be simpler if her thoughts had been a hallucination brought on by fever?

"Good." She sounded foolish, but it would be even more unwise to speak of how she had been ready to let him take her into his arms. It must be the weakness left by her illness and the loneliness of her broken heart. She would not make the same mistake with another man as she had with Abban. She had been shown how silly trust in a man could be. If

Abban had been alive when she reached New York with
the children . . .

"Then what's wrong?" Samuel asked. "Are you in
pain?"

"My head is aching." She would cling to the truth as
long as she was able.

"Maybe you should rest some more."

She hoped her voice did not sound as breathless to him
as it did to her own ears when his firm fingers curled
around hers, enclosing them in a warm cocoon of flesh.
"No, I want to spend more time with the children."

"They've worn you out." His smile was as paternal as
the one he wore when he teased Brendan.

"I've waited a long time for this. Now that I'm in Haven . . ."

"You're staying here?"

"I can't leave. I don't have enough money to pay for
even one train fare back to New York."

His expressive brows lowered. "You mean you bought
a one-way ticket?"

"It was all I could afford, and I didn't want to wait a
moment longer than necessary to find my children."

Samuel's shoulders grew rigid as Cailin's had been a few
minutes ago. Did she always have to put that slight em-
phasis on *my* when she mentioned the children? He did not
ask, because it might be his ears that were hearing that
stress on the word he had come to enjoy using when he
spoke of the Rafferty children.

"I'm sure you understand," she continued, her fingers
quivering in his.

Her hand in his? When had that happened? He released
her slender fingers, realizing he must have taken her hand
when he wanted to be certain she was not sickening again.

She hastily drew her hand away, holding it close to her
chest. His eyes followed the motion and took note of how
her breasts pressed against the borrowed shirt—his shirt—

with each breath she took. His own breathing was as unsteady as hers. Were they both out of their minds?

Lifting his gaze to a face that seemed to have no more
color than the pillows beneath her, he tried to imagine her
at Megan's age so he could finish this conversation with
what dignity he had left. It was impossible. Even though
her high cheekbones and softly rounded chin surrounded
by rich auburn hair were the same as the child's, he could
not ignore the pink invitation of her lips or the very adult
emotions in her dark eyes.

He mumbled something and went out of the bedroom.
As he walked toward the front door, he was not surprised
to hear the kitchen door open and shut and running feet
behind him. He paused in the doorway to see both Brendan
and Lottie vanishing back into the bedroom. A moment
later, her hands covered with flour, Megan followed them.

Walking out onto the porch, Samuel stretched his tense
shoulders as he gazed out over the fields of ripe corn. He
had spent too much time during the past few days standing
guard at Cailin's door so the children would not sneak in
and disturb her. Now he had work to catch up on. Lots of
it.

Good. That would keep his mind on something other
than dark brown eyes and soft lips. He had thought he had
learned his lesson, but it was clear he would end up being
taught the same lesson over again if he was not careful.

As he crossed the yard toward the red barn, he heard
laughter coming through the bedroom window. He paused
and listened to Brendan talk about the first stop the orphan
train had made, and how the older boys had tried to sneak
off the train to figure out where they were. This tale was
one Brendan had never told him.

Walking on toward the barn, he picked up a shovel. He
tossed it in the back of the wagon. He had gotten his life
to where he wanted it. He had the children to fill his days
with chatter. Teaching them their letters so they would be

able to keep up with the other children in Haven was a pleasure after a hard day's labor. Now everything was changed, because of a woman who was dependent upon him to take care of her until she took the children and left.

His hands curled into fists on the side of the wagon. She should not be able to come here and take them away so easily, not when her story had more inconsistencies than a felon's when facing a jury. Even without his legal experience, he knew she was hiding something from both him and the children. She had left the children in danger once. If she took them away, who could guess what she might do next?

There had to be something he could do. Tonight, when the children were sleeping, he would push aside the pocket doors to the back parlor and unpack the law books he had left in their crates. If there was anything he could do legally to keep her from endangering these children again, he would find it.

Four

As Cailin shifted the ragged gown on her lap, another section tore. She picked it up, wondering how many more patches she could put on it before she ran out of fabric from the sleeves she had cut unfashionably short. She ran her finger along the rent. This could be sewn back together. If she took the tiniest stitches she could, it might not be too obvious.

She looked down at the patches across the bottom of the skirt and laughed sadly. No one would take note of a single repair because the whole hem was now sewn together with so many pieces it looked more like a quilt than a dress.

The children's voices came from the front of the house. The heat of the day did not seem to slow them, but she was glad to be able to sit by the window to catch any bit of breeze that might climb up from the river.

She heard Brendan calling a greeting. Glancing where the sunshine shimmered on the grass before falling through the window to creep across the bedchamber floor, she wondered what Samuel was doing back from the fields when midday was two hours away. Was this his customary habit?

Cailin set the gown beside the chair. She had left her legs bare in hopes of being a bit cooler, but she could not have Samuel see her limbs if he entered the room. A silly thought, because he must have seen them when she was ill. That was something that could not be changed now. She would not compound their uncomfortable intimacy.

She reached down to pull the quilt up over her legs. Her head spun with the unthinking motion. When she had been able to walk the few steps from the bed to the overstuffed chair Samuel had brought into the room last night, she had fooled herself into believing she was almost well.

She ran her fingers along the chair's brocade arms. The dark blue fabric was shiny, not from wear like the furniture had been in the servants' quarters in New York, but from unimaginable luxury.

"I could become accustomed to this," she said aloud.

Her laugh halted when she thought about Samuel's few words when he had maneuvered the chair through the door. He had not looked at her until he had set it by the double window.

"I thought you'd prefer not to have the children bouncing on the bed when they come to visit you," he had said. "And, when you're well enough, you can sit here and enjoy the sunshine."

"Thank you." Her voice had been as distantly polite as his, sounding as if they had never spoken before.

"If there's nothing else you need tonight, I'll wish you a good night's sleep."

"No, there's nothing else I need."

When he had left, closing the door after him, she had stared at the lovely chair. Neither of them had spoken of what she knew was the real reason he had moved the chair into her bedroom. The chair was by the window because he knew that sitting on the foot of her bed was not wise. She had seen that realization in his eyes yesterday morning when she had snatched her hand away from his. She should be grateful for his quiet handling of what was troublesome.

And she was! Cailin told herself that again, as she had over and over since he had gone to do his chores. She had come here to get her children and find a way to earn

enough money to take them back to Ireland. Getting her
life ensnared with another green-eyed man would be stupid.

A knock came at the door.

"Who is it?" she called. The children would not knock,
and Samuel had not before.

"Emma Sawyer. May I come in, Mrs. Rafferty?"

Aware that she wore little more than a borrowed shirt,
she tucked the quilt more tightly around her and draped
her torn dress over her lap again before she called, "Please
do."

A blond woman who was growing round with child came
into the room. She was taller than Rhea, but not much. She
wore an apron over her blue and white gown. A simple
straw bonnet was tied under her chin with darker blue ribbons, and she carried a small box.

"Forgive me for the intrusion, Mrs. Rafferty," she said.
"I stopped by to deliver some supplies Samuel had ordered
from the store, and the children told me you were well
enough to receive callers."

Samuel . . . the children. Those words rang with famili-
arity. This was the woman! She belonged to the voice that
had filled Cailin's head and teased her by refusing to be
identified.

"Deliver supplies?"

Mrs. Sawyer smiled. "I run the store in Haven, and I
often deliver orders to my customers. However, that isn't
the real reason I came out here today, for Samuel usually
picks up his orders when he comes into town."

"But you were curious about what happened when I
came here."

She nodded as she put the small box on the dressing
table. She drew out the stool and sat. "And to apologize.
I fear I was so shocked at your questions when you stopped
at the store that I was terse."

"If you were, I didn't notice. To be honest, I don't remember much about that conversation." Cailin sat straighter, then put her hand to her forehead. The ache was fainter, but it was an ongoing reminder not to move quickly.

"Do you wish me to call some other time?"

"No." By now, she knew better than to shake her head. "I'll be all right." Forcing a smile, she said, "Mrs.—"

"Everyone in Haven calls me Emma, so why don't you? It looks as if you're going to be around here for a while."

Wanting to ask if Samuel had sent Emma to discover Cailin's plans, she swallowed the accusation. It did not matter because she had no idea what she would do when she was well.

"Thank you," she replied. "My name is Cailin."

"So I've heard." Emma folded her hands over her stomach, which suggested her baby would be born before spring. "Sean was quick to tell me every detail your son ever shared with him about you."

"Sean? Sean O'Dell?"

She smiled. "I must admit I seem to know more about you than would be deemed proper when we've spoken only once before this."

"You do?" Her hands clenched on the quilt; then she forced her fingers to relax. No one in Haven could know the one thing in her past that she wanted to keep secret. Not even the children knew of Abban's greatest betrayal, which she had discovered after the children were taken from Mrs. Rafferty's parlor, ostensibly to rest.

Emma's laugh urged Cailin to calm down even more. 'Brendan told Sean—and Sean hastened to tell me—about your favorite colors and foods. Nothing too personal, I assure you."

"Children like to gossip about their elders." She smiled genuinely for the first time. "I learned that lesson the hard way when Megan shared with everyone at church how I'd been sick the night before."

"Oh, that's not too bad. I've heard the most amazing—

and inappropriate—things from children who come into the store. I try to forget what I hear as soon as I hear it. Who knows how much of it is the truth and how much the child has mixed up?"

Cailin let her shoulders rest against the chair. It was impossible to remain tense when Emma was trying to put Cailin at ease. "I can already see Lottie mixes up a lot of what she hears. She repeats back words she doesn't know, and they have a whole new way of being pronounced. Yet somehow she makes herself understood."

"She's a darling child." Emma's smile faded when she said, "You must have missed your children greatly."

"I did. More than I could possibly say."

"Then why did you let them go on the orphan train?"

Hoping she would not have to explain to everyone in Haven, she said, "It was a mistake made by my husband's mother." She hated defending Mrs. Rafferty, but she would not let the woman's ambition hurt the children even more. "I was working in a different part of the city, and they were here in Haven before I knew they'd been put on the train."

"And your husband? Why did he allow it?"

She was better prepared this time. She hoped Emma did not notice how tightly clasped her fingers were when she answered, "He's dead."

"Oh, I'm so sorry."

"Don't be. He's been out of my life for many years now. Lottie's whole life, for he returned to America before she was born."

"And you came here to be with him not knowing he had died?"

"Yes."

"Sean didn't mention that." Emma sighed. "I'm sorry. I shouldn't have spoken of that."

"I guess Brendan has forgotten a lot about his father." Cailin touched a pocket on the dress she had worn when she worked as a laundry maid. It crackled, and she knew the cracked photo was still within it. She had planned to offer it to her mother-in-law but had changed her mind after Mrs. Rafferty made her cold announcements. Realizing Emma was waiting for her to continue, she added, "I doubt Megan recalls much of him."

"That's so sad, but they have you to share stories about him with them."

She nodded. What could she say about Abban that was not tainted with the truth?

"I'm glad you're here now," Emma said, her smile brightening. "The children are so happy to have you, and you can see how Samuel has cared deeply for them."

"I'm very grateful to him." She toyed with a thread on her gown, then said, "And to you for pointing me in the right direction."

"If I'd had any idea you were ill at the time, I wouldn't have let you come out here. Especially when a storm was approaching."

"I don't think you could have kept me from coming out here."

Emma laughed. "I understand that. If someone separated me from one of my children, I think I'd go mad." She put her hands protectively over her stomach. "But now you can make a new life with them in America, maybe even in Haven. I know my children and Kitty Cat would be happy to have them remain."

"Your cat?" she asked, puzzled. "Your cat is that fond of my children?"

"Kitty Cat is a little girl near your Megan's age. Her real name is . . ." She tapped her chin. "Now, let's see. What *is* her real name? Katherine Mulligan, I believe, but everyone calls her Kitty Cat. She came on the orphan train as well."

Cailin laughed. "Now I understand all the talk about Kitty Cat. I thought Megan was making up tales about a kitten. I couldn't imagine how a kitten could have a new pink dress."

"It's clear you've learned a lot about us already."

"Samuel said no one stays a stranger long in Haven."

"That's very true. Does that mean you're going to be staying?"

"For a while, at least." She looked down at her frayed gown. "I don't want to tear the children away from their familiar surroundings again until I'm ready to take them back home to Ireland."

Emma nodded and sighed. "I think you're wise. It'll give them time to say their goodbyes and for you to finish your mourning." Her gaze slipped to the dark dress on Cailin's lap. "Right from when I first saw you, I thought you needed to think about healing your heart."

Cailin shifted, uneasy with the turn of the conversation. Outside, the children were cheering each other in whatever game they were playing. She heard something hit a stick with a whack and more shouts. When Emma did not react, she did not jump from her seat to make sure nobody had been hurt.

Jump from her seat? She could hardly move without sending her head spinning.

"If I've offended you by my comments," Emma said, "I'm sorry."

"You haven't. I'm curious why you thought that about me." If she had betrayed herself and the truth to Emma, she might have done the same with Samuel. She did not want him to demand the truth when the children might overhear. The longer she could conceal her shame, the less likely it would be that anyone would discover it.

"I don't know. Just the hollow sound of your voice that night, even though you were clearly glad to be in Haven and so close to a reunion with your children. Now you've found them, so don't forget to take care of what's inside you, too."

"I won't," she said, touched by Emma's concern for a woman she had just met.

"I was a widow, too." Emma said the words so slowly that Cailin would have guessed she wanted to avoid speaking them. Was Emma mourning for her late husband even though she had remarried? "I know how hard it is to rebuild your life. If you wish an ear to listen, please come and talk with me."

"You're very kind."

"And I'm overstaying my welcome when you should be resting. Brendan told me not to stay long." She stood and put the stool back by the dressing table. "He's very protective. He said more than once that he wanted you to get well so you wouldn't die."

"They thought they had lost me once."

Emma nodded. "I can understand that."

But I don't! Cailin wanted to shout. *I don't understand how anyone could hurt a child by telling such a lie.*

"This is for you." Emma held out the box. "I saw you had only a small bag with you, so I thought you might need some things."

Cailin looked into the box. She picked up a comb from among the other personal items and smiled. "Thank you. I do need these things." She hesitated, looking from a lacy collar to Emma. "I'm not sure how I can pay—"

"These are a gift, Cailin." She raised her hands. "Don't look so chagrined. You don't know much about the folks in Haven yet."

She had no chance to answer as the door swung open again. She was about to greet the children when her eyes were caught by Samuel's. Once again, it was as if the rest of the world had dissolved. The children's voices, Emma's greeting, the sunshine hot on the back of her neck . . . everything dwindled into nothingness. Except for those green eyes that seemed to be seeking deep within her.

He looked away to answer Emma's greeting, and Cailin

saw his fingers were holding on to the door as tightly as she was her mending. Was he unsettled, too, by this odd connection that had nothing to do with the children? Or was something else entirely bothering him?

"Emma," he said in a voice that gave no suggestion of the source of any agitation within him, "I thought that was your wagon I saw coming up the road."

"Sean was eager to come out and see Brendan, and I wanted to visit with Cailin."

He released the door, leaving a greasy mark behind. With a grimace, he pulled a handkerchief out of his pocket and wiped off the door. His denims were covered with spots of grease as well, and his shirt stained with sweat. It clung to him, showing off every muscle. He dragged the handkerchief across his forehead before stuffing it back into his pocket. His hair spiked over his brow.

"If you aren't finished chatting with Cailin, I'll go and unload my supplies from the wagon." He smiled. "If you'll just tell me which things came in on my last order, so I don't take someone else's like I did last time I made that offer."

Emma laughed. "Actually you're my last delivery today, so everything in the wagon is yours. Now that I'm not delivering to River's Haven, you're the last stop in this direction. However, I hear that's going to change."

"Someone is moving in at River's Haven?" Samuel asked, surprised. He saw Cailin was listening, clearly trying to figure out what he and Emma were discussing.

"Rumor is that someone has bought all the property not taken by former members of the Community."

"There's a lot of good land left, although I think all the land along the river has been claimed. I know Wyatt has a large portion where he built his pier so steamships can dock there for repairs."

Emma shrugged. "As I said, it's just a rumor at this point. I'll let you know if I hear you're definitely getting new neighbors, Samuel." She smiled at Cailin. "I'm so glad to have a chance to talk with you again. I'm sure I'll see you in town one of these days."

"Yes, I'm sure you will. I look forward to it." Cailin's voice had a thready sound Samuel did not like.

Her face was almost colorless, save for those endearing freckles. Lines were furrowed in her brow, and he knew she was trying to do too much too quickly. He almost laughed. In that, she was much like her impatient son.

"Do you need help to get back to bed?" he asked.

"Bed?" Her eyes widened, before focusing on the dress she had draped across her lap. "No, no, I think I'll finish this now."

Samuel had no intention of arguing with her in front of Emma. Holding the door open, he followed Emma out of the room and onto the porch. She started to speak, but he shook his head and hooked a thumb back toward the bedroom.

They walked to the black wagon that had DELANCY'S GENERAL STORE, HAVEN, INDIANA, painted in white on the sides. Here their voices would be hidden beneath the children's loud ball game.

Even so, Emma asked in not much more than a whisper, "How are you, Samuel?"

"All right."

"Really? I think I'd be furious if someone came and claimed Sean and intended to take him away."

He picked up a box holding bags of sugar and flour. "I'm not happy about it. I intend to let Cailin know that as soon as she's feeling better."

"Be careful. She's frightened, Samuel."

"Frightened? Of me?"

Emma laughed as she reached for the horse's halter to turn the wagon back toward the road. "Of course not." She glanced at the house. "She must have married young, and she probably never wandered far from where she was born

until she came to the United States. When she found out
her husband was dead—"

"He's dead?" He set the box on a stump.

"You didn't know?"

"No." Putting one boot on the side of the stump, he said,
"I wonder what other things she hasn't gotten around to
telling me."

"She didn't act as if she were trying to hide anything.
It just came up in conversation." She patted the horse on
the nose, then called, "Sean, it's time to head back to Haven."

The children swarmed over them, all talking at once. As
he tried to separate one's words from the others, he swung
Lottie up onto his shoulders. The little girl squealed, getting everyone else's attention.

He put Lottie back on the ground as soon as the black
wagon was disappearing toward Haven. Picking up the
crate, he saw Brendan eyeing it, and said, "Don't get any
idea about catching more rabbits. One rabbit is one rabbit.
More than one is too many."

"What do you mean?" asked Megan.

"Ask your mother about more than one rabbit when she's
feeling better," he said gruffly.

The children stared at him in astonishment, but as he
carried the box to the house, he heard them laughing and
running toward the swing he had hung in the biggest tree.

Samuel left the box on the table in the kitchen and
walked to the guest bedroom. He started to open the door,
then rapped his knuckles against the raised panel.

"Who is it?" he heard.

"Samuel." There was a pause and the sound of fabric
rustling, then he heard, "Come in."

The moment he opened the door and saw her sitting
primly on the chair, he knew he should have gone back to
his chores instead of coming here. She was wearing his
shirt, a sight so enticing he could not help staring. Its collar

pushed up through her fiery hair, but drooped deeper than her prim dress's neckline. In spite of himself, he could not keep from thinking about how soft her skin had been when he rolled her stockings down her legs—legs that were bare beneath the shirt that must not reach her knees.

"Yes?" she prompted.

The wavering in that single word warned him that she had pushed herself too hard by sitting in the chair this long. "You should be back in bed!"

"I know." She sighed. "I tried."

How many more ways could she tempt him to forget his vow not to let another woman invade his life? Crossing the room in a trio of steps, he scooped her out of the chair. He thought she would protest, but she leaned her head against his shoulder with another sigh. He hoped it was with relief or fatigue, not a sensual sigh because he held her.

Cailin closed her eyes when Samuel placed her on the bed. The straw in the mattress below the featherbed whispered a welcome. She rested her head back against the pillows and opened her eyes.

He was too close. She mumbled something about being fine, but he did not move away. When he put one hand on either side of her and leaned toward her, she could not pull her gaze from his lips coming ever closer to her.

By all the saints! Was he thinking of kissing her? Had Emma said something to him that made him think Cailin would welcome his kisses? Honesty pounded through her. Emma had not needed to, because Cailin had curled up against his chest when he carried her here to the bed.

"Cailin . . ."

She waited for him to say something else, anything else that would send his warm breath along her lips like a tentative caress. She spoke his name as faintly as he had hers, but all other words faded into silence as his finger beneath her chin brought her eyes up to his.

His mouth on hers was gentle. Other kisses in other

times had not been like this. He was asking her to share her pleasure with him, not demanding. When her arm curved along his shoulders, he drew her up to him. His kiss deepened, thrilling her with its invitation and yet its restraint. A restraint she knew that was only because she remained weak. She combed her fingers up through the hair at his nape while he scattered kisses over her cheek and along her jaw. When the tip of his tongue brushed her ear, she could not halt the quiver racing through her. His breath, uneven and warmer than the day's heat, pulsed against her ear, swirling into her. As he pressed her back into the pillows, the mattress's rustling was a soft song beneath the pounding of her heart.

A young cry of outrage rushed in through the window. Cailin stiffened, but Samuel released her to go and look out. He called something to the children, but his words did not pierce the heated mist around her.

"They're all right," he said, walking back to her.

He glanced down, a smile matching the sparks in his eyes. With a gasp, she yanked the quilt back over her right leg.

"Don't look!" she gasped.

"I'll try not to . . . next time."

Now the warmth surrounding her was mortification. First she had let him kiss her. And kiss her well. Now she had let her limb be displayed as brazenly as a harlot's.

He drew the covers up over her. "There. You're properly concealed." Without a pause, he asked, "Why didn't you tell me your husband was dead?"

"You never asked," she answered, astounded at the question when moments before he had been kissing her.

"True." He gave her a lopsided grin. "One parent appearing out of nowhere was enough at a time."

"Samuel . . ."

"You don't need to look at me with an expression I expect to see on Megan's face when she does something naughty."

"I shouldn't have . . . we shouldn't have . . ."

"We did." He ran his finger along her lips. "Maybe it wasn't what we should have done, but it seemed so when you were draped over my arms."

"This is going to make what is difficult even more difficult."

"I know." He laughed again, but with little amusement. "I need to get back to work. Some fresh air might be a good idea."

"Yes." She had no idea what else to say.

When he walked out of the room, she turned her head on the pillow to stare through the window. She winced at the sound of Brendan's booming laugh. It was so much like his father's.

Tears pricked at her eyes as the sound brought Abban's image into her mind. She could have stayed in Ireland and struggled to make a home for her children on what was left of the land her father had farmed since he was not much older than her son. Athair had begged her to, but she had refused to listen. She had been too eager to come to America and make a life with Abban.

She had endured the long journey and the sparse food, giving the greatest share of whatever she could obtain to the children. She had thought the privation and trials would be ended when she reached Abban's mother's home. Then she had learned the truth from his mother on that horrible day she first called at Mrs. Rafferty's house. Not just of Abban's accidental death, but of his intentional betrayal.

She had told no one, not even the other servants in the magnificent house where she worked in the dank laundry, of Abban's darkest perfidy. On that one thing, she had agreed completely with his mother. She wanted no one to know her husband had married another woman after his return to America even though he had legally wed Cailin in Ireland. Unlike his mother, she had not cared about what his bigamy could do to the family's social standing. She cared only that her children not learn that Abban had never planned to send for them while he created a new family that met his mother's expectations. How could they understand their father doing such a thing? She could not.

The man she had known in Ireland had been quick-tempered and had spoken his mind, whether anyone agreed with his opinions or not. And he had loved her. She had believed that, and she wanted to believe it even now.

She wondered why he had changed so completely after his return to New York. When his mother had arranged for him to marry the daughter of a wealthy family, he had not told Mrs. Rafferty of his marriage and the wife and children who were waiting to join him. He had married, and, when he died, he had left his other wife with two children younger than Lottie.

Cailin's concern for those children as well as her own had been the reason she agreed with Mrs. Rafferty's plan to keep the truth hidden. It seemed so simple. Cailin would be hired out into a wealthy home to earn the money she needed to take her children away from New York. In exchange, her children would be allowed to stay with their grandmother, although none of the children would be told of the relationship between them and Abban's family.

Then she had been betrayed again, this time by Mrs. Rafferty, who had sent the children to the Children's Aid Society and lied to Cailin long enough so they could leave New York on the orphan train. When Cailin had last called at Mrs. Rafferty's house, Abban's mother had been unrepentant. Mrs. Rafferty was certain she had done what was best for all involved. Her *real* daughter-in-law, whom she never named in fear Cailin would contact her, would not be kept from making another match after her mourning was over. Her *real* grandchildren would continue to live in the luxury that was their due. Cailin's children would have a fresh start where they could not interfere with Mrs. Rafferty ever again.

And Cailin . . . Mrs. Rafferty suggested outright that Cailin return to Ireland, marry some ham-fisted farmer, and have the life a lowborn wench deserved. Instead Cailin had gone back to her job, determined to earn what she needed to follow the orphan train. If she had not wanted to hurt five innocent children, she would have whispered the truth among the servants. The truth would have reached the ears of the mistress of the house and then spread throughout the upper hierarchies of society, ruining Mrs. Rafferty's life as she had tried to ruin Cailin's.

She had held her tongue. Athair's voice filled her mind as clearly as if her father stood beside her. *A kindness done returns tenfold, an evil a hundredfold.*

Blaming Abban's mother for forcing him to marry would have been easy, but she could not. When Cailin was told that he had changed his name to a more acceptable Abner to enhance his family's standing among the Irish who had emerged from the slums to live in grand style in the shadow of the upper classes' mansions, she knew he had made the choice without coercion. He had wanted a life of being surrounded by splendor and comfort. While they sat together in the small cottage with its dirt floors, he often had spoken of when he had money and what he would do with it. He had denied his wife and his children to obtain the wealth he wanted.

She could have forgiven him if he had turned his back on them, but she could not forgive him for marrying another woman. Nor could she forgive him for letting her believe he would send for her and instead consigning her and their children to wait for the rest of their lives.

She had let Abban Rafferty beguile her . . . and lead her to this catastrophe. Now she was making the same mistake with Samuel Jennings, another man whose green eyes glinted with strong passions. She must get well and leave

this house before she made another decision that would
separate her from her children. She had been lucky to find
them this time. She could not count on being so lucky
again.

Five

Being rested and well was wonderful. Washing her hair and feeling clean would be even more delightful, but she had taken so much of Samuel's time already. She could not ask him if he could bring a tub in here so she could wash.

Cailin sat on the stool in front of the dressing table and finished pinning her hair into place. She stared at her reflection, noting new lines in her face since she had last had the luxury to appraise her appearance. That had been before she discovered what had happened to her children. But now that was behind her.

She smiled, and the lines vanished. It was so easy to smile when her children were here and she was well once more.

Standing, she smoothed her gown over her single petticoat. The patches were less noticeable in the lamplight than she had feared. Sunshine would pick out each stitch, but she would not shame her children by looking like a pauper.

"But you are a pauper," she said to her reflection. She took a deep breath and released it slowly.

Samuel had said no one in Haven was considered a stranger long, so that must mean he was familiar with everyone living along the river. If there was someone who was in need of help in their house, he might know. He would likely know as well if any house was vacant and available for rent.

Going to the bedside table, she picked up the sheaf of papers Samuel had given her when she first awoke. She lifted the topmost one, then let it fall back into place. The fine handwriting continued from the first page to the second. She saw a trio of numbers on the page. They matched the ages of her children. She ran her fingers across the letters next to them. *B-r-e-n-d-a-n. M-e-g-a-n. L-o-t-t-i-e.* Those letters must spell Brendan, Megan, and Charlotte. After the names were the letters *R-a-f-f-e-r-t-y.* She recognized those letters, for she had seen Abban sign his name the day they were married. Rafferty.

Cailin folded the papers again. She had been a fool to believe that Abban had taken those precious vows seriously. But how could she have guessed that, even then, he might have intended to return to America . . . without her?

"That's in the past," she murmured as she walked slowly to the door. "It's time to start over."

She hesitated as she put her fingers on the glass knob. The last time she had seen Samuel was when he had shocked her by kissing her with such fervor. She had not expected *that,* but she had not been able to think of much else since. He was so kind to the children. Maybe he considered his kiss as a kindness. If so, she needed to tell him that he was wrong. And she had to persuade herself it was wrong to want another kiss.

Cailin opened the door slowly. She had heard the children go to bed almost an hour earlier, so this would be a good time to speak to Samuel. Walking beside the staircase, she touched the banister at the lower end. It was as smooth as the well-polished wood on the bed.

She paused at the newel post that was topped by a brass sculpture of a dog sitting on its back feet and holding a up glass globe. Resting her cheek against the railing, she stared at what must be some sort of lamp. She had not guessed she was still this weak. She had walked around her room throughout the day, but now she panted as if she had run all the way from Ireland to Haven.

When the weakness passed, Cailin pushed herself away from the banister. To her right, she saw what appeared, in the moonlight, to be a dining room. A large table was surrounded by tall chairs. The kitchen must be beyond it. She looked to her left. A door set back in the shadows next to a long-case clock was closed. Another one was shut as well, but a broad doorway was open near the front door. She went there, guessing quite rightly that it was a parlor.

She looked in. The light came from a lamp in the room beyond. Taking care to edge around the furniture that filled the parlor, she paused and stared at the incredible fountain in the corner. It was larger than the one that had been such a source of pride in the house where she had worked in New York.

Was Samuel as rich as her erstwhile employers? Until now, she had been able to overlook the elegance of the furniture in the room she had been using. "The guest room," the children had called it. She had never heard of a house having such a room until she arrived in America.

Glistening in the faint light from the back room, the marble tabletops bespoke a wealth that contrasted with his worn workclothes. Everything she discovered about Samuel Jennings created more questions.

Cailin went to where pocket doors had been slid aside a short distance to grant entrance to a back parlor. She stared in astonishment at the disarray. A rolltop desk was set between the room's two windows, and glass-fronted bookcases lined the walls. All of them were empty. Several frames with pages covered with words hung on the wall, but she saw no photographs.

Books were piled on the floor by several crates that must have been opened recently, because the lids with the nails sticking out of them were leaning against the wall. She

doubted Samuel would have left those nails like this for
long; he would not want one of the children to get stabbed.

Turning, she saw many more crates stacked to the ceiling. If the pocket doors had been opened all the way, crates
might have spilled into the front parlor. She edged away,
not wanting one to topple on her.

Were they all filled with books? She bent to touch a
book on the closest pile. The leather binding was finer than
any pair of shoes she had ever owned. Gold leaf edged the
pages. Her employers in New York had been collecting art
they believed gave their house a cultured appearance.
Maybe Samuel collected fancy books.

"Oh, blessed morn!" she gasped when she saw that all
the books were covered with fine leather and gold leaf.
These must be worth more than Athair's farm.

Hearing footsteps, she stood. She started for the door,
then halted. Something had caught on her collar. She tried
to shift, but whatever held on to her clattered against the
wall. She strained to see what gripped the back of her collar.

"Cailin!" Samuel paused in the shadowed doorway. "I
thought you'd be asleep by now."

"I've slept my fill, I guess." She tried to edge to one
side, hoping whatever held her collar would release it.

He took a step into the room, and she could not keep
from staring. This was not the farmer she had met before,
but a gentleman. His vest beneath his light brown coat was
of gold satin. Trousers, a shade darker than his coat, par-
tially covered shoes that glowed, even in the dim light, with
a recent polish.

As he looked down at himself, he smiled. "I was on my
way into Haven for a meeting, but if there's something you
need . . ."

To be unhooked from whatever has me! She silenced the
thought, hoping she could figure out a way to get herself
free from . . . whatever.

"I wanted to return these papers to you." She held them out.

Taking them, he started to walk past her but halted when she moved only an inch to one side. She could not move farther. His brows lowered, and she smiled weakly. How could she explain that she was stuck?

"Do you have any questions about anything in them?" he asked as he edged around her and went to the desk. Rolling up the top, he drew a key out of a pocket. He pushed aside a pair of books. Opening a drawer, he put the papers inside and locked it again before lowering the top.

"No." Cailin struggled to look over her shoulder. More frames were lined up just behind her. One of them must have snagged her collar.

"So you can see now why I was surprised when you arrived?"

"Yes, of course." She wished he would leave so she could find a way to escape from whatever held her.

"I had thought you'd wait until morning before you started exploring." He leaned back against his desk and crossed his arms over his chest.

"Without the children underfoot, it was a bit easier."

"True." He smiled. "They do have a way of asking more questions than any one person can answer."

Why was he being as talkative as the children? She wiggled a bit to her left, hoping she could get free. "I hope you don't mind if I look around the house more in the daylight."

"Of course not."

"You have very nice furniture here." She pretended to be intrigued with the lamp set on a crate by the door. "So many of the things seem new. Did you buy them just before you left Cincinnati?"

"Yes."

At Samuel's terse answer, Cailin looked at him. What

was it about Cincinnati that caused this reaction? Maybe the children would know.

Quietly she said, "I don't want to keep you from being on time for your meeting."

"I should be going." He turned, his foot hitting a stack of books. When they crashed to the floor, he grimaced and bent to pick them up.

This was her chance. She slipped a hand up behind her, groping to reach the frame and free herself.

Broad fingers covered hers, and she looked up. Her nose bumped into Samuel's firm chin. She would have jumped back if she could have but froze when he laughed.

"Don't move," he ordered.

"I can't. Can you get me loose without ripping my collar?"

"I'm not sure I should. You make a nice addition to the wall."

She stared up at Samuel. His face was even more compelling at this distance, and more contradictory. Although he was smiling, his eyes had an intensity that unsettled her.

"I don't think this is funny," she replied. "You wouldn't think it was funny either if you were stuck."

"Probably not." He chuckled while he worked to detach the frame from her dress. A scent of some musky cologne drifted from him as he stepped back. "There. All set, and no damage to you."

Cailin realized she might as well smile, too. "Just my pride."

He laughed. When he reached toward her, she fought not to scurry away. She might get snagged again. The heat of embarrassment pumped through her as he straightened the frame behind her.

"And no damage to anything but my foot and some of these books." He gave her that cockeyed grin that sent something luscious swirling through her. "Next time, I'll watch where I'm going. But you must admit, a woman squirming up against the wall is distracting."

Her gaze was caught by his. She was going to have to watch what she said. He could be as smooth as a fresh coat of whitewash. "Really, Samuel!"

"Really, Cailin."

She realized he had not moved farther away. With his arm resting on the wall close to her, he had—if anything—inched closer.

"If you will excuse me—"

"I have so far, even when you poked your nose into my office."

"Your office? I didn't know farmers have offices," she said.

"This one does, for the lack of a better name for this mess."

"Have you read all these books?"

"Heavens, no!" He laughed and lifted one out of a crate. "These law books aren't easy reading."

"Law books? Are you a lawyer?"

"I have been." He dropped the book back into the crate. "But right now, I need to be on my way into Haven or I'll be so late the library committee meeting will be over." He did not move as he added, "We're trying to get a library established in the village. Then I can donate these books and get them out of my house."

"If you needed them—"

"They'd be right there. I just would have to go into town and get them."

She laughed. "So you have the villagers' appreciation and yet get what you want, too?"

"Exactly. I hope others aren't as insightful as you, Cailin." His voice softened on her name, turning it into a caress.

If he heard the gasp battering within her throat, he might . . . she had no idea what he might do. He truly was a contradiction. He read people well; perhaps that was a skill he had learned along with the law. Maybe he thought this honesty would make her trust him. She should put him to rights and let him know how thoroughly he was failing.

She did not trust him, and she did not trust herself when he was standing so close to her. She resisted glancing at the door to see if the children might have slipped down the stairs to eavesdrop. This room seemed so much cozier with the two of them here. Too cozy.

"I had another reason for looking for you," she said.

"Really?" He arched that single eyebrow, and she wondered if he had guessed how that fascinated her.

"Now that I'm well—"

"Better, but not well, I'd say by the look of you. You're pale."

"My Irish complexion." She laughed, but the sound fell flat.

"If your Irish complexion is gray."

"Samuel, I need to look for work to support myself and my children."

He scowled. "I've been taking care of the children for the past six months, and I don't intend to stop making sure they have food and a roof over their heads simply because you've shown up in Haven."

"I need to find work." She should not have mentioned the children; Samuel always got defensive when she spoke of them. "I thought you might be able to recommend someone who needs help in the house."

"Maids aren't *de rigueur* in Haven."

"What?"

His smile returned but was cool. "No one has a maid here."

"You have Rhea."

"Yes, but only to help two days a week. That isn't unusual. A full-time staff is. This isn't New York City."

Cailin bit back the sarcastic retort she wanted to make

when he acted as if she had no more sense than Lottie. "If that's the case, then I may have to leave Haven to look for work."

"Or you could take over the household here."

"Here?" She stared at him in disbelief. While she was ailing, nobody would think it strange for her to remain in this house with Samuel, but if she stayed once she was well, it would be very different.

As if he had heard her thoughts, he asked, "Do you really care more about what other people think than about your children?"

The words stung, for that was the very crime Mrs. Rafferty had been guilty of. "No!"

"Then stay and take care of the household. That will free me to catch up on my work in the fields. I'm behind because of caring for you."

It made sense. She would have a place to live, and her children would be with her and well cared for. Quietly she asked, "How much will you pay me?"

"Rhea gets fifty cents a week. I'll give you the same, as well as your room."

"That's too generous!"

"Do you want to accept it or not?"

Cailin could not miss the hope and despair mixed in his expression. He was offering her this job to keep her from taking the children and leaving. Didn't he realize the money she earned would be saved for passage to Ireland? She stared down at her clasped hands. It would take a very long time to pay for four tickets, but she doubted she could get better wages anywhere else.

"Yes," she said. "I'll accept it."

"Good." The satisfaction in his voice brought her head up. "That solves my problem of finding someone to replace Rhea."

"She's quitting?"

He did not meet her eyes as he said in an abruptly clipped tone, "She's getting married soon."

"To someone you don't like?"

"No, he's a fine young man."

She guessed this was another topic he did not want to discuss, so she said, "I don't want to delay you from your meeting."

"But you are." He stepped nearer.

"I can move aside now and let you by."

"Yes, I suppose you can." His hand curved around her shoulder. "Or I could just pick you up and set you aside as I do the children when they get in the way."

"I think you've carried me around enough." She tried to smile, but her lips seemed to have a mind of their own when he was touching her; all they had on that mind was being pressed against his. When she took a step aside, his arm drew her back to him. "I can find my way to my room and bed all by myself."

"Yes, I suppose you can."

"You're repeating yourself."

"Sometimes a man just has to keep doing something until he gets it right."

His mouth claimed hers, and he tugged her against him. As her hands glided up his firm back, he pressed her against the wall. She gasped against his mouth as his bold fingers grazed her side. Her dress wrinkled beneath his eager touch. When his tongue caressed her lips before delving within her mouth to sample every slippery surface, each touch created an escalating pleasure that urged her to sample more. She wanted to be closer to him, so close that not even a thought could come between them.

He raised his mouth. When she whispered a protest, he smiled. He brushed her hair away from her face as he examined every inch of it, lighting it with the blaze from his eyes.

"We could make a good team," he whispered.

Pushing herself out of his arms, she feared that he had kissed her only to entice her into staying. "I want to believe you, Samuel, but I don't know if I can."

He folded her fingers between his. She turned to look at him, and he smiled sadly. "You're afraid to believe me, but you'll come to see I'm being honest with you."

"You have more faith in me than I have in myself." A pang cut through her. She should tell him why. He deserved an explanation. She refused to listen to her heart which warned her of the danger she courted by craving his kisses when he wanted her children.

"Who are you?" he asked.

She stiffened. "What do you mean?"

Smiling, his finger traced a path across her eyebrow and along her cheek. "I mean who are you? I can't imagine a woman whose passion can barely be held within her allowing her children to be taken from her so easily."

"I explained what happened. Don't you believe me?"

"I'm trying to." His finger steered her mouth to his.

"Mama!" The cry from beyond the front parlor drove right into her heart.

"Megan!" Samuel gasped.

Needlessly, for Cailin recognized her daughter's panicked voice. She pushed away from him and ran into the other room. Crashing into a table, she shoved herself around it and rushed to Megan.

The little girl threw her arms around Cailin's waist and pressed her tear-soaked face against her. "Mama! Mama!"

"I'm here, *a stór.*" She lifted Megan, leaning the child's head on her shoulder, even though it took almost every ounce of what little strength she had regained. Megan's legs wrapped around her waist, her ankles locking together. "Hush, *a stór.* I'm right here with you."

"I dreamed you'd gone away and I'd never see you again." Her voice came out in broken sobs. "Not ever again. I dreamed you coming here was just a dream."

"I'm here, Megan, and I'm never going to leave you. Not ever." She buried her face in the little girl's hair. "Not ever," she whispered again.

Samuel stood beside the pocket door and watched in silence. Everything he had believed about the children was wrong. He thought they were happy with him. And they had been, until their mother found her way back to them.

When Cailin sat on the sofa, settling Megan on her lap and murmuring so softly he could not hear her words, he brought the lamp from the back parlor and set it on the table beside them. He was not certain either of them had even noticed until Cailin looked up and thanked him quietly.

"I need to leave for the meeting," he said, uncomfortable in his own house as he had never been before. This connection between Cailin and her children was stronger than he had imagined. Or he had wanted to imagine, for he had fooled himself into believing he could make them this happy.

"Go," she whispered as she cuddled Megan, who already appeared to be half-asleep. "She'll be all right."

Megan sat up. "I'm all right now, Mama." She wiped her cheek with the sleeve of her white cotton nightgown. "I thought you weren't here. I'm glad you and Samuel are here now."

"You should have only happy dreams from now on."

"Tuck me in, Mama?"

Samuel picked up the little girl. "Your mother is not completely better. Toting you up the stairs is too much for her."

"Then will you tuck me in, Samuel?"

His gaze caught Cailin's as he said, "I can't think of many things I'd rather do. While I do that, your mother can sit here and get some color back into her cheeks."

Cailin put her hand up to her face, and he almost

laughed. That expression, pensive and yet uncertain, was one he had seen on Megan's face often.

"Will you sit here, Cailin, while I pop this silly girl back into bed?" He flipped Megan so he was holding her by the ankles. As she squealed with delight, he set her on the floor and put his finger to her lips. "Quiet, so you don't wake your brother and Lottie."

"Lottie was snoring when I came down." Megan's nose wrinkled in disgust. "So much noise from a little girl. Did you know she snores, Mama?"

When Cailin's smile glowed in her eyes, he tried to ignore the twist of something pleasurable in his gut, something he had not felt since . . . He hurried to say, "Now you're dawdling, Megan." He gave her a gentle shove toward the door, but Megan ran back to Cailin. "Tell your mother good night and that she should sit quietly there until I come back down."

"Good night, Mama."

"Good night, *a stór.*" She kissed the little girl on the cheek, but her gaze rose again to meet Samuel's.

Cailin Rafferty was what his partner Theo would have called a second-looker. Not classically beautiful, but definitely worth a second look. And he gave her one, a slow perusal aimed at admiring every inch of her. She had a quirky smile and a figure that fit perfectly into a man's arms. Into *his* arms. Even in a ragged dress that had been patched as best as she was able, she had a regal mien.

An Irish princess.

He almost laughed out loud at the thought. She might have a pride that kept her chin high, but she was a ragamuffin who had had to leave her children in the care of people who had turned them over to an orphanage.

One corner of his mouth tipped up in a rueful grin. Would she be offended if he told her that the freckles on her pert nose had been the one thing that convinced him she was telling the truth? Any woman who did not try to hide them under a layer of rice powder must be honest.

"Mama!" Megan rushed to her mother again. "When will you be able to tell us some of your fairy stories?"

"You remember those?"

"I remember one about a little man with some gold."

"A leprechaun?" Cailin wanted to hug her daughter so long that the many months apart would be forgotten. "I'll be glad to tell you the story in the morning."

"You're dawdling again," Samuel said with a ferocious frown that brought giggles from Megan. "Off to bed with you."

"Will you read me a story tonight, Samuel?"

"I already have." He waved his hands toward the stairs. "Time to go to bed so I can get to my meeting in Haven."

"For the library?"

He nodded, then halted Megan by taking her hand as she was about to return to the parlor. "You can tell your mother about it in the morning. If you go to sleep now, she can, too. That way, she may be feeling well enough tomorrow so you can take her outside and show her your rabbit. How does that sound?"

Cailin did not hear her daughter's answer, for Samuel glanced back at her. She knew she should look away, but she could not. Her eyes were caught again by his, and her breath clogged in her throat. His build was perfect for denim and leather, but in his fancy clothes he was even more enticing. She thought of how he had asked her who she was. That was a question she should have posed to him. A gentle man and a gentleman. A man who was not afraid of hard work with his hands, but a man who had been a lawyer. Devoted to her children and yet not spoiling them as he taught them as if he were their father.

But even his good looks and his strong hands and his kind heart seemed incidental when she saw the strong emotions swirling in his green eyes. She was unsure how long they stared before he looked away. *With reluctance,* she thought. Because he had to look away or because he did not want to admit that the longing she had plainly seen in his eyes and tasted on his lips was dangerous?

She said nothing as he led Megan up the stairs. Seeing her daughter lean her head on his arm, she clenched her hands on her lap. No one could doubt the love between the two of them.

Samuel loved all three children, and they loved him. Would he try to keep her from taking her own children home? She looked toward the back parlor with the stacks of books that had been recently uncrated. He was a lawyer, so he knew the law well. Would he fight her for the children and win?

Six

Cailin yawned in spite of her efforts to hide her fatigue. She had not done much all day but sit on the porch and talk to the children. She had praised the rabbit's long ears and listened while Brendan seemed to tell her every detail of his cow's life. It had been more wonderful than she had imagined to become reacquainted with them. They had changed since she last saw them, Lottie more than the others, and she could not doubt they were happy here in Haven with Samuel.

"Why don't you rest, Cailin?" Samuel asked, putting down the newspaper he had been reading since he had come out onto the porch a few minutes before.

"It's so early."

"You sound like Megan when she doesn't want to go to bed."

The girl made a face at him, and Cailin could not keep from laughing. Putting her hands on the arm of the wooden chair, she pushed herself to her feet. She wobbled, and Brendan jumped to his feet to help her.

He was too slow, because Samuel was out of the rocking chair and had his hand under her elbow before her knees could fail her. As the children threw questions at her, he said under their fearful voices, "Trying to make up in one day for the time you've lost with them is going to make you sick again."

She could not argue with the truth, so she nodded.

"Can you stand on your own?" he asked.

She nodded again but held on to the back of the chair so she did not prove how uncertain she was. "Hush," she said to the anxious children. "I'm fine. Just tired."

"Not too tired for the bath that's waiting for you, are you?" asked Brendan, disappointment filling his eyes.

"Bath?" she asked.

Samuel said with what she knew was mock anger, "Now you've spoiled the surprise."

"A bath?" Cailin repeated, then smiled as Samuel and the children laughed at the breathless anticipation in her voice. Knowing there was no need to dissemble, she added, "I can't think of anything I want more at this moment."

Samuel slipped his arm around her waist. "Nothing?" he asked with a rakish laugh that set the children to giggling.

Cailin stiffened for a minute before realizing the children had no idea what he was suggesting. They were amused by his teasing laugh. Slapping at his hand, she said, "The water is getting cold while you keep me out here." She eased out of his embrace. She was astonished at how much she regretted that motion; his arm had offered a welcome she had never thought she would feel—or want to feel—again.

"Mama's going to have a bath?" asked Lottie, climbing up into the chair where Cailin had been sitting. "Can I wash the rabbit, too?"

"Rabbits can wash themselves, Quarter-pint," Samuel said as he swung her up into his arms.

Lottie whispered something into his ear.

With a grin, he said, "Folks can take baths when it isn't Saturday night." He set her down. "Now tell your mother good night and go upstairs and get ready for bed."

Cailin smiled when all three children began to protest. Telling them to obey Samuel, she gave each a hug and a kiss. "Pretty dreams," she said as they rushed into the house, each one eager to be first up the stairs.

In their wake, silence settled onto the porch, punctuated only by the chirps of insects. She said nothing while Samuel gathered up his newspaper.

He turned. "Your bath is going to get cold."

"Thank you," she said softly.

"For the bath? It's nothing. I figured you—"

She put her hand on his arm. "For making my children so happy."

"That was even easier than heating up bathwater for you." He folded the newspaper under one arm.

He did not move closer to her, but she was as aware of every inch of him as if he had pulled her against him. Her breath caught as her fingers were swallowed by his. Something stirred deep inside her, a sweet pleasure she had nearly forgotten. Pulling back, she clasped her hands behind her. She must not be tempted by a handsome man again. "I should go before the water gets cold."

"Yes, you should," he murmured, raising her hand.

She clenched her other hand as he brushed her knuckles with his lips. No kiss this chaste should seem so provocative, imploring her to forget her bath and the children and propriety while she let his mouth enrapture her.

"Good night." Slowly she drew her hand out of his and took one step toward the door. If he answered, she did not hear him as she hurried inside and to her room.

The lamp was casting its glow only into the middle of the room, leaving the corners in shadow. It reflected off the water in the tub that was far bigger than any she had ever used. She would be able to sit in it if she drew up her knees.

She waited for the pulse of excitement at enjoying such luxury, but it never came. Instead, she sat on a chair next to the tub and stared at the towels and the bar of soap sitting on the bed.

She had vowed never to let another man into her life, but from the moment Samuel had come out on the porch tonight she had struggled to keep her focus on Brendan's stories about raising his cow. Her thoughts kept wandering to where Samuel sat, reading his newspaper intently. She had noticed how he pushed his glasses up his nose with an impatient motion, and how his hair dropped down over the back of his collar. When he had rested one leg on the opposite knee, she had listened to little else than the rhythm of the rockers creaking against the porch floorboards.

Pushing herself to her feet so quickly that her head spun anew, Cailin gripped the footboard and waited for the room to stop rocking like Samuel's chair. She pushed the thought of him aside. Right now, all she should be thinking of was enjoying this bath.

She unbuttoned her dress with care, but, even so, another button fell off. It rolled under the bed. She bent to peer down and saw the button had come to a stop nearer the far side. Edging around the tub, she dropped onto her stomach and stretched her hand under the bed.

She pulled the button out and cautiously got to her feet. This time, her head did not spin. She must be careful until she was completely well. Setting the button on the dressing table, she put her dress on the chair. Just as she was about to lower the strap of her chemise, she heard a click and saw the door open. She grasped her dress, holding it in front of her as Samuel walked in as if there were nothing wrong with him being in her room tonight.

"What are you doing here?" she cried.

He tossed something onto the bed. It was, she saw, a man's dressing robe of dark red material that looked astonishingly like silk. "I thought that, once you were clean, you might want to wear something other than your dress tonight."

"I don't wear it to bed."

"You're wearing my shirt still?" His eyes glistened, and she knew he was imagining how she would look in that.

But he did not need to imagine. He had seen her wearing it when he came in here to help her while she was sick. She was no longer sick, and he should not be here. "Samuel, I don't think this is the time to discuss this."

"You're right." His gaze slipped along her.

She looked down to see that her legs from ankle to mid-calf were visible beneath the dress. Edging behind the tub, she said, "Thank you for the robe."

He held out his hand.

"What?" she asked.

"If you'll give me that dress, I'll wash it out. It should be dry in the morning when you get up."

"This dress?"

He smiled and turned to face the door. "Put on the robe and your modesty won't be compromised."

"But then it won't be clean when I am." That sounded petulant, but she had liked the idea of fresh clothes when she was done bathing.

Facing her, he said, "You are a troublesome woman. Wait here." He opened the door and went out.

Cailin did not move as she heard another door open. The one along the hall nearest to this room. When she heard a drawer opening and closing, she knew that door must open onto Samuel's bedroom. Only a single wall separated the two rooms. The thought of that intimacy was both unnerving and undeniably delightful.

Before she had a chance to warn her mind not to wander in that direction, Samuel strode back into her room. He held out a nightshirt that was of a soft gray flannel.

"This will be hot to wear tonight, but it'll keep you covered." He turned his back to her again. "You'd better hurry, or that water will feel as chilly as the ice down in the icehouse."

She kept the dress between herself and him and awkwardly pulled on the nightshirt. It dropped to cover the top of her toes. Sweat bubbled along her back, for the nightshirt was just as smothering in the evening's heat as he had warned.

"All set," she said.

He looked at her and chuckled. "I hope your suffering is worth it."

"If you'd leave, I could get into the tub and get cooled off."

"Give me your dress and I'll leave you to your bath."

She started to hand it to him, then reached into the pocket and pulled out the battered photograph.

"Is that a picture of your husband?" he asked quietly, the teasing gone from his voice.

"Yes."

"May I?"

Giving it to him, she watched as he tilted it toward the lamp.

He handed it back to her. "I thought he'd look more like Brendan."

"Brendan favors *mo athair*—I mean, my father." She put the picture on the dressing table. "I see more of Abban in Lottie than the other children."

"I hope that gives you some comfort."

She picked up the dress and handed it to him. "Thank you for your sympathy, but I don't need it."

"You don't need it?" His eyes narrowed. "Why not?"

Cursing herself for speaking so thoughtlessly, she answered, "It's time for me to think about the future, not the past."

"Wise advice. I hope you can follow it better than most people."

Cailin wanted to ask him to explain what he meant, but ending this conversation now would be the smartest thing she could do. Otherwise, her fatigue might lead her again into saying something better left unspoken.

"Bring the nightshirt along with your other clothes out to the kitchen when you're done bathing," Samuel continued, and she wondered if he was eager to finish this discussion that seemed to perturb him, too.

"You don't have to wash my clothes!" she said, even though she knew she should be silent.

"Have you been overcome by the heat, or is that a blush reddening your cheeks? I'll leave the laundry tub in the kitchen if you want to tend to your own laundry." He laughed as he reached for the doorknob. "Try not to take all night with your bath."

Cailin rushed to the door as soon as it was closed and twisted the lock. Now nobody could get in without clambering through the window. She crossed the room and drew the curtains. Moonlight washed through, diffused.

Peeling off the nightshirt and her underclothes, which were stained with sweat from her fever, she left them on the floor. She picked up the soap and stepped into the water.

"Perfect," she breathed as water flowed up around her legs to welcome her. She sat, and the warm water surrounded her. Even with her knees close to her chest, this was going to be the most luxurious bath she had ever had.

She trickled the water along her skin to savor its freshness, then began to scrub her arms. Soap bubbles surrounded her. She ignored them as she washed herself, then rested back to let the water lap up around her shoulders. This was the first time since she had left Ireland that she could let herself truly relax.

Being on a ship with three curious children had kept her busy. She had feared that inquisitiveness would end up with them falling overboard. When one of the sailors had offered to show them about, they had enjoyed the tour. She smiled. He had been not more than a dozen years older than Brendan, and he had seemed anxious to talk with her about his plans to ask his beloved to be his wife as soon as the ship docked in New York harbor. A happy ending to a love story.

Her parents' own love story had had a happy ending as well. They had not known each other long before they were married, and that marriage had lasted more than twenty years. She had been their only child, born long after they had feared their marriage would not be blessed with a child, and the affection they shared washed over onto her to create their love-filled home. Sometimes, there had not been enough food, but there never had been a dearth of caring.

She wondered how Athair was faring. She had known she would miss him, but she had not guessed how much. She missed his easy laugh and his love of fiddle music, a gift he had bequeathed to her, although she had had to sell her own fiddle shortly after she reached New York City to pay Mrs. Rafferty for providing for the children. When she had learned that one of the maids who slept in the crowded room along with her and three other women could read and write, Cailin had had her write a note to Athair, telling him of their safe arrival and Abban's death. The priest would read the letter to her father. She had said nothing of the icy welcome at Mrs. Rafferty's house, and the fact that she seldom saw her children. Worrying him would gain her nothing.

She had found her children.

And Samuel . . .

Everyone was astonished when Samuel offered to have the three children placed out with him. Three children for a bachelor!

Emma's voice played through her head again, but this time Cailin wondered why anyone had been astonished by Samuel's bringing her children into his home. His gentle heart was revealed each time he spoke to one of the children. Had he hidden it from the rest of the people living near Haven? He had not been able to conceal it from her.

Nor had he taken any trouble to make his desire to hold her a secret.

Sometime later, Cailin blinked and realized she had almost surrendered to her exhaustion. The water was now tepid, so she soaped her hair and rinsed it quickly. With reluctance, she stood and wrapped the towel around her.

She drew on the extra undergarments she had brought with her from New York after she had sold everything else to get the last few pennies for her fare. Slipping her arms into Samuel's robe, she relished the silk sliding along her skin like a cool caress. She tied it closed as she went to the dressing table. Drying her hair, she combed out the snarls. It hung down her back, so she tied it back with a ribbon from the box Emma had brought her. Gathering up her clothes, she left damp footprints behind her as she unlocked the door and opened it.

She stared out. Right in the hallway, Samuel was sitting on a blue wooden chair, reading his newspaper. "Samuel, I didn't realize . . . I mean . . ."

He came to his feet. "I didn't want the children to take it into their heads to intrude."

"Thank you." She tried not to think about how little she wore, but she was aware of every inch of herself, separated from him by little more than silk and air. "I'll empty the tub—"

"While dressed like that? If you get water splattered on you . . ." He took a step toward her, halting as suddenly as if a wall had suddenly appeared in front of him.

"It could ruin your robe," she finished. She knew, from the way his gaze edged from her head to her feet, that her words were not the ones he had halted himself from saying.

"Yes, yes."

She wondered if he was as grateful as he sounded . . . for any excuse to pretend nothing was out of the ordinary. She stifled a yawn. Maybe he was simply as tired as she was.

"Let me take your things," he said.

She smiled. "I'll wash them while you empty the tub."

"You can hang them over the chairs in the kitchen."

"It'd be more convenient to let them dry in my room."

"You're probably right."

She nodded, although he was studiously not looking at her. They were tempting trouble. An attraction was fun to think about, but fooling around with fire was a good way to end up with nothing but heartbreak. Abban had taught her that.

"Good night, Samuel." This time, the yawn escaped.

She heard him mutter something, and her steps faltered. "What did you say?" She half-turned before his hand on her arm twirled her against him. "Samuel, we shouldn't," she whispered, even as her arm slid around his shoulder.

He tossed the newspaper onto the chair. "You're right. We shouldn't." His fingers splayed across her back, drawing her even closer.

Slipping her hand along his nape, she teased the short hairs on the back of his neck. "I should go now."

"Yes, you should."

The robe wrinkled beneath his palm as his hand drifted up her back. She struggled to keep her breaths slow, but they grew rapid and shallow, each one brushing against his hard chest.

"Samuel . . ." His name became a moan when she dropped the clothes to the floor and steered his mouth over hers. All the many reasons why she should not be here with him, in his arms, kissing him, did not matter as much as the one reason why she should.

When his tongue brushed hers, she let the thrill sweep away her thoughts. His fingers combed through her wet hair, drawing it aside. She was sure the heat racing through her would dry it within seconds when his mouth moved along her neck. His hands scorched away the silk as they swept down her back. His hard arm pinned her to him, but she could not be still as a deep craving besieged her. Each motion brushed her against him, creating sparks between them.

She tasted the curve of his ear, and his breath caught. Exultation exploded within her as she offered him a share of the pleasure he was giving her. His fingers inched along her waist. As the robe gaped, she reached to pull it closed. He grasped her hand, drawing it away. His other hand curved beneath the robe before gliding up her back. Tugging her closer, he found her mouth with a longing she could feel along him. His shirt's coarse texture stroked the skin that was bare above her chemise.

He drew her toward the bedroom door, and her foot caught in the clothing she had dropped. She clutched his arms to keep from falling.

"Are you all right?" he asked as he steadied her. He chuckled. "I already know the answer to that. You're far better than all right."

Cailin pulled the robe closed around her, and the fire in Samuel's eyes dimmed.

He reached past her to pick up his paper. "I'll empty the tub. Good night." He laughed again, but this sound was as chilly as his eyes. "It could have been a good night."

"This is moving too fast. My gratitude to you doesn't go that far."

"Gratitude?" He brushed her lips with his fingertips. "I didn't taste any gratitude here." His eyes narrowed. "Nor any sorrow for your late husband."

Bending, she picked up the clothing. "I think we should both admit this was a mistake."

"And pretend it never happened?"

"Yes. That would be for the best."

"Are you this dishonest with everyone or just me?"

He walked into her bedroom before she could answer.

Cailin wanted to call him back, but that would be dull-witted, for she doubted she would be able to resist his

kisses again tonight. Abban had wooed her with kisses,
too. In astonishment, she realized she could not recall Abban's kisses being as fiery as these. She put her fingers to
where Samuel's lips had touched her's. The heat pulsed
through them, warning of the peril she invited when she
allowed him to hold her.

She saw something under the chair. A garment? She bent
down and drew out a crumpled newspaper page. She
started to call to Samuel but paused. Even speaking with
him again tonight might be trouble.

Taking the page and her clothes into the kitchen, she
saw her dress hanging over a chair next to a bucket that
was topped by the grease left by the soap he had used to
wash her dress. She put the page on the table and dropped
her chemise into the bucket.

She began to wash her underclothes, putting each garment into a pile on the table. When Samuel did not come
through the kitchen with the buckets from the tub in her
room, she wondered if he had decided to leave the task
until morning. That did not sound like him.

Just as she was wringing out her chemise, he walked
into the kitchen with the tub. He said nothing when he
opened the door and carried it outside. A hollow clang
sounded, and she guessed he had hung it up on a brad
nailed into the white clapboards.

She put the chemise on the table and bent to pick up the
pail. An arm reached around from behind her, lifting the
bucket before she could.

"Thank you," she said, straightening. When she bumped
into Samuel's chest, she grasped the handle of the bucket
before the water could splash out onto the floor. Her fingers clasped over his, and the longing careened through
her anew.

Edging away, she faced him. Slowly she lifted her hands
off the handle.

He set the bucket on the table, and he smiled. "How did

you manage to wash those clothes without getting the floor wet? I always have to mop up afterwards."

"You probably have more help than I did," she replied, glad his frown was gone.

"That's true."

She gathered up the washed garments. "And you clearly made the water in the tub magically disappear."

"I poured it out the bedroom window. It's easier than toting buckets through the house, and there's a flower bed outside the window that could use the water, since we haven't gotten much rain lately. Just the night you arrived."

"Thank you for arranging that bath for me."

"You're welcome." His smile widened. "You'd better hang up those clothes before the dripping water makes that whole robe transparent."

She looked down. Where water had dripped from the clothes, the robe was spotted, making the silk seem to disappear.

"Such a sight could make a man do something he knows he shouldn't." He grasped her arms and pulled her to him. The wet underclothes were squeezed between them as he kissed her soundly. Releasing her, he grinned. "I'd suggest you keep those clothes close to you unless you want to tempt me more than I can be tempted and resist."

She knew it was time to leave before he tempted *her* more than she could be tempted and resist. Something about him drew her to him, even when he was not looking at her. She had never met a man who could be so tender-hearted yet possessed such a captivating sensuality.

Bidding him good night again, she rushed to her bedroom and closed the door, but not quickly enough, for she heard his laugh follow her from the kitchen. As she sat on her bed, she glanced at the door and smiled reluctantly. The days ahead might be challenging, but she was sure of one thing: They would not be boring.

Seven

Cailin appraised the village of Haven, which was set on a bank high above the Ohio River. Her hazy memories of a town enveloped in darkness did not match the neat houses edging a village green. Today, with the sun shining, she saw a large white building on one side of the green that she had not even noticed in her blind need to get to her children.

Even though sweat dripped down her back, she shivered at the memory of that moment of being so close yet so uncertain of what she would find at what she hoped was the end of her journey. That uncertainty remained, but not about her children. Getting away from the farm and Samuel would give her a chance to clear her head.

She hoped.

The day had begun poorly when she had sat with the children on the porch. She had talked to them about Ireland and the journey to America, a subject that Lottie seemed to find boring. Only when Cailin had pulled out the cracked photograph of their father had she understood why.

Lottie had stood on tiptoe looking over the arm of the rocker. "Who's that, Mama?"

"It's your father." She told herself she should not be surprised that Lottie did not remember the picture Cailin had shown her often when she spoke of the father Lottie had never seen.

"Papa?" asked Megan and Brendan at the same time. Both rushed over to look at the photograph.

Cailin was startled when neither of them spoke. When she saw them glance at each other uneasily, she asked, "Don't you recognize him?"

"Yes," Megan said slowly. "Yes, I think so."

"I recognize him, Mama." Brendan added nothing more, not even to taunt his sister because he remembered something she did not.

That he changed the subject had unsettled Cailin more than anything else. She wondered what had been said in Mrs. Rafferty's house when she had not been there. Although she had tried to ask, Brendan kept returning to the topic of his cow and how she was certain to be judged the best at the fair.

On the white building, the letters *H-A-V-E-N-G-R-A-N-G-E* were painted over the door facing the green. A brick building next to it had a sign atop its door with the letters *H-A-V-E-N-P-U-B-L-I-C-L-I-B-R-A-R-Y.* The wood looked new, so she guessed it had been placed there recently. No one stood near it or on the green, which shimmered in the heat and humidity. At one end of the open space, a cannon was set into a flower bed.

"That's the Grange over there," Brendan said as he steered the wagon with a skill that impressed her.

"What's the Grange?" she asked, wiping a handkerchief across her forehead. She had not guessed it would be so unremittingly hot here in Indiana. When she had tried to sleep last night amid the heat, she had longed for the cool, gray days in Ireland.

"It's where the farmers around Haven meet."

"Why?"

He shrugged. The heat did not seem to bother him. "They have meetings, but I don't go. I'd rather play baseball with my friends."

"Baseball is the game with the ball and the bat, right?"

"Yep. Baseball is fun. Samuel said he saw the Red Stockings play in Cincinnati. That must have been exciting!"

"What are the Red Stockings?"

"They were a baseball team in Cincinnati. They haven't played in about five or six years, but I saw an article in one of his newspapers that said they might begin playing again. It depends on whether they can get enough money to pay the team."

"This team gets paid to play a game?"

He nodded. "Each side has nine players, and whoever gets the most runs wins. I like baseball. Maybe I'll try to get on the team when I get old enough."

Cailin marveled that every answer he gave her created two more questions in her mind. "I see," she said, even though she did not.

He grinned. "Pretty soon you're going to know everything you need to know to be an American."

"I don't think anyone will believe that as long as I speak with this accent."

"Americans have all kinds of accents. You should hear how differently they talk up in Chicago or on the other side of the river."

"You've traveled to those places?"

Brendan laughed. "No. Sometimes guests come to the Grange to speak with the Grangers. Some of them sound really odd." He pointed along the main street. "The store's over there, Mama."

"Emma's store?"

"Yep, and that's the livery stable just across from it."

"Where your friend lives?"

"Don't talk about that when we're in Haven!"

Cailin looked away so her son could not see her smile. Samuel had told her about Brendan's calf-love for a young girl named Jenny Anderson, whose father owned the livery. Hearing Brendan mumble something, she said, "Samuel says you got every word but two right last night when you were reading to your sisters."

"All but one!" His grin returned. "If I read to Megan and Lottie again tonight, will you come up and listen? I'm going to be the best reader in school when it starts this fall."

She wanted to hug him to show him how proud she was but knew she would embarrass him, so she just squeezed his arm. "I'd love to hear you read to your sisters."

"Then will you tell us one of your stories?"

"I'd be glad to do that, too. Do you want to hear one of the fairy stories?"

His nose wrinkled. "I'd rather have one with a giant or a monster in it."

Cailin laughed and looked around the village again. The church at the other end of the green was receiving a new coat of whitewash from some boys who clearly wished to be elsewhere. They stared wistfully after the wagon. One of them waved, and Brendan waved back.

"A friend of yours?" she asked.

"Yep. Jimmy."

"Did he come on the train with you and your sisters?"

"No, he's lived in Haven all his life." He gave a sigh that sounded too old for his years. "I wish I'd lived here all my life."

She put her hand on his arm. "Do you really like living here so much?"

"Yep."

"You keep saying that."

"That's the way Americans talk, Mama." His expression became pensive again. "I like being here in America."

"In New York—"

He grumbled something that sounded suspiciously like Samuel's favorite oath. "I hated it there. All those buildings and too many people. Here there are trees and the river and I've got my cow. I don't want to go back to New York."

Cailin knew she was risking an answer she did not want to hear, but she asked, "What about Ireland? Would you like to go back there?"

"Why?" he asked, stopping the wagon to let another pass by. "Here we've got a nice house, and I have my own room, without Megan and Lottie poking their noses into my stuff. We've got lots to eat, and I'm going to school." His grin returned for a moment as he said, "I don't always like school, but Samuel says a man can only get ahead if he's educated." He slapped the reins, and the wagon moved forward again along the main street. "If we went to Ireland, would Samuel come with us?"

She shook her head, then realized Brendan was so busy concentrating on his driving that he could not see her. "I don't think so."

"Then why would we want to go back there?"

"It's where we were born, and your grandfather is there." She was not sure what else to say, because, even though she had girded herself for this answer, she had hoped Brendan would be willing to go without Samuel.

"Wouldn't it be easier for Grandpa to come here?" His eyes lit up. "He'd like Haven, Mama. The folks here are nice, and they enjoy working in the fields and with animals as much as he does. Don't you think he'd like Haven?"

"Yes, I think he'd like it here." She would not lie to her son.

"Then why not ask him to come here?" He slowed the wagon in front of a brick house with tall, thin windows that was near the livery. "I can write to him if you want, Mama. Just tell me what you want me to say, and I'll write it to him. Then we can have Emma send it out on the next train."

"It's something to think about." Cailin gave him a smile, but she sighed when he looked back along the street. Her father had been furious when she decided to come to America. She had mentioned he would be welcome, too, in Abban's home. How innocent she had been then! Not that it mattered, for Athair had refused to leave his home and cross the ocean. He had said that after all his years of living on the farm, he intended to be buried in the churchyard near it. He had tried to persuade her to stay and wait patiently for a response to the latest letter Father Liam had written to Abban. She had considered remaining, because her father's health had been unsteady for years, but she had believed her place was with her husband. There had been no answer from Abban, just as there had been no answer to the three previous letters she had sent. She had feared there was a problem, but she could never have imagined the truth.

Brendan jumped down off the wagon. "Can I go and see my friends while you're talking to Doc Bamburger?"

"Just watch for when I come out. Supper will be late if we linger too long here."

He ran off with a shout, and she saw the boys by the church waving to him again.

Cailin straightened her bonnet, which was almost as bedraggled as her dress. She stepped down from the wagon. Dust rose from the road, clinging to her hem. More sweat trickled along her back, and she wished she had a parasol like the fancy ladies in New York. Any shade from the sun and any respite from the heat would be welcome.

Walking through the gate of a white picket fence, she went to the door that was painted bright blue. The door opened before she could knock.

The short man wore a red vest beneath his black coat. His dull graying hair contrasted with the glitter of sunshine on his glasses. He peered over them. "Mrs. Rafferty! This is an unexpected pleasure."

"Are you Doc Bamburger?"

He looked startled, then said, "A fair question, since you were not yourself when I saw you previously. Yes, I'm Doc Bamburger. Come in."

"Thank you."

As soon as she entered the house, she saw it was as grand as Samuel's. Paintings and photographs hung on the wall of the entry foyer, and more of those frames with words within them in the small room he led her to. Like the room Samuel called his office, this room had a desk. Two glass-fronted cabinets did not contain books. Instead boxes and bottles filled them. She guessed these were medicines.

"It's good to see you looking well, Mrs. Rafferty." He motioned toward a chair by his desk. When she sat, he pulled out the chair at the desk and did the same. "What brings you to see me today?"

"Lottie."

His smile vanished. "Is something wrong with the child?"

"No, I'm just curious about her eyes."

"It must have been startling for you to see her with spectacles."

"I'm very glad she has them. Mister—" She recalled how Lottie had said everyone addressed Samuel by his given name. "Samuel said you're quite confident she won't lose more of her sight."

"There's no reason to believe so."

"Good." She forced her stiff shoulders to loosen. "I don't question Samuel, you must understand. He has taken such good care of my children."

"But you wanted to be reassured yourself by hearing it from me."

She nodded. "Thank you for understanding."

"Lottie will need to have her eyes examined often, and if you see her seeming to have difficulty seeing, you must bring her to me right away."

"I will."

"How are you doing, Mrs. Rafferty?"

"I'm fine, thanks to you."

He shook his head. "Thank Samuel for that as well. He was determined you'd overcome that fever. He's a good man."

"Yes, he is." She was not sure what else she could say, because she was ill at ease discussing Samuel with the doctor. Coming to her feet, she said, "Thank you again, Doc Bamburger."

"Just keep an eye on that youngster. If she starts squinting, bring her in right away."

"I will."

He walked with her to the door. "But don't worry, Mrs. Rafferty. Lottie's going to be just fine. All of them will be."

She nodded again, but just like when she talked to Brendan, everything the doctor said created more questions in her head. She wanted to ask if Doc Bamburger was talking about the children being fine in Haven or when she took them back to Ireland. Instead she bid him a good day and went out to the wagon.

Brendan came loping across the green as she climbed up to the seat. All the way back to the farm on Nanny Goat Hill Road, he spoke nonstop about what he had talked about with his friends and the baseball game they would play during the next Grange meeting.

The wagon rattled into the yard, but no one came to meet it. When she saw the girls sitting on the shady porch, she smiled. At least, *they* had the sense not to go out in the bright sunshine. She needed to watch what the children did and do the same until she became accustomed to this weather.

Stepping down from the wagon, Cailin stepped to the side and away from the dust that billowed up even though Brendan led the plodding horse slowly toward the barn. She was about to go up to the house when a motion just to the left of the barn caught her attention.

Samuel was chopping wood on a stump that had been

cut to the exact height for him. She forgot the sun's heat
as a sweeter warmth boiled within her as she watched his
fluid motions, swinging the ax to split the log. He picked
up a piece, set it on the stump again, and sliced it in half.
Tossing the two chunks onto the pile, he took the other
half and broke it into smaller pieces.

Sweat glistened like a sheen of jewels along his naked
back, and his black hair shone blue-hot in the sunshine.
Muscles she had touched through his shirt knotted down
his arms and across his back. His skin was as bronzed as
his face, and she wondered how often he dispensed with
his shirt when he was working around the farm.

He heaved another section of tree trunk onto the stump
and raised the ax. Slowly he lowered it and turned, catching
her staring at him. He leaned the ax's handle against the
stump and pulled on the shirt she had not noticed lying
atop the wood waiting to be chopped. Not bothering to
button it, he walked toward her with the agility she had
seen when he wielded the ax.

"How was your trip into Haven?" he asked.

"Good." The word came out on a gulp.

He smiled. "There's cold water in the bucket by the well
if you're all choked up from the dust."

"Thank you." She tried to keep her gaze focused on his
face, but it kept drifting down along his chest and the firm
lines of his abdomen.

"Did Doc Bamburger ease your mind about Lottie?"

"Yes."

"I'm glad to hear that." He picked up his shirttail and
wiped his forehead.

"Oh, my!" she whispered as she was given a better view
of that strong chest. What was wrong with her? She had
been married. He was not the first man she had seen with
his shirt unbuttoned. Yet she could not stop herself from
staring.

A hand against her cheek tipped up her head so her eyes met his. "You look as if you're wilting, Cailin."

"It's the heat." She hoped he would misunderstand, thinking she spoke of the sun beating down on them.

"It is mighty warm today."

"Is it always like this?"

He smiled. "Lately."

"How long has this heat wave been going on?"

"Since you got here."

She started to reply, then saw the amusement in his eyes. He knew just how much he was disconcerting her . . . and he understood exactly what she had wanted him *not* to understand. Stepping back from the fingers that were stroking her cheek, she said, "You think you're funny, don't you?"

"It doesn't hurt anyone to laugh now and then." He eyed her up and down, and she knew her dress was clinging to her when his smile broadened. "I know you can laugh. You've got a very nice laugh. So why are you being somber now?"

"Because I don't like your idea of what's funny."

His eyebrows rose. "Do you want to explain that?"

"You think it's funny when you try to disconcert me by wandering about half-dressed."

He grasped her around the waist and tugged her closer. "I'm not trying to do anything to disconcert you, although it seems I am. I'm trying to get some chores done around here just as I did before you turned up in Haven and just as I'll continue to do. If you haven't noticed, it's as hot as Hades."

"I've noticed." The heat from his bare skin seared through her thin dress. "Will you release me before we do something stupid?"

"Like what?"

When she saw his lips tighten, she feared she had insulted him again. How could she know what to say or do? One minute he was distant and formal; the next he was treating her as if she had no more sense than Lottie. And, then the very next minute, he was touching her and creating the most bewitching sensations.

She peeled his arm from around her waist. "I've had enough of this silliness. I've got work to do, too." She started to walk away, then heard his laugh behind her. Whirling, she said, "I know you think you're irresistible, Samuel Jennings, but let me tell you something. You're not!"

"You're not telling me anything I don't already know."

She stared in openmouthed amazement as his smile vanished, and she saw pain in his eyes. Pain and grief and loss. She knew that expression well, for she had seen it, when she passed a mirror, on her own face since her arrival in America.

He walked back toward the woodpile. She took a single step to go after him and apologize for . . . for causing that heart-wrenching pain. She wanted to tell him that she had not meant to hurt him.

Or had she?

Pressing her hands over the buttons on her bodice, she bit her lip. She had needed to avoid succumbing to the easy sensuality that enticed her each time she was close to him. Her sole defense against it had been anger and sharp words.

As he picked up his ax and slammed it into the wood, she winced.

He's a good man. Doc Bamburger's voice now joined Emma's in her head. *Everyone was astonished when Samuel offered to have the three children placed out with him. Three children for a bachelor!*

She walked toward the house, not glancing back. That was the problem. He was a good man, the kind of man she had not believed, in the aftermath of Abban's betrayal, existed. She had thought Abban was a good man, too.

She must not allow another handsome man's charms—or

the pain she was tempted to ease for him as he had eased her fever—to bewitch her again.

* * *

Cailin smiled as she entered the kitchen. In the past week, this had become her favorite room in the house. Whimsical stenciled flowers danced across the pine cupboards. A half-dozen chairs surrounded the kitchen table, each a different style and color. Glass bowls in every shade and shape were set in a row near the ceiling along three walls. The fourth wall held a hearth and the stove. The mantel was bare.

Looking out the window, she saw wildflowers growing past the kitchen garden. Many drooped in the heat, but some in a glass would add color to the mantel.

She knew from the children that the bowls and the stenciling had been here when Samuel bought this farm. He had not changed it, and she wondered how long he had lived here before the children came to this house. Maybe he simply did not care about the kitchen, preferring to spend his time in the lavishly decorated parlor.

The kitchen was far cozier for her than the parlors or even the room where she slept. She liked the children's simple rooms, which were far nicer than anything they had had in Ireland, but not too elegant to unsettle her. The parlors and the grand dining room reminded her too much of Mrs. Rafferty's house, and she suspected Abban's mother would be jealous of Samuel's fine furnishings.

She pushed the thought of her husband's family out of her mind. In the past week, she had been so busy trying to finish the work that waited to be done while finding time every afternoon for a refreshing nap. Yesterday had been the first day she had not needed to sneak away for some rest.

With a laugh, she flexed her arm as Brendan did almost every morning.

"Checking to see if you're getting stronger?" Samuel's question was followed by a chuckle from behind her.

She whirled. "Do you have to sneak up on a soul like that?"

He paused in the doorway, clearly unsure if he would be welcome in his own kitchen. She could not blame him. Her retort had been chilly.

"I'm sorry," she said, falling back on the courtesy that had become her preservation. "You startled me. Come in." Pulling the green chair out from the table, she added, "You're late for lunch. The children were wondering where you were. They've already eaten and are off playing."

"The wagon busted an axle out in the cornfield." He rubbed the back of his neck with a stained handkerchief. "I'll have to get it fixed before I can do much more out there."

"I'm sorry."

"Why do you keep saying you're sorry for things that aren't your fault?"

"A habit, I guess. When I was working in New York, it didn't matter which maid made a mistake. I got used to saying I was sorry, even if it wasn't my fault."

"That doesn't sound too fair."

She went to the table and began to slice bread to make a sandwich of the roast chicken remaining from last night. "It's just the way it was. My employers didn't see us as individuals, just as the maids. They addressed each of us as 'Bridget.' "

"Why?"

"There were four Irish maids in the house by that name, so I guess they believed it was simplest to believe we all were named Bridget." Placing the slices of chicken on the thick bread, she put the sandwich on a plate and brought it to the table.

A wry grin on his face, he rested his elbow next to the plate as she went to pour him a glass of milk. "Being so accepting of the circumstances doesn't sound like you, *Cailin.*"

"What do you find funny about it?" she asked, then wished she had remained silent when his smile vanished.

"Nothing, I suppose."

Again her tone had been too sharp. She needed to find a way to speak to him that was somewhere between this sharp voice that suggested they were—and always would be—strangers and the invitation that softened every word when she gazed into his eyes.

Sitting across from him, she set the glass of milk by his plate. "I'm sorry again, and this time I have a reason for saying it."

"Maybe it's time we both stop giving each other a reason for saying those words." He picked up the sandwich and took a bite. "You haven't said anything at a temperature above freezing for the past week."

"I could say the same about you. I know it's bothering the children."

"That's obvious. I never saw them as quiet as they were last night at supper."

She sighed. "We both care about what happens to them."

"That's very true."

"So we should stop making them miserable by snapping at each other every time we say a word."

"Not every time we speak." He leaned toward her. "Maybe we're both afraid if we're nice to each other, we'll end up in each other's arms."

Warmth erupted through her, just as it had when he had freed her from being caught on the picture frame, and when he had held her after her bath, and when she had talked to him after coming back from Haven. Each time his face had been close to her, and she had dared to believe he was as wonderful as the children claimed. Since the conversation by the woodpile, she had not been sure if he was avoiding her, but *she* had been avoiding him.

It might be easier to continue doing so, yet it was silly to try. They were living together in this house. He was providing for her children while she took care of the housework. They had to find a way to make this seem normal, or the children would become even more withdrawn.

Dragging her gaze away from his, Cailin ordered, "Eat your lunch." She kept her tone as light as when she spoke with the children. "If you don't, I'll have to give the chicken to the cat."

"Cat?" His eyes widened. "What cat?"

"Lottie was carrying a cat around this morning. She told me it was hers."

"A cat?"

"A calico cat. I assumed it was living in the barn."

"We're going to have a complete menagerie here if the children keep finding animals that need a home."

Although she was not sure what the word *menagerie* meant, she guessed its meaning from the rest of his words. "I'll speak to her and try to discover where she found it. Maybe it can go back there."

"Let me talk to all of them, if you don't mind, before this is known as the Nanny Goat Hill Road Zoo." He took another bite and chewed pensively before saying, "Brendan has his cow and Megan has laid claim to the rabbit, so I guess Lottie wants a pet of her own."

"She tries to keep up with them." She laughed, standing and going to pour another glass of milk for herself. "One of these days, she'll surprise them."

"I think they're used to surprises by now."

She was startled to hear his voice from right behind her. She faced him as he rested his hand on the wall by her cheek. Her heart seemed to be thudding like a drum. Could he hear it? She shifted, and his fingers brushed her cheek so lightly, it could have been the caress of heat from the stove. Yet this warmth was more powerful.

She pulled back and bumped into his arm. Something

flashed through his eyes, but he looked away before she could see what it was. Not that she needed to see, because she already knew. It was the same sensation that blazed through her at every touch, even the most unintentional.

"It's my turn," he said quietly, "to say I'm sorry. What I said to you last week about not missing your late husband was cruel."

"You were angry."

"How you choose to mourn your husband is your decision and your decision alone."

"I'm trying to make things easier for the children."

"And what about you?"

"I've made my peace with the situation."

His brows lowered, and she knew she had said the wrong thing . . . again. He murmured, "That's an odd way of putting it."

"It's the truth." She looked down to avoid his gaze, and she saw that his shirt was misbuttoned. He had not been wearing it when he worked, yet he had made sure it was buttoned when he came in for lunch. It was a small kindness, but it touched her heart.

That longing to be in his arms with his lips on hers burst forth again. His kindness was not the only thing that had touched her heart.

"Thank you, Samuel," she said softly.

"Thank you? For what?"

"For trying to make this a good home for the children." She found smiling easier than she had suspected. "For all of us."

"It'd be a lot easier if you weren't so damn beguiling," he said. "That tattered Cinderella look is guaranteed to catch a man's eyes."

"Are you out of your mind?" she asked, looking down at her dress. She had put a new patch at the waist just this morning. When it tore again, she would not be able to repair it, because that had been her last piece of matching fabric. She should put a halt to this conversation, which was rapidly wandering away from the safe subjects of the farm and the house and the children, but she had missed his gentle teasing. She needed to tell him that she was sorry for overreacting when she spoke to him when he was splitting wood.

When she opened her mouth to apologize, he put his finger to her lips and shook his head. "Don't say it."

"Say what?"

"Don't say you're sorry again."

"How did you know what I was going to say?"

He smiled. "A good attorney learns to read faces well. He has to know when someone is lying and when someone is being honest. When someone is ready to make a stand and when someone is ready to apologize. We've both said 'I'm sorry' too often, because we've needed to. Isn't it time to stop?"

"Yes."

"I think so, too." He took her hand again and curved her fingers over his. Raising them to his lips, he kissed them with a light touch that contradicted the craving in his voice. "Like I said, this would all be so much easier if you didn't look as if your dress might fall apart at any time. It keeps taking my attention from what I need to think about, because I'd be a fool not to watch to see when the tatters win."

With a laugh, she shook her head. "Such words are sure to turn any woman's head."

His fingers tightened on hers. "The way you look is sure to turn any man's. You've got a softness about you, Cailin, that belies the steel within you. Your eyes are filled with a sensuality that's hard to ignore."

"Can you?"

"I don't know." He released her hand and sighed. "I honestly don't know."

"The children—"

"Forget the children." He pulled her into his arms and claimed her mouth with a feverish kiss.

She surrendered to the pleasure of his lips on hers, his arms sweeping up her back, his strong legs hard against her skirt. Yet, even as she ran her fingers along his shoulders and up into his hair, she knew they had simply traded one lie for another. Neither of them could ever forget—not even in the midst of a kiss—the children neither of them wanted to lose.

Eight

Samuel expected the looks when he arrived at the next meeting of the library committee and walked into the schoolhouse with the children . . . and Cailin. Why wouldn't everyone be curious about the woman who had followed her children and the orphan train to Haven?

Maybe he had been wrong to invite her here tonight. He wanted her to see Haven was a good place for her kids. Bringing her to the school would be a reminder of what her children had not had in Ireland.

Beside him, she was silent while she surveyed the room and the people gawking at her. He felt her hand brush his leg when she tugged carefully at her dress to twist the skirt enough to hide the line of patches down the left side. That was his other reason for asking her to come here tonight. He had hoped she would realize she needed to set aside her pride.

She had held tightly to that blasted pride when he had taken her with him to Emma's store two days earlier and picked a bolt of emerald green fabric off a shelf. He had asked, "Do you like the color?"

"I like any color as long as it isn't black," she had answered as they stood near the back of the store, where a woodstove was flanked by two rocking chairs.

He laughed. "Or pink?"

"Pink isn't one of my favorite colors either."

Looking past her, he said, "All right, Emma, we'll take the bolt, too."

Cailin gasped, "What?" She tugged on Samuel's sleeve and whispered, "I don't have the money to pay for that."

"I didn't say you were going to have to pay for it."

"I can't take it as a gift."

"Then consider it an advance on your earnings."

She hesitated, and he thought she would be sensible. Then she shook her head. "No, I can't agree to that either."

"Because you're saving every penny to take the children back to Ireland?"

"Why are you making it a question? You know that's why I'm working in your house."

He exchanged a long look with Emma, then said, "We won't be taking it."

"Are you sure?" Emma's face was lined with dismay. "I can't promise how long it will be here. It's such a lovely fabric."

"It is, but no thank you." Cailin picked up the newspaper and handed it to Samuel. "Good afternoon, Emma."

Bidding Emma a good day, Samuel followed Cailin out onto the porch and helped her onto the wagon seat. He was not sure if she would be furious or chilly, but he had not guessed she would be quiet with sorrow.

It might have been easier to insist she be sensible if he were not so uneasy about asking the questions that had been banging around in his head since she had fallen into his arms at the door. One thing he knew for certain—it would be a whole lot simpler if Cailin Rafferty was not so easy to look at. A man could get lost in her eyes, which were the brown of plowed earth on a rainy day. When they were sad, as they were now, he found himself longing to bring a smile back to her face.

A knife seemed to slice into him when, as they left the village, she said softly, "I thought you'd understand."

"I understand you're too proud to accept what you see

as charity. It's not charity. I wanted you to have something decent to wear." He plucked at her skirt. "This is going to fall apart one of these days."

She turned slightly on the seat so he could see her profile. "So this was just a way to persuade me to stay longer by having me work to repay you for the cost of the fabric?"

"If you'll recall, I told you that I intended to buy the fabric for you as a gift, but you were too stubborn to accept."

"It's not that I'm stubborn. I . . . I just can't."

"Now I don't understand." His eyes narrowed. "Or do I? You think I'm only pretending to be nice to you. Why?"

"You're wrong."

Samuel had not been able to get her to explain further. So he had brought her to this meeting, where she would have to look the facts in the face. Just as the others in the crowded room were looking at her.

"Samuel! Glad to see you here."

He smiled when he saw Noah Sawyer walking toward him. Noah's hair was several shades browner than Cailin's, and sawdust clung to one leg of his trousers. He must have come directly from working in his wood lot to this meeting.

"Noah, good to see you." He shook his friend's hand. Like Samuel, Noah was a relative newcomer to Haven, another who had been welcomed and made to feel so much at home that he cared deeply about what happened in the small town. "Noah, this is Cailin Rafferty. Cailin, Noah Sawyer."

"How do you do, Mr. Sawyer?" Cailin asked quietly.

"It's a pleasure to meet you, Mrs. Rafferty. Sean has told me how pleased these youngsters are to have you back with them." He ruffled Brendan's hair and smiled at the girls.

All three children giggled.

"Just a warning," Noah said, looking back at Samuel. "Some folks are already hot under the collar. Tonight might be the night to say what you told me when we last talked.

It's no night for you to stay mum. I know you don't like adding fire to an argument, but the library's future may depend on some common sense, and you've got that, along with the respect of some of these hotheads."

Samuel did not need to glance at Cailin, for her shock pierced him. He never withheld his opinions from her or avoided any exchange of heated words. Later he would have to explain how sometimes his words carried *too* much weight, because nobody forgot he had practiced the law before he came to Haven.

"I'll say what I have to say when the time's right," he replied. "I suspect tonight will be the night, Noah."

"If you don't speak up, there may not be another night to discuss a library for a very long time."

Nodding, Samuel steered Cailin toward the front of the room. All the seats at the back were taken. No one tried to hide their stares as they walked toward empty desks. He could hear Cailin's unspoken questions as if she shouted them, but now was not the time to explain her misconceptions.

She was not what he had imagined from the few comments the children had made. But, then, he could not expect a child to notice how all her curves were in the right places and the right proportions. For a moment, he enjoyed the gentle sway of her skirt while she listened to Brendan and Megan pointing out aspects of the classroom to her. Her skirt's motion complemented her reddish hair bouncing down her back, where it was tied with a bright green ribbon.

Megan tugged on her mother's hand and said, "This is where I sit, Mama!" She slid quickly onto the middle of the bench behind the long, low desk. "Brendan is on the other side and back a row. Come and sit with me, Mama."

"Me, too?" asked Lottie.

Before Megan's pout could be put into words, Cailin said, "I think there's room for everyone. Brendan, I hope you don't mind having to sit in this seat as well." She smiled. "Unless, of course, you'd rather go back outside and play with your friends."

Brendan nodded eagerly, gave her a kiss on the cheek, and ran out, with Megan close at his heels.

Taking Lottie's hand, she sat where Megan had been. "Lottie, let's sit where you'll be sitting when you go to school in a year."

"So you're planning on her going to school here?" Samuel could not keep from asking.

"I won't have fare for all of us by the time she's ready for school." Cailin's smile wavered as she helped Lottie onto the bench.

He sat next to her, although there was little space for his legs. He wondered how she managed to sit as primly as a lady overseeing a tea tray when she must be cramped, too. As he stretched his arm along the back of the bench, because he had nowhere else to put it, he heard a rustle of whispers behind him. Cailin's shoulders stiffened, so he knew she had heard it as well.

Noah sat behind them just as Reverend Faulkner walked up to where Alice Underhill usually stood when she was teaching. A man Samuel had never seen before walked behind the minister.

He stared at the stranger, just as the others had at Cailin. The man was shorter than most of the men in the room, although he was a head taller than the minister. His light brown hair was brushed back from his forehead, and his clothing clearly had been made by an excellent tailor of expensive material. Beneath his wool trousers, the toes of his boots had a sheen that suggested he had never worn them before.

"Who is that?" he asked over his shoulder.

"Lord Thanington," Noah replied.

"Excuse me?" *Lord* Thanington? He turned in his seat, wondering how he could have heard Noah so wrong.

Noah frowned. "Lord Thanington. He bought what was left of the River's Haven property last week."

"An English lord here in Haven?"

"Apparently he wants to get out from under his father's thumb. His brother will inherit the baron's title, so Lord Thanington decided to come here."

Before he could ask another question, Cailin said, "Then he isn't a lord."

"Excuse me?" he asked again.

Her gaze was focused on the man beside Reverend Faulkner. "Mr. Sawyer—"

"Noah," his friend corrected.

"Noah mentioned his father and older brother. His father is the holder of the title, and his brother might have a courtesy title as the heir. This man would not." She smiled tightly. "Save for one he gave himself to impress you."

Samuel glanced from her to Lord Thanington, who was holding court among the others crowding the front of the room. "He seems to believe he's *Lord* Thanington."

"He can't be."

"You seem very sure of that."

She met his eyes steadily. "I am. You Americans may have forgotten the intricacies of the British peerage, but in Ireland we're well-acquainted with them. As a baron's second son, he can't claim the title of lord."

Samuel said nothing, but stood and walked toward the self-styled Lord Thanington. That the man had come to this meeting might mean something more than just a chance to get to know his new neighbors. If so, Samuel wanted to know what.

He listened while others gushed over Thanington. People who should have known better were almost falling over each other and their own feet to ingratiate themselves with the man. Thanington offered a cool hauteur that suggested this was his due, but Samuel noted how his eyes glittered with pleasure.

Standing back, Samuel did not have to wait long for Thanington to take note of him. The man proved he was no fool, because he immediately tried to appraise Samuel, as if he could not comprehend why Samuel was not joining in with the fawning.

The minister motioned for Samuel to come closer. "Samuel, I know you'll want to meet your new neighbor. This is Lord Thanington." He glanced at Thanington. "Milo Thanington, correct?"

"Yes, that's correct, Vicar," the Englishman said with a cultured accent. His smile was exactly the right warmth when he added, "Forgive me. Vicar isn't an American term. I should have said, Reverend Faulkner."

"Lord Thanington," the minister gushed, as if he had invented the whole situation, "this is Samuel Jennings, who owns the farm on Nanny Goat Hill Road right on the border of your land."

"The farm between my land and the river?" Thanington asked, still looking at the minister.

"Yes." A bit of Reverend Faulkner's smile faded.

That and Thanington's curt question were all the warning Samuel needed. This man who had given himself a title had his eye on Samuel's land. Samuel could tell Thanington right now not to contemplate an offer for the farm. He was not leaving Haven. But if Cailin left with the children, would he want to remain in the empty, too silent house?

"Welcome to Haven, Thanington," he said, with smile he had not worn since the last time he had appeared in front of a judge. "It'll be good to have someone using what's left of River's Haven's property."

"Ah, so you are Mr. Jennings." Thanington did not hold out his hand. "You are the one who has been behind this little project."

"I'm one of several residents who believe a library would be a great asset to Haven." He would not let Thanington's condescending tone irritate him. In Cincinnati, he had learned such a ploy put one on the defensive, a poor position to take while sizing up someone else.

"I see." He smiled. "That must be your little family in the front row. Three children and such a lovely wife? You're a lucky man, Jennings."

Three children? He looked back. Cailin sat with Lottie on her lap and her arm around Megan. When Brendan sat where Samuel had, the boy leaned toward his mother. Protecting her? From what? Those were questions he might be better off leaving unanswered, along with why the older children were not outside with their friends.

Hearing a rumble of thunder, he chuckled under his breath. At least one question was easily answered.

Meeting Thanington's eyes squarely, he suspected the Englishman knew the exact situation at Samuel's farm. Thanington wanted to get Samuel off balance by having to explain that Cailin was not his wife even though she lived under his roof. Not sure what the man's ploy was, for everyone in Haven must know of Cailin's arrival by now, Samuel silenced his next chuckle. If Thanington thought he would embarrass Samuel, the man had a lot to learn about him and about Haven.

"I *am* a lucky man," he said. Looking past Thanington with an expression that dismissed the Englishman as no longer of interest, he asked, "Reverend Faulkner, may I speak with you privately for a moment?"

"Yes . . . yes, of course." The minister excused himself, backing away with as much deference as if Thanington had abruptly ascended to the British throne.

Cailin hushed her children as Samuel and the minister went to talk by a desk set at one side of the platform that was raised about four inches from the floor. She was interested in hearing how Miss Underhill listened to recitations at her desk, but she was more intrigued by what Samuel was saying to the minister. From where she was

sitting, she had been privy to every word said when Samuel
and the so-called Lord Thanington were introduced.

"Madam," murmured a voice in front of her.

She stared at the Englishman, who had come to stand
on the other side of the desk while she had been watching
Samuel. "Sir?"

"I was just speaking with Mr. Jennings and congratu-
lating him on his fine family, so I thought I'd come over
and introduce myself." He plucked her hand from around
Lottie and bowed over it. "Milo Thanington, Mrs.—"

"Cailin," she interrupted before he addressed her as
"Mrs. Jennings." The children would react to that, and
Samuel must have some reason why he had not told this
man the truth. "We're quite informal in Haven, sir."

"Irish, I hear from your accent."

"Yes, sir."

His eyes narrowed when she did not call him "my lord."
He opened his mouth to reply, but Lottie slid off Cailin's
lap and chirped, "Dahi! I—"

"Shh," Cailin cautioned. Before she could remind Lottie
that this was not the time to interrupt, Reverend Faulkner
hit a ruler on the desk to get everyone's attention.

Mr. Thanington went to sit by the opposite wall, near
enough to the platform that no one could mistake his importance to this meeting.

"Who is *that?*" asked Brendan. "Is *he* the high-and-
mighty fancy lord everyone was talking about?"

"Where did you get such words?"

"Grandpa used to use them when he was talking about
British lords."

Cailin smiled. "Grandpa wasn't fond of anything British, but we're in America now. You must be respectful to
all your elders."

"He wasn't too respectful to Samuel," Megan muttered.

"I'll survive, Half-pint," Samuel said, sitting on the

bench again. As the little girl grinned at him, he added, "Cailin, I know you heard what he said about—"

"Maybe it would be better to speak of that later."

He smiled and nodded.

She doubted Samuel would be so grateful if he realized why she wanted to avoid the subject. Too many eyes had watched her while she sat here. She should have guessed what would happen when Samuel invited her to come to this meeting tonight.

When Lottie shifted on her lap and she heard a thread snap on her dress, she tightened her hold around the little girl. Maybe she should have accepted the green fabric to make a dress. But how could she, when every kindness put her more in his debt? A debt she would repay only with grief at the moment she left with the children.

Nine

"Thank you for coming this evening," Reverend Faulkner began the meeting in a booming voice better suited for his church than this cramped schoolhouse. "There have been some concerns raised about the cost of establishing a public library in Haven, and the members of the library committee will be glad to answer them."

Hands rose, and the minister called on a man whose belly was barely contained by his suspenders. When the man spoke of other needs for the money, including a new pier down at the river to replace one damaged in a fire the past summer, heads nodded in agreement. A woman, so soft-spoken Cailin had to struggle to hear her, suggested that the money would be better spent on trees for the streets. Two other men suggested building a bigger school or a new train station.

The minister listened to each, giving them a chance to express their opinions, but glanced at Samuel with a clear order to speak up. Samuel said nothing, startling her because she had seen how eager he was to have a library built in the village.

Another man and two more women spoke. One of the women suggested the money be split—half for the library and the other half for trees—an idea that elicited grumbles around the room.

"Mrs. Anderson always tries to be the peacemaker,"

Samuel said quietly. "She should know better than to try to make both sides of this argument happy."

Not sure if he was talking to himself or to her, Cailin listened to thunder rattle in the distance. She hoped the storm would hold off until they got back to the farm. Then the rains could come and wash away this muggy heat.

When two more hands went up at the back of the room, Reverend Faulkner gave Samuel a desperate look before he called on the men. Neither gave a convincing argument for or against the library, because they both wanted to complain about raising taxes for anything.

"Samuel Jennings, you're next," the minister said with a motion for Samuel to come to the platform. "I think it's time to hear from the chairman of our library committee."

Cailin reached over and squeezed his arm gently. He glanced at her, and a smile sifted across his taut face. Standing, he walked up to the platform to stand next to the minister, then turned to face the room. She could not help but admire his easy command of everyone's attention.

"That's Samuel!" Lottie chirped into the silence filling the schoolhouse as everyone waited for Samuel to speak. "He's the chair's pin."

Laughter eased the tension as Cailin hushed her youngest. When Samuel glanced at Lottie and winked, she giggled. His gaze lingered a moment, holding Cailin's, and she smiled. He was glad she was here with the children, and she was, too.

"Ladies and gentlemen," he began, and looked down at the youngsters edging the room, "we aren't speaking of something that will benefit us like a new pier or a reduction in taxes. We are speaking of something that will benefit the next generation. Shady trees would do that, too, but a tree won't open a young mind and offer it the knowledge these children will need when they are our age." He walked to the edge of the platform. The sincerity in his voice could not be disputed as he continued. "The world is changing so swiftly, it's difficult to imagine what our children will face. Our country just celebrated its centennial. How it has changed since that day one hundred years ago when a small group of men read their declaration of the rights of Americans! Could George Washington have imagined a train like the ones that rumble into Haven? Could John Adams have envisioned our great cities that stretch from Boston to California? That would have been beyond their imaginations, just as the world our children will know is beyond ours.

"There is one thing we can be certain of," he said as he walked back and sat on the edge of the desk. "Our children will need to be able to compete in the new world ahead of them. To do that, they need knowledge. Not just the lessons they learn here in school, but knowledge that can be found in books the school doesn't have room for. A library is the gateway to that knowledge for them." He folded his arms in front of him. "We can either open that gate or close it. What we decide will have repercussions we can't see in the mists of the future, but we know they're there. It behooves us to think cautiously and decide if our children's futures are more important than trees or a new pier." He stood. "Thank you."

As he walked back to sit beside her, Cailin heard applause—at first scattered, then enthusiastic. She smiled at him as she clapped her hands and Lottie's together. Brendan jumped to his feet, cheering. Cailin did not tell him to sit down, although he was louder than anyone else in the schoolroom.

"That was wonderful, Samuel," she said beneath the clapping and conversation swirling around the room.

"An attorney learns how to sway opinion."

"I hope you have."

He stretched his arm along the back of the seat again. "I do, too. This matters more than words can say." His fingers curved around her shoulder, not quite touching her but creating a bond between the two of them and the children.

Reverend Faulkner grinned as he went back to the desk. "Thank you, Samuel. As always, you focus on the crux of the issue." He glanced around the room. "Does anyone else wish to speak before we adjourn? No? Then—"

"May I add to the discourse?" asked Mr. Thanington, rising.

Reverend Faulkner hesitated, glancing at Samuel, then nodded. "Of course, my lord."

Cailin bit her lower lip to keep from calling out that the man was no more worthy of the title of lord than she was, but she quieted the children, who were excited about the response to Samuel's words. She looked at Samuel, but his eyes were aimed directly at Mr. Thanington.

"Thank you, Reverend Faulkner." He gripped the lapels of his coat and struck a pose Cailin thought more appropriate for a statue. "I know I'm a newcomer to your fair village—"

Cailin tried not to roll her eyes. This man was as pompous as Lord Messier, who owned the land and the village where she had lived. The few times he had come to the great stone hulk of a castle that overlooked the sea, he had made a royal progress through the village to make sure no one failed to recognize him as the lord and master of his domain.

"But I do have some insights I'd like to share. First, you should know I agree with Mr. Jennings. A library is of primary importance to a village like Haven." His smile was aimed at embracing everyone in the meeting room. "That is why I wish to make an offer to your library committee."

Heads swivelled as whispers filled the schoolroom, but Cailin stared at Mr. Thanington. Lottie murmured something. Hushing her, Cailin waited to hear what the Englishman was going to say next. She was grateful he had not tried to undermine Samuel's comments, but she could not trust a fraud.

"I would like to speak with them first about it, of course," Mr. Thanington went on, "but, as money seems to be a common concern, I believe what I have to say to them will ease that problem."

More whispers rushed through the room. Cailin glanced at Samuel, and he raised that single eyebrow. She fought not to laugh. He saw, as she did, that Mr. Thanington was as bloated with self-importance as a Christmas goose.

Reverend Faulkner stepped forward to announce that the meeting was over and to thank everyone for attending. The buzz of questions and suppositions flowed out of the schoolhouse with the villagers.

"Cailin," Samuel said as he stood and held out his hand to help her to her feet, "I need to hear Thanington's offer before we leave."

"Don't you mean *Lord* Thanington?"

He chuckled. "I'll keep that in mind." Motioning with his head, he said, "Noah, a moment of your time, if you would."

"I wouldn't miss this for all the water in the Mississippi."

Keeping the children from following the two men who went to talk by a back window, Cailin glanced out the window as lightning flashed. She waited for the sound of thunder. It was no closer. The storm must be going around them, as others had since she had arrived. If just one would come through Haven, it certainly would wash away the sticky air.

She sent the wiggling youngsters to the blackboard on the side of the room, where they could entertain themselves with whatever small pieces of chalk they found. Wandering around the schoolroom, making certain she did not come too close to where Mr. Thanington was again surrounded by awed villagers, she glanced toward a shelf with a row of thin books set beneath a line of letters. She wondered if it was a long word, then saw none of the letters repeated. This must be an alphabet. She stared at it, for she had never seen all the letters arranged like this. She would ask Brendan to explain to her when Samuel was not nearby.

"Mrs. Rafferty, do you want to look at our readers?" asked a woman dressed in unrelieved black.

"Are you Miss Underhill, the children's teacher?" She tried to hide her consternation at talking to a teacher. She had to be careful to pick intelligent-sounding words, or her own lack of education was certain to be obvious.

"Yes." She smiled. "I'd be glad to show you what work your children were doing before the school closed for the summer. As you may know, I shan't be teaching in the fall because I'm getting married soon." Her smile grew warmer as she looked at a young man standing by the door.

Cailin wanted to sigh with relief. Here was the excuse she needed to keep the teacher from discovering that this was the first time Cailin had ever been in a schoolhouse. "I don't want to take any of your time, Miss Underhill, when you must be eager to spend time with your beau."

"Barry is accustomed to me lingering here in the schoolhouse." She laughed. "If I were to continue teaching after our wedding, I believe he might be less patient." Taking down a book from the shelf, she said, "This is what Megan has been reading." She turned a few pages and smiled. "Yes. She has read this far. As you can see, she has made slow but steady progress." She handed the book to Cailin and reached for another. "I've been pushing Brendan a bit harder so he can catch up with the others his age. Both children are good students and eager to learn as much as they can."

Cailin looked down at the page. Megan could read all of this? She listened as Miss Underhill spoke about what Brendan had been learning. The page in his book had many more words.

"You've got every reason to be so proud of them, Mrs.

Rafferty," the schoolteacher said as she put the books back among the others on the shelf.

"I am proud of them. Thank you for all you've helped them to learn."

"My pleasure, Mrs. Rafferty. Good evening." She went to where the young man waited.

Taking down the book Megan had been reading, Cailin sat on the closest bench and slowly turned the pages. The line drawings were simple. She guessed the words described the picture. Lottie came and rested on her lap while Cailin kept looking at the book. She ran her fingers over the combinations of letters which meant nothing to her. The letters blurred as tears filled her eyes. Her children knew how to read.

"Ready to go?" asked Samuel quietly. He put his finger to his lips when she started to answer. Pointing down, he whispered, "I think she had too much library meeting." He bent and picked up Lottie.

She stood. Sliding the book back among the others, she put her hand on his arm to adjust his hold on the little girl. Something about seeing this powerfully masculine man being so gentle with the child warmed her. Simply touching him allowed her to share that invisible sweetness. Her eyes widened as his arm moved to clamp her fingers between it and his body. The twinkle in his eyes dared her to pull away. She laughed softly. Let him think he had daunted her, but the truth was, she was glad for any excuse to be close to him. Denying that would be futile.

During the ride back to the farm and while they worked together to get the children to bed, Cailin wanted to pour out her heart to Samuel. Her eyes filled with tears again as she listened to Brendan read a story to Megan while Lottie slept. Tomorrow, she would ask him to show her this book and ask him some questions that might unlock the magic of reading for her.

She brought two glasses of lemonade into the parlor

where Samuel was sitting. For once, he was not reading
his newspaper, although it sat beside him on the table.

Thanking her for the glass, he drew her down to sit beside him on the sofa. "I can't believe Lottie never woke
up through the jostling ride and Brendan's reading."

"She was sound asleep."

"It'd be nice to be so oblivious to everything else in the
world." He took a drink, then bent to pull off his boots.
Wiggling his toes, he said, "I think I've stepped on every
rock in that cornfield in the last two days."

Putting her glass on the table, she knelt by the sofa. His
socks scratched her palms as she rubbed his toes between
her hands.

"You don't have to do that, Cailin."

At the embarrassment in his voice, she looked up to see
a baffled expression on his face. "Does it help?"

"More than you can know."

"Good." She lowered her eyes as she asked, "What did
Mr. Thanington have to say?"

"I don't want to talk about that now." He caught her by
the shoulders and drew her up to sit beside him. "I want
this."

His mouth slanted across hers, and she gladly went into
his arms. Her fingers sifted through his thick hair. It sprinkled through her fingers, setting each throbbing with longing. No, a desire . . . a need to give the same joy to him.
It was all of those and more.

So many things she wanted to ask him, so many she
yearned to tell him. Every thought was stifled by the escalating beat of her pulse.

She sighed as his lips touched her cheek. She curved her
arms up his back when his mouth over hers pressed her
against the strength of his embrace. She exulted in the
brawny breadth of his chest against her.

When he leaned her back into the sofa, she brought him
atop her. Her fingers crept beneath his shirt to explore his

firm muscles. At her touch, his breath burned into her mouth, mingling with her fevered gasps, igniting the passion that had refused to lie quiescent since he had roused it. His lips swept along her throat, sparking pleasure on each brief caress, and she whispered his name softly. To be with him and in his arms was heavenly.

Her joy erupted into a blazing craving when his fingers roved upward along her bodice. Shimmering sensations rippled through her as she clung to him, overpowered by his touch. Her fingers tightened on his back as his fingertip roamed in a meandering path along her breast.

The virile lines of his body sent her deeper into the cushions, surrounding her with the rapture she had despaired of ever feeling again.

Again?

With a moan, Cailin pushed him aside far enough so she could scramble from the sofa.

He sat up and asked, "Cailin?"

"No," she said quietly. "No, this is wrong."

"You are wrong." He pulled her back down into his arms and curved a finger back up over her breast. When she sighed with delight, he whispered, "This is right."

"I can't!" She jumped to her feet.

He grasped her arm, keeping her from fleeing. "Cailin, you're frightened. It can't be from these few kisses. What's wrong?"

"This is wrong. You and me."

"You're lying." He scowled. "Tell me the truth!"

From the corner of her eye, she saw a hand rise. Time collapsed on itself, and she was being held by another man who was upset with her. Not upset, furious. Lifting up her other arm to protect her head, she cried, "Don't!"

Samuel released her, horrified to see this proud woman cowering before him when he had been about to put his fingers to her cheek to comfort her. As she sank to the sofa, hiding her face in the seat, he squatted down beside her.

"Cailin?" he whispered. "Cailin, what is it? Who hit you?" Even as he spoke the words he wanted to believe could not be true, a rage threatened to strangle him as he wished his fingers could be around the neck of the person who had struck her.

Her fingers settled on her right arm. "Abban—"

"Your husband?" Disgust sent nausea through him. He wanted her to deny that her husband—the father of the children he loved—had beat her.

"Yes, but only a few times."

"Only a few? How many times would have been too many?"

"I don't know."

"I do. Even once is too many. The children never said anything about this."

She raised her head and dampened her lips. "I don't think they knew. It never happened when they were nearby, other than that last night when I asked him to take all of us with him to America." She shuddered. "I never had seen him so angry, although there had been whispers of him being involved in fights at the tavern and making threats. I discounted them as drunken tales until that night. Maybe I was foolish to insist we continue the discussion outside, away from the children."

His hand beneath hers cradled her right arm as he brought her up to sit against him. "And he hurt you?"

"He was furious."

"How bad did he hurt you?"

Running her fingers along her forearm, she whispered, "He broke this."

Samuel swore. "You forgave him for *that?*"

"He apologized, begging my forgiveness and blaming his anxiety at the long sea voyage through a wintry sea, as well as his despair at leaving me and the children behind.

I forgave him. What else could I do when he was leaving for America?"

"And you followed so he could beat you some more?"

"I had planned to tell him that he must change, but I never thought about leaving him." She looked toward the stairs. "He was the father of my children. I had to think of them. I thought they'd have a better life in America."

"Did you have to think of the children?"

She gasped. "Of course I did."

"Maybe," he said, cupping her chin in his hand, "just maybe once you should think about Cailin Rafferty." He stroked her cheek. "And maybe you should think about the fact that I would never hit a woman, no matter how much provocation she gives me."

Drawing her into his arms, he tasted her trembling lips before she could ask the questions he saw in her eyes. He must not think of the past or the future when, if she had her way, she would find the money to leave with the children.

As she stood and bid him good night, he wanted to laugh. A sad laugh, for he knew neither of them could take his advice. He might want her, and she might long for him, but the fear of losing the children stood between them . . . and would not be moved.

Ten

"Rhea brought her here for *me*," Lottie said in answer to Cailin's question as she hugged a black kitten that scrambled, hissing, out of her arms.

Cailin caught it before it could run under the stove. Calming the frightened kitten as she cradled it in the crook of her arm, she said, "If you're going to have a kitten, Lottie, you must learn how to hold it correctly."

"So I can keep her for my very, very own?"

"If Samuel says it's all right."

"Samuel, can I keep her for my very, very own?"

He pushed back from the kitchen table and lifted the little girl to sit on his lap. "You'll have to take care of her and the other cat, making sure they have food and water and a warm place to sleep."

"Like you take care of Mama and us?"

"Yes."

Cailin said nothing when Samuel looked past the little girl toward her.

A bewitching smile slid along his lips as he went on, "And how your mother takes care of all of us."

Lottie jumped down from his lap and ran to Cailin. Putting the kitten in the little girl's arms, she said, "Now be careful. She's just a baby."

"I will. I promise, Mama."

Cailin went to the table to pick up the rest of the plates.

They had eaten in the kitchen this evening in hopes of savoring even a hint of air from the back door. The dining room seemed as hot as the stove.

When she reached for a plate, hands at her waist brought her down onto Samuel's lap. She laughed. "How do you expect me to get my work done?"

"I don't care about your work." His mouth caressed hers, but he pulled away at a crash.

On the other side of the kitchen, the two girls wore chagrined expressions. The kitten vanished beneath the stove again, with a frightened mew, and around two pair of feet were the shards of a plate.

"Megan! Lottie!" gasped Cailin, coming to her feet. She heard Samuel push back his chair as he stood behind her.

"I didn't mean to, Mama," Megan said. "I just wanted to show it to the kitten." Tears oozed out of her eyes.

"Are you hurt?" Cailin asked, keeping her eyes focused on her daughters. She did not want to see Samuel's reaction to the absurdity of showing off a plate to a kitten.

"No."

"Good."

Cailin pulled out her handkerchief, dabbed Lottie's face, and then handed it to Megan. Asking Brendan to try to coax the kitten out from under the stove, she began to pick up the biggest pieces of the broken plate.

"Look out," Samuel said. "I'll sweep it up."

"Let me." She stood and took the broom. "Samuel, I can replace it—" She stopped herself. She had no money to buy a plate or even the food to put on it. If Samuel had not allowed her and the children to stay here, she was not sure what they would have done to survive.

Out west they are looking for women like you.

She tried to banish her mother-in-law's vicious words from her mind. *Women like you.* She had not asked Mrs. Rafferty what that meant, for she suspected she did not want to know.

"No need to replace it." He picked up more of the bigger pieces and dropped them into the trash. "Don't worry. None of these plates are worth much."

"I'm sorry," Megan whispered, wiping her cheek with the back of her hand.

Samuel gave her a bolstering smile. "I know you are, Half-pint. I hope the sound of the breaking plate didn't scare you much."

She grinned. "I wasn't scared of that!"

"You're getting to be a big, brave girl, aren't you?"

"I am!" She held up her arm. "See my big muscle?"

He turned her toward the stove and gave her a playful swat on the bottom. "Then help your brother get that kitten out from under there before it cooks."

Cailin bit her lower lip as Lottie teased for him to ask her to help, too. Samuel brought out a joy in her children that had eluded her since she had left Ireland. It was dismaying to think how long she had been separated from these bright, innocent smiles. When she thought of what could have happened to them . . .

"It's no tragedy," Samuel said as she put the last china pieces in the trash. "It's just an old plate. You don't need to look so upset."

"I'm not upset about the plate." She tried to smile. "In fact, I'm thinking happy thoughts."

"If that's your happy expression, I'd hate to see your sad one."

She hastily turned away and leaned the broom against the wall.

"Cailin, I didn't mean that as it sounded," he said to her back.

"I know you didn't." Facing him, she locked her fingers together at his nape. "Let's just talk about something else."

"That sounds like a good idea." He pulled her closer then grimaced. "I'm going to get you sweaty."

"You're too late. I think we're all soaked. Are the summers always this hot here?"

"I suspect so."

"We're going to melt away in this heat."

"We need to do something about that." Keeping his arm around her waist, he raised his voice to get the children's attention. "How about some ice cream?" He smiled at Cailin. "If it's all right with your mother."

"Is it all right, Mama?" Brendan asked.

"How can I say no?" She laughed. Before she had gone to work in New York, she would have had to ask what ice cream was. She had seen it but never tasted it. The children's faces revealed that they had, and they had enjoyed it.

"Take the kitten out to the barn, Lottie. I'm going to need you to help turn the ice-freezing pail," Samuel said, his eyes twinkling with merriment. "What do you say to blackberry ice cream?"

"Blackberry?" Cailin asked.

He pointed to the small bucket by the door. "There seems to be a bumper crop on its way, but most of them are green and hard. I picked some early ones on my way back from taking the broken wagon axle to Wyatt to be repaired."

"Another broken axle?" Cailin asked.

"I tried to repair it myself and didn't do a very good job. Wyatt Colton's going to work on it. He can fix just about anything mechanical."

Lottie jumped up and down. "I love backberries."

"Blackberries." Samuel chuckled. "Have you ever had them?"

"No, but I loved storeberries." She twirled around.

"Strawberries?" Cailin smiled.

"I guess so. Whoa there," Samuel said, putting a hand on Lottie's shoulder. "One broken dish is enough for today. Wyatt can't fix those, too."

The children burst out talking at once, and Cailin stared at them in amazement. What were they asking about?

Samuel held up his hands. "I can't hear any of you when all of you are talking. Yes, I went out to have Wyatt fix the broken part on the wagon. No, I didn't see Kitty Cat."

She smiled, at last understanding. "Do you mean the little girl Kitty Cat?"

"My friend," said Megan proudly.

"Got it!" shouted Brendan, standing up as a cloud of soot billowed out from him and the kitten.

Samuel waved aside the soot. "Take the kitten out to the barn and bring in that bag of ice I broke up earlier."

As the children rushed out, Cailin called for them to wash up before they came back inside. She swept the floor, trying not to stir up the soot again. Samuel whistled a light-hearted tune as he edged around her to get the ingredients they would need to make the ice cream.

He did not touch her, but there was something, something intangible, something compelling, drawing her toward him. She wanted to ignore it, but that was impossible. She hoped she could continue to resist it tonight.

She was horrified at the way she had acted last night in the parlor. Samuel might have reacted with anger when she cringed away, fearing he was about to strike her. She wished she could find the words to apologize. Just speaking of it threatened to open the barely healed wounds within her heart.

"All set. Just have to prepare the berries," he said as he opened a cupboard. He lifted out a pewter pot, setting it on the table. "As soon as the kids return, we'll begin. Have you ever had blackberry ice cream?"

"I've never had any kind of ice cream."

He looked amazed, then said, "Then you're in for a treat you won't soon forget."

"What can I do to help?" she asked as she put away the broom.

He did not answer, and she looked at him. Her question, which should have been a commonplace one, took on new meaning when his eyes glowed with passion. An answering craving billowed through her. When she pretended to be busy straining the blackberries through a sieve as he requested, she was grateful Samuel had not replied with a suggestion that would have had nothing to do with ice cream. *Don't think of that!* She had to keep her own thoughts tightly under control.

The children burst in, slamming the screen door. Brendan handed Samuel a canvas bag, and Lottie held up a pail. Megan put a much smaller bucket of cream on the table.

"Spoons are in the drawer by the dry sink," Samuel said as he picked up the bag of ice and dumped it in the pail. He added a few handfuls of saltpeter.

The cool air struck her face, easing the fire along her cheeks. Oh, was she blushing? Nobody seemed to notice, so she guessed it was the heat scorching her each time Samuel looked at her with an invitation in his eyes.

"Spoons?" she asked, trying to sound nonchalant. "Is it ready already?"

Megan giggled. "Mama, we all need to help stir it so it freezes."

"Don't tease your mother," Samuel said. "Think how impatient you were when I first made ice cream with you. You didn't want to wait for it to freeze all the way through."

Cailin watched, fascinated, as he set the pewter pot into the ice and then poured the cream, sugar, strained berries, and some raspberry jam into it. He put a lid on the pot and told them to be patient. The children vied to be the first to stir the mixture fifteen minutes later. Lottie was given the honor because she would not have the strength to stir as it froze harder.

Samuel turned the pot in the ice each time the children stirred. When even Brendan could not move the mixture within the pot, he gave it one more turn and said, "It's ready."

Taking out the ice cream pot, he set it on the table. Lottie was leaning on the table, an expectant smile on her face. Beside her, Brendan and Megan wore the same eager expressions as they held out dishes.

"Your mother first," Samuel said. "She's never had ice cream before, so we'll let her have the first taste."

She reached for a spoon, but froze as solid as the ice cream when he dipped his finger into the blue mixture and held it out to her. His other hand took the spoon and set it back on the table.

"Mama," Brendan said, "hurry up. We want some ice cream, too."

"You heard him." Samuel's words had a husky edge that matched the warmth of his smile. He stepped closer. "Don't you want to try it?"

The children's excited voices vanished into the frantic beat of her heart while she opened her mouth to allow his finger in. The ice cream was sweet and cool on her tongue. His finger was warm and rough as he drew it away.

"Do you like how it tastes?" he asked.

"Yes," she whispered, knowing that neither of them were speaking of the ice cream.

"Would you like more?"

"Save some for us!" cried Megan, and the connection between them shattered.

Cailin stepped aside as the children held out their bowls eagerly. She shooed them out onto the front porch as each one got a serving.

Lottie paused, turned around, and came back into the kitchen. "Can I have some extra for Dahi?"

"Lottie," Cailin said, "asking for more before you have eaten anything is not polite." She did not let her amazement show. Before they came to America, none of the children would have asked for another serving, because they had known there was nothing more.

Samuel pulled another spoon out of the drawer. "Why don't you and Dahi share? If you finish it all, I think there may be a bit more."

She shouted and twirled about again.

Cailin caught her by the shoulders and prompted, "Lottie?"

"Thank you, Samuel. Can Dahi and me—"

"Dahi and I," corrected Samuel with a smothered laugh.

"Can Dahi and I sit on the tree swing?"

"Just be careful you and Dahi don't tip off the tree swing and lose your ice cream in the dirt."

She nodded, then said, "I think we'll sit on the steps."

He chuckled as she followed her sister and brother outside.

"I've been meaning to ask you," Cailin said as she took the bowl he offered her. "Who is this Dahi? Is it another child? Daihi is an Irish name, which is close to the way she pronounces it." She laughed. "She mispronounces so many other words."

He set the pewter pot back into the remaining ice. "I thought you'd be able to tell me the answer to that. She talks about Dahi all the time. Apparently he's some friend only she can see."

"The Irish are renowned for their grand imaginations and storytelling."

"I don't think it's a story to her. She believes he's there." He laughed, and she knew her disquiet was visible. "No need to worry. Alice tells me it's not unusual for a child to have an invisible friend."

"Alice?" She was pleased at how natural her question sounded because a jolt had struck her as she thought of another woman here with him and her children.

"The schoolteacher in Haven. You talked to her at the meeting last night. Alice Underhill."

"Oh."

"Is that a green-eyed monster I see in your brown eyes?" he asked. "Jealous?"

"The only green-eyed monster here is you." She stepped around him.

He laughed, and she had to smile. This man was just too charming for her to stay vexed with him. As she carried her bowl into the foyer, he held the front door for her.

She sat on a chair near where the children were prattling between bites of ice cream. He took another chair and put his feet up on a low stool. Taking a spoonful of ice cream, she let it melt on her tongue. It was luscious, but, without the added zest of his skin, it seemed to be lacking.

"Lottie?" She motioned to the little girl. She had to think of something other than the tempting taste of Samuel's finger.

Lottie bounced up onto the porch, threatening to send the rapidly melting ice cream flying everywhere.

Cailin steadied her daughter's bowl, then put both bowls on the porch floor. Picking up the little girl, she set Lottie on her lap.

"Tell me about Dahi," she said.

"He's my friend." Lottie stared at her ice cream.

"Tell me what he looks like."

With a giggle, Lottie crowed, "But, Mama, you know what he looks like! He's tall." Her eyes widened. "He's very, very tall."

"As tall as Samuel?"

She nodded. "And he washes over me so I'm all right."

Translating *washes* to *watches,* Cailin asked, "Is there anything else you can tell me so I'll know Dahi when I see him?"

Lottie giggled again. "Mama, he's indibble."

"Invisible," Samuel said as he sat in the chair next to them.

"That's what I said!" Lottie slid off Cailin's lap and put

her hands on her hips. "Indibble! But one day, Mama, he'll be dibble—dizzle," she corrected herself with a laugh. "Then you'll see I'm right."

Bending down to get the little girl's bowl and hoping Lottie did not see her smile, Cailin said, "I'm sure I will. Just let me know the day he's visible." Cautioning her daughter to be careful as she went to sit on the stairs, she looked at Samuel.

He shrugged. "That's more than I ever knew about Dahi, her indibble friend."

"It doesn't seem to be doing her any harm to believe in him."

"Not when she smiles every time she talks about him." He picked up her bowl and held it out to her.

Cailin sat back in her chair and watched her children enjoy their ice cream. Silence settled on the porch as twilight crawled out from beneath the trees beyond the barn. Insects began their nightly song, a more frantic tune with the hot evening. In the distance, heat lightning danced across the sky as swiftly as the lightning bugs. A glorious spark, then it was gone.

She toyed with her spoon, knowing she should say something to Samuel but not sure what. The easy camaraderie they had shared while the children churned the ice cream had disappeared. It was just as if she and Samuel were much younger and he had come calling at her father's house. As if they stood by the cottage's front door and were trying to decide if he would try to kiss her and if she would let him.

This was absurd! She was a grown woman.

She turned to look at him, but whatever she might have said went unspoken. His gaze enveloped her in a luscious warmth as sweet as any embrace when his broad hand curved along her cheek.

"Would you like some more ice cream?" he asked, his

thumb trailing across her lips and setting off a storm of sensations.

"Just ice cream?" She knew she should put an end to this, but his mix of teasing and sensuality enthralled her.

"Ice cream and whatever else you'd like." His hand settled on her arm. His fingers were as firm and less yielding than the chair. She wanted to touch the rough planes of his tanned face, to trace his lips as he had hers. And not just with her fingertip, but with her mouth.

"Mama! Look at this!"

Cailin pulled back as Samuel swore softly. She understood his frustration because she shared it. Yet she had to be grateful each time the children's intrusions reminded her of the cost of trusting another man with her heart.

Admiring the lightning bug Megan had captured, she looked up when Samuel said, "Brendan, go and get the book on the table in the parlor."

"A lesson now?" he asked, obviously disgusted at the very thought.

"I thought you might want to read to your sisters again tonight." He smiled. "Do you think you can read all of the next chapter to them?"

His eyes glistened with pride. "Yes, sir! I can read all of that and more."

"One chapter will be enough. It's late."

Cailin smiled as each of her children hugged her and gave her sticky kisses. She watched while they did the same to Samuel. Anyone witnessing this scene would think they were a family, no different from any other. That thought was surprisingly pleasing. She was captivated anew by the idea of staying on this farm where her children were happy . . . and where Samuel was.

Calling after the children to leave their dirty dishes on the kitchen table, Cailin stood. She set her dish on the seat of the chair and went to the railing to look out into the night. In the few weeks since she had stumbled up the road, this place had seeped into her heart. It resembled Ireland so slightly; only the scents from the fields brought back memories of her life there. Still, this farm at the end of the dirt road had become a place she would always hold dear. It would be a sweet memory . . . if she left.

Where had that thought come from? It should have been *when* she left, not if. Yet, as she gazed out into the night, she knew she had already begun questioning whether she wanted to return to Ireland. Here her children could go to school. Here they could grow up to be whatever **they** wanted to be. Here was where Samuel lived.

"You're wearing that pensive expression again," Samuel said, coming to stand beside her as if she had spoken his name aloud. He leaned his arm against the post holding up the roof. "I hope your thoughts are happy ones."

"Do you know how lucky you are to have found this place?"

"Yes."

"How *did* you find it?"

He laughed. "I looked on a map and saw the name of the village and decided this was where I wanted to live."

"Haven?" She looked up at his face, which was shadowed by a day's growth of whiskers. "Why were you seeking a haven, Samuel?"

"Aren't we all searching for one?" He ran the backs of his fingers along her cheek. "A place where we can set aside our troubles and revel in happiness."

"Have you found it?"

"I thought I had."

"Until I bumbled into your life."

He laughed again. "Not you. Thanington."

Leaning against the rail, she asked, "What offer did he make to you and the library committee?"

"Money. Lots of it."

"With what conditions?"

"I should have guessed you'd be much more clear-thinking than Reverend Faulkner and Alice, who were so thrilled with the obvious solution that they wanted to accept it last night. I talked them into asking for a week to consider Thanington's offer." He rested a hand next to hers on the railing as he asked, "Why is it you're suspicious of his generosity?"

"In Ireland, the English aren't our favorite people, especially one who has anointed himself with a title he doesn't have the right to claim." Putting her hand over his, she asked, "What does he want?"

"He hasn't said, because I brought the discussion to a quick end. I figure he wants at least his name over the door."

She rested her head against his arm. "That isn't too much of a price to pay to get the library you want Haven to have."

"If that was all he wanted, I'd agree wholeheartedly. That much money must be aimed at getting him more."

"You're a suspicious man, Samuel Jennings. Always looking a gift horse in the mouth."

He drew her to her feet. "It comes from my years of reading the law, I'm afraid. I learned the good side of people often is only a way to conceal greedy hearts."

"Do you really believe that?"

"I did. That's why I came to Haven. To persuade myself there's a lot of good in a lot of hearts." He curved his arm around her waist. "And I think I'm getting persuaded until someone like Thanington comes along."

"He may be harmless in his delusion of being a fancy lord."

When she ran her fingers along his chin, he smiled. Her own smile vanished beneath his lips as he kissed her with a slow, deep yearning. It urged her to succumb to the need to make love with him until their minds fell from the precipice of sense into the sweet madness of passion.

He drew back, and she moaned a denial. Propping up

her face on his thumbs, he said, "You must decide, Cailin, if you're going to look for good, too, or just see the bad. When you make your decision, let me know."

"I will."

"Good night." After a swift brush of his mouth against hers, he picked up the dishes and went into the house.

She looked back out into the darkness. Lightning flashed, distant and impotent, so unlike the fiery craving within her. Glancing at the door, then down at her tightly clasped hands, she knew she must figure out what she wanted. Samuel Jennings was going to be part of her life for as long as it took her to earn enough money to pay for train tickets to New York, so she must get her life back on track—and headed in the right direction. It would be so much easier if her heart stopped beseeching her to trust Samuel even as her head warned, over and over, what had happened when she last had fallen under a handsome man's spell.

Eleven

Brendan called out, "Samuel, where are you?"

Looking up from where he had been checking an ear of corn, he waved to the boy. He smiled as Brendan rushed up to him. "You're just the person I wanted to see. Can you—?"

"What did you say to my mother?" he asked, his arms clasped over his chest. "She's looking so sad."

"I don't recall saying much to her other than good morning." He tossed the ear into the half barrel he was using to collect the corn until his wagon was repaired. "What did she say before she started looking sad?"

He shrugged.

"What were you talking about?"

"Oh . . ." He gulped. "My Grandpa O'Shea."

He ruffled the boy's hair and said, "I'll see what I can do to cheer her up."

"Samuel, I'm sorry." Brendan stared down at his bare feet. "I shouldn't have accused you of upsetting her, but you and she—you, well, you know."

"I know." He pointed to the row of corn, not wanting to discuss the uneven course of every conversation between himself and Cailin. "Start here and see if you can finish the row before lunch."

"Mama wants me and the girls—the girls and me—to go into Haven for her."

"Do that, and then finish up this row."

"Yep." His grin returned as he raced off, leaving a small dust storm in his wake.

Samuel wiped his forehead on his shirt before tucking it back into his trousers. If this hot, dry spell had come a month ago, the crops would have been ruined. Harvesting in the heat was no fun, but at least he would have something to feed the cows he had planned to buy this fall.

As he opened the screen door into the kitchen, which smelled of that morning's eggs and coffee, he smiled. Cailin was humming the tune he often whistled while he finished a chore. Even in that blasted patched dress, she was beguiling as she swayed to the music. He wondered when the next dance would be at the Grange Hall.

"Busy?" he asked.

Cailin halted in mid-note as she looked over her shoulder. She dried off a plate and put it up on the shelf. "I'm done with the dishes. I'm going to do some cleaning. By the time I'm done, the bread will have finished raising, and I'll bake that. There's a cake Brendan's been asking me to make for dessert, so I need to prepare it."

He raised his hands and laughed. "I wasn't accusing you of not having anything to do. I was wondering if you wanted to take a few minutes and go for a ride."

"A ride? Where?"

"I've got to see Wyatt Colton to get the axle for the field wagon. Do you want to ride along?"

"Is it far?"

"No, so you'll be back before Brendan and the girls return from Haven."

She nodded. "It shouldn't take them long to pick up some chocolate and the mail."

"And you accused me of spoiling them."

"You accused yourself, if you'll recall. Sending three children into town to pick up some supplies isn't exactly spoiling them."

Holding up a single finger, he said, "One box of chocolate. Three kids. That seems like a couple too many for the job."

"All right." She draped the damp dishrag over the back of the chair. "You've discovered the truth. They were anxious to play with Emma's children, so I figured the errand was a good excuse to let them run off some of their energy on a hot day. Brendan promised he'd be back in time to help you in the cornfields later this afternoon." Scanning the sky through the door, she asked, "How long does it stay this hot?"

"The weather should break sometime toward the end of September."

Cailin groaned. "That's weeks away." She hesitated. "Samuel?" She drew a wrinkled page of newsprint out of her pocket. "I found this in the parlor. I'll talk to the children, so they don't make a mess of your newspaper again."

He took the crumpled page and tossed it into the air, catching it easily before dropping it back onto the table. She was not fooled by his apparent indifference, because his smile looked forced. When he answered, his voice was strained. "I told them they could have the old newspapers for the rabbit's hutch. This one is one I've already read." He glanced at her. "You didn't want to read it, did you?"

"No!"

Her fervor was too much, she knew, when he said, "I guess that's a definite answer."

"Let's go to pick up that axle before it gets much hotter."

"An excellent idea."

She started for the dining room, but paused when he moved in front of her. His hand settled on the door frame only a finger's breadth from her. Even though his smile did not change, his eyes narrowed ever so slightly.

Just enough so she had to wonder if he still was talking about the axle when he murmured, "I'll have to come up with a few new ideas, won't I?"

She backed away, hitting the kitchen table hard enough to make it rattle. He walked out of the kitchen, whistling the very tune she had been humming before he came in. Astonished, she realized she had heard it first when he whistled it. Samuel Jennings was becoming a part of her life in so many ways.

Leaning in the doorway, she watched through the window as he strode toward the barn. The confidence in his step was not arrogance, and his smile was sincere. He was unquestionably beguiling, and his kisses burned on her lips for hours after he was no longer holding her. He was everything she had dreamed about when she was a young girl. A man who thought she was beautiful in spite of her freckles and her height. If only she had met him before . . .

Cailin shook those silly thoughts from her head. She started to untie her apron, then left it on. The white apron was stained, but it covered many of the patches along the front of her dress. She got her bonnet. By the time she came out into the yard, Samuel had the horse harnessed to the wagon.

He drove slowly, so the dust raised by the horse was not smothering. Even so, she began to cough as she waved the particles away from her face. When he offered to stop the wagon, she motioned for him to keep on going.

"You're a stubborn woman," he grumbled, but he slapped the reins on the horse as they turned down a road leading toward the river. He pulled out a handkerchief and handed it to her.

Her coughing disappeared as the road became a grassy trail. When they came over a small hill, she saw a cottage. Its whitewash glistened in the sunlight, and she was astonished to see a bright red door set in the center of a porch with a single rocking chair.

As they stopped, her gaze was pulled toward the river. A steamboat was docked at the small wharf reaching out into the river. On the sidewheel *The Ohio Star* was painted in bright red paint around a blue star. The sound of a hammer striking metal came from somewhere on an upper deck.

Samuel helped her down from the wagon and shouted, when the hammering paused for a moment, "Wyatt, are you around?"

A dark-haired man peered over the railing on the middle deck. "I should have guessed you'd be right on time." He walked with easy confidence on the deck, which rocked with the river's current.

Samuel's hand on her arm guided Cailin down the hill and onto the wharf. Her first tentative steps told her the boards were not going to crack beneath her.

As he reached the stairs, the man on the boat called, "Check the boiler now, Horace, and see what pressure you can get."

An older man peered out of a door on the bottom deck. "Give me a few more minutes."

The dark-haired man crossed the lower deck and jumped across a narrow finger of water to the wharf. As he walked toward them, he pushed back his hair and settled his cap in place.

He put his fingers to the brim as he looked at her. "Ma'am."

"This is Wyatt Colton," Samuel said. "Wyatt, Cailin Rafferty."

"There's no doubting you're the mother of the Rafferty kids," Wyatt said with a deep laugh. "Same red hair. Rachel and Kitty Cat are in Haven. Rachel is helping Anderson with his books."

"Books?" Cailin asked. "Is she going to work in the library when it's built?"

He wiped his hands on a cloth he pulled out of a pocket. "I should have said Rachel is helping with his financial books. She did all the finances for the River's Haven Community, and now she's working for folks around the Haven area. They're going to be sorry they missed you. Rachel has been wanting to meet you." He put his foot against the boat's railing. "We've been pretty busy since *The Ohio Star* tied up here."

"Where is it headed?" Cailin asked, fascinated by the ship with its large paddlewheels on either side.

"Up the river to Cincinnati, so putting in for repairs here was sensible." He smiled. "Anything you need picked up in Cincinnati, Samuel? *The Ohio Star* can bring it back on her way down river to Louisville."

"Nothing, thanks." Samuel's reaction to the word *Cincinnati* was so restrained, Cailin doubted if Wyatt had even noticed it. She would not have, if she had not seen it before. Samuel had admitted he had come here looking for a haven. From what? Not just from the life he had known as an attorney.

She silenced her questions as she walked back up the hill with the two men. While Wyatt showed Samuel the repairs he had made, she gazed along the river. Its silvery thread glinted in the sunshine. She saw clouds rising over the horizon to darken it to the west. Maybe the long-awaited storm would come tonight.

"That's damn—blasted heavy," Wyatt said as he closed the back of the wagon. "If you roll it out, I don't know if it will stay together."

"Brendan can help me," Samuel said. "The boy's gotten to be a great hand to have at the farm. He's learning faster than I can teach him."

"Right now, Kitty Cat seems to be an expert on looking for trouble." He laughed. "Something she's had a lot of experience at." He tipped his cap again. "Glad to meet you, Cailin."

"And you." She smiled as she let Wyatt give her a hand up onto the seat while Samuel swung up on the other side. "One of these days, I'm sure I'll meet Rachel and Kitty Cat."

"I'm sure you will." With a grin, he walked back toward the steamboat.

Samuel steered the wagon onto the road. Waving his handkerchief like a limp fan to keep the dust away, Cailin thought about the ice cream they had enjoyed. Maybe she would take the girls and see if they could find enough berries to make more. Or maybe they could make ice cream with some of the chocolate.

She sat straighter as the wagon turned into a road that angled back toward the river. "Where are we going? This isn't the way to the house."

"You're right." He rested his elbows on his knees as the horse went along at a pace appropriate for the hot day. "I have one more stop to make."

"Where?"

"Curiosity killed the cat," he teased.

"A fine sentiment if my name was Kitty Cat. However, it isn't."

"I know. It's Cailin O'Shea Rafferty."

She regarded him with bafflement. "Why are you babbling?"

"Brendan came out to the cornfield to let me know you were wearing a sad face. He was upset enough to accuse me of doing something to hurt you."

"You didn't do anything." She put her hand on his arm. "We were talking of Athair."

"So he said, after he calmed down."

"My father's birthday is tomorrow, and I hate not spending it with him."

"I'm sorry."

She smiled sadly. "And I'm sorry Brendan accused you of something that wasn't your fault."

He did not reply as he drew the wagon into a small grove of trees. Stopping, he jumped down and came around to her side. He held up his hand.

It was a summons her heart refused to allow her to ignore. Putting her fingers in his, she turned to step down. He released her hand and grasped her at the waist. Lifting her off the seat, he lowered her slowly until her feet touched the ground. Then he took her hand again and pressed his mouth to her palm.

She whispered, "I don't like being irritated with you."

"And you make it blasted difficult to be angry with you when you look at me with those brown puppy-dog eyes. I guess I'm just going to have to accept that you don't trust me."

"How can I trust you when you've made no secret of the fact that you want my children?"

Running his finger along her sleeve, he whispered, "The one I want now is you."

"You're making this even more awkward." She walked along the wagon to put some space between them but did not step out into the punishing sunshine. "You shouldn't say things like that."

"Do you want me to lie to you, Cailin?"

"No."

"Then what do you want?"

She faced him, not surprised that he was less than an arm's length away. "You'd like me to say you, wouldn't you?"

"I wouldn't mind a bit." His finger slipped across her shoulder to wrap itself in a loose strand of her hair. "But it was an honest question."

"I'll give you an honest answer. I want to go home and pretend I never came to America."

He laughed coolly. "I should have known better than to ask you for the truth if I didn't want to hear it."

"Samuel, I'm glad we've had a chance to meet. That's honest. But your life is here, and mine is in Ireland."

"Where your kids never had a chance to go to school and you lived in a house with a dirt floor?"

She wrung her hands in her apron until she heard the

thin fabric rip. "I want my children to go to school. With learning, they can be whatever they wish to be, but my father is back there all alone. We should be with him."

Taking her hands in his, he did not move closer. "There's no sense in letting this gnaw at you when you're a long way from having the money to go back."

"If I asked you—"

"I thought you didn't want anything from me."

"It would be a loan."

He shook his head. "You know I won't agree to anything that takes the children away from Haven a minute sooner than necessary."

"I know."

"So we're at the same stalemate we've been from the beginning. Shall we call a truce, Cailin? We'll both stop trying to distrust the other. That would be a good start."

"I will try."

"And so will I." He released one of her hands but held on to the other as he led her through the trees.

"Where are we going?" she asked as she let the cool shadows wash away the day's heat. A faint breeze rattled the leaves against each other, and the grass was soft and green beneath her feet, not brown like the stalks drying in the sunlight.

"Just for a walk."

"We both have chores to do."

"And the hardest one is trusting each other, isn't it?"

She sighed. "I don't want to talk about that again."

"Then shall we talk about the heat?"

"Not when it's so pleasant here beneath the trees. Let's talk about something else."

"How about you? Can we talk about you?" he asked as he swung her hand.

"I'm a duller subject than the weather." She smiled.

He stroked her fingers. "That's strange, Cailin. I don't

find you the least bit boring. You're an endless puzzle to me."

"Me? A puzzle?' She laughed. "I'd say it was the other way around."

Instead of answering, he continued to lead her through the grove. Dappled shadows darkened his hair and dripped along her gown, hiding the patches. When they emerged from beneath the trees, the pungent smell of ripe fields ready to be harvested combined with the aroma of the muddy riverbank. Trees whispered like children laughing together. The sound was diminished by the whine of insects in the bushes.

She held up her hand to protect her eyes from the sun's reflection on the pond in front of them. It was big enough so the house and barn could have been placed in the middle. Looking along the river, she saw the familiar barn not far away. She had not guessed they were so close to it.

"What a pretty spot!" She turned slowly. "I'm surprised you have a pond when your farm is near the river."

"The river looks closer than it is. A bluff drops down to the riverbank. The pumper from Haven, even if it could get here in time to fight a fire, wouldn't be able to get water from the river to the barn or house. From here, there's a chance." He laughed. "Assuming the fire burns very slowly."

"Very, very slowly." Squatting down, she put her fingers in the water. "It's cold!"

"There's a spring in the bottom so the water stays cold all year round. I widened the bowl it was sitting in to make this pond." He kneaded his shoulder. "That job almost persuaded me I didn't want to be a farmer. I never wanted to see a spade again."

"This must be what Lottie was talking about when she asked me if a water spirit lived nearby." She stood. "I've told them stories about spirits who live in springs in Ireland."

"Do you think that's her friend Dahi?"

"Who knows? She apparently inherited her grandfather's gift for storytelling."

Again he took her hand. As they walked through the tall grass that reached almost to her knees, he said, "I've been thinking that, with the house being so blasted hot, we might have a picnic some evening here by the pond."

"A picnic?"

"Haven't you ever been on a picnic?"

"I've eaten in the fields when I helped my father on our farm, but never on a whim."

He smiled. "We'll have to do something to rectify that. We'll bring the children and come here with a basket and a blanket to enjoy a cool meal on a hot night."

"That sounds wonderful." She wiped her forehead. "I hate to complain, but—"

"It's hot." Walking toward the trees that circled the pond on three sides, he laughed. He sat her on a rock and dropped to the ground beside her. "I think I'll let the sun pass by a little before I fix the wagon."

"Look." Cailin smiled as she stood and walked around the nearly perfect circle of stones at the edge of the wood. "I used to call those fairy circles. There was one not far from our farm. I'd go there hoping to capture a fairy."

"Not a leprechaun?"

"These are *fairy* circles." She laughed. "The little people are more likely found along a country lane where they might trick a foolish mortal into giving up his last coin."

"You sound as if you believe in such things."

"I don't disbelieve." She sat on a log just outside the ring of stones. "Who knows what I might have chanced upon?"

Coming to his feet, he put one foot on the log next to her and rested his arm on his knee. "This is a side of you, Cailin, I haven't seen before. You're usually so practical."

"In Ireland, it seemed practical to allow for possibilities."

"I don't think it's so different here. There are always possibilities one needs to consider."

"Is that why you're here in Haven instead of being a lawyer in Cincinnati?"

"I hadn't looked at it that way."

She nodded. "Is Cincinnati near here?"

"It's up the river in the state of Ohio." Her bafflement must have been obvious because he added, "To the east of here. By a steamboat like *The Ohio Star,* you could be there in a day or two, depending on its stops."

Cailin said nothing. When he sat beside her on the log, she wondered if he was searching for a way to answer her question or a way to circumvent answering it. She chided herself for that thought.

"My possibility," he said, "is deciding I'd rather be a farmer."

"Were you right?"

"Yes."

She wanted to believe him but saw undeniable regret in his eyes. He was honest about his yearning to move away from the city; she had seen how he liked the harder life on the farm. Something else had persuaded him to leave what must have been a more luxurious life. Only once had she met an attorney. That man had worked for Abban's mother, and his attempts to intimidate her had been too successful.

"But you opened those crates, so you must have been reading those thick law books." She saw color rise up out of his open collar. For so long, she had been anxious to ask this question. Now, when she had the opportunity, she hesitated. Even asking the question might destroy everything between herself and Samuel, but she must know. "Were you looking for a way to keep the children?"

"It seems you're good at guessing, too."

"When it's easy." She picked some white blossoms from

beside the log. Dropping them onto her skirt, she began to shred the leaves off the stalks.

"You aren't curious about what I found?"

"No." She continued to pull off the leaves. "I don't go looking for bad news."

"You just let it find you?"

She raised her eyes to meet his. "It has too often."

"Yet you don't buckle under."

"I can't." In spite of herself, her voice caught as she said, "Not as long as I have my children. Are you going to continue to look for ways to take my children away from me?"

He shook his head. "No. I haven't considered doing that since the night you came into my office with the papers from the Children's Aid Society. Anyone can see how much Megan needs you." A sad smile tilted his lips. "Even someone who didn't want to see it."

His hand, as gentle against her chin as it was when he teased Brendan's hair, kept her from looking away. She was not sure if she could have when she saw the naked pain on his face. Slowly, her fingers glided along his cheek. Words of comfort filled her mind, but this touch—this incredible communication that needed no words—spoke them far better.

"I know how much they mean to you," she whispered when he sighed. "I'm sorry this has happened."

"Don't be sorry. I'm not." He plucked another flower. "Have you ever viewed these in the moonlight?"

"Why would anyone do something so ludicrous?" She laughed as he grimaced playfully. "You can't see colors at night."

His arm circled her waist and pulled her closer. "Cailin, you're wrong. I can see the golden-brown fire in your eyes even in the midst of my dreams. Is there anything else I truly want to see?"

The genuine longing in his voice warned her of the danger she was courting by remaining here. He lifted her hand away from his cheek. For a moment that could have been a single heartbeat or an eternity, he looked at her over it. He released it and captured her face between his hands. His lips stroked hers.

She ceded herself to the powerful urgency awakening within her. Not reawakening, but as if for the first time, because the thrill of his kisses reached depths she had never known. His lips trailed along her neck in a scintillating path. Every inch of her ached to be touching him. Her hand under his open collar caressed the firm skin along his shoulders. She should push him away, but she held onto him as waves of tempting heat flowed over her.

"You feel so sweet against me," he whispered, so close his lips brushed hers on every word.

Slowly her eyes opened as he raised his head to smile down at her. She blinked, but her glazed vision refused to focus. Not that it was necessary; her heart knew every line of his face. Her finger quivered as she traced his stern nose and the unyielding heat of his lips. They captured hers again. As his breath burned into her mouth, she heard a strange sound.

With a laugh, she drew back and patted his stomach. "You sound hungry, Samuel."

"Yep."

She chuckled again when he used the word Brendan had. "The children are probably back and waiting for their lunch, too." Standing, she held out her hand to him. "I think we'd better get back to the house."

"I think you're probably right, even though I hate to admit that." He took her hand as he got up. "After you feed them, how about taking care of the hunger inside me?" He pressed her hand against his stomach. "I don't mean the hunger here."

She could not misunderstand *this*. He made her long for him as no other man had ever done. She wanted him, but in her heart as well as her arms, and she could not allow that. "I can't, Samuel. Not now."

"I know." He cupped her chin. "Don't blame me for trying to persuade you over and over when one of these times you're going to agree."

"You sound pretty sure of yourself."

"A good attorney always knows what the results will be in an open-and-shut case." He laughed, then said, "I wish I could convince you right now to sample rapture with me."

His words sent a swell of desire rushing through her, but when she said nothing, he walked to the front of the wagon. Putting her hand in his, she let him help her up onto the seat. He climbed up after her. He reached for the reins, then, with a moan, pulled her back into his arms. His lips moved across hers, teasing her into forgetting every obligation but the one to the desire growing between them. She must not, but she wondered how much longer she could resist.

Twelve

"Are you ready?"

At the question, Samuel looked up from hooking the horse to the wagon he called a rockaway. Cailin and the children were silhouetted against the sunlight that was becoming less unbearable with the end of the day. As he led the horse and carriage out of the barn, he smiled at Cailin's astonishment.

"I thought," he said, winking at the children, "that as you have everyone Saturday-night clean and pressed, we should go to town in style."

"This is yours?" She ran her hand along the black side and touched the tufted dark red cushions on the front seat.

"I haven't used use it much since I left Cincinnati, but I figured tonight was a good night to take it out." He lifted Lottie and Megan onto the back seat. Brendan jumped up to sit next to them. The children giggled when he bowed to Cailin and said, "Ma'am, I'd be right pleased to hand you in."

Cailin's eyes were wide as he assisted her. She raised her fingers to run them through the bright red trim hanging along the edge of the roof.

"This is as fancy as the tassels and piping I've seen on draperies," she said in awe.

"And it doesn't hold up to the rain any better than fancy velvet drapes. That's why I don't take this rockaway out when I suspect it may storm." He sat beside her on the cushioned seat and set the horse along the road. Hearing the children's excited voices, he said more quietly, "I thought you'd like a treat. You've been working hard lately."

"As you and Brendan have out in the cornfield."

"We all deserve a treat." Holding the reins with one hand, he slipped his other arm around her waist. She leaned against him, and he wished they had left the children at home.

The children began singing in the back seat, and he listened as Cailin hummed softly. He wanted to urge her to sing with them, because he suspected her singing voice would be as warm as her speaking one. Instead, he guided the horse and let the song fill the air. More than once, he felt Cailin glance toward him, but he was not ready to tempt ruining this evening. Not yet.

Lights blossomed from the Grange Hall as they drove into Haven. Wagons of all sorts were parked in a haphazard pattern around the Grange and along the green. The children jumped out almost before the wheels of the carriage stopped and were running across the green to join the other children playing tag.

Offering his arm to Cailin, he put his hand over hers as he walked with her to the front door. Conversation, mingling and tangled, poured out. The Grange's windows, which lined both side walls, were thrown open to catch any breeze from the river. Most of the chairs were filled, and people leaned against the walls between the windows. At the front, a platform like the one at the school usually had a podium on it, but tonight the piano had been pushed out into its center. Again, as when they had gone to the meeting at the schoolhouse, curious eyes followed as he and Cailin went to a pair of seats at the far right.

"Nobody's going to eat you alive," Samuel murmured as she seemed to draw in upon herself. "There's no reason to be shy when Brendan has probably told you tales about half the people here."

"Maybe knowing so much is a good reason to be shy."

He laughed and watched heads turn toward them again. Taking a book from the stack one of the Grange members was passing out, he offered it to her.

"It looks as if we're going to start the evening singing," he said.

Cailin opened the book slowly and stared at the page as if she could understand the letters between the musical notes. "I doubt I know any of these songs."

"You'll learn the music pretty quickly, and, as you can see, the words are simple."

"Yes."

As soon as the pianist began playing, she realized Samuel was correct. The words *were* simple, and she recognized several songs she had already been taught by the children. Sitting beside him, holding the music book between them, following his lead in singing, she was enveloped in a quiet joy. When Lottie ran in, Cailin set her youngest on her lap and listened to Lottie's sweet voice. She saw Samuel smile when Lottie added a few of her own unique lyrics.

Cailin could have let the evening of singing go on forever, even if they had to sing the same songs over and over. She would be able to pretend that nothing was amiss beyond these four walls, and she could ignore the pretty dresses the other women wore. Too soon, the piano was pushed back to one side of the platform. The chairs were folded and put away or arranged in a single row along the walls. Cider was poured, both sweet and hard. Any youngster who got too close to the jugs of hard cider was warned away with smiles and a cup of the sweet cider.

When Samuel was drawn into a discussion with Noah Sawyer and several men she did not know, Cailin selected a chair along the wall. It gave her a good view of Lottie, who was talking earnestly with a blond gentleman. He patted her on the head before she ran out the door to find the other children.

Cailin opened the music book and ran her finger down the page. *D-a-y.* She would ask Brendan to tell her what that combination of letters meant. She looked at another word. A longer one. *U-n-i-t-e-d.* She shook her head. That one looked too hard. Smiling, she touched the next word. *S-t-a-t-e-s.* Two of the letters were used twice. That surely would make it easier to learn and remember.

"Cailin?"

Her head jerked up, and she shut the book hastily. Seeing shock on the faces of the two women in front of her, she tried to smile.

"Are we disturbing you?" asked Emma, her blond hair clinging to her cheeks with the heat.

"No, no. I was just looking at the music." She glanced at the other woman, whose hair was as black as Samuel's.

Emma smiled warmly. "I thought you'd like to meet Kitty Cat's mother."

"That sounds silly, doesn't it?" the woman said with a laugh. "I'm Rachel, and you must be Cailin. I've heard a lot about you from Kitty Cat."

"The children seem to have a very efficient way of sharing news." Cailin stood and put the book on the windowsill behind her chair. *D-a-y* and *S-t-a-t-e-s.* She repeated the letters over and over in her mind, so she would not forget them.

"More efficient than a telegraph," Rachel replied. She glanced at Emma, then turned back to Cailin and added, "I understand you spent some time in New York City before coming here."

"Yes." She fought not to tense. If everyone in Haven believed, as Samuel had, that she had abandoned her children and then changed her mind, she wondered how she could ever feel truly welcome here.

"I can't imagine how horrible it must have been for you to learn your children had been lied to and sent away," Rachel said.

Cailin wanted to give her a hug. Rachel's few words swept away any hint that Mrs. Rafferty's treachery had stalked Cailin to Haven. Knowing she was further beholden to Samuel, for he must have made sure the truth was known, she said, "I try not to think of it."

"Then I'm so sorry to have reminded you." Rachel hesitated, then said, "Many of us with children from the orphan train are curious about what they experienced before they came to Haven." Again she looked at Emma.

Quietly, Emma said, "The children are reluctant to speak of what life was like there. We can't blame them for not wanting to remember such an appalling time in their young lives. Yet sometimes they act unexpectedly."

"What do you mean?" Cailin let her shoulders ease from their soldier-straight stance and smiled. "I have to admit, whether well-behaved or naughty, my children act pretty much as they always have." *Except when they treat Samuel as if he's a real part of our family.*

"It isn't a matter of misbehaving; it's odd behavior. For example, Sean often takes food and hides it under his bed, even though we always let him know he can have as much as he wants to eat. He doesn't eat it, and if the cats and dog don't have a feast, it rots. I can't understand why he keeps doing it."

"You have never been hungry. Truly hungry." Cailin looked across the room to where her children were giggling as they drank cider and chattered with their friends. She wondered which of these children had come here on the orphan train. "If you'd ever been truly hungry, you'd know how wise it is to hoard food in case the bounty comes to an abrupt end."

"That makes sense." Emma smiled. "Thank you so

much. Now that I have an idea of what he might be feeling, I can help him. This is going to be very helpful."

She laughed, surprising herself. Talking with these women was not like talking to strangers. It was true; nobody could stay a stranger in Haven for long. "I'm only guessing."

"It's a good guess. Better than anything any of us have considered."

Rachel added, "If you'd be willing to speak with some of the other people who have had children placed out with them, I know anything you have to say would be gratefully heeded. We could invite everyone here to the Grange Hall, and you could enlighten—"

"No!" gasped Cailin, shaking her head. "Please don't suggest I stand up in front of people and talk to them. I could never, never do that."

Emma patted her shoulder. "No one would ask you to do something that makes you uneasy. Shall we make it just the women? Would that put you more at ease?"

"Maybe."

"Good. The women meet here occasionally after a Grange meeting to clean up. Would you be willing to answer their questions when you come and help us day after tomorrow?"

"If I can." Even though she knew she should change the subject, she heard herself saying, "I didn't live in the part of New York City where most of these children were found, but I'll be glad to help in any way I can."

"But you said you knew about being hungry . . ." Rachel halted herself. "Forgive me, Cailin. I didn't mean to pry."

"It's all right," she said, meaning the words more than she ever had. "One of the reasons I brought my children from Ireland was to escape the deprivation there. Although they didn't live hard lives in New York as the other children on the train did, they understand how lucky they are to be here."

"Samuel has welcomed them as if they were his own flesh and blood," Emma said, smiling. "And he's been kind enough to let you stay until you can decide what you want to do. Not many men would be so generous."

Noah stepped out of the crowd and put his arm around her shoulders. "Are you tarring all of my gender with a single brush?"

"Not *all*." Emma laughed before excusing herself and Noah.

Cailin continued talking with Rachel and was introduced to Kitty Cat, a clearly mischievous imp with Irish red hair, before the children ran back outside to play hide-and-seek in the thickening dusk. For a moment, Cailin was intimidated by Rachel's obvious high level of education, recalling that this woman assisted with business affairs around Haven, but she relaxed again as they spoke of the children.

They were interrupted by the sound of a bow being drawn across fiddle strings. A hand settled on Cailin's waist, and she smiled as she looked over her shoulder. She did not have to guess who stood there. No one but Samuel could create such luscious longing with even a chaste touch.

"Ready?" he asked after greeting Rachel.

"For what?" Cailin returned.

"Dancing to start with." He led her to the center of the room, adding softly, "Where it goes from there is up to you."

She had to fight her own body, which wanted to melt against him. Her voice trembled as she said, "You're a rogue tonight."

"Any night you wish." He raised his voice again to its customary level and asked, "Do you know how to square dance?"

"No, but I learn quickly."

"So I've seen."

"Maybe one of these evenings, I'll teach you some of the dances we do in Ireland."

"That would be fun." He squeezed her hand as he brought her to stand on his right across from another couple.

Two other couples filled out the square, and Cailin was pleased to see Wyatt and Rachel were on her right. She listened to Samuel's quick instructions, which ended with, "Just heed the caller and follow what the rest of us do." Many of the steps he described she knew from Irish reels.

The bow was pulled across the fiddle again, and she was astonished to see it was being played by Doc Bamburger. Beside him stood the man who had waited for Miss Underhill after the meeting in the schoolhouse. She heard someone call him Barry.

Raising his hands, Barry called for everyone to honor their partner, then their corner.

Cailin laughed as she curtsied first to Samuel and then to Wyatt, both of whom bowed to her. Then she took Samuel's hand and tried to keep up with the steps that were a bit more convoluted than she had guessed. The others were patient with her mistakes, and by the time they had completed the first dance, she could keep up with them.

Her patched skirt whirled out around her ankles as Samuel spun her about. She smiled up into his eyes when he pulled her a bit tighter before they swirled apart to be swung by others in the square. When she went around the square, one person taking her right hand and then the next her left as they wove through the dance's pattern, she was amazed that coming back to Samuel, who twirled her again, could be as splendid as coming home to a warm hearth on a cool, rainy day. She wanted to be in his arms, to hear him laugh, to share this special moment with him.

She applauded with the others when the dance ended. Glasses were passed around, and she sipped the sweet cider that was, she knew, such a treat at this time of year. She hurried to empty her glass and put it on a windowsill as Doc Bamburger picked up his fiddle again. The melody he played this time was slower.

When Samuel laced his fingers through hers, she walked with him to where couples were waltzing. He did not ask her if she knew these steps, just pulled her to him and led her through the circular sweep of the dance. Her fingers rose from his shoulder to comb through his hair. He smiled and kissed her lightly.

Her feet faltered, but he did not let her stop. When his hand stroked her waist, bringing her even closer, she stiffened. He drew back, and his smile vanished.

"Dancing is supposed to be fun," he said quietly.

"It was."

"Until?"

She pulled her hands out of his. He caught them, repeating his question.

She owed him an answer, but she asked, "Can we talk about this later?"

"I suspect it'd be better if we didn't let this fester." Releasing one hand, he guided her past the other dancers.

Eyes followed them yet again. Glancing back, she saw smiles and quickly averted gazes. She wanted to shout that no one was hiding anything from her. They thought she and Samuel were leaving to have a tryst. How wrong they were!

The air seemed even closer outside than in the Grange Hall. When Cailin started to call to the children to meet them at the rockaway, Samuel halted her. He saw her astonishment, even in the darkness. Or was it just that he knew her face and its many expressions so well that each one was printed indelibly in his mind, to be recalled whenever he needed?

Pausing by the carriage, he said, "Please explain what just happened. I thought we were having a good time."

"We were."

"Until . . . ?" he asked as he had before. This time he did not wait for her answer. "Until I kissed you."

She nodded.

"You've liked my kisses up until now, so I can only guess that either you've developed a distaste for them or you don't want me to kiss you when anyone else is around."

"They'll think—"

"I don't care what *they* think. I care about why you care about what they think."

"There are already enough suppositions about what's taking place at the farm."

"You're right. Anyone who has given the matter the least bit of thought most likely assumes we're lovers. Is the idea so horrible?"

Shaking her head, she whispered, "Of course it isn't horrible, but—"

"Gossip might hurt the children."

She nodded.

He tipped her chin so he could see the tears glistening in her eyes. "Cailin, listen to me. No one's going to blame the children for anything you and I do. I think you're more worried about what they'll think of *you*."

"You're wrong!"

"Am I?"

"I admit I was worried, but after talking to Emma and Rachel, I'm not any longer. They asked me to come back and speak to the ladies who have had children placed out with them. They hope I have some answers to what their youngsters have experienced. Even if I don't, they asked me if I'd help."

"As well they should, but that doesn't change anything. If you want to know what I think, it's that you'll use any excuse to avoid admitting the truth that you want me as much as I want you."

He thought she would fire back a sharp answer, but she pushed herself away. Running her fingers along the side of the rockaway, she said, "If you want to know what I think, I think it's time the children went home and to bed."

"And us?"

Her fingers tightened on the side of the rockaway, and he heard her sharp intake of breath before it shuddered out of her. Her words could deny the truth to him all she wanted, but each reaction told him that he was right. She was eager to be in his arms as they sought ecstasy. If he . . .

Was he crazy? Working the farm and trying to keep the children happy kept him busy. He did not need to complicate his life with Cailin, even if she was willing to be a complication, which she was trying to prove to him—and herself—she was not. It was tempting to toss aside sensible thoughts and capitulate to the craving for her, but he knew how high the cost of that pleasure could be. To protect the children from gossip, she might flee Haven. She would do anything for them—even deprive herself and him this chance for happiness.

He took her hand to help her into the carriage. Her fingers quivered like a leaf caught by the wind, and he saw uncertainty as she tipped back her head to meet his gaze. Moonlight danced on her hair, but the flame in her eyes was even brighter. As if from a great distance, he could hear the children playing on the green.

A single step would bring her into his arms. All he needed to do was tug on her fingers. Would she come willingly? Would she soften against him? Her parted lips were an invitation to taste them. His fingers were tickled as he brushed wisps of hair away from her cheeks.

Wrong move, Samuel knew, because Cailin stepped away and climbed into the rockaway on her own. He heard fabric rip and what sounded like a curse, but she did not look at him as she sat with her hands primly folded in her lap.

Sitting next to her, he did not touch her. He took the reins to keep his fingers from exploring her bewitching curves. His elbows rested on his knees as he said, "All right. You've made yourself clear, but I've got a question. What now?"

"We should leave things as they are."

He snorted his disagreement. "Do you think I'm going to be satisfied with a few kisses whenever we can no longer keep ourselves from slipping into each other's arms? Do you think *you* will be?"

"We should leave things as they are," she repeated, not looking at him.

"What is it? Burned once, you learn to look before you leap from the frying pan into the fire?"

"Yes."

His eyes narrowed as he noted how Cailin drew back into herself. The question had touched a nerve, one that still hurt. Her hands curled into fists in her lap. That as much as her clipped tone told him how badly her late husband's betrayal continued to wound her. He damned Abban Rafferty. He silently repeated the oath at Cailin who mourned, despite her assertion otherwise, for the man who had hurt more than her heart.

Samuel shouted for the children before saying in a lower voice, "So we'll go back to the way it was in the beginning."

He thought he heard a sob in her breath as she answered, "You must agree that would be for the best. You'll provide my children and me with a home. In exchange, I'll tend to all that needs to be done in the house."

Tossing down the reins, he swept his arm around her waist and turned her to face him. Her soft breasts stroked him as she drew in a deep breath. It took every ounce of his strength not to shove her back on the seat and make love with her right there. He caught her chin between his fingers and smiled coolly. He kept his voice too low for the children to hear as they bid their friends good night. "Cailin, you're very wrong. You don't tend to all that needs to be done in the house."

"I believe you've had too much hard cider, Samuel."

"You may be right. I may have had too much cider." He brushed a fingertip along her brows before curving his palm across her cheek. "But one thing I know, I'd much rather drink of you."

"Poetry won't persuade me." Her rapid heartbeat contradicted her cold words.

"Then what will?" He ran his tongue along her lips before his mouth covered hers. "Will this?"

"Samuel . . ." His name was no more than a breathless whisper.

But it was enough for him. He pulled her against him and kissed her as if he never would have the chance again. Losing himself in the thrill, as she softened and slipped her arms up his back, he knew this was what he needed as a salve for the pain he had brought with him from Cincinnati. Making love with Cailin would help him forget the events that had ripped apart his life. Maybe they could forget together. A pang cut through him as he wondered if she wanted to use him in the same way.

He released her and picked up the reins. Ignoring her astonishment, he said nothing on the way back to the farm. His fury was now aimed at himself. He knew what it was to be deceived by a woman. He had vowed never to make that mistake again. It was a vow he must keep, even if it cost him the rapture he dreamed of discovering in Cailin's arms. How simple it had been to make that promise to himself as he left Cincinnati—and how difficult it was going to be to keep when every thought focused on how much he wanted her.

Thirteen

The house was oddly quiet. From upstairs came only the sound of the children's footfalls. The customary chatter was missing. Through the open windows, a slight breeze that had come to life at sunset carried insect chirpings from near the river. A distant rumble might be thunder or a train arriving late in Haven.

In the parlor, Cailin tried to ignore the near silence as she lengthened a pair of Brendan's trousers. Her son had gone up to his room after supper without a word. She had thought he and his sisters would come back down from the rooms that had to be stifling in the day's last heat. An hour remained before they needed to go to sleep. Maybe he was waiting for Samuel to leave for the library committee meeting in Haven.

She looked up when Samuel appeared in the parlor doorway. He had changed into a clean shirt, which he wore beneath a dark green vest, but he wore his workboots.

"Will you be back in time to tuck Megan and Lottie into bed and read them a story?" She tried to sound casual, although her heart thundered at the very sight of him. Trying to push him away last night had been futile, for she had not persuaded either him or herself. She wanted to be in his arms. She stood, setting the trousers on the arm of the sofa. "The girls would like that." She smiled weakly as she whispered, "So would I, Samuel."

She doubted he heard her whisper when he replied, "I hope so, but I can't promise. The meeting may go long. If Thanington is there, he's sure to try to gain control of it, as he did at the last meeting."

"Tell him you don't have time for such nonsense. You started working before dawn this morning, and you plan to do the same tomorrow."

"That's a farmer's life. If I can't get back in time tonight, I promise I'll read to them tomorrow night. I think they'll understand."

"I think they will, too."

"Good." He smiled. "Why don't you read the next chapter to them? They can show you where we left off."

She steeled herself not to flinch. "That's something special you share with them. I think they'd prefer for you to continue reading the book."

"I think they're happy to have any time with you. They didn't realize how much they missed you until you came back into their lives."

"They were mourning because they believed I was dead." She did not try to keep emotion out of her voice this time. "I don't know if I'll ever be able to forgive Abban's mother for the sorrow she brought upon my children."

"She failed at what she was trying to do."

"Did she?" She wiped her palms against her stained apron. "She wanted the children far away so no one would know of them. I once thought they were the most unfortunate children ever to be born. Now, I see they aren't." She put her hand on his arm. "Thank you for caring so much about them, Samuel."

"They made it easy."

"It's their O'Shea charm." She smiled. "My father could coax a rabbit right out of the ground."

"Really?"

Happy he was teasing her again, she asked, "Samuel, must you take me so seriously?"

He chuckled. "Now you're the one taking *me* too seriously. I enjoy pulling a leg or two, you know." His eyes narrowed as he gripped her arms, tugging her to him. "I'd especially enjoy putting my hand around your ankle, which must be as slender as your wrist."

"You want to pull my leg?" she whispered, letting herself be caught up in his passion . . . her passion . . .

"No." His voice lowered to a raw whisper as his fingers trickled down her sleeve. He put them around her wrist for a moment as he said, "This is what I would like to do with your leg." Slowly, sinuously, his fingers slid up her arm, pushing her sleeve before them, so his palm caressed her skin. "With all of you."

She breathed his name just before his mouth slanted across hers. This was the very worst madness she could imagine, and it was the sweetest pleasure she had ever known. Her arms curved up around his vest, delighting in the muscles he had honed through long hours of work. When his lips moved along her neck, she clenched her hands on his back. How much longer could she persuade herself that this was all she wanted from this beguiling man?

His words were uneven as he said, "Now I must leave or I'll be late for the meeting." He kissed her swiftly. "Very, very late. Don't wait up for me."

"But—"

"Promise me that you won't wait up. You've been working hard."

Unsure what else to say, she whispered, "I promise, Samuel."

"Good," he repeated. Releasing her, he opened the door and walked out onto the porch.

She ran after him and put her hand on his arm. As her eyes adjusted to the thickening twilight, she said, "Promis me you won't linger to argue some point. You need your sleep, too."

"That's not what I need."

She quivered. "Please promise me, Samuel, that you'll come home as soon as you can. I don't want to think of you getting hurt out in the field because you're too exhausted to watch what you're doing."

"All right." The back of his hand stroked her cheek. "I promise I'll do everything I can to be back before ten."

When he pulled her into his arms, she savored his eager mouth on hers. He groaned as he released her. He did not go down the steps, and she wondered if he was as unwilling as she to let this moment end.

The screen door opened, bumping into Cailin. As Samuel steadied her, Megan came out onto the porch. Cailin heard her daughter, but paid no attention to her words as she touched Samuel's cheek. He smiled and walked toward the barn.

"Yes, yes," Cailin said to her daughter's impatient voice.

"Yes? Both of them can?" asked Megan, excited.

"Both of them can what?" She watched Samuel get into the wagon and drive toward Haven. The lantern on its side twinkled like a star that had fallen from the sky.

"Come upstairs to our room."

Cailin looked back at her older daughter. "Both of them who?"

"My bunny and Lottie's kitten. We'll be careful, Mama, and—"

"No, you can't take the rabbit and the kitten upstairs. You know they sleep in the barn."

"But you said—"

"Megan, you know better!"

Her daughter's face crumbled into tears. "But you said we could."

"I didn't mean you could take your pets to your room."

"But you said we could!" Megan threw the door open.

"Just like you said we could come to America and have a home together."

"Megan, why are you angry about that? I thought we'd be with your father, too."

The little girl ran into the house, letting the door slam behind her.

Cailin let her shoulders droop. If she had listened to Athair and stayed in Ireland until she heard back from Abban, her children would not have been subjected to all this pain. She opened the door and went inside. Unsure what she could say to Megan, she knew she had to think of a way to explain without revealing the truth of their father's denial of them. She had thought the simple falsehood of Abban's only crime against them being his dying before they could see him again would protect her children from misery, but she was no longer sure.

Going to where Megan perched on the lowest step, crying, Cailin sat next to her. She smoothed back her daughter's bright red hair and said, "Megan, I'm sorry I was cross with you."

"You said—"

"I know I said you could bring the pets upstairs, and it seems I changed my mind. The truth is, I didn't heed what you were saying to me because my mind was elsewhere. That was very rude of me, and I'm sorry."

"How can your mind be elsewhere? Isn't it in your head?"

She tried not to laugh at her older daughter, who was almost as literal as her younger one. Before she could answer, she heard a rustle from beyond the kitchen door. She glanced at Megan, who suddenly looked frightened. As she rose to make sure a dog was not digging in the garden, Megan grabbed her arm.

"Don't, Mama!" she ordered in a desperate whisper. "Sean said there's a band of thieves prowling around the river."

"You shouldn't be frightened of rumors."

"What if it isn't just a rumor?"

She could not mistake her daughter's fear. Telling her to stay where she was, Cailin went into the kitchen. She grasped the handle of a cast-iron pan. She inched toward the door and raised it as the door opened.

Her wrist was grasped as Megan let out a screech. She stared at Samuel, who shouted, "It's just me! Put that down!"

She drew her hand out of his grasp and set the pan back on the table. "What are you doing back so soon? Did you forget something?"

"Yes." Looking past her, he said, "Megan, you should put that knife down, too."

"Knife?" Cailin spun to see her daughter by the dining room door, a large blade in her hand. Behind her, Brendan and Lottie, both wide-eyed, were rushing into the dining room. As Megan put the knife on the table, Cailin hugged her. "Thank you for trying to protect us, *a stór.*"

Megan grinned. "Will you come up and listen to me read? I can do it, Mama."

"Only a page or two, because you need to go to sleep before you fall asleep right where you're standing." She put her arm around Megan's shoulders and said, "Tell Samuel good night, and—"

Samuel stepped past her. Scooping up Megan, he then picked up Lottie under his other arm and carried the two giggling girls upstairs. Brendan chased after them, trying to tickle his sisters' noses.

Cailin smiled when she heard the laughter from the children's rooms. Taking them from here would make them as unhappy as when they had been sent away on the orphan train. They adored Samuel, and he was an important part of their lives. Nothing would change that.

When she reached the girls' bedroom door, Lottie ran to her and grasped her hand, bringing her into the room where not a breath of air moved. The little girl tugged her toward a chair set between the beds.

"Samuel, you're going to be late for your meeting," Cailin said.

"You worry too much." He laughed and, with a gentle push on her shoulders, sat her down. "It's time to read another chapter of the story now."

Confused, because he had not yet explained why he had come back to the house, she nodded. "Go ahead."

"Me?" He laughed and looked at Megan.

The little girl picked up a book and knelt on her bed. She held it out. When Cailin took it, Megan asked, "Mama, will you read to us tonight?"

Cailin's fingers tightened on the leather binding. Read? Their father's treachery was not the only secret she had been keeping. She said, offering the book to her older daughter, "You were going to read."

Megan reached out to take it, then shook her head as her siblings glared at her. "You read tonight, Mama." She opened the book and pointed to a page where the words started partway down. "Begin right here, Mama."

Cailin stared at the letters. None of them seemed to be familiar. She put the book on the bed, stood, and left the room.

Samuel saw the children exchanging worried glances. Picking up the book, he handed it to Megan and said, "Read the next page to your sister and brother."

"But, Samuel—"

"Read what you can and make up the rest, then blow out the lights and go to sleep." He paid no attention to their startled expressions. Walking down the stairs, he was not surprised to see the screen door closing, for Cailin always went out on the porch when she was distressed. He was not sure why she considered it a sanctuary, and now was not the time to ask.

He opened the door and shut it quietly behind him. Even

before his eyes adjusted to the darkness, he heard her soft sobs.

As he walked to where she stood by the railing, she asked, "Did you get what you forgot to take with you?"

For a moment, he had no idea what she was asking. Then he remembered what he had told her when he came back into the kitchen. Instead of answering that question, he said, "Megan is reading."

"Good."

"I know she'd like to have you there to listen."

"I know that, too." She continued to stare up at the sky, where the first stars were poking through the darkness. "You're going to be late for your meeting, Samuel."

"Megan would appreciate some help. This book is harder than any she's read before." He put his hand on her arm. "Why don't you—?"

She shook it off and snarled, "Why don't you just leave me alone? Go to your meeting, and leave me alone."

"I'm not going anywhere until you explain why you're acting like this."

"Then you're going to be very, very late." She started to move along the railing, but he moved to step in front of her. "Samuel, will you leave me alone?"

"I can't." Framing her face with his hands, he said, "Tell why you stormed out of the room."

"I can't read!"

He stared at her, not sure what to say.

"I wanted to learn to read," she continued, "but there was no school near us. My father could play any song on his fiddle after just a single hearing, but he couldn't read or write, so he couldn't teach me." She sat on the rocker. "I was so excited to come to the United States, where my children would have chances they'd never have had in Ireland. That I never had." She dabbed her apron against her eyes. "I'm so proud they're learning to read and write their names and do their ciphering."

"You can learn, too." He leaned against the railing.

"Me? I'm too old for school." She flung out her hands. "Can you imagine me sitting in that schoolroom with the children?"

He smiled. "That's an interesting image."

"I'm glad you're amused. I don't find this in the least bit funny!" She came to her feet.

He put his hands on her shoulders to halt her from leaving. "Cailin, you need to stop being ashamed."

"I can't help it."

"Why? Because your mother-in-law made you ashamed of your life?" He could feel her breath catch before her shoulders shook again.

"She's so elegant, with her nice home and fancy furniture. The children and I didn't match her grand house."

"Would you have wanted to?"

Cailin stared at him, her eyes widening. As Samuel's hands shifted on her shoulders, she was glad he did not draw them away. She needed this connection and this compassion.

In a near whisper, she said, "No, I didn't want that hypocrisy. I'm proud of what I am and how, all by myself, I brought these three children across the sea to America. I kept my promise. Not like Abban, who married another woman after he left—"

"He married here in the United States while he was wed to you?" Anger laced the question.

"Forget I said that. Please. Please forget it, Samuel." She pulled away. She had let his comforting words make her speak without thinking . . . because she trusted him.

"How can I forget something like that?"

"I'm trying to."

He walked toward the door. She bit her lower lip to keep from calling out to him not to abandon her—as Abban had.

He slammed the flat of his hand against the wall and demanded, "The children don't know, do they?"

"Of course not."

"Are you trying to protect them or their father?"

Cailin took a step back from his fury, then snapped, "That's the silliest question I have ever heard! There's no need for the children to know how their father betrayed me."

"And them."

"Yes!"

He shook his head as a frigid smile settled on his lips. "So their father can remain a saint to them."

"They barely remember him." She looked up at the porch roof, imagining the two rooms at the top of the low-slung house. She could hear Brendan reading now to his sisters. As long as she and Samuel kept their voices low, the children would not hear what was being said on the porch. "Lottie has no memory of her father. When I showed Megan Abban's picture, she didn't recognize him. Brendan said he did, but I think he wasn't certain. They don't talk about him unless I bring up the subject, so I don't believe they have any attachment to him any longer."

He walked back to her, but her hope that he would hold her faded when he asked, "Do you love him still?"

"He was my husband, and I can see him in our children. There weren't just bad times, Samuel."

"Except when he beat you and married another woman."

She sank to the chair again. "Yes."

"So answer my question." He rested again on the railing next to her. "Do you love him still?"

"No."

"That was a quick answer."

"I've had more than a year to consider it. When we were married, he told me how he longed for a big family because he had been an only child. I had no idea that he intended to have children with another woman."

Samuel put his foot on the arm of her chair, halting it

from rocking. In a tone she had never heard him use, he asked, "There are children from his second marriage?"

"Two. It's because of them, as well as my own children, that I agreed with Abban's mother's plan for me to work in another house to earn the money I needed to support my children until we could leave New York."

"The same offer I made you." He leaned forward and stroked her cheek. "I'm so sorry, Cailin. Now I know why you were reluctant to agree to what—to me—seemed an obvious solution to our problems."

"You didn't know." She wove her fingers through his. "One thing I know is that I want nothing more to do with Mrs. Rafferty."

"Nothing? Your children are your husband's heirs."

"His other family—"

"Are, in the eyes of the law, without a legitimate claim to a single penny of his estate." He laughed, warning her doubt must have been apparent. "You can definitely trust me on this, Cailin. I know the law."

"I know you do, but I don't want anything from Mrs. Rafferty."

"Your anger is making you shortsighted. Your children deserve a part of their father's estate."

"How do you know Abban had an estate?"

He laughed coldly. "If you were wearing that naïve expression when you met your mother-in-law, she must have been delighted. Didn't you just say Abban was an only son?"

"Yes."

"You've mentioned his mother, but not his father."

"Abban's father is dead."

"When his father died, some part of his estate must have been set aside for his son. Now it should belong to his children, but it seems his mother was determined it would go to his children by his other wife." He laughed again, the sound even icier. "No wonder your mother-in-law was so eager to put you into service and send your children somewhere where no one would know about them. That you went compliantly and were willing to protect all the children from their father's sins made you the best ally his mother could have wished for."

"I never guessed."

"That's exactly what she hoped." He chuckled. "I think I'll write to a friend in New York. He's an attorney, and he'd enjoy calling on your mother-in-law and her attorney."

"No."

"No?"

"No," she repeated. "I don't want money or anything else from her."

"But you could give your children a very comfortable life if even a portion of what you saw was theirs."

"I know, but the price of their souls would be too high."

"You're still thinking of taking them back to Ireland, aren't you?"

She heard the anguish in his voice at the thought of the children leaving. Just the children, or would he regret her going, too? If she told him how she wanted to take the children—and *him*—to Ireland, what would he say? He had made it clear he liked the haven he had found here. Even though she had no idea what he was running from, she had seen how he valued the friendships and roots he had here.

"Cailin, are you? Are you planning to take them back to Ireland?"

She discovered that keeping her hand from settling on his knee was as impossible as not yearning for him to take her into his arms. She saw, in the light from the parlor lamp near the window behind her, the shadow of loss in his eyes, and wondered again whose leaving had left this pain upon his heart. "I'm thinking about it."

Snarling an obscenity, he stood.

"Just thinking," she said, rising. "Who knows when I'll ever be able to afford passage?"

"All you need is enough to pay your way back to New York City."

"I don't want to go there unless I'm about to embark on a ship from the harbor. There's nothing for us there."

"Yes, there is. You want passage for you and the children to Ireland. Your mother-in-law would gladly give it to you."

Cailin looked up at his taut face. "Are you out of your mind? She wants nothing to do with us."

"That's true, so she'd see the cost of shipping you back across the Atlantic as a small price to pay for never seeing or hearing from you again." He folded his arms over his chest and gazed toward the river. "You probably could get even more if you reminded her how bad it would be if it became known that she'd sent her own grandchildren away from New York on an orphan train. Then you could live very comfortably in Ireland."

"Is that what you think I should do?"

He leaned forward to put his hands on the railing. "Yes."

"You want us to leave now?"

"Whether you leave now or later, you plan to leave."

She raised her hands to put them on his shoulders again, then drew them back before she touched him. "Samuel, I don't know what I plan to do. Not any longer."

"Let me contact my friend in New York."

Sliding between him and the railing, she wrapped her arms around his shoulders. "I don't want to resort to blackmail."

"It could be amusing," he murmured as his arm curved around her waist.

"That's not how I want you to amuse me."

"No?"

She framed his face with her hands and said, "Samuel, I don't want to talk about leaving or Mrs. Rafferty or anything else tonight."

"What do you want?"

"To spend the night with you."

He chuckled, but she heard the craving barely hidden
beneath his humor. "Are all Irishwomen like you? Playing
coy, then going after what they want and not mincing
words?"

"I don't know. I just know what *I* want." Stroking his
cheeks where a day's growth of whiskers tickled her fingertips, she said, "And what you want."

"Are you so sure of that?" He pressed his lips to her
neck.

"Yes. I've been lying to you—and to myself—for too
long. I want to be completely honest tonight . . . with you."

She closed her eyes as he sprinkled kisses across her
face before capturing her mouth. With a moan, she answered his hunger with her own. Sliding her hand beneath
his shirt, she delighted in the smooth skin over his muscles.
She moaned against his mouth as his finger etched a heated
path across her breast. She wanted him to hold her, to be
part of her, to give all of her being to the ecstasy she could
find with him.

When he stood and reached for the door, he held his
other hand out to her.

She put hers in it, then paused. "Your meeting!"

"Forget my meeting."

"Forget it? But you came back because you needed
something, and it must have been something very important."

"I did need something, but it had nothing to do with the
meeting. When I saw the longing in your eyes as I was
leaving, I'd hoped you would come to your senses." He
chuckled. "As you have."

"You came back for that? Were you so certain?"

"I was so hopeful." He drew her inside. Closing the
door, he said, "Tonight and every night."

"Don't ask more of me than tonight," she said.

"I won't promise that."

"I don't know if I have more to give."

"Then I'll take tonight, but tomorrow, I'll ask for anoth
night with you."

She tried to copy his single arched brow. When l
laughed, she did as well, overjoyed at how easy it was
jest with him.

"Maybe you won't want another night with me," sh
said as she put her hand on his again as they moved alor
the hallway. The children calling good night to each oth
added to her joy. For a moment, *this* moment, she cou
not imagine any other place they belonged.

"I don't think you need to trouble your head with th
thought." He opened the door to his room.

She stared in amazement at the splendid room th
seemed more out of place than any of the others in t
farmhouse. Beneath her feet, the thick carpet had an a
stract pattern of red and blue and green, but her gaze w
riveted on the bed set in its middle. Four tall posts of da
wood supported an uncovered canopy that was carved
an intricate pattern of spirals. Starlight reflected on t
ivory satin coverlet and the black marble tops of the tabl
set on either side of the bed. He lit a lantern to burn soft
on the closer one.

"One bedroom tonight," he whispered as he drew h
into the room. "One bedroom and one bed."

He captured her lips, daring her to surrender to her ov
uncontrollable need. As he pinned her against his fir
body, her fingers inched up his back, holding herself
him, wanting to be a part of his fantasies as he was p:
of hers. A fantasy that, tonight, could be made real.

Gasping into his mouth, she shivered as his tong
delved deep past her lips to inflame her with its fiery touc

"Tell me this is what you want, *a stór*," he murmured
he loosened her hair to fall in a ruddy storm around the:

She drew back. *"A stór?"*

"It means darling, doesn't it?"

"Yes." Her breathless voice faded beneath the poundi

f her heart as his hand moved along her breast. With his
ingers' inviting caress, he lured her into his arms and into
apture.

"Then let me call you that tonight." He gave her a ro-
;uish smile as he took off his glasses and put them on the
able beside the bed. His eyes were an even more brilliant
hade of green without them. "Or for however long."

"For however long." She was willing to promise any-
hing as long as he continued enthralling her with his eager
ouch. It created a tempest through her, fired by every
eated breath.

His fingers sought the buttons closing her dress, but he
id not undo them. He whispered her name against her
ips, and she knew he was offering this last chance to stop
rom further entangling her life with his. She wondered if
ny other man could be so tender and yet so enticing. She
anted more than to entangle her life with his. She longed
o entangle herself with him.

Her hand stole along his chest to find the first button
n his vest. She said nothing as she loosened it. As silently,
he released the next and the next, until the front of his
est fell back.

When he bent to taste her lips, she held up her hands
ith a soft smile. He frowned, perplexed, then grinned as
ne began to loosen the buttons on his shirt. When her
ngertips swept along a chest bared by his gaping shirt,
is mouth covered hers.

She quivered when the powerful surge of uncontrollable
raving washed over her as her fingers swept across his
nest. The firm muscles beneath his skin reacted to her
ouch, inviting her to discover more. When he shrugged
ff his loosened clothing, she admired his strong body
ove his well-worn denims, which outlined every mascu-
ne angle. She wanted to uncover and explore every bit of
m.

"Let me see all of you, *a stór,*" he whispered against her throat as his lips left sparkles of delight on her skin.

"Yes," she murmured as she reached for her gown's buttons.

He drew her hand away and turned it palm upward. His mouth's feverish caress on it dissolved her within a fragrant flame. She wanted his mouth on every inch of her. Raising his head, he held her gaze with his emerald one. She became the pulse of his heartbeat, which she could sense with every breath. They were no longer separate, but not yet one. She ached for the consummation of the rapture promised by his smile.

Swiftly, he unbuttoned her gown and let it fall to the floor, forgotten. A soft cry of astonishment burst from her when he whirled her away from the wall and pushed her not ungently onto the bed. He leaned over her, smiling with devilish desire.

She was sure he would speak and waited for his teasing words. Instead he whispered, "Hush, *a stór.* I don't want to share you with anyone tonight, not even the children."

"Just you and me tonight."

"And maybe tomorrow night."

She laughed, but her voice softened to a mew when his hand settled on her knee and crept upward in a slow, undulating path. She wrapped her arms around his shoulder and drew him down onto her. Even as his fingers stroked the sensitive skin along her inner thigh, his lips sampled the curves above her chemise's low neckline. It was a dual assault on her senses.

He pulled the strap of her chemise along her arm, lowering it down along her breast. His gaze held hers as his eyes crinkled. She waited for his next jest. When he lifted her right hand and drew her first finger into his mouth, his tongue wet its length. Her breath shuddered through her when he guided her finger to wander his cheek. He held up his own hand.

She pulled his finger into her mouth, letting her tongue learn every rough texture she had only sampled when they made ice cream. When she withdrew it and raised it toward his face, he laughed and caught her finger. He ran it along his finger, dampening his own skin, then swept his finger along her breast, the heat of his touch evaporating the moisture. She shivered as he lifted his hand again. Before she could grasp it, he bent to place his mouth against her breast.

Her pleasure burst from her in a low, throaty gasp. His tongue slid in a meandering journey to its very peak. When he drew it into his mouth, her hands curved down his back to his lean hips, wanting to draw him into this incredible joy within her.

His mouth continued down as he drew her shift lower. Sliding his hands beneath her bottom, he pulled off her shift and tossed it aside. His eyes glistened with the powerful passions she had seen the first time their gazes locked, and he stripped away her stockings, tossing them over the bottom of the bed. Lightly his fingers drifted along her thigh, leaving a dazzling blaze in its wake.

Desperate to explore him before she was utterly consumed by his enchanting touch, she rose to kneel on the bed and, with a laugh, shoved him onto his back. He clasped his hands behind her neck and pulled her down over him. With her breasts against his chest, she fought to breathe. Then his mouth slanted across hers, and she did not care if she ever breathed again. All she could think of was his skin on hers.

Her leg brushed his denims and she lifted her mouth from his. "One of us is improperly dressed," she whispered against his ear before her tongue curled around its whorls.

"And what are you going to do about it?"

"This." Her fingers settled on the button at the top of his denims.

A shiver raced along him, and she smiled. Looking down

into his eyes, she relished his reaction as she loosened the
top button, then the next. Her questing fingers stroked him
sending renewed waves quaking through him, each one ca
ressing her.

Suddenly, with a groan, he pushed her over onto he
back. He yanked off his denims and threw them on th
floor before pressing her into the soft mattress. His lip
demanded exactly what she longed to give him. The lengt
of his body against hers was intoxicating. When he ben
to trace his tongue down her abdomen, she gripped hi
shoulders. His fingers stroked upward along her thighs t
seek the source of the fire burning within her. A soft cr
of delight burst from her but vanished when his mout
claimed hers.

He drew her beneath him and, as his tongue slid alon
her lips, he melded them together. Each stroke created
rhythm deep inside her, a rhythm that was of him, yet wa
of her and the need they could never deny again. Movin
to it, becoming a part of it, becoming a part of him, sh
tasted his straining breath swirling through her. The exqui
site sensations soared, taking her with him into an ecstas
made all the sweeter when he gasped her name as he shud
dered against her in consummate rapture.

Cailin opened her eyes to a scintillating smile. As he
lethargic fingers traced Samuel's lips, he kissed the
lightly. Stretching her arm across him, she rested her chee
against the welcoming pillow of his chest. Beneath her ea
his heart beat as rapidly as hers. Even now, they were t
gether, fused within the crucible of their passions until the
could be completely separate no longer. She could n
imagine any happiness greater than this.

"You are quiet, *a stór*," he said.

"I don't want to say anything to put an end to this joy.

"The night has only begun." He chuckled as his ar

curved around her, holding her close. "And you are mine for this whole night."

"As you are mine."

He rolled her back into the pillows and gave her a roguish smile. "A most appealing idea when you are a most appealing sight."

Wrapping her arms around his shoulders, she said, "I was wrong."

"Wrong?" His brow tilted, and she laughed.

"I told you poetry wouldn't move me."

"And now it does?"

She nodded.

When he sat and swung his legs over the bed, she watched in amazement as he stood. He walked toward a shelf set beside a door she suspected led to a closet.

Sitting up, she admired his well-sculptured body, each angle accented by starlight. She wondered if he had been as rugged before he came to work on the farm. While she watched the flow of his muscles with every movement, she quivered, yearning to have them against her again.

He came back to the bed and sat beside her. Putting his arm around her, he handed her a book covered with reddish leather. Gold letters were tooled into the spine and across the cover.

"Open it," he said.

"Where?"

"Anywhere."

She did, then looked at him. "What's this?"

"A very good choice. Listen." He read:

> "Thus can my love excuse the slow offense
> Of my dull bearer, when from thee I speed;
> From where thou art why should I hast me thence?
> Till I return, of posting is no need.
> Oh, what excuse will my poor beast then find,
> When swift extremity can seem but slow?

Then should I spur, though mounted on the wind;
In winged speed no motion shall I know:
Then can no horse with my desire keep pace;
Therefore desire, of perfect love being made,
Shall neigh no dull flesh in his fiery race;
But love, for love, thus shall excuse my jade;
Since from thee going he went willful slow,
Toward thee I'll run, and give him leave to go."

She ran her fingers along the words. "That's lovely. What is it?"

"A sonnet. One of Shakespeare's, to be exact."

"I've heard of Shakespeare, but I thought he wrote plays."

"And a few sonnets." He pointed to each word as he read the first line again. "If you want, I'll help you learn to read."

"This?"

He smiled. "Eventually."

"I'd like to be able to read to my children before they go to bed."

He tossed the book onto a table and swept her back into the pillows. "But not tonight, *a stór.* Tonight all your stories are for me."

"For you or *with* you?"

His answer was an enthralling kiss, and she gave herself to the passion once more. She knew one night would not be enough.

Fourteen

Would she faint? Would she stumble over her words? Would she even remember any words at all? Would someone notice how, under her apron, there was a patch of a completely different color because she had cut out a piece to fix a section along the side that had torn when Samuel had undressed her last night?

While the children scampered from the wagon and ran up the street toward Emma's house, where Sean and his sisters were waiting for them, Cailin rubbed her icy hands and stared at the Grange Hall. Its whitewash glistened in the bright afternoon sunlight.

Broader fingers covered hers, and Samuel said as he helped her down, "It'll be all right. You've met most of these ladies, and you know the people in Haven are good-hearted. They're only looking for what help you're willing to give."

She hoped no one could hear her frantic heartbeat, but it seemed loud enough to reach into the Grange Hall. Her head was light, and she knew she should breathe more slowly and deeply. Was it the idea of speaking to these women, or was it because Samuel's hands remained on her waist?

Last night had been a wondrous joy, but she was unsure what would happen now. Everything had seemed so simple when she came west on the train. She would get her children, find a way to take care of them until she could earn the money to take them home to Athair, and then try to remake her life. Then she had opened her eyes to see Samuel, and her world had gone topsy-turvy all over again.

"It'll be all right, Cailin," he said, drawing her eyes back to his sympathetic smile.

"I-I-I-I hope so."

He put his hands on either side of her face and tilted it up so she could not look anywhere other than into his eyes. "It will be all right, Cailin. You don't think I'd have brought you into Haven if I thought it wouldn't be all right, do you?"

"Sometimes I think I don't know you very well."

"Yes, you do." He gave her a crooked smile. "You just are trying to convince yourself you don't."

"Why would I do that?" She wondered how long she could keep this conversation going so she did not have to enter the Grange Hall. And so she could gaze up into his eyes, which were as welcoming as the green hills she had left behind.

"So you don't have to admit that I'm not the horrible beast you first thought I was."

"I never thought that!"

"No?" That single eyebrow rose.

"I didn't think you were a beast."

"Just horrible?"

She laughed. "Now you're trying to put your words in my mouth."

His face lowered toward hers as he whispered, "Words aren't what I want to put in your mouth."

When he brushed her lips with a swift kiss, his tongue slipped between them. A mere suggestion of the delight they had shared, it sent a quiver ricocheting through her.

"A kiss for good luck," he murmured.

"Is a kiss lucky?"

"It is for me when I'm kissing you."

"Samuel, I should . . . I should go. They—they—"

He gently tightened his clasp. "You aren't getting away that easily."

"They're waiting for me."

"So they are." He released her with a sigh worthy of the hero of a melodrama. "Go and have fun."

"Cleaning the Grange Hall?" She laughed. "You have an odd idea of fun, Samuel."

He grasped her hand as she was about to turn away. "If you're willing to give us another night, I'll be glad to show you more of my idea of fun."

"I'd like that."

"But first you need to go and speak with those ladies."

Walking with him to the door, she smiled when he laced his fingers through hers. She had not realized how mired she had become in unhappiness and fear until he reminded her of joy.

As they had before, voices surged out of the Grange's door. Today, they were feminine and mixed with laughter.

She paused and smiled at Samuel. "I doubt we'll be long when there are so many hands here to help."

"Take all the time you need. I can always call on Reverend Faulkner and get his thoughts on Thanington's offer to the library committee." He gave her a rakish grin. "After all, I missed the meeting last night."

"Should I meet you there?"

"Why don't you get an idea of how long you'll be here first?"

Nodding, she went to the door. She paused at the steps and walked back to him. "I do want another night with you, Samuel."

He brought her hand to his lips for a lingering kiss before whispering, "I had hoped you'd say that."

Cailin wanted to stand there and let herself disappear into his eyes. She gave him a swift smile as she forced her reluctant feet to the steps. Climbing them, she stepped into the Grange Hall. She blinked as she tried to get her eyes to adjust from the brilliant sunshine.

"Surprise!" echoed around her.

Cailin squinted, recognizing several faces. "Surprise what?"

"Surprise!" came the shout again.

She stood there, dumbfounded. When Rachel took her hands and drew her toward the others in the middle of the room, Cailin said, "I don't understand. What surprise?"

"A surprise for you."

"Me?" She glanced over her shoulder and saw Samuel resting one shoulder against the door. He was smiling as broadly as the children had when he brought them home a bag of candy after his most recent meeting in town. He must know what was going on. "I don't understand."

Alice stepped forward. Over one arm, she carried light green flowered fabric. A dress, Cailin realized when the schoolteacher lifted it to show it off. Mother-of-pearl buttons closed the front of the flowered bodice, and a pair of ruffles decorated the dark green skirt. When Alice turned it, Cailin could see it had been made to be worn over a small bustle, for more ruffles dropped along the back.

The schoolteacher held it up to Cailin and said, "Perfect!"

Her fingers trembled as she touched the sleeve. At the cuff was another mother-of-pearl button, as well as a hint of lace to match what decorated the collar.

"Do you like it?" Rachel asked, smiling.

"It's beautiful." She could speak no louder than a whisper.

"It looks as if it'll fit you well." Alice smiled.

"Fit? Me?" Cailin took the dress as Alice pushed it into her hands. Looking down at it, she wondered if, even in her dreams, she had imagined owning such a splendid garment.

Rachel led Cailin toward where the women were stepping aside to reveal a table topped with three more dresses, undergarments, and even an umbrella. "Do you like these other dresses, Cailin?"

She nodded, unable to speak. Her mind was frozen as she stared at the table.

Picking up a blue dress with strips of darker blue velvet accenting its sleeves, Rachel said, "This one looks as if it'll fit you perfectly, too."

"Too? This is for me, too?"

Emma reached across the table and took Cailin's hand. "This is for you," she said as gently as she would have spoken to a child. "We heard how you sold almost everything you owned except the clothes on your back to get here to find your children, so we thought we'd help." She motioned toward the table.

"This is unbelievable. I don't know what to say." She touched the small buttons on the cuff of the dress she held, then whispered, "Thank you."

Hearing delighted laughter around her, she slowly turned her head to look at the door where Samuel still stood. Her gaze was caught by his, and it seemed as if they were the only ones in the room. The women's excited voices diminished as her uneven breathing grew as loud as thunder.

Then he was gone. She was unsure how long she had stood there, connected to him in a way that defied definition.

Emma's hands on her shoulders gently brought Cailin back to the table. Then she motioned to the other women. Curtains were drawn at the windows and the door was closed. A woman stood in front of the main door and another by the door on the side near the platform.

Cailin did not need coaxing to strip off her worn gown and pull on the green dress. As it dropped to the perfect length atop her scuffed shoes, she ran her fingers along the skirt. "It fits just right! How did you know?"

Laughter burst forth around her again.

"Samuel advised us on your size." Emma chuckled as she hooked up the back. "I'd say he's a very good judge of your measurements."

"When a man looks at a woman as much and as long as Samuel looks at Cailin," Alice said, "he becomes quite the expert."

Throwing open the windows and doors, the women brought out cake and iced tea to enjoy while they caught up on the news they had not had a chance to share before. Cailin accepted a plate and a glass. She sank to sit by the wall and set the food on the next chair.

"May I?" asked Alice.

"Please." She motioned to the chair on her other side. "I think I'm too overcome to be able to eat at the moment."

The schoolteacher laughed. "When Emma came up with this idea after your visit to her store, we all set to work. We spoke to Samuel at the library committee meeting, and told him to keep it a secret."

Cailin knew she was blushing. Even though Alice was being circumspect, the visit to the store she mentioned must have been the one when Cailin had refused to let Samuel buy her the bolt of cloth.

"This is too grand a gift," she said. "I don't know how I'll ever repay all of you."

"There's no need. We take care of each other in Haven." Alice leaned toward her. "To tell you the truth, much of the clothing Rachel brought from River's Haven. It was left there when the members of the Community fled from the diphtheria outbreak." She smiled. "It would have been easier to make you clothes from theirs if you'd been shorter."

She lifted the hem of the green gown. "It doesn't look as if you added fabric to this."

"Actually, we ended up taking the clothes apart and using the material. You'd have looked silly with ten inches or more of fabric beneath the original hem."

"Ten inches?" she asked, astonished. "Were they all as short as children?"

"The Community members chose to wear clothing a bit different from the rest of us." She looked to where Rachel had Kitty Cat perched on her lap while they shared a piece of cake. "If you're curious, you can ask Rachel about it. But please wait. It has been such a short time since she left the Community, and I think, no matter how happy she is now, she regrets the decisions she had to make. Please wait a few months."

Cailin continued to finger the soft wool. "I don't know if we'll be here in a few months."

"Are you planning to leave? The children were so happy to have you arrive."

"I'm not leaving my children behind if I go."

Alice frowned. "If you take them, Samuel will be shattered. He loves them as if they're his own."

"But they are *my* children."

"And they are his now, too."

"Did he tell you to talk to me about this?" She started to stand.

Putting her hand on Cailin's arm, Alice said, "Of course he didn't ask me to speak to you about this. Samuel Jennings is too private a man to do something like that."

Cailin sat back on the chair and sighed. She was making a mess of this. "I know."

"He loves the children deeply."

"I know that, too."

"He's looking to the future of Haven because he now has a part in it. There's no doubt that his determination to get the library built is because of your children. He was only mildly interested in a library for Haven before he took them into his home. Before they were placed out with him, he seldom came into Haven, and when he did, he said so little, some folks thought he might have left his voice behind when he moved here."

Cailin did not try to hide her surprise. Then she realized this should be no surprise at all. "He's been a good influence on them, too."

"They certainly are more focused on their schooling than they must have been before. It was as if I had to start from the beginning with both of them." She smiled. "They've been so eager to make him proud of them. Now they'll work to please you, too."

"I know."

Alice hesitated, then said, "I know it's none of my business, but the best thing you could do for those children is to let them put down roots here. It wouldn't be such a bad thing for you to do the same."

"I've given it some thought," she replied, choosing her words with care.

"And so has Samuel, if I'm any judge of the man." She laughed. "His smile as you were dancing at the meeting made that obvious. You two look as if you truly belong together. He has shoulders just the right height for you to lean on. Certainly that thought crossed your mind, at least for a moment?"

Cailin did not answer because she did not want to lie. That thought *had* crossed her mind many, many times. Each time she reminded herself she did not need any man—handsome or not—in her life. Only idiots made the same mistake twice. Yet had it been a mistake to spend last night—and tonight—with Samuel?

Alice came to her feet and smiled. "I see you're listening to someone who knows better than I do."

"Excuse me?"

"Your expression tells me you're listening to your heart, and it's listening to his."

Again Cailin remained silent. She did not have to worry about anyone noticing, because several other women came over to join them. After they had asked some questions about New York, and Cailin had given them what answers

he had, the conversation turned to Alice's wedding, which
vas set for the following Wednesday evening.

It was impossible not to get caught up in the excitement
s the women spoke about what dishes they would be
ringing to share. Cailin was included, and when she hesi-
ated, Alice told her that everyone in Haven—including the
hildren—was invited to the wedding, which would be the
ast event of the summer. The fair and school opening
vould herald in the fall.

She thought of the new potatoes waiting to be dug in
he kitchen garden. A pot of potato and leek soup, chilled
or this hot weather, would be a good dish to share at the
vedding. She would have to ask Samuel if he knew where
he might find some leeks. Onions could be substituted,
ut she preferred savory leeks.

Just as she was about to offer to bring the dish, she heard
shout and her son crying. She jumped to her feet, rushing
the door. Brendan ran in, holding one hand against his
ft cheek. His sisters and Emma's children and a boy
omeone called Jesse followed, all of them shouting as if
nly the loudest would be heeded.

Cailin ignored everyone but her son. He reeled, nearly
ollapsing. She caught him and exclaimed, "Brendan!
Vhat happened to you?"

Megan cried, "Sean hit him! Knocked him right down
nto the ground."

"He hit me first!" Sean fired back, his fists at his sides.

"That's because you said—" Brendan bit off his words
nd leaped toward his friend.

Cailin grabbed him. "That's enough."

"Tell him to shut up!" shouted Brendan.

"All I was doing was telling the truth." Sean raised his
in. "Right, Jesse?"

The other boy shuffled his feet and wisely kept silent.

"If you don't want to hear the truth," Sean snarled,
don't listen."

"That's enough, Sean." The male voice startled Cailin and she saw a slight, light-haired man standing behind her. He tipped his cap to her. "I'm assuming you're Mrs. Rafferty, ma'am."

"Yes."

"I'm Sheriff Parker."

"Sheriff?" she choked.

Emma patted Cailin's arm and asked, "Lewis, did you have to get involved in this spat?"

"Jesse came and got me." He put his hand on the third boy's shoulder.

"Jesse is Reverend Faulkner's nephew," Emma said softly.

"They were rolling about in the dirt on the street," the sheriff continued, "and I didn't want them to get run over by a wagon." He smiled before frowning again at the boys who were glaring at each other.

Cailin released her anxious breath. This sheriff clearly was not like the one she was familiar with in Ireland. That man had taken his job of overseeing the lord's tax-collecting too seriously, and breaking a few heads was his method of stopping a fight.

"Thank you, Lewis." Emma put her hand on Sean's shoulder. "I think it'd be best if we discussed this at home, young man." Looking at Cailin, she added, "I'm sorry."

"I am, too." She frowned at Brendan. "Whatever made you think hitting your best friend was a good idea?"

"He was talking about stuff he didn't know anything about."

"So you decided to teach him a lesson?" She handed him one of her new handkerchiefs to put against his scraped right cheek. "That was silly. Haven't I told you that words are the best way to end an argument?"

"I saw Papa come home several times with a bloody nose, and his eye was black the next day."

She looked away before she said the words burning o

ter tongue. In that way, she had hoped her son would not
grow up to be like his father . . . and hers. Both of them
could not be halted from vengeance if they thought their
pride was being belittled.

"Megan," she said, "go and find Samuel. He should be
at Doc Bamburger's house now."

"Don't you want Brendan to go and see the doctor?"
Megan asked.

Fearful of what she would see, Cailin drew his hand
away from his face. He tried to hide it, but she could see
the scarlet imprint of Sean's knuckles on Brendan's face.
She wanted to ask what had started the fight. However, she
would follow Emma's lead and wait until they got home.

"Go and get Samuel," she said.

Megan ran out and then popped right back in, holding
Samuel's hand. "He's right here, Mama."

When he asked no questions as he herded the children
out of the Grange Hall, Cailin was astonished. She thanked
the women, who gathered up the clothes and put them carefully into a pair of wooden crates. Samuel returned to take
them out to the wagon.

He handed Cailin up onto the seat. When Megan started
to talk about the fight, his glance in her direction silenced
her as quickly as if he had snarled an order at the child.
Lottie crawled up onto the seat and into Cailin's lap. The
little girl shivered, and Cailin wondered what had happened
before the boys struck each other.

Samuel's terse order sent Brendan to the well behind the
kitchen to wash his face before going to his room. Megan
and Lottie hung back for once. Heaving the two crates out
of the back of the wagon, Samuel carried them into the
house and set them in the front hall.

"Cailin?" he asked.

She paused with her hand on the banister. "Yes?"

"Let me talk to Brendan."

"He is—"

"I know he's *your* son, but this isn't *your* problem." He motioned for her to follow him into the front parlor.

"I don't know how you can say that." She ignored his gesture for her to sit on the sofa. "He has done something he shouldn't have. The sheriff was involved!"

"Don't fret about that. Lewis Parker likes to keep things from getting out of hand."

"It's my place to correct Brendan."

"No, it's not."

Cailin stared at him, too shocked to speak.

Resting his folded arms on the back of the chair where he sat each evening to read his newspaper, he said, "It's my place to correct him because this isn't the first time this sort of thing has happened since you last saw them."

"It isn't?" She sank to the sofa.

"Brendan presents a cheery face to anyone he meets, but he has occasionally been very unhappy."

"But you said the children were happy here."

"They are. Most of the time." He sighed. "He was very hurt and very angry when he first arrived in Haven. Pretending they're unchanged by what happened to them is a waste of time. You saw how protective Megan was of Lottie when you arrived here. Megan tried to act as Lottie's surrogate mother. She's no longer doing that, because she's relinquished that role back to you. Brendan is having a harder time. I've handled this before. Let me handle it now."

"All right. We can talk to him—"

"Let *me* handle it. I warned him before what the consequences would be if he got into another fight. This is something that's better said between a man and a boy."

Cailin clenched her hands in her lap. "You're asking me to relinquish my place as his mother."

"I'm asking you to trust me enough—just once, Cailin—to do what's right for him."

She searched his face and saw his sincere concern fo

rendan. Wanting to tell him she had always trusted that
is love for the children was genuine, she nodded.

"Thank you," he said quietly.

"If there's something—"

"I'll call for you." He glanced toward the hall as foot-
eps sounded heavily on the landing upstairs. "Why don't
ou get some supper started for us while I speak with Bren-
an?"

Slowly she stood. "Samuel—"

"Trust me."

The plea pierced her right to the heart, and she nodded.
I do trust you to do what's right for Brendan."

"I guess that's a start." He reached toward her, but she
it up her hand to halt him.

She was unsure what her heart might persuade her to do
hen her emotions were as unsteady as Brendan had been
a his feet. He caught her fingers and drew her to him. In
e glow of the sunshine through the windows, his eyes
immered like green fire. His fingers grazed her jaw.

"Promise me one thing," he whispered.

Or at least she thought he whispered. Her pounding heart
nothered all other sounds.

"What?" she asked as softly, wanting to lose herself in
s bewitching fire.

"You'll consider trusting me in other ways."

"I'm trying to trust you more."

"I know."

"And are you willing to trust me, too?" she asked.

"I do trust you."

"Do you? Do you really?"

As he had done too many times, he looked away.

Putting her hand against his cheek, she tipped his face
ward her and whispered, "Don't ask of me what you
en't willing to ask of yourself."

She hoped he would say something, but he turned toward
e door in a silent command. Knowing the conversation

was over and she would get no more from him, she walke
with him as far as the stairs. He looked at her for a lon
moment, then called up to Brendan.

Cailin went into the kitchen, not pausing when she hear
her son come down the stairs. While she made a meal c
cold meat and fresh vegetables, Samuel took Brendan int
the back parlor and closed the door. She hoped she ha
done the right thing, agreeing that this discussion woul
be best handled by him. She had been ready to argue unt
Samuel mentioned that this was not the first time Brenda
had gotten into a fight. Now he must face the consequence
Samuel had set.

The food was ready, and the door to the back parl
remained closed. She fed the girls and sent them out
play, and the door remained closed. She washed the dish
and called the girls back inside to get ready for bed, an
the door remained closed.

It finally opened a few minutes later. Brendan sat at th
dining room table. The bruise on his cheek was alread
swelling, but he kept his eyes downcast. She set a pla
and a glass of milk in front of him. He began eating witho
a word.

Looking from the boy to the door, she was not surpris
to see Samuel there. She picked up the plate she had wai
ing for him, but he motioned for her to put it down a
stay where she was. When he came into the kitchen a
closed the door that had always been open since she h
arrived here, she was astonished.

He picked up the plate she had prepared for him and s
at the kitchen table. "Brendan understands what he did w
wrong. He'll think twice before hitting someone el
again."

"He looks so chastised," she answered.

"I told him that if he's so foolish again, he won't
taking his cow to the fair to be judged. He needs a ca
head for that, and, if he got upset over some criticisms

his cow, he'd lose everyone's respect and cost himself any chance for a ribbon." He reached for the jug and poured some milk into a glass. "The very thought of losing that privilege punched a hole in his bravado." Taking a drink, he wiped his mouth with the back of his hand. "Tell me something."

"If I can." She handed him a napkin and smiled.

His expression remained somber. "Did their father get into fisticuffs often?"

"What does that have to do with anything?"

"Brendan said his father wasn't reluctant to settle an argument with his fists." His voice lowered in anger. "You've told me he wasn't reluctant to hit you. Did he get into fights with others?"

She wrung out the cloth and tossed the dishwater out the back door. "What does it matter, Samuel? That's in the past."

"But if Brendan thinks it's permissible to settle his differences that way, he needs to learn better ways."

"You make it sound so simple. It was different in Ireland. We didn't have lawyers to handle disagreements."

"There's no need for you to drag me into this argument just to give his father an excuse for his actions."

Cailin looked at him. "Do you think that's what I'm doing?"

"It sure sounds that way."

"That wasn't what I meant. I want my children to have the opportunity to be better than we had the chance to be in Ireland."

He stood and spat a curse, shocking her. "But your husband wasn't from Ireland. He had, from what you and the children have told me, every possible advantage. One thing keeps puzzling me. Why did he go to Ireland in the first place, and stay as long as he did?"

"I don't know." She searched her mind for an answer to

that and found nothing, astounding herself. "Samuel, I honestly don't know."

"You could contact your mother-in-law—"

"No! I won't ask anything of that woman who told my children I'd died. She'd just lie to me, too. I won't ask anything of her, not even the truth about why Abban came to Ireland."

"You never asked him?"

"No, and I'm not sure why I didn't."

"Because you trusted him." He paused, then added, "As I want you to trust me."

"A blind trust?"

"No, a trust that doesn't have to be asked for every day."

"I'm trying, Samuel."

"I know you are, and I'll try as well."

He held out his arms, and she rushed to him, pressing her face to his shoulder. His arms surrounded her with a comfort she wanted to savor forever.

"Are you going to be all right about Brendan?" he whispered. "I saw how upset you were."

"Yes. I can accept that my sweet son has been in fist fights before, so I'm going to be all right here." She put her finger against her temple, then touched the center of her chest. "But I'm not so sure I'm all right here."

"I think you're all right here." His wide finger covered hers.

She gasped as the brush of his hand against her breast sent a quiver into her very depths. When his lips covered hers, the flame of longing burst to life, melting her to him. Only when the long-case clock in the hallway chimed the hour did he release her. She gazed up into the fathomless pools of his eyes.

When he said something about getting ready for the library committee meeting that had been postponed when he did not arrive last night, she tried to force her mind to focus on his words. All it wanted to do was imagine Samuel kissing her again . . . and not stopping. Last night had not been enough. Tonight would not be enough. She wanted a lifetime of nights with him, but she wondered if he wanted more than the arrangement they had now.

Fifteen

Samuel tapped his fingers on the desk in the school-room. After being put off another night, the library committee was finally meeting, but he could think of only Cailin. In the three days since he had first brought her to his bed, he had looked forward to each evening and the game of asking her for one more night. Tonight, by the time he returned to his farm, she might already be asleep.

A smile pulled at his lips. Waking her with kisses would be fun. When her eyes were heavy with sleep, he would let her make one of his favorite dreams come true.

"Samuel?" asked Reverend Faulkner. "Are you with us?"

He shook himself and smiled. "Sorry. It's been a long day."

The minister nodded. "I understand. I'm sorry, too, that it's taken us this long to make this decision. It should have been done long before the harvest."

"What were you asking me when my mind drifted away?"

"Do you think we should turn down Lord Thanington's offer?"

Samuel looked down at the papers before him. The offer had been outlined by a competent attorney. In exchange for Thanington's donation, the library would be named in his honor. That was no problem. However, the rest of the restrictions put on the donation were. The village green would be turned into a garden, which, although it said nothing in this letter, would have as its centerpiece a statue of the benevolent Thanington. If that was not bad enough, Thanington stipulated that no child under the age of sixteen could borrow a book, and anyone who misplaced a book would be banned from the building.

"Yes, I think we need to turn it down," he said quietly, looking from the minister to Alice, who wore a dismayed expression. "I'm sorry. If all he wanted was to have the Haven Public Library named the Thanington Library, I'd be begging you to have this signed right away. As it is, I can't. The next thing you know, he'll be asking to rename the town after him."

Alice gathered up the papers and stacked them neatly. "I agree, even though it breaks my heart not to accept this offer."

"It *is* an offer." Samuel took the papers from her and picked up a pen the minister had in front of him. "What do we want? We leave that and cross out the rest and send it back to him."

"Can we do that?" she asked.

"What do we have to lose?" He laughed and began scratching through the items that bothered the committee. Dipping the pen into the ink again, he drew more lines down the second page. He had forgotten how much he enjoyed the negotiating he had done when he worked with Theo in Cincinnati. For the first time in weeks, he wondered how his partner was faring. Theo had never enjoyed bargaining and compromise but would research through stacks of dusty tomes to get an answer on a property dispute.

Reverend Faulkner chuckled. "This is going to be quite a shock. I can't wait to see his response."

"Neither can I." Samuel continued to read and rewrite or delete other items. When he was finished, he handed the papers back to Alice. "I asked for a response by next Wednesday."

"Next Wednesday?" Alice glanced at the minister. "Samuel, I'm getting married next Wednesday. Did you forget?"

"No, no," he said, coming to his feet. Taking the last page, he wrote in a date a week later. "How's that?"

"Much better. Thank you." Alice smiled.

Samuel got through the rest of the meeting and the good nights, but as he drove home along the quiet, dark road, he was not sure how. He sighed. He had lambasted Cailin for holding on to her shame, and here he was doing the same.

"And your shame wasn't because of anything *you* did," he said, as if Cailin sat beside him.

He looked at the newspaper on the seat beside him. Would he find Beverly's name in it again? It seemed the newspaper had become focused on her every action, reporting which parties she attended and which charities were benefitting from her generous donations of her husband's money.

A single light burned in the hallway when he entered the house. He blew it out before going to his bedroom door. When he opened it, he discovered another lamp was burning even more dimly. He was surprised the room was empty. He had expected Cailin would be asleep at this hour. Tossing his coat over the back of the chair, he stretched to loosen the muscles tightened by fatigue and frustration.

He sat and pulled off his boots. He stared out the window, wishing Cailin had been waiting. She would laugh with him about Thanington's silly posturing and remind him that continuing the battle was worthwhile. He needed her warmth, which renewed his soul as her faith in him strengthened his belief in himself. She would be rankled at Thanington's latest tactic, but, as Samuel did, she would see that this counteroffer might be the swiftest and only solution to the stalemate.

Rubbing his eyes beneath his glasses, he wondered where she was. Maybe Megan had had another nightmare. Maybe he should go and make sure everything was all right.

As he pushed himself up from the chair, the door opened. Cailin slipped inside, and he stared at her. This was not the prim woman who had so insisted on proprieties that she had been willing to wear a patched gown rather than let him buy her fabric for a new one. She was dressed in little more than a chemise that did not reach far past her knees.

"Why do you look so surprised?" she asked, flicking her fingers against the skirt. "I told you that I'd teach you to dance as we do in Ireland."

He gasped, "You dance dressed like this?"

"No," she whispered in a sultry enticement as she walked toward him, letting her fingers trace a path along the bed's upright in a motion he ached to feel upon his own skin, "but I'll show you what I learned from a gypsy woman who sought shelter at our farm for a few days until Father Liam discovered she was there and asked her to leave."

Samuel smiled. Who would have guessed this proper woman had learned to dance from a gypsy? Cailin had some mischief in mind. Her chemise was lathered to her by the heat. He let his gaze slip along the curves that boosted his own temperature. He swallowed roughly, trying to withstand the demands of the mischief on *his* mind when he looked at her.

The low-cut ruffle across her bodice tempted him to touch her, and he wanted to dispense with anything but laying her back on the bed as he tasted her luscious skin. When his gaze returned to her face, he saw the easy provocativeness of her challenging pose. He doubted if he could resist her beguiling beauty for long.

"Show me, *a stór,*" he replied as softly.

Cailin clapped her hands. Slow at first, the rhythm increased in tempo with the flare of her chemise as it belled around her. In the close confines of the bedroom, she could not leap with the wild turns she had learned. As she watched Samuel's face, she knew it mattered little that she could not execute the most intricate moves.

Discovering that, she abandoned herself to the erotic cadence flowing from her heart to her hands. When she had been a young girl and had learned the steps, she had not realized how they imitated the motions of a woman teasing a man. Her hands grazed his face, his shoulders, the curve of his ear as she whirled close, then away. As if they had become winged, her bare feet flowed across the carpet. All the while, her fingers kept up the mesmerizing beat that took control of her body. She and the rhythm and the need to be loved had become one.

Her eyes closed as she slowed to sway to the throbbing within her. Slowly they opened when she sensed Samuel approaching her. Her gaze took in the loosened collar of his shirt, his firm, stubborn chin, the luscious shape of his lips and his eyes' jade flame. She lifted his glasses off his nose and put them on the bureau. He smiled, and she doubted she had ever been happier than she was at this moment. When he ran a fingertip along her face, the answering tingle exploded in her most secret depths.

He drew her toward him, letting her swaying stroke him as eagerly as her fingers had. Taking her hands, he kissed one, then the other. His arms enfolded her, and she could only think of his muscular body against her. His insatiable mouth refused to taste only her lips.

He raised them away from hers far enough to ask, "Does this mean you are giving me one more night?"

"This night and any others you want," she whispered

before his mouth reclaimed hers. As he leaned her back on the bed in the faint moonlight, she wondered if he had heard her offer to be his . . . for the rest of their lives. Then, as his kisses deepened and as he taught her a very special dance only they could share, she forgot everything but their euphoria.

Cailin called for Brendan to carry an armful of supplies to the wagon outside the store. As he bounced in, with Sean on his heels, gathered up the supplies, and ran out, she laughed.

"It looks as if they've forgotten their differences," she said to Emma, who was shaking her head and smiling.

"Whatever upset them is obviously no longer important."

"Do you know what caused the fight?"

Emma put aside the paper where she had calculated Cailin's order. "Sean was very closemouthed about it. He said it wasn't his business to talk about whatever set them off. Has Brendan said anything?"

"No, although I've been waiting for him to. Maybe I should ask him directly."

"Good luck in getting more from him than I got from Sean." She wiped her hands on her apron.

"I'll let you know when I see you next week."

"Aren't you coming to Alice's wedding? I thought you and the children would."

"Samuel hasn't said anything about—"

"He won't come to the wedding. And don't try to change his mind about this, because you won't."

Cailin frowned. "But he admires Alice very much, and he has spoken well of her future husband."

"True, but he won't come." She rested her hands on the counter. "I consider him a good friend. He shares many of my hopes for Haven's future. Yet, when I was married, he didn't attend either the ceremony or the reception afterward at the Grange Hall."

"If he was busy, or one of the children was sick—"

"It's not that, Cailin. He never comes to town for weddings. He attends events at the Grange Hall or the church, but he's always somewhere else when there's a wedding." She sighed and came around the counter. Sitting in the rocking chair by the stove, she put her hands over her rounded belly. "I tried talking to him once about it, but he just changed the subject."

"He does that every time someone probes too close to whatever he's trying to hide."

"He's hiding something?" Emma stared at the wall and mused, "I didn't know he had come to Haven with something to hide, too."

"Too?"

Emma waved aside her question. "Just mumbling to myself. Maybe your arrival has changed his mind and he'll come to the wedding, but don't count on it."

Cailin nodded and bid Emma a good afternoon. In truth, it was closer to evening, because chores had delayed both her and Brendan from finishing their errands.

Her smile returned. Brendan was spending every free moment he had with his cow. He brushed its black and white coat until she feared he was going to wear it right off. With care, he selected everything the cow ate. He was obsessed with every detail, and she knew Samuel had been right to insist on her son being on his best behavior if he wanted to take the cow to the fair.

Sweat bubbled up on her forehead and slipped down her back as she stepped off the store's porch and into the sunshine. Even at this hour, the heat was hardly bearable, and dust rose with every step. She glanced toward the western sky, but no clouds were thickening there. How much longer could this heat and drought last? She hoped Samuel was wrong when he said it could be for several more weeks.

Brendan climbed up onto the wagon's seat at the same moment she did. When she motioned for him to take the reins, he grinned. He loved every opportunity to drive.

She waved aside more dust as he turned the wagon back in the direction of Nanny Goat Hill Road. Slapping her skirt, she watched a brown cloud surround it. Everything was infested with dust.

"Mama?"

Cailin looked up at Brendan. "Yes?"

"I heard you and Samuel talking before we left and . . ." Color splashed up his face, although it could not hide the dark bruise around his eye and down his cheek . . . as Abban had worn more often than she had admitted to Samuel.

She did not want to see anything of his father in Brendan, but he had the same cleft in his chin and the same square hands. Putting her fingers over one of them, she said, "I assume you saw Samuel kiss me before we left."

"I've seen him kiss you lots of times before." He gave her a wry grin. "After all, Papa's dead, so it's all right for you to kiss another man."

"It sounds as if you've got it all figured out."

"I talked it over with Megan and Lottie. Then I talked to Sean this afternoon. We agree it's all right."

"Thank you. I'm glad you don't mind my kissing Samuel."

"Not kissing him, Mama. I mean it's all right for you to marry him."

"Marry him?" she gasped.

"Sean says that's what grown-ups do who live in the same house." He lowered his voice and looked over his shoulder, as if he expected someone to be following to eavesdrop. "He says it's not right for you to be at the farm with Samuel for this long if you aren't married, but I told him you wouldn't do anything wrong."

"Is that why you punched him?"

He nodded, hanging his head.

She put her finger beneath his chin and raised it. Seeing tears in his eyes, she said, "Brendan, Sean is the very best friend you have ever had. I know it hurt your feelings when he said something you disagreed with."

"I didn't disagree with him, Mama. You and Samuel should get married." His smile returned, tremulous at first then brightening as he said, "It'd be perfect. We could stay in Haven, and you and Samuel could have some more babies if you want."

"You seem to have it all planned out."

"I do!" He chuckled. "All you have to do is tell Samuel you want to marry him, and everything will be perfect."

"I know it sounds that way to you." She sighed. "But it isn't quite that easy."

"Why not? Don't you love him? You wouldn't kiss him if you didn't love him, would you?"

"It isn't quite that simple."

"I don't know why not." His brows lowered in an expression he must have borrowed from Samuel. "You like kissing him and he likes kissing you. Shouldn't you do what's right, even if it's difficult?"

She almost laughed at her son's innocent assumptions. "Is that what Samuel told you about avoiding another fight with Sean?"

"Yes, and isn't it the same?"

"I wish it was." She hugged him and repeated, "I wish it was."

"Will you think about it?"

She was tempted to tell him that the idea of marrying Samuel had not been far from the front of her mind since the night she first shared his bed. "Yes, Brendan, I'll think about it."

When Cailin had finished the dishes and tucked the children in after Brendan had read to them, she came back down the stairs. She knew she had to tell Samuel what Brendan had said, but she was not sure exactly how. If Samuel was as skittish about weddings as Emma claimed, the very topic might be ticklish. She recalled how he had reacted when he spoke of Rhea not working here any longer because she was getting married. He had looked as if someone dear had died.

Cailin paused in the parlor doorway. On this long, hot day, the breezes drifting through the open windows were a balm. A parade of insects danced about the lamp in front of one window, but she ignored them.

She was not surprised to see Samuel reading his newspaper. When he looked up, he smiled. He stood and tossed the newspaper onto a crate in his office. He picked up a sweating pitcher from the table beside his chair and asked, "How about some tea?"

"Iced, I hope."

"It's far too hot for anything else."

"A good thunderstorm would sweep the air clean." She took a glass and sat on the sofa.

"Cailin, we can talk about the weather all evening, but I'm more interested in what kept you mute through supper. Are you going to keep on avoiding whatever is bothering you?"

"No, I want to talk about it." Her knuckles bleached on the glass. "Samuel, we need to talk."

He sat beside her and murmured against her ear, "Do you want me to tell you about how my fingers could glide down your back like this?" He ran his hands lightly along her back.

"Don't," she whispered.

"Don't?" He regarded her with astonishment. "Don't what? Talk about touching you or touch you?"

"We need to talk about us."

"What about us?" He twirled a strand of her hair around his finger.

She reached up and unwound the strand. Standing, because she had to put some distance between them, she said, "Brendan told me why he fought with Sean." She put down the glass and clasped her hands, so she could not touch him. "Sean repeated the rumor that there's something wrong about you and me living here as we are."

Samuel shrugged. "Kids like to repeat what they hear, even when they don't completely understand it."

"But they do completely understand it." She blinked back the tears she had been determined not to let fill her eyes. "If I was still just your housekeeper, I could have consoled Brendan and told him not to worry."

"You were never *just* my housekeeper."

"True, but . . ." She had to say it. Holding it back would only make the strain worse. "The children want us to get married, so their friends and their friends' parents will stop gossiping about us."

"Married?" Samuel stood, wanting to believe he had misheard Cailin. When she did not withdraw her words, he snapped, "If this is your way of coercing me to—"

"I never would force you to marry me. How could you even suggest that?"

"Cailin—"

"No, you'll listen to me for once!" Her eyes were brilliant with fury and unshed tears. "How could you think I would use my children to make you marry me? What gives you the idea that I even want to marry you?"

"The way you kiss me."

"It's the same as the way you kiss me, and you don't want to marry me, although you've been quite happy to bed me. Now my children are the laughingstocks of Haven." She put her hands up to her face. "Why did I listen to my heart again?"

"Your heart?" He grasped her shoulders. "Cailin, how could you be so foolish? You know this was meant to be just until you left."

"No," she whispered. "I didn't know that." Her face hardened. "Or was making love to me your way of persuading me to stay so you didn't lose the children?"

"Is that what you think? What you really think? I don't want to hurt either you or the children."

"Then you failed." She drew back. "Good night, Samuel." She walked out of the parlor.

He heard her bedroom door close with a click. Not a slam as he had thought. Or as he deserved.

Sixteen

Samuel looked over the newspaper he had started to read last night before Cailin left him to deal with his thoughts. He did not want to believe he had been using her, but he had been delighted that she was not looking for any permanent ties. They could be happy with each other and not involve their hearts again. When the time came for her to go, as she seemed determined to do, she could do so without leaving him with nothing but humiliation.

He had thought it was the perfect solution to his unquenchable desire for her and his determination not to get mixed up with wedding plans again. As each minute passed during the eternally long night, he had been reminded how imperfect his plan had been. He had avoided the embarrassment but not the pain. And, worst of all, he had hurt her.

He slowly came to his feet as Cailin stood framed by the parlor doorway. Even in her old dress, she had possessed a certain tattered gamine appeal. Now, she wore a suit that hugged her curves before flaring out over a bustle. The brown fabric was the exact shade of her eyes, and her hair beneath her matching bonnet had become a ruddy flame. As hot as the one burning within him.

Her slender face would not be considered as beautiful as Beverly's classically perfect features. Cailin had a pert nose and sparkling eyes framed by that fiery hair. More importantly, Cailin offered an outpouring of laughter and warmth to everyone she met. She did not need to have her name in a newspaper, for her efforts were aimed at helping quietly.

As she had wanted to help him.

Was he a fool to prevent her from helping him? She had trusted him with the greatest anguish within her heart, and she waited for him to do the same. And waited and waited.

"You look lovely," he said, pushing aside his nagging thoughts.

"We're going to Alice and Barry's wedding. Are you coming?" Her voice was cool, and he noticed that she wore rice powder in an attempt to hide the circles beneath her eyes. She must have found sleep elusive, too.

He did not answer when he saw the children grouped behind her. All three had clean faces, and Megan and Lottie wore white ribbons in their neatly brushed hair. Dressed in their finest, the clothes he had had made for them to attend a recitation at the Centennial celebration at the schoolhouse on Independence Day, they were awaiting his answer with unusual patience.

"Well?" she asked when he said nothing. "Are you coming to the wedding with us?"

Again Samuel did not reply for so long Cailin began to believe he was hoping she would give up and leave without him. Or did he expect the children to do something outrageous and pull her attention from him? She could have told him that they were as anxious to hear his answer as she was.

"No," he said quietly. "I made a vow a while back to avoid weddings and all the silliness that goes with them. I don't see any reason to break that vow."

Lottie rushed to wrap her arms around his leg. "Samuel, Dahi and me—"

"Dahi and I," he corrected as he put his hand on her head, but his gaze never wavered from Cailin.

"Dahi and me and I . . ." Lottie giggled. "We're going to see Miss Underhill get merry, so Brendan and Megan can have a new teacher."

"Get *married.*" Brendan took her hand and led her back to stand beside Megan. When Lottie began to protest, he put his finger to his lips. "Shh!"

"Brendan, bring the soup pot." Cailin held out her hands, and each girl took one. "We'll see you this evening then, Samuel."

She hushed the children's questions as she herded them to the door. She looked back to see Samuel standing in the same spot. When he sighed, she wanted to run back and plead with him to come with them. She would be glad to help him face whatever kept him away from this happy day in Haven. Whatever had kept him away from her last night.

On each step toward the wagon, she yearned to hear him call for her to wait, that he had changed his mind. The only things she heard were Brendan's cow's bell and the birds singing in the trees. Lifting the girls into the back of the wagon, she set the soup pot in a crate so it would not spill. Then she turned to help Brendan so he could climb up without getting his dark suit dusty.

"We're going without Samuel?" he asked, incredulous.

"Yes."

She thought he would argue. She feared he would refuse to go unless Samuel joined them. When he picked up the reins, she climbed up beside him.

"Go ahead," she said.

"If you talk to Samuel, maybe he'll listen to you. He has before."

"Samuel doesn't want to come, and I know you're excited about seeing Miss Underhill married."

"Ask him again, Mama. Please."

She had not guessed her heart could break again, but it did when she said, "No, Brendan. Let's go."

He nodded and gave the horse the command to go. Behind them, Megan and Lottie were busy imagining all that would happen at the wedding. They were debating how they could arrange to get the piece of cake with the most frosting.

Cailin looked back at the house. On the porch, Samuel leaned his hands on the railing as he watched them go. His face was long with a frown, but he did not call out to them to wait. He was standing there when the cloud of dust behind them obscured the house.

"A beautiful wedding," announced Reverend Faulkner as he handed Cailin a glass of punch.

"Yes, it was." She waved a paper fan that someone had handed her when she walked out of the church onto the green where the guests were gathered. It moved the heavy air very slightly.

He laughed as he looked past her, and she saw Megan and Lottie lining up with the young, unmarried women who were waiting for Alice to toss her bouquet. Before she could call them away, Alice threw it. Applause rose as it fell into Megan's hands. Several of the young women looked aghast at the idea that the little girl would be the next among them to be married.

Megan ran over to them, with Lottie bouncing after her, and cried, "Look what Miss Underhill—I mean, Mrs. Hahn—gave me!"

"They're lovely." Cailin hesitated, then asked, "Reverend Faulkner, should she give the flowers back? She and Lottie shouldn't have been there."

"Mama!"

Reverend Faulkner patted Megan's head. "Of course she shouldn't give the bouquet back. She caught it fair and square."

With a cheer, Megan held out the flowers to Cailin. "Mama, will you hold these?"

Cailin took them, and pulled out one and stuck it in Megan's hairbow. "Now you look like a flower fairy."

Megan danced away, twirling so the flower was in danger of flying off her head.

"Me, too?" asked Lottie.

"Of course." She laced another stem through Lottie's bow. "We'll leave the others here."

"Flowers need water to go. Samuel says so."

"Go?" Cailin smiled. "Oh, you mean grow. Yes, flowers do need water."

"Dahi and me—Dahi and I will get some water."

She nodded. "Get a cup and fill it. Water, not punch. Flowers don't like punch."

"Silly flowers." She grabbed a cup and ran toward the church.

"Megan looks so pretty," said Alice as she picked up another glass of punch. Unlike every other time Cailin had seen her, Alice was not wearing black. For her wedding, she had chosen a pale yellow gown. "Not quite the person I thought would catch my bouquet, but I doubt if anyone else would enjoy it more than she will."

"I think you're right," Cailin replied with a laugh.

"Are *you* enjoying yourself?" She glanced at the minister, then said, "I thought if anyone could induce Samuel to change his mind, it'd be you, Cailin."

"He didn't want to come, but he sent his best wishes." She added the last when Alice's face grew bleak.

Music sounded across the green as Doc Bamburger's fiddle announced that the dancing was about to start. When the groom came to collect his bride for the first dance, Alice said, "Tell Samuel I'll see him at the meeting next Wednesday."

"I will." Cailin kept her smile from vanishing as the two walked toward the center of the green, where the guests had gathered to watch them dance for the first time as husband and wife.

When someone called the minister away, Cailin nodded absently as he excused himself. She was glad for a moment alone, a moment when she did not have to pretend it was all right that Samuel had not come to the wedding. Sitting on a bench by a table burdened with food, although the guests had already eaten, she sighed.

What she said last night had needed to be said. She could not regret a word, but she was very sorry that whatever he refused to share with her had created a chasm she was unsure if she would be able to cross again.

"Good afternoon, Mrs. Rafferty."

Cailin raised her eyes to discover Mr. Thanington smiling at her. Today, she could have almost believed his lie of being a British lord; his clothes were even more elegant than those he had worn to the meeting at the schoolhouse. Gold glittered on his fingers and across his stomach, where a watch fob ended in a pocket on his vest.

"Good afternoon," she said.

"Would you stand up with me for a dance?" He gave a half-bow toward her.

"Dance?"

"If you would be so kind, Mrs. Rafferty."

She stood. "Thank you, Mr. Thanington."

"Mister?"

She did not answer, and he began to smile.

"Mrs. Rafferty?" He motioned toward where the others were already dancing, then offered his arm.

Putting her hand on it, she almost laughed out loud at this ridiculous situation. The very idea that Cailin O'Shea Rafferty was about to dance with the son of a British lord would have sent her father into peals of laughter.

Mr. Thanington held her at a proper distance as he led her through the steps of the waltz. The dance, which had seemed so lusciously intimate with Samuel, was far more commonplace now. Mr. Thanington's hand was smoother than Samuel's, and she wondered what work he did on the many acres he had purchased from the River's Haven Community.

"I would be wise not to underestimate you, Mrs. Rafferty," he said. "Now I understand why my generous offer to the library committee wasn't accepted."

"I'm not on the committee."

"But you do have Samuel Jennings's ear." His smile was cool. "I assume you have informed him of my little charade."

"Samuel wouldn't make any decisions about the library based on anything but the best interests of Haven."

"I understand Jennings is an attorney."

"He was."

He either did not notice her taut response or chose to ignore it. "I could use the services of a good attorney."

"Are you in trouble?"

"Not as you're thinking, I assure you, Mrs. Rafferty." His smile warmed. "My queries have gained me information that Mr. Jennings has extensive skill in resolving property and inheritance issues. Do you think he would be interested in such work here in Haven?"

"I can't say. You'd have to ask him."

"Where is he?" He chuckled. "I didn't think he would be willing to let your first dance be with anyone but him."

"Samuel couldn't attend today."

"I see," he replied, although his puzzled expression revealed that he did not. As the music faded, he released her hand and smiled as he bowed his head again. "This has been very pleasurable, Mrs. Rafferty. Please let Jennings know I'm considering his comments about the donation for the library."

"I will."

Cailin stepped aside as another dance started. Now, when everyone was busy, would be the best time to slip away. She found Brendan first and sent him to get the soup pot. Megan was showing off her flower to the other children, and she pouted for a moment when told they were leaving. Her smile returned as she went to collect the rest of the bouquet.

Where was Lottie? She was not here with the other younger children.

Looking where the dancers were twirling now to a reel, Cailin did not see her daughter among them. She fought the slimy fingers of anxiety closing around her throat. Lottie should not have gone far when there was so much here to enjoy.

Ten minutes later, she had not found the little girl. She told Brendan and Megan to remain by the wagon, trying not to let them know she was uneasy. Through her mind played the memory of Lottie's determination to get water for the flowers. Lottie had not been by the bucket beside the church's well. Nor had she gotten water from the pail set on one of the tables for the guests.

Cailin swallowed her moan when her eyes were caught by the sunlight glistening on the river as brightly as on Mr. Thanington's gold rings. If Lottie had gone down to the river alone . . .

Gathering up her skirt, she ran along the street leading toward the railroad station on the bluff above the river. She hurried past Emma's store, then paused. There, on the porch, Lottie sat with a young man she recognized from the Grange, even though her agitated brain could not recall his name.

"Lottie!" she called. "Why did you go off without telling me?"

The man looked up from where he had been talking with Lottie. He tilted his broad-brimmed hat, and she saw his hair was a blond so pale it was nearly the color of the ripples on the river.

"She's fine, ma'am," he said, smiling. "She was just telling me about her friend Dahi."

"Dahi is here!" Lottie ran to Cailin and grasped her hand. "Mama, Dahi is here. Right here."

She squatted down and put her hands on either side of Lottie's face. *"A stór,* Dahi isn't here."

"No?" She looked at the man. "Dahi isn't here?"

"No. Why don't you come with me and we'll look for him on the way home?"

"We're going home? Then I can show Samuel my flower." Lottie's face brightened, and she ran back toward the green.

"I hope she didn't bother you," Cailin said, standing.

"Of course not. She's an adorable little girl. You're a lucky woman."

"Thank you," she replied, although she did not feel the least bit fortunate. Bidding him a good day, she went to where the children waited by the wagon.

Cailin did not have to worry about them noticing her silence, because they chattered like songbirds from the moment they left the green until they pulled into the yard in front of the farmhouse. Brendan offered to put the horse away while he checked on his cow. Megan decided she must make sure her rabbit was all right, too, and Lottie ran to get water for the flowers she handed Cailin to carry into the house.

Opening the front door, Cailin took a deep breath of the motionless, quiet air inside. She set her bonnet on the peg by the umbrella stand and walked to the parlor door.

She was not surprised to see Samuel was holding a newspaper, although she wondered if he had been reading it the whole time they were at the wedding. What astonished her was to see a bottle of whiskey beside him. It was half-empty. Had he had a little or a lot? She had never seen him drink anything but hard cider.

"Samuel?"

He lowered the newspaper. Unlike when she had last

seen him standing on the porch, his face was bare of emotion. "I see you caught the bouquet."

"Actually Megan did." She put the flowers on the stairs. "I thought you'd change your mind and come to the wedding, or at least the gathering afterward."

"I told you I wouldn't."

"You missed a lovely wedding. The children enjoyed themselves."

"That's good to hear."

He picked up his glass. Taking a deep drink, he refilled it. "Don't," he said.

"Don't what?"

"You're wearing that scowl you wear every time you scold one of the children for doing something you believe they should know better than to do." His voice remained crisp and unslurred, so she guessed he had not had much to drink.

"I wasn't going to scold you."

"No? Then why are you standing in the doorway staring at me?"

"I was staring at the newspaper."

"And reading it?" He stood, tossing the newspaper down, and laughed sharply. "Have you suddenly made such great strides in your reading lessons that you now can read the *Enquirer?*"

"You know I haven't."

"Then you must have been staring at me." He walked toward her, resting one hand on the molding beside her. "Or you're lying."

She pushed past him and picked up the newspaper. She pointed to a drawing on the back page. "I was looking at this advertisement." Throwing the newspaper back onto the chair, she said, "It was far more interesting than you are when you're being petulant, if you wish me to be completely honest."

"I wish you to be completely honest." His arm swept

around her, pulling her to him. His kiss threatened to steal her breath from her, but she would not let him use this pleasure as a weapon. She pushed herself out of his arms. "You're drunk."

"Not yet. I suspect I will be soon." His laugh was harsh. "Do you want to join me?"

"Having a drink of whiskey? Yes."

"Yes?" His eyes widened in shock.

She went into the kitchen. Returning with a glass, she held it out.

"You want some whiskey?" He seemed abruptly as sober as a preacher on Sunday morning.

"You offered me some. Are you saying you don't want to share?" Reaching past him, she picked up the bottle and splashed a generous serving into her glass. She clicked it against his before downing it. "That's fine whiskey, Samuel."

He frowned. "I had no idea you were an expert on spirits."

"My father taught me to respect whiskey." Setting down the glass, she said, "Apparently your father didn't do the same."

"Ah, now comes the scold."

"Quite to the contrary." She shook her head. "I don't know what's upsetting you enough to drink alone, Samuel. I don't know if it's the wedding or something else, but it's clear you'd prefer to accuse me of things I have no intention of doing rather than be honest with me this evening. If you'll excuse me . . ."

Samuel knew he would be wise to let Cailin walk out, not just out of this room, but out of his life. She was a woman who did not know how to leave well enough alone, and she was tempting him to spill his reservoir of pain. What would she do then? Laugh at him for being so distressed by what had happened in Cincinnati on a day not very different from this one? He had lost the woman he loved to another, but her husband had betrayed her far more appallingly.

"Where are you going?" he asked.

"Do you really care?"

He bit back his answer. Yes, he did care for a thousand different reasons, but he said only, "Just curious if you're going to stay with me tonight."

When sorrow filled her eyes, he wondered what he had said wrong now. He had thought she wanted to continue to play the game she had begun. He had hoped she would admit that last night had been too long when she was not with him. As he looked down at his glass, contempt at his bout of self-pity sliced through him. He put the glass on the table.

"I'm sorry, Cailin. I'm taking out my anger on you."

"Anger? At what?"

He shook his head. "It really doesn't matter. I've got better things to do than sit here and feel sorry for myself."

"Samuel, if you'd tell me what's haunting you, I'll listen. Sometimes it helps to talk about the things that plague our hearts."

The things that plague our hearts? She was too perceptive. The sweet smell of some fragrance drifted from the hair that curled along her neck. He would like those strands grazing his fingers as he drew her mouth to his.

When he did not speak, she said, "Mr. Thanington was asking about you."

"Thanington? Why?"

"He was curious if you'd be interested in doing some work for him. Legal work."

He laughed without humor. "He'll have to find someone else."

"He said also to tell you that he's considering your comments on the offer he made to the library committee."

"That's a surprise. A very pleasant surprise."

"I thought you'd think so." A half-smile tilted her lips. "And Lottie thought she had found Dahi."

"Found Dahi? I thought she could see him whenever she wished."

"Why don't you ask her?"

As she turned again to leave, he said, "Cailin, there must be a way to work this out so we're not both miserable."

"Just you?" she asked, facing him.

"I'd rather not be miserable."

"I think you revel in your misery. I don't know why, but you do. I wanted to help you as you've helped me deal with—" She paused as the children rushed up the stairs to change out of their good clothes so they could play. "It's time for me to heat up what's left of the soup for supper."

"And that's that?"

"Yes. I don't want to be unhappy, Samuel, and you don't want to be happy. Supper should be ready soon." She picked up the bottle and poured another serving of whiskey. Taking it with her, she went back to the kitchen.

He looked at the nearly empty bottle, then walked out of the house. He had a long overdue errand to run, and now was the time to do it, before the whiskey sifted from his head and he talked himself out of it. The telegraph office must still be open. If it was closed, he would search Haven for Kenny. It was time to send a message immediately to New York.

Seventeen

"D-e-l-a-n-c-y spells Delancy, Mama," Megan said with a smile.

Cailin laughed and gave her daughter a hug. When Samuel's newspaper crackled beneath her elbow, she shoved it to the middle of the kitchen table. He must have been finishing it while he had breakfast before any of the rest of them had gotten up this morning.

"Can you tell me what all the letters on the side of Emma's wagon spell?" she asked, to keep her thoughts on her children who were sitting around the table.

"Delancy's General Store, Haven, Indiana," Megan answered with pride.

Glancing at Brendan who nodded, Cailin said, "You're learning more and more. Your new teacher is going to be impressed with all you can read."

Cailin was not sure how Brendan had become aware that she could not read. She had asked him what certain letters spelled, but as she was doing with Megan, she had pretended she knew the answers to her questions. Suspecting he had overheard her and Samuel the night she admitted the truth, she was glad he had not said anything to the girls. Neither Megan nor Lottie were good with keeping secrets.

The back door opened, and Samuel asked, "What does *b-l-a-c-k-b-e-r-r-i-e-s* spell?"

Megan screwed up her face in concentration, then asked, "Is it blackberries?"

"Yes." He held out several pails. "Lots and lots of them are ripe along the old road leading down to the river." He smiled at the children. "Shall we go and see how many we can pick before nightfall?"

They tumbled out of their chairs, each grabbed a pail, and ran out the door.

Samuel held up one of the two pails he had left. "Do you want to come with us?"

"Yes." She took one pail. "Thank you."

He held the door so she could precede him. Closing it, he said, "I thought you'd say no."

"If you hadn't wanted me to say yes, you shouldn't have asked."

"Whoa!" He held up his hands. "I didn't say I didn't want you to come with us. I said I didn't expect you would. You've been keeping a lot of distance between us during the past week."

"How better to put some distance between us than in a briar patch?"

He laughed, and she was astonished to realize she had not heard him laugh in far too long.

She sneezed as dust tickled her nose. "If it doesn't storm soon, this whole road will blow away."

"And the pumpkins won't grow any more. Until Megan took over care of the rabbit, she'd planned on taking the biggest pumpkin to be judged at the fair. It's a good thing she's forgotten that, because they're going to be a pretty small lot."

"You love working this farm, don't you?"

"It's an endless challenge. Next year, I want to have more than a couple of fields planted. Brendan plans—had planned—to raise some pigs to sell to the markets in Cincinnati."

She did not answer. So many plans would now have to be changed, not just Brendan's.

Handing her the other bucket, Samuel picked up a washtub from beside the well. He stuck out his crooked elbow. She put her hand on it and walked with him toward the waiting children. He said nothing as the children called excitedly to them. Then he answered their questions about picking berries.

As if she were hearing and seeing him with the children for the first time, she noted the bonds that had grown between her children and him. To tear them away from him would hurt them so deeply. Yet how could she stay when he had been honest that he had no place for her in his life other than as his mistress? She wanted a home—just like this one—and a family—just like this one—and a man she could love forever—just like this one. It should have been perfect, but it was just the opposite.

When they reached the massive wall of blackberry bushes, Samuel set down the washtub and said, "Before you start, you need to remember that there are prickers on the bushes. They'll hurt if you get one stuck in your finger."

"I don't want to get my fingers sucked!" cried Lottie.

She tried not to, but Cailin could not keep from looking at Samuel as Lottie's words reminded her of her first taste of ice cream. His eyes burned with the craving she knew too well. Too many nights had passed since she had last slept in his arms.

"Just be careful," Cailin said, knowing that was advice she needed to take for herself.

Megan picked a berry and popped it into her mouth. "They're yummy."

"Try not to eat all you pick." Samuel laughed, but the intensity in his gaze had not lessened. "Megan, why don't you come with me? We'll start at the far end."

Knowing he was wise to put some distance between

them, even though she wanted nothing between them,
Cailin said, "Brendan, you and I'll start here."

"Me? Me?" asked Lottie, spinning in her excitement.

"You have the whole middle."

With a whoop, the little girl raced along the bushes and
picked off one berry. She held it high in the air before
dropping it into her bucket. Then she ran to another spot
and pulled off another berry.

Cailin saw many of the berries had shriveled on the
twisting vines. The heat would soon dry out the rest. She
pushed those hard, black nobs aside to look for berries
hidden more deeply within the briars. Batting away a buzz-
ing insect, she pulled off the berries and let them fall with
a steady plop-plop into her pail. Sweat glided down her
back and dripped from her forehead, and she thought of
the sweet ice cream they could make with these berries.

Brendan inched closer and grinned. "We're going to
have lots of berries, Mama."

"Maybe we can make some blackberry jam."

He licked his lips. "That sounds delicious!" Squatting,
he plucked berries from the lowest vines. "Did you talk to
Samuel about it?"

"About what?" She wove her fingers past the briars to
pick another berry.

"About you two getting married."

She gasped, hoping Samuel was not close enough to
hear. "Brendan, I thought you understood that that decision
is between me and Samuel."

"It seems as if you've decided. We're in Haven."

"You know why we haven't left."

"Because you don't have the money to pay for our passage?" He frowned. "Samuel would give you the money
if you really wanted it."

"No, he wouldn't." She sat back on her heels. "He
doesn't want to lose you and your sisters. He loves you
very, very much."

"And he loves you. Jenny said so, and she always knows about these things. She knew Jesse Faulkner was sweet on her sister Miranda before anyone else did."

Cailin smiled gently. "I had no idea Jenny was so wise."

"Don't make fun of her, Mama!"

Putting her hand on his arm before he could whirl away, she said, "I'm sorry, Brendan. I didn't mean to insult her. She clearly has insight into young hearts."

"She says you're in love with Samuel. Says she's seen it with her own two eyes when you've been in Haven." He scuffed his foot in the loose dirt. "She wants to know, too, why you two haven't gotten married."

"Is that so?"

"She says everyone in Haven hopes you'll decide to get married because they're all curious if Samuel would attend his own wedding."

"Brendan Rafferty!" She stood and looked down at him. "You need to learn the difference between gossip and hurtful gossip. If Samuel heard you say that, you'd hurt him greatly."

He tried to look repentant as he said, "I'm sorry, but I'm curious, too. He hasn't gone to a wedding since we got here, and you can't get married if he doesn't go to your wedding, can he?"

"That's enough talk about weddings. Let's just pick berries."

Cailin thought he would say something else, but he nodded. She saw the disappointment in his eyes. She almost hugged him and told him she felt the same way. Burdening the child with her very adult quandary was wrong, even if Brendan could have done anything to change Samuel's mind.

Brendan suddenly cursed. Before she could chide him for using such language, he spit a berry into his hand and grimaced.

"What's wrong?" she asked.

"Ants." He pointed to the insects wiggling on the berry. "They were trying to walk around in my mouth." He spat again. "I never want to feel a tickle like that again."

She laughed as he tossed the berry back into the bushes. "Next time, look before you put a berry into your mouth."

"Mama!"

Giving him the hug she had wanted to give him before, she held out her pail. "Try another. Go ahead," she urged when he hesitated. "Just check it inside first."

He gingerly picked up a berry and tilted it to see under its cap. Popping it into his mouth, he grinned. He grabbed his smaller pail and went off to another section of the bushes.

Cailin wiped more sweat from her forehead, then unbuttoned the cuffs of her gown. She rolled up the sleeves. She might get scratched, but a few scratches would be better than roasting.

"Now you look as if you're ready to get to work," Samuel said as he dumped his pail of berries into the washtub.

"I'm ready for a dish of blackberry ice cream."

When he slipped his arm around her and pressed his lips to her nape, she did not fight her yearning to soften against him. He whispered, "How about a cool bath?"

"That sounds heavenly."

"It would be if you'd let me wash your back."

She looked at where the children were spread out around the thatch of blackberry bushes. Putting down her pail, she took his hand and led him toward a trio of trees across the narrow road. Only when she was certain they were out of the children's earshot, she said, "Please don't say things like that. They're already upset enough about the rumors. If Lottie repeated what you'd just said, the gossip would bother the children more."

"Is there new gossip I haven't heard?"

"You know what's being said!" she snapped, abruptly irritated that he was making this difficult for her.

"It appears that they're wondering if the reason we haven't gotten married is because I wouldn't attend my own wedding."

She gasped. "You were listening to me and Brendan!"

"You weren't whispering." He put one foot on a stone. "And maybe the gossip isn't all wrong."

"I don't care if it's right or wrong. I don't want the children injured by these comments that are certain to become more pointed."

"And do you expect me to drop to one knee and ask you to be my wife?"

She shook her head. "Getting married just for the sake of the children wouldn't be good for them either."

"You're right." Samuel muttered the curse Brendan had used. When her eyes widened, he whispered, "Cailin, I'm not sure how much longer I can wait to hold you again."

"You know that would make things more difficult." She looked down at her hands.

Taking the pail, he set it on the ground. He looked down into her earthy eyes that told him how much she ached for him. "I don't care, *a stór.*"

He gave her no chance to answer. His fingers combed through her hair and tilted her mouth beneath his. With a slow pleasure that dismissed the trouble beyond their embrace, he teased her lips with the tip of his tongue. As they softened, he tasted within her mouth the flavor of blackberries that was sweetened by her own flavor. As her breath became swift and eager in his mouth, he tightened his arms around her. He wanted to sweep aside her clothes and hold her with her silken skin against him.

His hand brushed her breast, and she gasped against his lips. Delighting in her arousal, which fired his own, he stroked her supple curves until she quivered with the need tantalizing him. He savored her lithe body against him and longed for the moment when he could hold her in private.

Megan screamed.

He released Cailin, who looked frantically in both directions.

"Megan! Where is she?" Cailin cried.

"This way." He ran toward where the bushes curved into the field.

Megan screamed again.

Running after Samuel, Cailin looked beyond the end of the bushes. She saw Megan swiping at something and crying out in pain and horror. Bees! Megan must have disturbed them.

Samuel shouted as he grasped Lottie to keep her from going to her sister, "Stay back, Cailin!"

She did not slow. Megan needed her help.

He bellowed for the rest of them to stay back. She pushed past him. Those could not be bees! They must be wasps, for they were swarming up out of the ground.

Then the wasps attacked her, too. She tried to swat them away and reach for Megan at the same time. Savage fire seared her arms below her sleeves. She could not see through the swarm as tears flooded down her cheeks, which were burning as fiercely.

"Megan!" she shouted.

"Mama! Mama! Make them stop!"

She somehow found Megan's hand. Yanking the child into her arms, she choked as the wasps stung through her clothes. She did not take time to push them away. Holding her daughter close, she tried to escape the attack.

She could not see. All she could do was feel the unending pain and hear Megan's screams.

Hands grasped her waist. Samuel! He tugged on her, and she lurched after him. She hoped he could see more than she could.

He shoved her to the ground. The earth was cool against her ravaged skin. She kept her arms around Megan, trying to protect the child and herself at the same time. Wiping away the wasps, she moaned as more stung. Samuel swore, and she knew the wasps had not given up their vicious attack.

When he grabbed her arm and jerked her to feet, she gathered Megan up in her arms. She raced after him as fast as she could. Her hair had fallen to cover Megan, keeping many of the angry wasps away from the little girl.

She heard Samuel shout to Brendan to bring Lottie. With a moan, she tried to see where her other children were. He did not give her a chance. Taking Megan from her, he seized Cailin's hand and pulled her away from the swarm. She was not sure how far the wasps would follow.

When he slowed, she sank to the ground, gasping for breath.

"No, no," he mumbled. "We need to get into the house until they calm down."

She pushed herself to her feet. A hand cupped her elbow, and she heard her son urging her to hurry. She winced as Brendan's hand brushed one of the spots where the wasps had stung her, but she reeled after him.

Something buzzed close to her ear. With a choked gasp, she ripped off her bonnet. A trio of wasps whirled out of it. She swung her bonnet at them. They flitted out of her reach, then flew away, clearly no longer interested in the battle.

"Inside!" called Samuel. His order was oddly distorted. Was it his voice or her ears?

Cailin pulled the screen door closed behind the children, then shut the wooden door. Leaning back against it, she took a steadying breath before asking, "Do you have any hartshorn, Samuel?"

"No." His voice was distorted, she realized, for hers had sounded almost normal.

"Brendan, get some baking soda and mix it with whatever water we have in the kitchen. Make it into a thick paste." She wobbled to where Megan was lying on the floor. "Lottie, get me an onion." Kneeling, she winced.

Only now was she discovering that the wasps had stung through her thin stockings.

Samuel knelt beside her. "Megan?" he called softly.

"Are they gone?" the little girl whimpered.

"Yes."

Megan raised her head, and Cailin was glad to see there were only a half dozen stings on her face. There were probably twice that many on her arms. Taking the bucket with the baking soda paste in it, she scooped out some and plastered it on Megan's face. The little girl yelped, then relaxed as the paste cooled the hot stings.

"Brendan," Cailin said, "peel the onion Lottie has and cut it into big slices."

She heard him do as she asked, while she continued to lather the paste on Megan's arms. When she asked where else the little girl was stung, she was relieved to hear that she had put the paste everywhere.

"Go and sit quietly in the parlor. I'll bring you something cold to drink as soon as I tend to Samuel."

"And I tend to your mother," he said, his words sounding even stranger.

Cailin stared at him as she stood. Or tried to. Her eyes were swelling shut, but she could see red welts had risen over most of his left cheek.

"What were they?" she asked, setting the bucket on the table and motioning for him to sit.

"Yellow jackets." He grimaced when she put some of the baking soda paste on his face. "They're especially vicious this time of year. I should have warned you before we left the house."

"If you had, we wouldn't have gone for berries." She tried to smile when Brendan handed her a plate with the sliced onion, but each motion added to the pain across her face. She sprinkled salt on the onion.

"What are you going to do with that?" Samuel asked.

"If you had some hartshorn, I would use that to draw

out the stingers and ease the pain, but the onion and salt will have to do, along with the baking soda plaster."

"Here, Mama." Lottie held out another bowl with the baking soda paste and water. "It's my kitten's water dish." She pointed to a spot on her arm. "I'm stinged, Mama."

"So I see. Thank you, *a stór.*" Cailin took the bowl and stuck her fingers in it, so glad the touch cooled the agonizing burn. Gently she dabbed the mixture on Lottie's arm. Handing the bowl to Samuel, she picked up Lottie.

"Let me," Samuel said. He held out his arms for the child. They were even more heavily covered with welts than his face.

"No, you're hurt worse than I am," she replied, although she wanted to accept his offer. Every motion added to the pain searing her. "You need to be tended to right away."

When her son offered to take Lottie into the parlor and read her a story, Cailin nodded. "Thank you, Brendan," she murmured. "Are you certain you don't just want to escape from slicing more onion?"

He laughed, and she smiled, in spite of the pain.

"Sit down, Samuel," she said quietly as the children left the kitchen. "Let me get some of this on your face while I can recognize it as your face. Rub this slice of onion on your arm while I do something about your cheek."

He sat and set his glasses on the table. She was horrified to see one lens was cracked.

"How did that happen?" she asked.

"I'm not sure. I'm surprised they aren't worse. How are Lottie's?"

"I think they're all right."

"You think?"

"I didn't check them."

"Because you can't see them?"

"I've been a bit busy, as you should recall."

He caught her hand. "Her glasses are fine, but you

aren't. You're staggering about almost as much as you did when you arrived here. Sit down."

"I think that's a good idea." She groped for the chair, knowing it must be nearby.

"Here." He cupped her elbow and sat her in the chair. "You don't have to pretend any longer."

She closed her swollen eyes as he spread cooling salve on her arm. "Pretend what?"

"Acting as if you don't hurt even worse than Megan and I do."

"You were stung more than I was."

He shook his head. "I don't think so. Of course, we could count the stings on each other to make sure." His low laugh offered an invitation she might not have been able to ignore if she did not hurt so bad.

Trying to keep her voice light, she said, "No thanks. I don't want to know which one of us was more foolish."

"That's easy. You were. Hands down."

"What's that supposed to mean?"

He gently lathered the back of her hand with the paste. "You need to trust me to watch over the children, too."

"I do."

"Then why did you keep trying to help Megan when I yelled to you to stay back?"

She opened her eyes as widely as she could. "Would you have stopped if our situations had been reversed?"

"No, but that's different."

"Why?"

"Because I trust you."

She shook her head. "No, you don't. You don't trust me to take care of my own children."

"You're wrong. If I hadn't trusted you to take care of them, I'd have sent you on your way when you were well enough to travel."

"With the children." When he did not answer, she

sighed. "We've had this discussion before, and it went nowhere."

"You're wrong," he said again. He put his fingertips on hers, and she knew he was trying not to hurt her by chancing to touch one of the welts along her arm. "I listened to what you said, and I've seen you with the children. I know you need them and that they need you."

"And they need you."

He chuckled. "You'd make a fine lawyer, Cailin. You can argue every point until it's just easier to give up and give in to you."

"Not every point."

"That's true, but you've given me cause for ideas I haven't thought in a long time."

"Since you came here from Cincinnati?"

A screech from the parlor silenced his answer. When he told her to remain where she was while he checked to see what was upsetting Lottie, she nodded. She watched him leave through the narrow slits of her swollen eyes.

Groping for the baking soda paste, she did not find it. She stood to check whether it was on the other side of the table. When she moved, she stepped on a paper on the floor. She bent to pick it up, although she knew what it must be even before she peered at it through her burning eyes.

She unfolded the crumpled newspaper. Looking from the words she could not read to the door through which the man she could not understand had gone, she wondered if the paper had fallen out of his pocket or been left on the floor. She folded it and put it in her apron pocket. As soon as she could, she would ask Brendan if there was anything similar written on this one and the paper she had found crumpled up before. Maybe her son could help her discover if the answer was there. If it was not, she feared she might never persuade Samuel to unburden his heart so she might find a place within it.

Eighteen

Samuel squinted through his broken glasses. Hitting his thumb when he was hammering in this nail would be stupid. When he had offered months ago to help build the judging barn at the fairgrounds just outside Haven, he could not have imagined all the turns his life would take in the meantime.

"What happened to you?" asked Lewis Parker as he brought another board cut to fit this section of the wall. The sheriff had been working on the smaller building and the seats around what would become a boxing ring. Samuel had heard some of his neighbors taking bets on how many opponents Lewis would knock out this year. Despite his slight build, the sheriff was reputed to be an excellent boxer. "You look as if you lost a fight with a cat."

"Yellow jackets." He smiled. "Can you run the lot of them in and lock them up?"

"No thanks!" He laughed. "Why aren't you home letting Cailin take care of you?"

"Cailin doesn't look much better than I do. Megan escaped with the least number of stings, and she's the one who stumbled into their nest."

"That's what you get for playing the hero."

"You can be sure I'll think twice next time."

Lewis's smile slipped away. "That's not likely. You'd risk anything for those children."

Samuel nodded and went back to trying to hammer in nails without striking his fingers. He had rushed into the swarm not to rescue Megan—Cailin was doing that—but to help Cailin escape the wasps.

Working on the side away from the sunlight, he was able to see well enough through the broken lens to help build the long, low building where the livestock judging would be held. He smiled. Lottie had told him that he could share her spectacles. Pretending to consider her suggestion, he had declined as seriously as she had offered. The memory warmed him. Not just Lottie's generosity but also Cailin's laughter, which had, for that moment, torn down the wall between them.

"Why don't you head home?" asked Noah, coming up behind him. "You've been here for hours."

"The interior needs to be finished."

"We've got plenty of volunteers." He smiled. "And Emma is concerned that Cailin needs some help after what she's been through with the wasps."

"Is this Emma's way of telling me I should be resting, too?"

He laughed. "Not Emma. She'd be much blunter than that. She's worried about Cailin and your little girl."

Samuel fought not to react to his friend's words. Before Cailin had arrived, he had been pleased each time anyone had called Brendan, Megan, and Lottie *his* children. Now each mention reminded him how unsettled matters remained, more than ever since Cailin had first shared his bed.

Handing the hammer to Noah, he said, "There's no sense in getting Emma upset."

"Take care of yourself." Noah smiled, then winced. "I remember the first time I came upon a hornet's nest in some wood I was getting ready to work on. I won't be that stupid again."

Samuel had to admit he was grateful for the excuse to

get in out of the sun. Its heat seemed to exacerbate the burning stings. He would be glad to get back to the farm and plaster on more of that baking soda. Even so, when he reached the village, he drew the wagon to one side of the street.

He walked into the telegraph office. As soon as he opened the door, he could smell the pomade Kenny Martin put in his hair. The young man seemed to think he had to look slick as goose grease to impress his customers. Samuel doubted many folks paid any attention to Kenny's smooth hair and pristine white shirt when they came in to send a message or wait for one.

"Wow!" Kenny said as he stood up behind his counter. "I heard you'd had a run-in with some wasps, but I didn't know you'd look this bad."

"I'm better than I was yesterday." He folded his arms on the counter, then, wincing, straightened. "I thought I'd stop in and see if there's any answer to my message."

"Nothing yet. I'll send word out to you as soon as something comes in."

"Thanks." As he went out and closed the door behind him, he heard Kenny's snicker. He could not fault the telegraph operator. The very sight of his wasp-stung face had brought peals of laughter as well as sympathy from everyone he had met today.

Driving his wagon along Haven's main street, he frowned. He had sent that telegram to Lloyd Sanders more than a week earlier. By this time, Lloyd should have gotten the answers he needed and sent a reply back to Haven. If he heard nothing by the time the fair was over, he would send another, more pointed telegram to his friend. He had waited too long on this already.

Brendan was bounding out of the barn as Samuel drew the wagon to a stop. Waving to the lad, he swung down and called, "I could use some help."

"With what?" His smile wavered, and he looked at his feet.

"Go and get your sisters to help," Samuel said, pointing to the back of the wagon. He knew he should ask Brendan what was wrong, but he held his tongue. If the boy had done something he should not have, the truth would come out soon enough. "There's too much for you and me to carry." A motion in the barn door caught his eye, and he was glad. Even if she looked the worse for the stings, Cailin was a sight he enjoyed as often as possible. "Cailin, come and see what was put in the wagon while I was working at the fairgrounds."

He handed Brendan a cake and a box. When he held out another pair of boxes to her, she asked, "What's all this?"

"Noah told me Emma is concerned about how you're faring. It wasn't until I hit a chuckhole on the way out of town and heard the clatter in the back that I realized she was determined you wouldn't have to cook tonight."

She opened a box. "Do you know what this is?"

"Fried chicken," Samuel said with a chuckle. Peeking into the other, he took a deep breath and smiled even more broadly. "And potato salad. Have you ever had either?"

"No."

"Then you're in for a treat."

"Emma did this?" she asked as tears filled her eyes again.

Samuel put his arm around her shoulders and steered her toward the house. He hushed the children, who were distraught to see her weeping.

"It's all right," she said when they entered the kitchen. Stepping away from him, she put the boxes on the table. "And I'm all right. I'm just so pleased not to have to cook supper. The heat from the stove makes everything hurt more."

Shooing the children back into the parlor with instructions for them to play quietly, Samuel placed a milk pail on the table. He opened it and chuckled. "Lemonade to go along with the food."

"I can't believe she did all this." She stared at the bounty on the table. "No, I can believe it. I've never seen such generous people as in Haven."

"We do take care of one another."

"So I've seen." She motioned toward the door as she wiped her eyes cautiously on her apron. "Go and sit with the children while I get this on some platters. Then we can eat out on the porch."

He nodded. As he watched her walk about the kitchen, he noticed that she was as unsteady as he was if he moved too quickly.

With Brendan's help and Lottie's attempts to help, Cailin prepared five plates and poured five glasses of lemonade to take out onto the porch. Samuel and Megan joined them outside.

Samuel laughed as the children reached for the plates that were lined up along the top step. When he saw Cailin exchange a glance with Brendan, he noticed neither looked at him.

He was about to ask what was troubling them, but Megan exclaimed, "Mama, try the chicken. It's so good!"

Cailin took a bite of the potato salad and then one of the fried chicken. "These are delicious. I'll have to persuade Emma to share her recipes." She seemed as determined as the children to enjoy the meal.

He decided to do the same, remembering that he had not eaten much at midday. As Brendan helped his sisters divide up the final pieces of chicken before going inside for second helpings of salad, he said, "Brendan is becoming quite the diplomat. He handled that without creating a single outcry. Maybe he's feeling sorry for us."

"He is." Her voice was so hushed, he almost asked if she was hurting worse. As she stabbed her fork into a chunk of potato, she took a bite and looked across the lawn.

"He has a good reason." He flexed his right hand. "I haven't done that much hammering in a long time. I missed the nail as many times as I hit it." Adjusting his glasses, he said, "I'm glad I didn't break both lenses. You'd be leading me around to do my chores."

Cailin gave him no answer before the children hurried back out onto the porch.

His brows lowered when he saw Brendan glance at her several times, an uneasy expression marring his face. When she spoke of nothing more important than how good the cake was, he wanted to believe he was reading more into her silence than he should.

He was grateful when it was time for the children to go to bed. As they scurried into the house, he said, "Cailin, you rest here while I take the last of the dishes into the kitchen."

"Leave them. I'll take them in later."

He dropped to sit on the railing beside her. "Are you as tired as I am?" he asked with a chuckle. "Even with all the help we had, building that judging barn took a lot longer than I'd anticipated."

"I *am* tired." She hesitated so long, he thought she had something vital to say. When she did speak, she said, "I love evenings like this. Sometimes Athair and I would sit out on summer nights and play the fiddle and sing to the stars."

"Sing to the stars?"

"I guess I should have said sing under the stars. It was a nice way to pass an evening."

"Then why don't you sing? You've got a lovely voice, and it'd be a nice way to spend the evening."

"I'd rather talk."

He leaned forward and rested his elbow on her chair's arm. "About what? About how lovely you are when the setting sun glistens on your hair?"

Cailin reached into her apron pocket and drew out the

two newspaper pages. Without a word, she handed them to him.

Even in the dimming light, Samuel could see a name circled on each page. Beverly's name! He stood. His voice hardened as he asked, "Who helped you read these? I hope you didn't ask someone in Haven."

"I wouldn't do that." She gripped the arms of the chair. "I asked Brendan to read them to me. He helped me find something in common in these two pages that you crumpled up and threw on the floor."

"So I see." He folded the pages and put them in his pocket.

"Who is she, Samuel?"

"Beverly Newsome."

"Very funny!" She folded her arms in front of her but stayed sitting in the rocking chair. "You crumpled these pages with her name on them. In anger?"

"I don't want to talk about it."

"Why not? Ever since I arrived here, you've been trying to dig up every detail of my past and help me banish my heartache. Why won't you let me help you do the same?"

"Because I don't need help."

"Do you want to spend the rest of your life destroying pages of the newspaper with Mrs. Newsome's name on them?" She clearly did not intend to let him avoid her questions tonight.

"Just because you wandered, penniless, into my house doesn't mean you can tell me what I should do with the rest of my life." He cussed under his breath when he saw her eyes widen as far as they could at his cold words. He could tell her that he had not meant them, but it was too late. They were spoken now.

"It isn't just your life!" she fired back. "It's the children's and mine, too, while we're here."

"While you're here? Are you still planning on leaving?"

She waved aside his words. "Don't change the subject. Please be honest with me."

"I'll be honest and say I don't want to talk about it."

"With me?"

Samuel could not ignore the thrust of something like a well-aimed fist in his stomach. Her question was so soft and so heartfelt that he knew he owed her an answer. More importantly, he owed her an honest answer.

"If I were going to talk to someone about it, you'd be the one I'd talk to."

"Tell me, Samuel. Trust me at least this much." She put her hands over his on the arm of her chair as he sat on the top porch step. "It's nothing more than you've asked of me."

He wanted to tell her that, of course he trusted her, but she had to trust him about this being the one thing he needed to keep to himself. When he gazed up into her eyes that remained swollen, showing she had been unafraid to protect her child . . . and him, he knew he could not be less courageous.

Taking the pages out of his pocket again, he looked at the circled names. "As you guessed with Brendan's help, I do know Beverly Newsome. I know her well."

"Is she the reason you left Cincinnati?" She swallowed so hard he could hear it.

"I'd become weary of being an attorney, so I'd been looking for something else to do." He chuckled sadly. "My partner, Theo, thought I'd gone mad, after years of study and building our business. I wanted to find something that challenged me more."

"So you decided to become a farmer?"

"It wasn't what I'd planned at first. I considered becoming a teacher because I enjoyed being with children. Opening my own school for young boys who were interested in learning what they needed to go to university would have been a challenge I would have enjoyed."

"But you didn't."

"No."

"Because of Beverly?"

He leaned against her leg when she stroked his hair. There was something so liberating about her touch, which asked no more of him than he wanted to share. And, he was astounded to discover, he wanted to share with her the truth about what had hastened his decision to leave Cincinnati.

"Yes," he said, "because of Beverly. We were supposed to be married."

"Did you love her?"

"Very much."

"Do you love her still?"

Looking up at her, he saw she was biting her lower lip, a motion that brought Megan instantly to mind. He knew Megan did this when she was trying to avoid saying something. Was that a habit she had learned from her mother?

"That's the same question I asked you," he said.

"Yes."

"A question you answered with such honesty. I'll do the same. I don't think I love her any longer."

Her voice caught. "You don't think?"

With care so he did not hurt her or himself, he put his arms on her knees. "I thought I was able to let those feelings go." He pulled out the pages. "You see the result."

"I see that this is festering inside you. I see that you thought you'd found the perfect family here. Children you loved without the hindrance of a woman who could break your heart again."

"Now you know why I wasn't pleased to find you on my doorstep."

She brushed his hair back from his forehead, not touching any of the welts. "Tell me the rest."

For so many long months he had hidden the truth, ashamed of anyone discovering it. Now her gentle smile invited him to do the very thing he had thought he could never do . . . trust another woman.

"We were to be married," he said, "but she changed her mind."

Something flickered in her eyes, but he could not determine what it was before she asked, "After your plans were announced?"

"After I arrived at the church."

"She jil—changed her mind on your wedding day?"

He folded her hand between his. "You can say the word, Cailin. She jilted me at the altar. She decided she didn't want to marry a mere lawyer when she could have a glamorous life as the wife of the son of a rich man, one of the richest in Cincinnati."

"You're lucky."

"Really?"

"She could have decided that *after* she married you." She looked away.

Reproaching himself for not realizing how his explanation would add to Cailin's pain at her husband's duplicity, he drew her down to sit on the porch next to him. He held her as the stars appeared and then faded as the moon rose. While they both were so sore from the stings, he must do no more than hold her and talk.

But soon they would be healed. . . . He smiled. Then he would hold her far closer and he would keep her lips busy with his. And then . . . His smile faded. He had told her the truth, answering each question she asked, but, as he had learned to in court, he had not offered any information. One question she had not asked. If she had, he was unsure what he would have told her. He did not know if he could ever trust another woman—even Cailin—with his heart, even if he wanted to.

At the rattle of a wagon coming up the road, Cailin wiped water off the window she was washing. She saw the black delivery wagon with *Delancy's General Store, Ha-*

ven, Indiana on the side. Dropping the rag back into the bucket of water, Cailin hurried out of the house and waved to Emma.

"Do you want something cool to drink?" Cailin called as she pushed her heavy braids back over her shoulders. She had hoped wearing her hair like this would ease the day's grinding heat, but she was not sure anything could.

"That sounds wonderful." Emma stepped down from the wagon and reached into the back.

"Come up on the porch and I'll get some iced tea."

By the time Cailin had brought out the pitcher of tea she had made for the children's return from helping Samuel gather up the last of the corn in the larger of the two fields, Emma was sitting in the rocker.

"Thank you," Emma said as she took the glass Cailin had poured.

"Thank *you* for all the delicious food you sent out earlier in the week."

"My pleasure." Drinking, she smiled. "Perfect."

"You should be careful on these hot days."

"Now you sound like Noah."

Cailin sat on the chair Samuel usually used. "You should listen to him. Lottie was a summer baby, and even in Ireland, where it's far cooler, I knew it was important to take care."

"This baby won't be here for several months, but he or she is already making it clear who's in charge." She laughed. "And it isn't me. You're looking better than I'd expected when I heard about the wasps."

"We didn't look better earlier in the week." Cailin blinked. "I could barely do this two days ago."

"At least you have some blackberries for your pains."

"Plenty. Brendan and Lottie went back and picked more, so I have enough to make jam. I'll send you several jars."

"That would be wonderful." She held out a long, thin

box. "This came in on the train this afternoon. I thought you'd want it right away."

Cailin took it and stared at the lettering across an envelope affixed to the front, recognizing her name at the top of the address. Looking up at the wagon, she matched the letters of Haven, Indiana, to the ones written beneath her name. The rest of the words made no sense to her. Some were crossed out, but she could not guess why. The package must have had a tough journey, because it was almost as ragged as her dress had been when she arrived here.

"You're lucky to get this," Emma said, pointing to the writing on the front. "It has followed you all the way from Ireland to New York and then here."

"Ireland?" She ran her fingers along the writing on it. Someone must have seen the package when it was delivered to the house where she worked and sent it on to her here. One of the Bridgets, she guessed. She almost asked Emma if it was from Athair. She would have Samuel read it when he returned. Looking up at the sun, she knew it would not be for several hours.

"I was certain you would want it straightaway." Emma stood and set the glass on the railing. "Now I need to deliver an order out to Thanington Hills."

"Thanington Hills? I hadn't heard Mr. Thanington had named his farm."

"Farm?" Emma laughed. "I suspect he envisions it as a fancy English estate. Enjoy your mail, Cailin."

"If you see the children along the road, would you send them home right away?" She could ask Brendan to read the letter that must be in the envelope to her if he arrived home before Samuel.

"Gladly. Enjoy your news from home."

Cailin stroked the envelope and nodded. Waving as Emma went back to her wagon, she sat in the rocking chair and opened the envelope. She drew out the letter, which was only a single page. She silenced her disappointment, reminding herself that the handwriting was small, so there might be a lot of news on that one page. Folding it up, she slipped it back into the envelope.

She started to open the package, then knew she should wait and see what the letter said. It had been put on top of the box, so maybe she should know what was written there before she saw what was inside the box that was almost as long as her arm and about as thick as her clenched fist.

She took the package into the house and put it on the mantel in the parlor. There, it would not get splattered as she washed the windows and did the rest of her chores.

Time after time, during the afternoon, Cailin went to look at the package. Once she knew what the letter said, she would have Samuel help her write back to her father, for this package must have come from him. She could sign her own name now, and Athair would be so proud of her. Not even the day's oppressive humidity could steal her smile as she finished washing the front windows and began to cut fresh vegetables for supper.

When she met Samuel and the children at the door, she grasped his hand and pulled him into the parlor. He put his arm around her waist and asked, "So eager? I like this."

"Read this to me." She smiled at the children as she lifted the package off the mantel. She pulled the envelope off the front and then held the box to her chest. "Read it to us."

He wiped his forehead with a handkerchief before taking the letter. He whistled as he looked at the writing on the front. "This came all the way from Ireland."

"That's what Emma said. Is it from Athair?"

He held out the envelope and pointed to some writing in the upper lefthand corner. "It's from a Father Liam. Do you know him?"

"He's our priest in Ireland." Setting the box on a nearby table, she took the envelope and pulled out the letter. "What does it say?"

He scanned the letter and drew in his breath sharply.

"Samuel, what is it?" She gripped his arm. "What does it say?"

"I think we should discuss this alone."

A chill that swept away the day's heat congealed inside her. As if from a distance, she heard herself telling the children to help each other get some supper from the platters on the table. She saw Samuel's mouth tighten as he looked at the letter again.

"What is it?" she asked as soon as the children ran into the kitchen, along with the promise that they could have the rest of the fresh blackberries for dessert.

"It's about your father."

She put her hands to her mouth as she whispered, "Is something wrong with Athair?"

"Cailin . . ."

The truth was in his eyes. She closed hers. "He's dead, isn't he?"

When he took her hand, he said, "I'm sorry."

"Did Father Liam say what happened?" she choked out.

"Yes." He touched the center of the letter. "Your father had been to the public house and had a convivial evening. When he didn't come to church the next day, Father Liam went to check on him. As you asked him to."

"As I asked him to," she repeated.

"Father Liam found your father in bed. He apparently died in his sleep." Samuel brushed a loose hair back from her face. "Father Liam says his face was peaceful, so there must have been no pain."

"Oh . . ."

"Cailin, I'm so sorry."

"Read it to me."

"What?"

She tapped the letter. "Read it to me. Every word."

"Cailin, the children may hear."

"Read it quietly. Please, Samuel. Please read it to me."

He picked up the letter and read in an expressionless voice:

Dear Cailin,

It grieves me deeply to have to write to you at this time when you are embarking on your new life in America. I hope the journey to your home with your husband and his family has brought you all the blessings and joy you believed awaited you there with Abban.

Your father passed on to his heavenly reward sometime during the night. He went, as was his habit, which you know so well, to the public house and enjoyed the company of his friends. When he left, he seemed unchanged. Then, this morning, when he did not attend mass, I went to your house to make sure nothing was amiss. Your father never missed morning mass.

I found him in his bed. His face was so peaceful, I knew he was already with your mother in the arms of the angels. I know these tidings are sad for you and your family, but he told me more than once, he would not go to his reward and to your mother until he was certain you were with the man who would give you and the children everything you needed . . . everything he believed he could not give you himself. He promised your mother when he stood beside her deathbed that he would take care of you until he could trust someone else to do so.

He was a good man, and I know he loved you and the children with all his heart. You were the joy that put lightness in his step and kept the devil's own despair from his heart after your mother's death.

As your father requested, I am sending you the possession he prized most—his fiddle. I hope it reaches you in one piece.

God bless you and your family. I will pray for you that you found everything you hoped for in America.

Samuel put the letter back into the envelope. "It's signed with Father Liam's name."

Lowering herself to the sofa, she took the envelope and ran her fingers over it. "Athair had been suffering some pains in his chest, but he assured me that he was well." She swallowed around the grief clogging her throat. "He insisted on continuing his work on the farm, so there was always food for the children and me. There might not have been much to eat, yet there was always something."

"And he sent you this." He picked up the box and held it out to her.

She fought her trembling fingers to untie the strings and undo the paper around the box. She opened the lid. Her father's fiddle case was within. Lifting the leather case out, she opened it and touched the strings of the fiddle he had always loved playing. She looked into the box and saw the bow. She picked it up and put it across the fiddle.

"It was his most precious possession," she whispered.

"Other than you and the children."

"Yes."

"So he did as he promised your mother and took care of you."

With a sob, she turned her face against his chest and clutched his shirt. He gently stroked her back. He said nothing, and she was glad. False platitudes would have been painful.

She had never known that Athair had made such a promise to her mother. Each time he had suffered from a painful heartbeat, he had reassured her that he was not ready to go yet. But she had been married to Abban. . . . Had her father seen some streak of treachery in her husband that she had failed to notice? Athair had not wanted her to go to New York, and at the time she had been sure it was because he did not want to be alone. Maybe it had been something more.

Lifting her gaze to where Samuel was watching her with

the gentle compassion she had first seen in his eyes when she told him of her trials in New York, she whispered, "When did my father die?"

He took out the letter again. "It's dated a little over a month ago."

"Around the time I was leaving New York to come here." She touched the paper. Had Athair somehow known she would find Samuel, a man who would reawaken her deadened heart at the end of the train journey to Haven? Her father would have liked Samuel and respected his knowledge, but most of all Athair would have appreciated how Samuel opened his house and his life to Brendan, Megan, and Lottie . . . and her.

"Will you tell the children?" Samuel asked, and she knew, for once, he had not guessed the course of her thoughts.

"I must." She put the letter on the table beside the case and rubbed her hands together. "This loss isn't like with Abban. Their memories of him are sparse at best. Lottie may not remember Athair well, but the other two will."

"Do you want me to get them?"

She almost said no, because she did not want to tell them when her cheeks were red with the stains of her tears. Then she nodded. She would not hide her grief from them. Not about this.

Samuel's taut face must have warned the children that something was amiss because they were silent as they came into the parlor. When she held out her arms to them, they ran to her. She embraced them as she told them about their grandfather's death.

Sitting next to Cailin, Samuel took Megan onto his lap and held her as she wept. Lottie wore a lost expression, and Cailin guessed her youngest was uncertain how to respond. When Samuel set the little girl on his other knee, she cuddled close to him.

Cailin looked to where Brendan had stood and saw him

walk to the door opening into the back parlor. Rising, she went to him and put her arm around his shoulders. She was astonished when he shook it off.

"Brendan, I'm—"

"Don't say you're sorry!" he snapped. "You're the one who dragged us away from Grandpa and brought us to America. Then you left us after telling us Papa had died. Then they said you died, but you didn't. Now you're saying Grandpa died. What if he didn't? What if he's still alive?"

She heard Samuel draw in a sharp breath. "Brendan . . ." he began, his voice as rigid as his face.

Waving him to silence, Cailin knelt in front of her son and folded his hands between hers. They trembled as fiercely as his words had. "You were lied to about what had happened to me. I'm not lying to you. You believe that, don't you?"

"But you didn't die!"

"No, that was a lie. I wish I could tell you that the letter was another lie, but it isn't." She reached up to frame his face—his face that looked so much like a youthful version of Athair's. Swallowing her sorrow, she whispered, "Brendan, you know I'd never, ever lie to you."

"Like Papa did?"

"Your father?" she glanced at Samuel, who had come to his feet, holding each girl by the hand.

"I know what Papa did," Brendan said. "I knew before we left New York, Mama. We saw Papa's other children come to the house. Mrs. Rafferty told us who they and the lady with them were."

Samuel swore, but Cailin only asked, "Why didn't you tell me that you knew?"

Brendan looked at his sisters, then said, "We didn't want you to be upset, Mama." He barely paused before he asked, "Are you going to die, too?"

"Do you mean soon?"

He nodded.

"No." She struggled to smile. "I'll be here to tell you to pick up your clothes and eat your vegetables for many, many more years."

He threw his arms around her.

"Tá grá agam duit. I love you," she whispered. She leaned her head on top of his and looked across the room to Samuel, Megan, and Lottie. "I love all of you."

The little girls ran to throw their arms around her again. She knew the danger of letting Samuel's gaze capture hers, but she could not look away. Did he know her words had been for him, too?

She could not guess, for Megan tugged on her sleeve.

"Yes?" Cailin asked.

"Can we? Can we now?" Megan's tears fell down her cheeks.

Cailin nodded, coming to her feet. As the girls grasped her hands, she said, "Samuel, we're going down to the river. Will you come with us?"

"Why are you going there?"

"When someone died," she said, her voice catching, "we tossed flowers into the stream on the farm and watched them flow down to the sea. It's sort of a tradition in our family. Will you come with us?"

He nodded and picked up Lottie. Taking Cailin's hand, he started toward the door.

She drew her hand out of his and went to get the fiddle. Taking it and the bow, she followed Samuel out of the house. Brendan trailed after them. They paused only long enough to pick some wildflowers by the fence, then walked down the hill to the river.

Where the riverbank dropped sharply into the water, Cailin quickly twisted the flowers together in a garland. It would not hold together long, but it did not need to. She handed it to Brendan. He was the oldest, so he should have the honor. When the girls did not protest, she wanted to draw them into her arms and hold them until every hint of their pain was gone.

Picking up the fiddle, she drew the bow across the strings. A few quick turns tuned them, and she began to play. Samuel's eyes widened as her fingers flew across the strings in a lighthearted tune. First Megan, then Lottie began to clap along.

She lowered the fiddle. "Samuel, don't think I'm a horrible daughter to play such a happy song. It was my father's favorite."

"I'm not shocked because of what you played, but how. I had no idea you could play so well."

"Athair began teaching me when I wasn't much older than Brendan." She touched the fine wood. "I'd intended to start teaching him on my fiddle, but—"

"You had to sell it when you got to America."

She nodded, then turned to Brendan. "Now you should toss the flowers into the river. They'll eventually reach the sea."

"Down the Ohio to the Mississippi," Samuel said quietly. "Then they can drift back to Ireland."

"Yes," she whispered, slipping her hand into his.

"Careful," he added as Brendan eased closer to the edge of the bluff. He shot a quick smile at Cailin. "Sorry. Habit."

"A good one. Go ahead, Brendan."

He held up the garland. "Good-bye, Grandpa. We'll miss you." He flung the flowers out toward the water.

Somehow, the garland hung together as it hit the river and was swirled into the currents. The children cheered. As Brendan and Megan told their favorite stories of their grandfather and asked her to play more of the songs they remembered, Samuel squeezed her hand. She had never guessed she could be so happy and so sad at the same time.

Nineteen

As her daughters got into bed, Cailin hushed them, but they kept talking about the fair that would be starting in two days. When she blew out the light in the girls' room and went onto the landing, she was not surprised to hear soft footsteps behind her. She looked back to see Lottie climb into bed with Megan. Immediately they were giggling.

Leaving them to their mischief, for their laughter was a wondrous sound, Cailin looked in to see that Brendan was already asleep. Or pretending to be asleep, because he had agreed to go to bed early tonight so he could spend tomorrow night at the fairgrounds with his cow. That would allow him to rise early and be ready for the judging on the first day of the fair.

The everyday sights and sounds eased her grief over her father's death. Athair would not have wanted her to weep. He had always believed in celebrating every minute of life. So had she, until Abban's cruelty and then his mother's drove all joy from her. She would not allow it to be stolen again.

A light was on in the back parlor, and Cailin went to the door. Samuel was sitting at his desk, squinting as he tried to see what he was writing on a paper in front of him.

"Is it important?" she asked.

He looked up. "This letter? I want to get it in the mail,

but it can wait until the end of the week. If you want some company, I can set it aside."

"I don't want some company." She drew the door closed behind her and walked around a crate to his desk. Lifting his glasses off his nose, she placed them carefully on top of the letter. The letters of her name tried to catch her attention, but she smiled at him. "I want you."

"Here?"

"Why not?" With her foot, she shoved away a short stack of books. "You've got a nice carpet here, Samuel."

"You're a brazen woman."

She ran her fingers along his face, tipping it up to her lips. "Are you complaining?"

"I'll never complain about this."

When she knelt on the floor and held out her hands, he dropped from the chair to sit beside her. He cupped her face and kissed her tenderly.

"Don't hesitate," she whispered. "I'm not asking you to hold me because I want to forget about my father. I want you to hold me because I was a fool to storm away when we could have had these nights together."

"Counting our stings?"

She laughed. "As long as we did it lying side by side."

"I like the way you think." He started to kiss her again, then said, "I don't want to hold you—"

"What?"

He laughed. "Let me finish. I don't want to hold you to banish another woman from my mind. I want to hold you because I was a fool to let you storm away when we could have had these nights together." He laughed again. "To count our stings or whatever. It doesn't matter as long as you're lying by my side."

"Is there an echo in here?" She laughed as she swept her arms up his chest to curve over his shoulders.

"Just of two people yearning for each other." His fingers stroked her face. "Can I tell you a secret?"

"A happy one?"

"A very happy one." He teased her ear with the tip of his tongue. When she shivered with delight, he whispered, "Sometimes, on the nights when you were with me, I'd wake up and watch you sleeping. I wanted to make sure you weren't only a dream."

She rested her cheek against his as his arms enfolded her. "Sometimes I did the same. I burst into your life so quickly that it swept my breath away."

"As I want to do now."

"Here?" she teased, copying his astonishment.

He laughed huskily, his longing naked in his voice. "I hadn't planned on making love with you in my office, but, *a stór*, does it matter where we are as long as we're alone here?" Standing, he twisted a key in the lock she had not noticed.

As he walked back to her, she held up her hands to him. He took them as he knelt again beside her. Saying nothing, he reclined her back and leaned over her. He lifted her braids and slipped his finger into the plaits. His gaze held hers, promising her that they would share every pleasure, and his finger slid along a braid. It loosened, scattering her hair around her. Pulling her other braid over her, he began to undo it.

She quivered as his finger glided along her, grazing her neck and stroking her breast. When her hair drifted about her, he smoothed it away. His fingers traced a meandering path of delight along her body until they curved around her face.

"My sweet Cailin," he whispered.

"Samuel, *a ghrá mo chroí*," she answered as he brought her lips beneath his. She welcomed his kiss, glad he had not asked her to translate, for she was unsure how he would react to knowing she had called him the love of her heart.

Putting her arms around him, she held him to her. His hair caressed her face when his hungry lips elicited plea sure along her neck. She traced the curve of his ear, and his rapid breath seared her skin.

He impatiently loosened her gown and pulled her clothes from her and tossed them, unnoticed, beside his on the floor. When she leaned over him, she sighed with the deliciously powerful satisfaction of his skin against hers. The sensation became more splendid each time they were together and had haunted her dreams when she had not been with him.

His eyes burned with emerald desire as she ran a single finger across his lips and over his chin. The bronzed skin along his chest could not conceal his accelerating heartbeat when her fingers sought the lean line of his hips. When he writhed beneath her light touch, she bent forward to taste the fire on his lips. Her tongue stroked his mouth as lightly as her fingers moved along him, then flicked scintillating sparks on his skin, taking the same sensual journey her finger had.

Moaning her name, he tangled his hands in her hair. She explored his firm skin's warmth and a ticklish spot along his ribs, setting him to laughter amid his quick breaths. His laughter faded into a gasp when her tongue swirled along him in a wave of incredible, intimate ecstasy.

Wanting only to give him the rapture he offered her, she discovered anew how bringing her most devilish fantasies to life fueled that bewitching flame within her. The essence of his skin, the roughly silken texture of it against her mouth, the musky scent of his desire immersed her in a flood of craving.

His strong hands on her shoulders brought her over him again, brushing her body along his. When his hands framed her face, he stared into her eyes, his gaze glazed with yearning. Slowly he guided her lips over his. His hands set her afire with their lustrous caress. Settling them on her hips, he kept her mouth busy with his probing tongue while he pressed her down over him. As he delved deep within her, she moaned his name into his mouth, conquered by the tempest of passion.

Melded together by the power racing around and through them, she moved with him. Lightning hot, the yearning became need, the ecstasy became torment. It whirled her with him into an immeasurable eddy of rapture, dissolving her into it and into him. It was everything she wanted.

The day of the fair dawned as hot as any in the middle of summer and with a squeal when the bedroom door crashed open. Lottie clambered up onto the bed and over the top of Samuel to announce, "I'm four. I'm four. It's my birthday!"

Cailin sat up, halting her. It was too late to worry that Lottie had discovered them here together. She would need to watch Lottie closely to make sure she did not speak of this at the fair. "Lottie, you shouldn't be disturbing Samuel before the sun is up over the horizon."

"Samuel," the little girl said, "tell Mama that today is my birthday."

"That's a fact she's more likely to know than I would." He tugged on Lottie's braid. "Go and feed your kitten, Quarter-pint."

"When are we leaving for the fair?" she asked, bouncing up and down.

"After breakfast." He picked her up and dropped her to the floor. "Go and feed your kitten, Quarter-pint."

Skipping out of the room, Lottie crowed again and again that it was her birthday.

"I'm sorry she woke you," Cailin said, swinging her feet to the side of the bed. "I should go. Lottie's celebration is sure to wake her brother and sister, if they're not already awake and anxious to get to the fair."

He threw off the sheet and hooked an arm around her drawing her to him. She trembled when his bare ches brushed her. Lifting aside her braid, he pressed his lips to her nape. He loosened one button, then another on her collar and pushed it aside as his lips swept along her skin. His hand rose to cup her breast at the same moment he whispered against her ear, "Brendan is at the fairgrounds. Remember?"

"How . . . How . . . ?" She moaned when his fingers toyed with the curve of her breast.

Laughing, he released her. "Can you talk now?"

"You like unnerving me, don't you?" She smiled as she ran her fingers up his bare chest. "I don't think I've ever seen Brendan as happy as he was last night when we left him at the fair with his cow."

"His prize-winning cow, as I think he told me a dozen times."

"I hope he won't be disappointed if his cow doesn't win a ribbon."

"What makes you think she won't win?" Rolling her onto her back, he smiled down at her. "Don't you think I've taught him to do everything he can to get what he wants?"

Cailin laughed softly.

"What's so amusing, *a stór?*" he whispered.

"Not funny. Happy."

"I'm happy, too. To have you here with me." His smile faded as he said, "I haven't asked you, and you haven't said, but I need to know. Are you continuing with your plans to return to Ireland?"

"There's nothing back there for me."

"Your father's farm—"

"It was a tenant farm, so someone else will already have claimed it. His fiddle is his only legacy to me."

"Are you still planning to go back there?" he asked again.

Running her fingers across the whiskers on his cheeks, she repeated, "There's nothing back there for me."

"Are you staying in Haven?"

"Do you want me to?"

"That's an absurd question."

"Please answer it."

He leaned across her. "Cailin, I don't want to lose any of you."

"The children—"

"Not one of you." He combed his fingers through her hair. "I thought I'd never be able to wait until you welcomed me into your arms again. All I could think of was carrying you off."

"If you carried me all the way to your bed, you would have exhausted yourself so much that you wouldn't have had any energy left."

"I wouldn't say that!" With a rakish laugh, he leaned over her. The unending desire in his eyes washed over her, urging her to stroke his back again. "No matter what happens, I'll always have this ache to make love with you again and again and . . ."

His words vanished into her lips as she drew him to her again. She had no idea how much longer this magnificent joy would be hers, but she was going to enjoy every moment of it, not worrying if it was the last. She had lived too long worrying about the future—waiting to hear from Abban, sailing to America, working to obtain money to provide for her children. Now she wanted to think only of this minute and this man.

Cailin waved aside dust as she stepped down from the rockaway carriage at the fairgrounds. What had been an empty field edging up to the river held more people than she had guessed lived around Haven. Animals, in even greater number than people, were making every possible sound they could, and the fairgoers were talking over them.

Aromas of food being prepared mixed with the scents from the barns.

Two barns were set beside a large, roped-off oval where horse races would be held later in the day. In the opposite direction was the boxing ring and hints of music. She could not see what was making it, but the sound added to the joyous mood. The western horizon was emphasized by a low, gray line. She hoped, after they had waited so long for rain, that the storm could stay away until the day's entertainment was over.

"Let's take my rabbit to be judged!" shouted Megan as she jumped down, sending more dust floating around them.

Putting Lottie on the ground, Samuel adjusted the little girl's bonnet. "Why don't we find Brendan first? Rabbit judging isn't for a few hours." He lifted the cage from the back seat. "We'll take your rabbit into the agricultural building where he can be cool; then we'll find Brendan."

The two girls raced toward the bigger building where the animals would be judged. The smaller building held domestic items, such as food and needlework.

"You should have entered some of your delicious blackberry jam," Samuel said as he offered Cailin his arm.

"I don't think the children would have let more than the two jars I sent to Emma leave the house." She smiled, placing her hand on his elbow. "With Megan and Brendan both having their pets judged, that's enough suspense for this fair."

"Maybe I should enter you in the kissing contest."

"There's a kissing contest here?"

Laughing, he said, "If I were smart, I'd say yes and that we need to practice."

"You're teasing me again."

"Maybe I'll suggest such a contest for next year."

"Do that."

"We'll have to practice a lot between now and then."

She laughed along with him, liking the idea that she

would be in Haven a year from now. Staying here to watch
the seasons unwind one after another was so tempting.
When she saw the girls pausing to talk to a boy, she wondered how she could wrench them away from this place
they now considered home.

That she now considered home, too.

As she walked around extra pens that had been set up
at one side and into the barn, she smiled at people she
recognized from the Grange Hall or the village. Their cor-
dial greetings were mixed with commiseration about having a run-in with wasps.

"Mama! Samuel!" Brendan's voice rang out over the
others. "Over here."

Cailin hurried through the maze of pens inside the barn
to where her daughters were chatting with excitement as
her son grinned broadly. The dark circles under his eyes
and the pieces of straw in his hair warned that he had spent
the night tending to his cow and getting little sleep. Yet
she had never seen him look happier.

"You're just in time," he said. "They've already started
judging." He pointed to empty pens closer to the open area
at one end of the barn.

"Good luck." She hugged him, plucking out the straw
at the same time.

Samuel balanced the rabbit's cage on the wooden post
at one end of the pen, where a lantern hung from a brad.
"We'll be cheering for you, Brendan." He offered his hand
to the boy, who took it with an even wider smile at the
acknowledgment that he was old enough to have earned
the respect of one man for another.

A man called from closer to the judging area, and Brendan changed back into a young boy.

"That's me!" he cried. "I mean, that's us! I have to go."

"Go!" Samuel stepped aside, then asked, "Where are
the rabbits?"

Brendan pointed with his elbow toward the other wall

of the barn. He bent to check the black and white cow's rear right leg.

Cailin herded her daughters ahead of her in the direction Brendan had indicated. Quickly, they arranged for the rabbit to be added to the list to be judged. Then they hurried to the open area to find a place around the rope separating it from the pens.

"Why didn't you build a bigger barn?" asked Cailin as she inched through a space where the aisle narrowed to barely enough room for her to pass.

"The planners must not have known so many entries would be here on fair day." Samuel picked up Lottie and set her on his shoulders when they reached the rope and the crowd gathered around it.

Megan squeezed in front of him and applauded enthusiastically when Brendan led his cow into the judging area.

Cailin watched, so proud she feared her exultant smile would not fit on her face. When Samuel put his arm around her waist, she saw a matching smile on his face. He should be proud; he had inspired Brendan to work toward this moment.

More quickly than she had guessed, the judge walked around each cow. He pulled out three ribbons. He handed the white one to a man whose hair was the same color, then walked across the area to give the red one to Brendan. She cheered so hard that she did not see which entrant got the first-place blue ribbon.

"We'll meet him outside," Samuel said as he motioned for them to follow. "It'll be quicker than trying to go through the barn. I don't think we could cram ourselves through the crowd again."

"But my rabbit—" Megan began.

"We'll check on it later. The rabbit judging won't begin until the cattle and sheep groups are completed late this afternoon."

Slipping her hand into his, Cailin held out her other one

to Megan. She looked toward the west. The clouds were no closer, but they appeared a deeper, more malevolent ebony. The longer the storm remained away from Haven, the longer they had to enjoy the day.

Brendan ran up to them, along with his friend Sean and Jesse Faulkner. "Look! A ribbon! A red ribbon!" He was jumping up and down like Lottie.

Cailin hugged him, half-expecting him to flinch away while his friends were watching. "I'm so proud of you."

Samuel gave his shoulder a squeeze. "You've worked hard, Brendan. You've earned that ribbon."

A man called to Brendan from the barn. Grinning, the boy hurried to see what the man wanted.

"He did it," Samuel said with a chuckle.

"With your help," Cailin replied.

He bowed deeply, sending the two girls into peals of laughter. " 'Tis my pleasure to be able to assist, Mrs. Rafferty."

"We're most grateful, Mr. Jennings." She curtsied, and the girls giggled more.

Putting his arm around her waist again, he whispered, "I'll be glad to let you show me just how grateful you are later."

"Then it will be *my* pleasure."

"Ours, *a stór.*"

She kissed his cheek lightly. "Most definitely ours." She stared at the longing in his eyes. Was there more than desire there? *Oh, please let this be love I see in your eyes.*

"Samuel!" came a shout.

Cailin turned to see Reverend Faulkner and Alice Underhill—no, Alice Hahn—along with her new husband hurrying toward them. With them was Mr. Thanington, whose expression was somewhere between a smile and a grimace as they steered him across the dusty field.

Putting her hand on Lottie's shoulder before the little girl could race to meet them, she hushed the child, who was talking about her invisible friend Dahi and wanting to show him the rabbit. Lottie gave her a puzzled glance but subsided as the others reached them.

"Samuel," said the minister, panting from the exertion of rushing on such a hot day, "we need you to hear this."

"This?" he asked, looking at Mr. Thanington.

"You're a dashed difficult man," the Englishman said, chuckling. "I didn't expect to have my offer to the village returned to me with so many comments."

"Then I assume you've read them."

Cailin hid her smile of pride as Samuel responded in an affable tone. Only his hand tightening at her waist told her how anxious he truly was to hear Mr. Thanington's comments.

"I read them," Mr. Thanington said as he wiped dust from his rooster-red vest. "I can't say I appreciated your questioning some of my suggestions. However, I've come to see the sensibility of them." He held out his hand. "It's agreed, then."

"Just like that?" Samuel asked, clearly astonished.

"Unless you want to negotiate some more."

"No, I know when to quit."

Mr. Thanington laughed. "I do as well, but do think, Jennings, about reconsidering my request to help me with clearing the title to Thanington Hills."

"Your attorney—"

"I haven't hired one in the United States, and, to be honest, I find your legal system somewhat confusing."

Samuel smiled. "I can suggest an excellent attorney for you. He's in Cincinnati, so it wouldn't be too much of a journey for him to come and speak with you."

"Do call at your convenience. I look forward to talking with you about this attorney." He tipped his hat to Cailin. "Good day, Mrs. Rafferty."

"Mr. Thanington," she said.

His eyes twinkled, and she guessed he was amused at

the way she had undermined his attempt to pass himself
off as a lord. Bidding them all a pleasant day, he walked
away, his gold-tipped cane glistening in the sunshine.

"We've got our library. We did it!" Samuel twirled her
about and set her on her feet, kissing her soundly. The
children laughed, and Reverend Faulkner offered his hand
in congratulations.

Pumping his hand, the minister said, "This is even more
than I'd prayed for."

"It's wonderful," Alice added. She glanced at her husband. "I told you that miracles can happen."

"I think we're all sure of that now," Reverend Faulkner
replied.

As the three walked away, discussing when they would
start building the shelves for the library, Cailin heard a
distant rumble of thunder. She glanced toward the western
sky. The clouds were climbing up from the horizon, but
slowly.

"Shall we eat?" she asked, seeing Samuel look at the
sky, too. "Then we can visit the rest of the fair."

He halted the girls' protests. "That sounds like an excellent idea, Cailin."

By the time he had retrieved the basket from the carriage, Brendan had joined them. Cailin opened the basket
and lifted out the food inside. The children held their breath
with as much anticipation as on Christmas morning, even
though they must have smelled the aromas coming from
the kitchen yesterday. Or maybe they had been so absorbed
in their preparations that they had taken no notice of hers.
A potato-and-carrot pie was warm as was the sliced ham.
Butter for the rolls came from deep within the bed of
mostly melted ice that also had kept the lemonade cold.

Lottie peeked in. "Is my chocolate birthday cake in
there?"

Cailin tugged on the little girl's ear. "You're going to
have to eat your lunch before you see what's for dessert."

"But it's my birthday, Mama!"

"And you need to start growing for another year." She relented and said, "Your cake is in there, Quarter-pint."

"That's what Samuel calls me!" She giggled.

"And for you, Samuel," she said, drawing out a bottle of beer. "I thought you might enjoy it for our celebration today."

He chuckled. Holding up the bottle, he said, "To Lottie on her birthday, to Brendan and his red ribbon, and to the new library in Haven."

After they clinked cups of lemonade against the bottle, Cailin served everyone. She knew better than to offer them too much, because the children could barely sit still. Even the birthday cake got scanty notice before they were begging to walk around the fairgrounds.

Samuel took the basket back to the carriage. As soon as he returned, all three children bounded to their feet and scurried toward the smaller barn. Only his shout to wait slowed them.

"This is such an exciting day for them," Cailin said as she put her hand on his arm.

"What about you?"

"Me? I'm having a grand time." She stared as they came around the back of the smaller barn. A round platform was topped by wooden horses. Above them on the circular roof, bits of gilt paint glittered. The clatter of a steam engine rumbled beneath the excited voices all around it. "Oh, my!"

"It's a carousel," Samuel said.

"I've never seen one before."

"Nor have I."

"You haven't? But didn't they have fairs in Cincinnati? I thought you said it was a city."

He chuckled. "Before I came to Haven, I never visited a fair. I was too busy with work."

Megan raced up to them. "May we ride?"

"Yes," Samuel replied with a grin, "all of us."

"All of us?" Cailin asked.

He lowered his voice as the children cheered. "I know you'll want to make sure neither Megan nor Lottie fall off their chargers, so we'll have to stand beside them to keep them on their horses."

"But that will cost extra."

"I think I can afford it." He chuckled. "I'll take the penny out of your wages if you'd prefer that."

"No, I don't prefer that."

"So you'll accept *this* from me?"

"I don't think it will start too many new rumors."

"This may." He gave her a swift, sweet kiss before going to buy tickets for the carousel.

Cailin shared her children's excitement as they waited to ride. When she stepped up onto the platform, which was smooth from hundreds of feet before hers, she lifted Lottie onto a horse that was painted white with flowers twisted through its mane. Telling the little girl to hold on tightly, she heard Megan's squeal as Samuel put her on the black horse behind them. Brendan scrambled onto the red one just in front of Lottie's.

With a jerk and a sputter of steam, the carousel began to turn. Lottie bounced up and down on the horse as if she expected it to come to life and take her off on a great adventure.

Cailin laughed, looking over her shoulder. Samuel's hand curved around her side, and she wanted to nestle closer to him. As the carousel continued to twirl, its steam engine spitting and hissing like a maddened snake, she looked from her children's ecstatic faces to Samuel's smile.

She could not imagine leaving Haven and this life she had never guessed she would find here. All she needed was for Samuel to ask her to stay.

Twenty

"Did you have a fight with a pincushion?"

At the question and the laugh that followed, Samuel turned. He had been on his way to see the boxing matches, something Cailin had refused to witness. She had taken the children to look at the exhibits in the smaller barn.

A dapper man was stepping out of what must have been the livery stable's finest buggy. Theo Taylor had not changed a hair since Samuel had bid him goodbye and good luck in Cincinnati more than a year earlier. His thick mustache was a black smudge on his face, and his clothes, though well-made, hung on him, for he was as thin as a scarecrow.

"Theo!" He clapped his onetime partner on the shoulder. Sneezing as the fitful wind sent dust twirling around them, he said, "You're a sight for sore eyes."

"And you've got a sore one, so you should know. What happened to you?"

"A few days ago we intruded on some yellow jackets."

Theo shuddered. "Spare me the details. Just looking at you is bad enough." He drew off his unblemished tan leather gloves. "Aren't you going to ask me why I'm here? I didn't come all the way out here just to see how you're doing."

With a laugh, Samuel asked, "Why are you here?"

"To find out if it's true that you've gotten yourself a family."

"I wrote to you months ago about having three orphan train children placed out with me." He motioned toward the agricultural hall, where he could see Cailin and the children talking with Thanington. Lottie was jumping from one foot to the other, and he wondered what Thanington had said to make her so excited. "There they are right now, those three young redheads."

Theo smiled. "The ones with that pretty gal?"

"Cailin is their mother."

"Mother?" He frowned, grasping his bowler before a gust of wind could pull it off his head. "I thought they were orphans."

"I thought so, too, but I was wrong."

"And?"

Samuel chuckled. "It's a long story, but suffice it to say, she's really their mother."

"Cailin Rafferty, right?"

"Yes. How did you know?"

Theo reached under his black alpaca coat and drew out a letter. "This came to the office. It was addressed to you, but I opened it, thinking it might be some matter we'd dealt with before you got the silly idea of throwing everything away and moving out here to be a farmer. I had no idea why else anyone would be writing to you from New York City."

"New York?" He snatched the envelope out of Theo's hands. Seeing the fancily embossed return address, he withdrew the pages inside. He scanned them quickly and chuckled.

"I thought you'd be pleased to get this," Theo said. "What did you say to those folks to persuade them to part with a penny for the Rafferty kids?"

"Me? Nothing. I had Lloyd Sanders pay them a call and remind them of the truth. The bastard was their father. He

AFTER THE STORM   301

owes them at least three-fifths of his inheritance." He put the pages back into the envelope and stuck the envelope into his pocket before it could blow out of his hand. He looked about. "Did you see in which direction Cailin went?"

"No." He grasped Samuel's sleeve. "Wait! There are a couple of other things I need to discuss with you."

"I want Cailin to hear what this letter says."

"Just a minute."

"What's so blasted important?" he asked, irritated. This had been one of the reasons he had left their partnership. Theo insisted on being heard, no matter if something else was more crucial.

"What can I say to convince you to come back to Cincinnati, Samuel? Your brain must be rotting out here."

"Actually, I've found it quite a challenge to stay one step ahead of the weather."

Theo waved his words away. "Bah! Any fool can do that. You have a mind trained for the law."

"You're wrong, Counselor. Not just any fool can be a successful farmer. There are more skills in farming than in the law." He shook his head, then pushed the hair out of his eyes. The wind was getting stronger, warning that the storm would soon reach Haven and put an end to the dry spell. "If you came here to persuade me in person to come back to be your partner, you've wasted a train ticket."

"Two."

"Two? Who else did you bring along to convince me?"

Theo looked toward the hired carriage, and a sinking feeling dropped through Samuel's gut. Was it Theo's smile or the faint scent of perfume—an aroma that once had been so familiar—that warned him who had used the second ticket? He glanced over his shoulder to see Beverly walking toward them.

She was every bit as beautiful as he remembered . . . as he had been unable to forget. From her clothes, which were made to accent each of her superb curves, to her perfect, pale complexion that was hidden from the sun, as always, by a stylish bonnet, she looked exactly as she had the last time he had seen her. The night before the wedding that had never taken place.

"Gentlemen," she said with a warm smile. Putting her hand on his arm, she added, "Samuel, you're looking well."

"As you are, although I never thought I'd be saying that to you here. Welcome to Haven, Beverly."

"Your haven?"

"The town's name is Haven." He remembered the discussion he had had on this very subject with Cailin. It had been so easy to confide his pain to her, but the words refused to form on his lips when he looked at Beverly. Amazed, he realized he had never confided anything of importance to her, except when he had asked her to marry him. "What did Theo do to persuade you to come here?"

"I persuaded *him* to let me travel with him. I felt it was time for me to apologize to you."

"There's no need for an apology." The words were not just trite ones, he was astonished to discover. They were genuine.

"Is that so?" Beverly smiled when Theo bent toward her and whispered something quickly. The only word Samuel could discern was *Cailin.* "I'm glad, Samuel. You're a good man, but not the man who would have made me happy. You wanted a life away from the city, and I couldn't live in the country."

"You should have told me that."

"I was a coward because I didn't want to hurt you. Nor did I want to destroy your dreams."

"So you married Newsome?"

"I made a mistake, I'll admit," she said, startling him with her unexpected honesty. She put her hand up to hold her bonnet in place as a gust tore at the flowers on it. "But it's my mistake to live with. I want you to keep from throwing your life away, too."

He looked from Beverly's sincere face to Theo's expectant one. "What makes you think I'm throwing my life away?"

"You were a brilliant lawyer."

"And now I'm a brilliant farmer." He shook his head. "Nothing either of you can say will persuade me to change my mind. Coming to Haven is one of the best decisions I've ever made. Bringing the Rafferty children out to the farm was also one of the best decisions I've ever made."

"What was the very best decision you ever made?" she asked.

"One that I can't talk about yet." He was unable to halt his smile as he thought about what he had decided while he had ridden the carousel with Cailin and the children. "But it is, without question, the very best decision I've ever made."

"I'm glad, but I wish it meant you were coming back to Cincinnati."

He shook his head. "No." When Theo opened his mouth to speak, Samuel shook his head again. "No."

"That's pretty definite." Theo frowned.

"Very definite. Why don't you come and see my son Brendan's prizewinning cow?"

"*Your* son?" asked Theo.

Beverly glared at him as she shuddered with something that looked like horror. "No, thank you. Theo, if we stay here much longer, we're going to get soaked."

Samuel looked up to see the clouds rising rapidly to overtake the sun. Lightning flickered across the sky, and thunder boomed from not very far away. The storm was approaching even more quickly than he had guessed. He needed to get Cailin and the children back to the farm before it broke—if that was possible.

"Are you staying in Haven?" he asked to bring the conversation to a close.

"At the hotel." She shuddered again. "Such as it is. We'll be taking the train back to Cincinnati tomorrow."

He smiled. "Theo, there's a gentleman—a wealthy gentleman—here looking for some legal advice on securing a legal claim to property he has bought. I'm sure it's just the sort of complex problem you like to unravel. Let me see if I can arrange for him to stop by before you leave. I'll say goodbye to you both, then."

He bent to kiss her cheek, but she tilted her face so his mouth brushed hers. He jerked back, unsure if he was more startled by her brazen motion or his lack of reaction to it. "Beverly . . ."

He heard a gasp and looked over his shoulder. Cailin was standing not far behind them. The children were grouped around her, but he paid them no mind as he saw her shock.

"Excuse me," he said, leaving Theo and Beverly to stare after him. Running to where Cailin was herding the children toward the agricultural barn, he called her name. He thought it might have been swallowed by another crash of thunder because she did not turn.

Then Megan did. He saw the little girl pull on Cailin's skirt. With clear reluctance, Cailin paused.

"I'll meet you by the rabbit's cage," he heard her say as she sent the children on toward the barn. She faced him, tears filling her eyes.

"It's not what you think," he said.

"I think I saw you kiss that woman and call her 'Beverly.' Is that Mrs. Newsome?"

"Yes, and Theo Taylor, who was my law partner. He brought her here to convince me to go back to Cincinnati."

He put his fingers to her soft lips. "Don't say what I see in your eyes. I'm not Abban Rafferty, Cailin. I didn't lure you into my bed and then plan to go off with another woman."

"You were kissing her."

"I meant to kiss her cheek, but she kissed me. Even so, it was just a good-bye kiss among old friends."

"I don't kiss *my* old friends on the mouth."

"Things are different in the city. We—" He sighed. "Why am I trying to explain? You won't believe anything I say, will you? You've never trusted me. You think I'm just like Abban Rafferty, who tossed you aside to marry a rich woman. Did you ever really trust him either?"

When she choked and pulled away, he released her. She was going to ignore his question.

"Cailin," he said, "you need to see this."

"I've seen enough."

He drew out the letter and handed it to her. "You need to see *this.*"

"You know I can't read any of this."

He stabbed a finger at the first line. "You can read these words."

"The children's names." She met his eyes steadily, and he could see she was torn between wanting to know what was in the letter and striding away with what dignity she believed she had remaining. Anxiety filled her voice as she asked, "What does it say about them?"

"It says that three-fifths of Abban's estate now belongs to your children."

"I told you I didn't want anything from the Raffertys."

"Dammit, Cailin! *You* aren't getting anything." He held her gaze, refusing to let her look away. Did she think he had never seen her pain before? He did not want to see it ever again, but she must let it go. She had told him she had, but her reaction to both Beverly and this letter told him that she had not. "The money is for the children. It's not much, not much more than a few hundred dollars each, because everything the Raffertys own apparently has been heavily mortgaged, but it's rightfully the children's. Are you going to let your pride deny your children their inheritance?"

Her eyes widened as she looked down at the paper.

He jabbed his finger at the second paragraph. "And there's the answer why your saintly Abban Rafferty went to Ireland and figured he'd never come home."

"What does it say?" Her trembling voice was almost swept away by the rising wind.

"He killed a man in a fight." At her gasp, he took the letter back. "My friend writes that Rafferty claimed self-defense, but witnesses stated otherwise. They testified that he struck the man first. The man had come into the tavern looking for Rafferty. He said your husband had badly beaten the man's sister, who had been one of Rafferty's mistresses. Rafferty beat him, leaving him for dead. Then he fled and returned only when his family's influence and money greased enough palms to clear his name."

Her face was ashen as she whispered, "I never guessed."

Stuffing the letter into his pocket, he clasped her face. "Cailin, why should you even consider accusing a man you loved of such abominable behavior?"

"I never guessed," she repeated, then shivered. "Yet I accused you of—" She stiffened when thunder crashed so close that the ground reverberated.

More lightning crackled overhead.

Megan rushed to them and hid her face in Cailin's skirt, and Brendan raced across the field, shouting, "We need to get inside before the storm hits."

Samuel grabbed Megan and ran to the rockaway. All around him, others were racing for their carriages. Tossing Megan onto the front seat, he hefted Brendan up beside her. He turned and motioned to Cailin, who had not moved.

He rushed to her. "Don't be so stubborn that you'll stand out in the storm simply because you're mad at me, Cailin!"

"It's not that. Where's Lottie?"

"She was with Megan." Rain struck them, as piercing as the wasps' stingers.

"But where is she *now?*" Tears brightened her eyes, but he knew all her thoughts were on the little girl.

"She was going toward the barn. She'll be—" He yelped as something hard banged against his head. He put up his hand, wondering if he had been hit by a baseball. Then hail clattered around him. "C'mon, Cailin. Now!"

For a moment, he thought she would refuse to listen. Then she ran with him to the carriage. The hail battered them in a shower of icy pebbles.

"Megan," he called as soon as he was within earshot, "do you know where Lottie is?"

"She was going to go and see if our rabbit got a ribbon."

"If she's in the barn, Cailin, she'll be all right."

He did not give her a chance to answer. Handing her into the rockaway, he jumped up beside her. He pulled her into his arms, turning so he was between her and the barrage. The children crouched beneath the dash. In his arms, Cailin shook. Was it from fear, or was it because she could not deny, even in the midst of her belief that he had betrayed her as Abban Rafferty had, how much even the simplest touch fired their yearning for each other?

The carriage rocked as a savage gust struck it. He heard Brendan and Megan scream, but could only hold on as the right wheels rose off the ground. They dropped back to the grass with a crash that reverberated through him.

"No!" Cailin shrieked.

He raised his head to follow her horrified gaze at the larger barn. The wind lifted the roof. It struck the ground, smashing into kindling. For a moment, there was silence, save for the hail that rattled around them.

Then screams came from every direction. Human

screams. Animal screams. Thunder burst like cannon fire overhead. The pens by the barn shattered as the terrified beasts broke through them. The walls of the barn shook, and he knew other animals inside it must be trying to flee.

Cailin pulled away from him.

He halted her. "Stay here."

"I'm not staying here!" She started to slide off the seat.

"Stay here." He caught her face between his hands. "Trust me this time to save one of your children, Cailin. Trust *me!*"

"Samuel—"

"Trust me! Please."

It was only a second, but it seemed like a lifetime before she nodded. "I'm trying to trust you. I really am." She put her hand on his cheek. "Go!"

He did not give her time to change her mind or for himself to enjoy this hard-won show of her faith in him. He leaped out of the carriage and raced across the open field, which was rapidly becoming a mire. Through the rain that was falling as swiftly as if the Ohio surged up over the bluffs, he saw others running toward the barn.

The wind knocked him from his feet. He stood, then ducked as debris soared toward him. Spitting out mud, he scrambled to his feet. He put his arms over his head to protect it and ran to the barn.

Cows and goats ran through a hole in the wall. He jumped aside before one could plow him down. He heard shouts for help from inside the building. Running to where a door had been ripped off by the wind, he threw himself inside.

He fell to his knees as he was freed from fighting the wind. Hoofs grazed his side. With a groan, he pushed himself out of the way of the panicked animals.

"Lottie!" he shouted.

He heard his name cried in a high-pitched voice. He ran to his left. Or he tried to, because he was shoved back time after time by the animals. He clambered up the side of a pen, vaulted over the sheep in it, and catapulted out on the other side. Seeing several unmoving forms on the ground, he ran past them to Lottie, who crouched in a corner where two pens came together.

He pulled her into his arms as the wind tore the boards off the wall like someone peeling a potato. Huddling with her, he realized someone was stretched out beside her on the ground. Lightning flared against the darkness.

Thanington!

Samuel held on to the little girl, wishing he had let Cailin and the other children come with him. He tried once to look over the top of the walls protecting them, but rain and wind knocked him to his knees again. In his resolve to force Cailin to admit that she trusted him, he had left her and the children to this storm. Then he realized he had to trust *her* to protect Brendan and Megan.

With a crash, the back wall fell. Then there was silence again, broken only by the patter of rain. Not like the violent storm of moments ago; this was the steady rain they had been hoping for.

Shouts came from every direction. Calls for help for those who had been hurt, and more from folks searching for those who had been separated in the abrupt storm.

Standing, Samuel scanned what remained of the barn. Other people were coming to their feet, soaked, muddy, some with blood on their faces. All of them stared about in disbelief.

"Samuel? Lottie? Samuel, where are you?"

Cailin!

"Over here!" he called back.

She ran to him, drenched and with her broken bonnet bouncing on her back. Brendan followed. He tugged his sister after him. When Megan turned and darted toward the back of the barn, he gave chase.

"I found Lottie," Samuel said.

Cailin dropped to her knees and hugged her youngest. "Lottie, dearest Lottie." She could not say anything else but those two words as Lottie clung to her.

"You scared us, quarter-pint."

Samuel's voice broke through her hysteria, and she saw him beside Mr. Thanington. Her first thought that the man was dead vanished when she saw him lifting his hand to his forehead and moaning.

"I think," Samuel said, "we all survived. What a mess to clean up after the storm passes."

"Is Dahi all right?" Lottie asked.

Cailin stared at her daughter. How could Lottie be talking about an imaginary friend now? Gently she said, "Lottie, Dahi isn't here."

The little girl pointed to Mr. Thanington. "Dahi is right there!"

"Dahi?" she repeated in astonishment. When Mr. Thanington sat, shaking mud from his light brown hair, she asked, *"He* is Dahi?"

"Isn't he, Mama? You said the others weren't Dahi, so he must be Dahi."

"I can't see your friend."

"But you know all about him, Mama."

"Pretend I don't. Tell me everything you can about him."

Lottie screwed up her face. "Mama, you know. He lived in Ireland with us and then he went to 'merica. We went to 'merica, too. But you couldn't find him in New York. He was lost, so I wanted to find him for you."

"Dahi?" she asked softly, thinking of the many words Lottie misunderstood. "Like *do athair?"*

"Dahi!" exclaimed the little girl with excitement, mispronouncing the words as she had so many others. As Cailin looked at Samuel in astonishment, Lottie continued "You told me Dahi had pale-colored hair and was tal and—"

Cailin drew her younger daughter into her arms. "Lottie, do you know what the words *do athair* mean?"

She shook her head.

"It is Gaelic for 'your father.' We came here to be with your father—your papa, but he died before we got here."

"Then I don't have a papa?" She pondered for a moment, then said, "If I don't have one, I should be able to pick out one for myself."

"It doesn't work like that, *a stór.*"

"Maybe it should," Samuel said as he drew Cailin to her feet.

She gazed into his eyes, wanting to believe what she saw there. He had been wrong when he said she had never trusted him before today. She had dared to trust Samuel with her heart. Not blindly, as she had Abban, but through the pain and doubts. Even through her fear that having this man in her life would be a short-lived joy. He had proven that every foreboding was unjustified.

"I'm sorry," she whispered. "I shouldn't have jumped to conclusions."

"You've got plenty of excuses not to trust a man."

"But I trust you, and I really like trusting you." She took a deep breath, then said, "Because I love you."

"Do you now?" he asked, copying her Irish accent. "Then, *a stór,* there seems nothing else to do but . . ." He took her right hand and dropped to one knee. "Will you marry me, Cailin O'Shea Rafferty?"

She stared at him, astonished. Hearing chuckles around them, she paid them no mind as she gazed down into his smile. "Marry you? You want to marry me?"

"I just asked you, didn't I?"

Ignoring Lottie, who was dancing about with excitement, she said, "I thought you never wanted to get mixed up with weddings again. That's what you told me when you refused to come to Alice and Barry's wedding."

"Are you trying to talk me out of this proposal?"

She knelt, facing him as rain poured down over them to wash away the sorrows of the past. "No."

He released her hand and cupped her chin. "What do you say, *a ghrá mo chroí?*"

"You know those words?"

He chuckled. "You aren't the only one in Haven who speaks Gaelic. I remembered you speaking them at a very tender moment, so I wanted to find out what they were. 'Love of my heart,' right?"

"Yes."

"And you love me."

"Yes."

"And I love you. Will you be my wife?"

"If you are asking me because of the children—"

As if on cue, she was interrupted by a shout of "Mama!" She saw Megan and Brendan hurrying toward them. Megan was carrying a very wet and very unhappy rabbit and a white ribbon. She was grinning broadly. Brendan was leading his cow, which seemed unhurt, although straw was sprayed over it.

Samuel brought her face back to him. "This has nothing to do with the children. I'm asking because I want *you* in my life, Cailin. I love *you.* The children are a bonus, like in any marriage." He chuckled. "They were just an early bonus. So will you marry me?"

"Yes." She could not imagine what more she would want to say, for that one word said everything her heart longed to sing out with joy.

He pulled her into his arms, and his mouth caressed hers with a promise of rapture that needed no words. Around them, applause and cheers sounded. Not just from the children, but from the extended family they had found in Haven.

Drawing back, she said, "I must ask you one question."

"What is it?"

"Will you forget your vow to avoid weddings and come to our ceremony?"

He ran his finger along her cheek as he murmured, "I'll be glad to trade that vow for another—to love you for the rest of our lives."

Author's Note

This is the concluding chapter in the *Haven* trilogy that began with *Twice Blessed* and *Moonlight on Water*.

Next month, look for something slightly different. *A Rather Necessary End* is the first book in a romantic mystery series from Zebra Regency. When Lady Priscilla Flanders, a vicar's widow, discovers a dead man in her garden, she must depend on her friend Sir Neville Hathaway to help her uncover the truth. She wants to protect her three children from being the next targets and to clear her own name. And it certainly would be simpler if her aunt was not trying to run her life. . . .

Readers can contact me at: P.O. Box 575, Rehoboth, MA 02769. Or visit my web site at: www.joannferguson.com.

Thrilling Romance from
Lisa Jackson

_Twice Kissed	0-8217-6038-6	$5.99US/$7.99CAN
_Wishes	0-8217-6309-1	$5.99US/$7.99CAN
_Whispers	0-8217-6377-6	$5.99US/$7.99CAN
_Unspoken	0-8217-6402-0	$6.50US/$8.50CAN
_If She Only Knew	0-8217-6708-9	$6.50US/$8.50CAN
_Intimacies	0-8217-7054-3	$5.99US/$7.99CAN
_Hot Blooded	0-8217-6841-7	$6.99US/$8.99CAN

Stella Cameron

"A premier author of romantic suspense."

__The Best Revenge
   0-8217-5842-X $6.50US/$8.00CAN

__French Quarter
   0-8217-6251-6 $6.99US/$8.50CAN

__Key West
   0-8217-6595-7 $6.99US/$8.99CAN

__Pure Delights
   0-8217-4798-3 $5.99US/$6.99CAN

__Sheer Pleasures
   0-8217-5093-3 $5.99US/$6.99CAN

__True Bliss
   0-8217-5369-X $5.99US/$6.99CAN
